DEEPER THAN THE OCEAN

Other titles by Mirta Ojito:

Finding Mañana: A Memoir of a Cuban Exodus

*Hunting Season: Immigration and Murder
in an All-American Town*

DEEPER THAN THE OCEAN

MIRTA OJITO

UNION
SQUARE
& CO.

NEW YORK

UNION
SQUARE
& CO.
NEW YORK

UNION SQUARE & CO. and the distinctive Union Square & Co. logo are trademarks of Hachette Book Group, Inc.

© 2025 Mirta Ojito

All rights reserved. No part of this publication may be reproduced, stored in a retrieval system, or transmitted in any form or by any means (including electronic, mechanical, photocopying, recording, or otherwise) without prior written permission from the publisher.

This is a work of fiction. Names, characters, businesses, events, and incidents are the products of the author's imagination. Any resemblance to actual persons, living or dead, or actual events is purely coincidental.

ISBN 978-1-4549-6190-1 (hardcover)
ISBN 978-1-4549-6191-8 (e-book)
ISBN 978-1-4549-6192-5 (paperback)

Library of Congress Control Number: 2025940452

Union Square & Co. books may be purchased in bulk for business, educational, or promotional use. For more information, please contact your local bookseller or the Hachette Book Group's Special Markets department at special.markets@hbgusa.com.

Printed in Canada
2 4 6 8 10 9 7 5 3 1
MRQ
unionsquareandco.com

Cover design by Jared Oriel
Cover images by Shutterstock.com: Here, ilolab, Tama2u, U-Design

*To my mother, Mirta Muñoz Quintana, the original storyteller.
And to her mother, the real Catalina of my life.*

In the dead of night when the sky is deep
The wind comes shaking me out of sleep
Why does it always bring to me
The far-off, terrible call of the sea?
—Sara Teasdale, "The Sea Wind"

Part I

My bounty is as boundless as the sea,
My love as deep; the more I give to thee,
The more I have, for both are infinite.
— *Romeo and Juliet,* William Shakespeare

Mara

Santander, Spain
July 2019

Last night I was searching for my daughter again.

The anguish was so palpable I knocked down my nightstand lamp as I thrashed about in bed. In my dreams I was running after her in what seemed like an old house. I rushed room after room but couldn't find her. As I ran, I could feel the polished wood against my bare feet, the texture of the floral wallpaper against my fingertips—soft, like vinyl—and I furiously rubbed my hands over and over the surface as if my daughter were trapped in that endless field of yellow wildflowers.

When I woke up, I was gripping the blanket so hard my fingers hurt as I stretched out my hand to pick up the phone. It was screeching with that old-fashioned ringtone I assigned to my boss at the newspaper. Glancing at the screen I saw it was 4:02 a.m. A call in the middle of the night is never good news for most people. But for people like me who make a living reporting, it often means a chance at our next story.

"Mara here," I said, trying to sound alert and professional.

"Mara dear," said Carl, my editor. His tone told me everything I needed to know.

Somebody, somewhere on my side of the world was indeed receiving very bad news.

"Yes, where is it?"

"Not far from you," he said, trying to sound upbeat, though for him, almost four thousand miles away in New York, it was already 10 p.m.

I was struggling to keep my eyes open; the Ibuprofen PM I had taken at midnight was finally kicking in. My neck had been bothering me for almost ten years and, lately, the middle of my back had joined the fray. It seemed that, at fifty-five, my body had decided it was time to start falling apart.

"Where?" I repeated, eyeing the two packed bags I kept near the foot of my bed. The small backpack was for short assignments; the larger one could serve me for a week or longer if I was careful.

I jotted down the grim details of the assignment: a boat had been found off the coast of northern Africa with seven dead bodies inside, including a child. For now, Carl wanted only a brief story, but a freelancer in Côte d'Ivoire had told him that dozens of people had taken to the sea in the last few days. "It may be a repeat of 2015. Who knows?"

"You think?" I said, immediately regretting my sarcastic tone. But sweet, polite Carl didn't seem to notice. Four years ago, a wave of refugees had overwhelmed the Canary Islands, a Spanish archipelago closer to Africa than to the Iberian Peninsula. Hundreds of people had died at sea. The harrowing photos on the front pages of most newspapers were impossible to forget.

"Keep an eye on it, would you?" Carl urged before hanging up.

I put the phone down and closed my eyes, trying to hold on to the still vivid details of my recurrent nightmare. I was determined to write it down as my therapist had repeatedly asked me to do, but I never did and, invariably, I ended up forgetting the dream. This time, I had the sense I was running, searching for something or someone. My daughter! But I don't have a daughter. I have a son. Am I subconsciously pining for the baby girl I never had? I didn't think so but perhaps. Certainly something to discuss with my therapist next time.

I couldn't go back to sleep now. The nightmare was receding, but the assignment I had just received loomed large. An assignment is like a marching order to focus hard and fast. I untangled the sheets from my body, and, using the phone, I booked a one-way ticket from Santander, the city where I live in Spain, to Madrid and then to Tenerife in the Canary Islands, flinching a little at the price. I knew the paper would pick up the cost, but I've always been frugal, more so now that I'm no longer on the payroll. As a freelancer, you don't want to spend too much, so that the assignments keep coming. Then I called my friend Nina Blau, a talented Madrid-based Israeli photographer I often worked with. Nina was ready to go. She had received the information from a contact and had already booked a seat on the same flight to Tenerife. "I was about to call you," she said, sounding more alert than I was. After a quick chat, we arranged to meet at Barajas Airport.

Next, I called my mother, Lila, putting her on speaker. I always refer to her as *Mima*, which is close enough to her name and a much sweeter variation of *Mother*. She is seventy-nine years old and, since my father's death a decade ago, lives alone in Miami in the beautiful home they bought shortly after I left home. I'm her only child, and the one rule she requires of me is to call her every day. If I forget, she calls. At any hour.

In a rush I told her about the new assignment and that I was on my way to the Canary Islands. She was quiet for a moment. The pause was so unusual that I had to ask if she was still on the line as I laid out my clothes on the bed and headed for the bathroom.

"Yes, yes," she said. "It's just that I've been meaning to ask you for a favor for a while now, but I know you're busy and I didn't want to interfere with your work. Now I can finally ask. It shouldn't be so difficult for you."

A favor for my mother could be anything from getting her a tube of condensed milk, the kind she was certain you could find only in Spain, to pills to stave off osteoporosis to a cute baby outfit for her friend's granddaughter—never mind that one could buy perfectly beautiful baby clothes in Miami. For her, quality items came only from Spain. But she wasn't after anything like that this time.

What she needed from me was simple, she explained. She wanted me to find her maternal grandmother's birth certificate. The Spanish government had passed a law allowing the children and grandchildren of Spanish citizens to claim citizenship if they had a way to prove the nationality of their ancestors.

My great-grandmother, Catalina Quintana Cabazas, had been born in the city of Santa Cruz in the Canary Islands. She had traveled to Cuba in a ship in the early twentieth century, but the details were fuzzy. Catalina had raised my mother, and, though there were no pictures of her, my mother claimed all she had to do was look in the mirror to see the beloved face of her grandmother: she had inherited Catalina's curly red hair, unusually tall height for a woman, heavy-lidded brown eyes, and skin so pale that a day at the beach was a torment for her.

"It won't be easy to get such an old birth certificate," I said. "I mean, do you even know what year she was born?"

My mother thought for a moment.

"Of course I do," she said. "She was born April 29th, 1919."

"Is there anything else you know?" Out of habit I reached for my notebook, ready to jot down details. "Do you have anything of hers?"

"No, of course not. You know that we left it all behind when we left Cuba," she said. "But I remember her parents' names. She mentioned them once."

"Once!" I scoffed.

"Once is enough if it's important, Mara. She rarely talked about her past."

"Yes, I guess that's true," I said, suddenly feeling the poignancy in her words. But I quickly got back on task. "Well, what are her parents' names?"

"José Angel Quintana and Inés María Cabazas," she replied.

"Fine, this'll have to do. Anything else you remember might help," I said, both amused and pleased that, three months before turning eighty, my mother had decided to rescue her past. I asked her why now, and she explained that two passports were better than one.

"You never know what can happen," she added, and hung up, leaving me facing the mirror over the bathroom sink. Only then did I realize I had forgotten to tell my mother about my nightmare. Already, the details were blurry, like the ghostly images that used to emerge from the photographers' bins in the old darkrooms. But the feeling of dread was still with me as I stepped into a steaming shower.

Catalina

Tenerife and La Palma, Canary Islands
February 1888–October 1903

It began with a gust of wind, a flurry of leaves spiraling before her eyes, and Inés María immediately felt her throat was scratchy as if grains of sand had lodged in the recesses of her mouth, her nose, her ears, even her eyes. She feared she was choking. Her nostrils constricted, denying her the breath she desperately needed. Inés María turned to her mother, unable to speak, but doña Elena didn't know what to do. The air around them had turned yellow, then, quickly, orange brown, like clay. The wind battered them from all sides and shook them about as if they were marionettes in a macabre dance. Doña Elena Cueto de Cabazas wrapped an arm around her daughter's shoulders and pushed her toward the first person she saw at the port of Tenerife, a tall man with an affable face who was bent slightly at the waist against the wind and held on to his hat with both hands. As he grabbed the young woman, his gray felt hat tumbled to the ground and flew off to the sea.

Before she passed out in the arms of the man who would become her husband, Inés María saw the world turn red.

This is how Inés María Cabazas and José Angel Quintana would later recount the beginning of their courtship to their children.

"I had no choice. Your grandmother flung your mother into my arms. What was I to do?" José Angel used to say with a glint in his eyes.

By the time Inés María came to, sheltered under the awning of a shuttered café near the port, José Angel had already decided he couldn't let her go. At the time, she was eighteen and he was twenty-four, an imperceptible age difference because Inés María, with her sad dark eyes, slightly curved back—a foolish attempt to hide her full height—and long hair so pale blond that it looked white from a distance, seemed at least as old as José Angel, a strongly built redheaded native Canarian with blue eyes, a long straight nose, and a dimpled chin.

His ancestors were Guanches, men and women who had migrated from the north of Africa and found refuge in the caves of Tenerife, the largest of the Canary Islands, which had sprouted from volcanic activity at the bottom of the sea millions of years ago, as if they were ancient trees, their canopies full but their roots shaky. At least once a century they would erupt, altering the topography of the islands and rattling the hardy men and women who trusted the land and God to keep them alive.

To live on those islands, one needed to be finely attuned to the most minuscule vibrations of the ground, alert to winds that seem to come out of nowhere, and attentive to the form and crest of waves, the rustle of tree leaves, and the flight patterns of native birds. Any rumble could signal an active volcano. A sudden squall could make the difference between life or death. A flock of birds suddenly flying away could indicate a disastrous storm was approaching. Sometimes, swarms of locusts from Africa would rain down on the islands like hail, with the power to devour millions of acres of cropland in a matter of hours.

José Angel was such a man: strong and watchful, yet optimistic; deeply devout, yet confident in his own prowess. He thought that his fate was in his hands, and his hands were never idle. When troubled, he looked up to the heavens, searching for God, but he also looked eastward, toward Africa, which was a mere two hundred miles away. Though he couldn't see it, he knew all his strength, all that he was, came from his ancestors—men brave enough to tame the rocky soil of these islands and fight a succession of invaders until they lost their independence to Spain in the late 1400s. This is why the descendants of Guanches like José Angel spoke Spanish, like almost everyone else on the islands, but with a lilt that Inés María, who was from the north of Spain, found enchanting.

She had traveled to the Canary Islands aboard the *Coruña*, a ship that once a month carried passengers and merchandise from ports in peninsular Spain and its islands to Puerto Rico and Cuba. But before the ship arrived at the port of Tenerife, its last Spanish stop, Inés María's father, don Carlos Cabazas, suffered a fatal heart attack one evening at dinnertime. The two women held on to the body for a day, but ultimately doña Elena was forced to tell the captain she had no money to properly bury her husband of twenty years. All their savings had been used to book passage to Cuba on that gleaming new ship. There, on the Caribbean island said to be the prettiest human eyes had ever seen, they had planned to forge a new life.

After the captain ordered them to prepare the body for burial at sea, doña Elena lovingly washed her husband's face and hands and removed his shoes, but she did not change his clothes. Don Carlos would be buried wearing his best outfit, the dark gray woolen three-piece suit he'd had made for the journey, the one he had worn for dinner every night since they left home. During the short ceremony the captain himself cast the sheet-enshrouded body of don Carlos off the ship. Heavy rocks attached to his legs with thick ropes made the bundle quickly disappear as Inés María and her mother embraced, horrified that the captain had refused to wait until they reached land to give the body a proper Christian burial.

"May God forgive you," doña Elena hissed at the captain, keeping her eyes on the waves that had swallowed up her husband's body but speaking forcefully enough for all gathered to hear. "Because I never will."

It was the last time she spoke to any man other than her future son-in-law or a priest during confession. Mother and daughter then retreated to their small second-class cabin and did not resurface until they felt the ship approaching port.

Inés María and doña Elena arrived in Tenerife, heartbroken, ashamed, and penniless. The sea had not delivered them to the new world as they had hoped; instead, it had robbed them of the man central to their lives. But the sandstorm blowing in from the Sahara Desert as they debarked, a weather phenomenon known in the Canary Islands as *la calima*, would end up saving them and sealing their fate.

José Angel Quintana was not a wealthy man, though he had inherited a farm on one of the islands of the archipelago, La Palma, a speck of land shaped like a heart with a beating dormant volcano in its center, and treacherous mountains protecting it from the sea. His grandparents had lived and raised their families on that land, but his parents had moved to Santa Cruz de Tenerife after their wedding and had never wanted to return to the more isolated and rural La Palma permanently. For them, it would have been a step backward.

José Angel, on the other hand, saw a life in La Palma as both a rightful return to his roots and a leap forward. In fact, when *la calima* deposited Inés María in his arms he had been on his way to arrange travel to La Palma. Three days later, when the sky once again returned to its usual flawless blue, José Angel went to the port to book passage to La Palma, but this time he bought two additional tickets. "You are coming with me," he told Inés María, pressing his mouth to the curled fingers of her left hand. It never occurred to him to ask her if she agreed. He took her quiet demeanor for acquiescence.

Inés María and José Angel married on March 11 of 1888, exactly twelve days after they met. Ordinarily, doña Elena would have opposed such a rush to the altar, but these were not ordinary times. Without her husband, she felt that José Angel Quintana was, for the moment, the only person she could trust, though she wasn't sure why. In his face, she saw kindness, and his very name seemed to confirm his goodness and her faith. Doña Elena was a devout woman, and she was certain God himself had put an angel on their path. One evening, when she detected doubt in her daughter's eyes, doña Elena took Inés María's hands in hers and asked, "Who else but someone with the name of Angel could have saved us from penury and a sky so red it looked as if heaven itself was raining down blood?"

To that, Inés María, who was reticent to share her thoughts and moved through life in her mother's shadow, had no concrete response, only the vague feeling that her mother, though exaggerating, was probably right.

The wedding was held at a small church in Tenerife, near the guesthouse where Inés María and her mother had found refuge on the day of their arrival. José Angel had offered to pay for their accommodations, but doña Elena was proud and prudent, selling her wedding ring instead to pay for the accommodations. For her wedding, Inés María wore a simple light blue dress with a high neckline and three-quarter sleeves, which she had planned to wear upon their arrival in Cuba, and the black mantilla her mother had packed for the trip. They had no money for flowers, but José Angel took care of that, thrusting a beautiful bouquet of wildflowers in Inés María's hands the moment she reached him at the altar, accompanied only by her mother.

Because both were illiterate, Inés María and José Angel signed their wedding certificate with crosses, as if God was guiding their hands, if not their lives. When she said, "I do," the priest had to ask her to speak up. She was so mortified, she looked to her mother, and doña Elena said the words on her behalf. The priest, content with a response he could hear, did not even notice that Inés María's lips had not formed the words. Until the day she died of a fright, alone in her bedroom, but much loved by her family, José Angel would tease doña Elena that she was the one married to him, not her daughter.

When, newly married and with doña Elena in tow, they arrived at the plot of land José Angel had inherited, Inés María felt she had made the wrong choice and that perhaps that was why she had lost her voice on her wedding day. She was supposed to be in Cuba, the dreamy land of possibilities, not in this barren, desolate part of the world. In the area of northern Spain where she grew up, a peaceful valley near the old port city of Santander, apples grew unbidden from the fertile green earth, blessed by almost continuous rain. So did beans, tomatoes, onions, lettuces, leeks, kiwis, pears, cabbages, cauliflower, and chard. Here, in La Palma, the land was hard and uneven, and the sun brutal. She couldn't imagine this soil would ever yield anything.

But José Angel had a plan.

"I have no intention of selling onions or bananas," he said after a pause, as the two made their way back to the house. "My ambition is grander."

He told her he wanted to plant mulberry trees. The leaves of those trees—dark green and wide as fans—were the only food consumed by silkworms, tiny spinners of the finest threads that, woven together by the expert hands of La Palma's women, would be turned into garments to clothe the clergy and the wealthy all over Europe.

"Can't others do the same?" asked Inés María, sensibly, bending down to poke at the parched land with the tips of her fingers. When she looked up, she saw José Angel from a different angle. As he spoke about his dreams, he seemed somewhat taller and more handsome to her. Her heart began to expand, and love planted its roots in an organ that, until then, had merely pumped blood. Now, a warmth originating there began to spread until it reached every recess of her body. Inés María blushed. Gently, José Angel took her hands and helped her to her feet. Standing upright, they were the same height.

"No," José Angel explained kindly. "Not everyone has access to those trees, but our land is blessed with the kind of soil, elevation, and light these delicate trees need to thrive."

José Angel knew this because his grandfather had passed along the information as if it were a family secret. The old man himself had never planted the much-coveted trees because he had feared failure, but he knew his grandson feared only God. And God, José Angel was certain, had always been on his side, especially since the day Inés María had fallen into his arms.

"The trick to keeping mulberry trees alive and thriving is to plant them in the right spot," he told his bride. "Too much sun and their leaves burn and drop to the ground, dry and brittle. Too little and they wilt in the shade."

As a response, Inés María pressed her fingers into his, and José Angel was startled by the strength he felt from this warm hand that only two weeks before he hadn't known existed.

From then on, all their hopes were centered on the mulberry trees. They weren't pursuing wealth, just hoping that the trees would provide them a decent living and peace of mind.

After they rebuilt his grandparents' house with José Angel's meager savings and money borrowed from an uncle, all they had left was the furniture they could salvage from the grandparents' old house: a metal framed bed with a straw mattress, which they kept for themselves, and an old bed with a coiled-spring mattress, for doña Elena. They also had a solid wood kitchen table whose surface bore the scratches of a lifetime of chopping vegetables and cleaving meat, four wobbly chairs that José Angel hammered into shape, three black cast-iron cooking pots, ten *reales*, and the fifteen mulberry seeds they had purchased to plant. Within a month, ten of the fifteen seeds had sprouted. Seven eventually grew to maturity. In time, from the bark of those trees, José Angel took softwood cuttings and planted others.

Mulberry trees, José Angel knew, had become inextricably linked to silkworms. Though he was no scientist, he was convinced that the leaves released a substance that altered the chemistry of the worms and made them dependent on those trees for their survival. The same substance, perhaps, deterred other insects from feeding on the leaves; therefore, no pests or other animals ever attacked the Quintanas' trees. What José Angel feared were the acts of God: the wind, especially when the saplings were small, or a sudden fire, a constant worry in this part of the world where a tossed cigar or errant lightning could ignite and destroy an entire forest in hours.

From sunup to sundown, José Angel worked on his farm, tending to his vegetables but, especially, to his trees as if they were his children. And, in some ways, they were. For what are children if not the essence of optimism? Children, like his trees, would forever extend his life into a future he couldn't yet fathom, but deeply believed would be exceptional.

While the mulberry trees grew and multiplied, Inés María withered, as her body rejected the lives that she so coveted. She would get pregnant, and the couple would pray for a boy, a strong boy to help them with their growing mulberry tree business. But, every time, the babies squeezed out of her body too soon, often during the night, soaking the bedsheets with the blood that had nourished them in her womb for weeks, sometimes months. In desperation and shame, Inés María turned to her mother, whose hands alone were healing but who also had a talent for making tinctures and teas for all her daughter's ailments since childhood.

"Mother, mother!" she yelled the first time she miscarried, standing in the kitchen, a wooden spoon in one hand and the handle of a bubbling pot in another. She was petrified. The second time it happened, she called out to her mother as she lay alone in the bed, her hands wadding the sheets between her legs in a futile attempt to force the clots of blood back into her uterus. By the third time, while she was resting under the sun, her back against a tree, Inés María didn't call for anyone. She waited for the clots to trickle out of her body, and, when the pain allowed her to get up again, she went to her bedroom and cleaned herself. Then she knelt under the wooden cross on the wall opposite the marital bed and asked God for a miracle.

There was not much doña Elena could do for her daughter. She had not yet become acquainted with the ways of the Canary Islands. Her prayers from the north, whispered over her daughter's rounded belly, were lost in the air, like smoke rising over their heads, never settling on the object of their shared obsession: a healthy womb for Inés María to nurture her babies until they came to term.

The last two babies Inés María lost—a set of twins—were in her body for so long that when they left her, she raised herself on the bed, putting all her weight on her elbows and closely examined the lifeless bodies between her legs. Though tiny, they were already fully formed boys. Their nails were transparent and their ears softer than silk. One had a pink birthmark on the lid of his right eye. Inés María made the sign of the cross with one hand and with the other she covered the baby's entire body. The other baby seemed like a beautiful angel in repose. If he had stayed in her body only a little bit longer, he would have survived, she was certain of that. She had seen women who delivered prematurely wrap their babies in banana leaves and keep them close to their bosom for months, feeding them as if they were birds in a nest until God and all the saints decided to bestow a soul on them and allow the babies to thrive. But Inés María had no such luck. When her mother helped her burn the useless afterbirth, she threw in the pile the banana leaves she had gathered once she had felt the first stab of pain. Then, she bound her breasts with a long strip of cloth until they stopped leaking.

She hated to say that she had lost her children. She had not; she knew exactly where they were. Inés María had insisted on burying them herself. She wrapped their tiny bodies in white silk and delicately placed a piece of cotton over each eyelid, forever sealing eyes that had never witnessed the glorious light that bathed their corner of the world. Eyes that would never see how pain had ravaged their mother's face: her cheeks now hollow, and her full mouth thinned out and haggard.

After each miscarriage, Inés María hoisted the shovel over her shoulder and walked to the shadiest spot on their land, under a magnolia tree, surrounded by the fiery orange and red blossoms of the *pico de paloma* flowers that grew wildly on the island. Every time the shovel hit the hard ground, she felt her entire body convulse as if, once again, her babies were leaving the safety of her womb.

In the first three years of their marriage, five crosses poked up from the ground to remind her daily of her failure and her sadness. When she ventured outside their home, which wasn't often, she could feel the eyes of the townsfolk on her. She knew the whispers traveling from mouth to mouth about her barren womb or her impotent husband. In the river, where she joined other women weekly to wash her husband's soiled work clothes and their white sheets against the rough edges of river rocks, the women ceased talking or singing when she approached. She sensed they feared her fate was contagious, as if her mere presence would also leave them childless and dry, unable to keep a home or a husband. For what was the purpose of the union between a man and a woman if not to fill their hands and their hearts with the sweet plump bodies of babies?

One night, after a hearty meal of white bean stew and goat meat grilled with peppers, onions, and olives, Inés María waited for her mother to leave the table and then implored her husband to bring the river to her.

"I'm choking with anger and despair," she said bluntly, looking directly at his eyes. "I don't want to see them anymore."

"What are you saying?" José Angel thought he knew but he needed to hear her say it.

"The women," she said, almost spitting out the words. "I don't want to see all those women and their children."

José Angel bowed his head, as if ashamed, but he obliged. The next day, before dawn, he built a pedestal with discarded wood under the myrtle tree and placed a concave river stone on top. On laundry days, he would bring pails of water from the well and pour them in the stone, which he had smoothed out with his farm tools to protect his wife's still delicate hands.

Absconded in her house with her mother and loving husband, Inés María tended to her grief as if it were a garden. She paid close attention to it and fed it memories, expectations, and truncated hopes. As she went through her daily chores—caring for the animals, weeding the vegetable patch, helping her mother cook meals and clean the house, washing clothes and pressing them with a flat iron heated by coals—she grew sadder and more pensive. It was clear to her that God was punishing her. For what, she wasn't sure, for she considered herself a virtuous woman and a devout Catholic, already faithful to *La Virgen de la Candelaria*, the patron saint of the islands, and to *La Virgen de las Nieves*, the virgin venerated in La Palma. It became clear to her that, despite her frequent prayers to the Blessed Mother, she would never bear another child. The thought pierced her soul for in their solitude and misfortune, Inés María had grown to love her husband. She cherished his stubbornness toward the land, his optimism, his sense of humor, and his essential goodness, but she especially loved the way his eyes shone with gratitude when she gave herself to him. In his eyes, she saw the reflection of her own growing desire for him and for the family that God had denied them.

There was only one thing to do and that she did. She started to refuse her husband. At night, when José Angel stretched his thick arms under the covers and tried to arrange her body under his, Inés María turned away from his insistent kisses and kept her legs closed as her mother had told her to do before marriage. José Angel never gave up, though. For eight years he would hold her and gently dry her tears—and his as well—for theirs was a true love.

Then, one day, as she was settling down for the night, it occurred to Inés María that José Angel was coming home later and later every night. In fact, the thought hadn't occurred to her, but it was planted in her head by her mother, who, as she was setting the table that evening, only for the two of them as was ever more common, quietly asked her daughter, "Why is your husband working in the dark?"

Inés María hadn't replied, out of respect for her mother, but also because she wasn't sure what to say. She knew the work on the farm was grueling, but had it become more so lately? She couldn't remember if he had always come home this late. That night she waited for him, alert in the darkness of their bedroom. When she felt him near her, she turned toward him.

"It's not my intention to make you uncomfortable," she began timidly, "but why must you work so late?"

José Angel could feel her dark eyes boring into his and decided to tell her a version of the truth.

"I was not working, woman. I was having a drink," he said. "Sometimes my bones need a drink; not my mouth or my throat or my head, but my bones."

Inés María nodded, knowing he couldn't see her assent but sensing he could feel her understanding. And yet, she had a keen sense of smell and she had not detected the repugnant smell of alcohol on him. She had, however, breathed in a different aroma on his neck when he kissed her, as he always did before turning on his side to sleep—a pungent smell of onions with a hint of lavender and a dash of lemon. There was no lavender on their farm. And so, this time, before he rolled away from her, Inés María pressed her body against his. José Angel, surprised but elated, embraced her as if he were a drowning man and she the last lifeboat in the ocean.

Nine months later, just four months into the new century, she gave birth to a baby girl after a glorious pregnancy that returned her husband to her arms and purpose to their lives. They named her Catalina, for she was born on the 29th of April, the feast day of Saint Catalina of Siena. The baby's second name was Candelaria, to honor the virgin Inés María so worshiped.

From the moment of her birth, Catalina de la Candelaria Quintana Cabazas became their cherished miracle baby, so strong and healthy that she came out crying and hardly seemed to stop for a year. Inés María and José Angel didn't mind. Catalina had saved their marriage and lifted the curse of the family. Thirteen months later, Simona de las Nieves was born, and two and a half years later, Lucía Hilaria.

There were now three precious girls on the Quintana farm, but no one in the family ever doubted who among them would one day break everyone's heart.

Mara

Santander, Spain
July 2019

As usual, my mother's words had left me feeling morose. It was true that life had a way of surprising you. "You never know what can happen," she had said. With that, I had to agree.

There was a time, thirteen years ago, when I had a family and we lived in an elegant pre-war apartment on the Upper West Side of Manhattan. I had a full-time job at one of the world's most respected newspapers, where I covered the immigration beat, which usually meant I wrote about the displaced and the poor for a living. My husband, Nelson Salas, a network news producer, was busier than I was—often traveling on very little notice. We had a son, Dylan. Content and alert from the day he was born, Dylan became the center of our lives.

Back then, I dreamed of being a foreign correspondent in Africa. I was drawn to the continent since childhood for reasons I couldn't really explain; it helped my ambition to know that all the correspondents I admired had worked there at one time or another. But that dream ended when my husband died, unexpectedly and crushingly, of a massive heart attack while walking to work through Central Park. He was forty-two. At the time of his death, we had been together for twenty-four years, ever since we were high school seniors.

My Nelson was the kind of boyfriend who brought me flowers every time he picked me up in his old beat-up VW. He wrote me poems and left them in my schoolbag, and he made me mixed tapes of the music he liked and hoped I would, too. With him, I learned about classical music, English poets, and Argentine tango. In the years we lived together, he always took the butter out of the refrigerator in the morning so that, by the time we sat for breakfast, it would be soft, just the way I liked it. He made me cappuccino with foam and cinnamon every single morning of our life together. The morning I got the call from the hospital, I had not yet washed my coffee mug. For a long time, I didn't wash it, because it had been the last thing he had touched in our home. I was in the bathroom when he left that morning and I didn't kiss him goodbye, as I always did.

But, it seemed to me, I had been lucky after all. Most people don't get to experience in a lifetime of dating what I had with Nelson. Yes, we should have grown old together, but that wasn't the way my life had turned out. Thankfully, he left me the most precious of gifts: Dylan, our son. If it were not for Dylan's tangible presence, I probably would have thought my relationship with Nelson was like a mirage, a shimmering pool of water in the desert of my heart. In the years we had together, I was whole, the one time when all the pieces of my self were gathered neatly under the tent of our love.

I was numbed with pain, but because I had a six-year-old to look after, I would not allow myself to crumble. The day Nelson died I went straight from the hospital to Dylan's school to pick him up. I took him to the playground for a while until I could summon the courage to tell him Daddy was no longer with us. Dylan was too young to comprehend death, but old enough to mimic my behavior. If I was sad, he was sad as well, and if I cried, he cried with such feeling that his sobs stopped my tears. I was afraid my son would be scarred because of the absence of his father, so in those first confusing days after his death I vowed to keep living with joy and a sense of adventure, as Nelson had, as he would have wanted us to go on.

But I was so lost without him. In the mornings I didn't know what to wear because he always read me the weather report before I opened my closet. He was the gregarious one in our marriage, the one who knew everyone in the building, even on the block. Walking by myself in our neighborhood after his death, I felt unseen. It was as if someone had thrown a switch and left me in complete darkness.

There was no funeral or burial. Nelson wouldn't have approved. Instead, his body was cremated, and his coworkers had a very sweet gathering on Central Park's Great Lawn to celebrate his life about a week after. There was music, poems, and plenty of good red wine, just as Nelson would have liked. Of course, I attended, and I took Dylan with me, but we left quickly. My pain was so raw, and Dylan was so small, there seemed to be no point to any of it. What could they possibly say that we didn't know? What memories or stories could they share that would top my own? I had lost the love of my life, and my son had lost his father. No violin concert, such as the one at the park that day, and no amount of wine, could assuage my pain.

For years, I kept his ashes in a cedar box in the closet. Later, when Dylan entered his teenage years, we would talk about what to do with the ashes, as in "What are we going to do with Daddy?" I always thought I'd wait until Dylan was older so that he'd help me decide, but that moment passed, and he didn't. That cherished box is now tucked away in the bottom drawer of my dresser, here with me.

By the time my son left for college, my days began to lose their shape and order once again. I no longer wanted to cook. While I had once been the enthusiastic cook for three, and later became the loving cook for two, now I couldn't even shop for one. Milk would go bad, lettuce wilted in the bag, pears rotted in the bowl before I could get to them. I spent most days in a daze, alternatively feeling giddy at all my new freedom and terrified of being alone. The two-bedroom apartment suddenly seemed enormous.

My mother called several times a day, but I avoided her calls until I couldn't anymore because, even I could tell, I needed help.

"What you need is a boyfriend," she said, after I explained my malaise. I pulled the phone away from my ear and considered hanging up on her. Instead, I silently counted to ten in my rusty French, so that it would take longer. I had been on a smattering of dates since Nelson's death but never more than once with the same man. I kept comparing them to Nelson, and all fell short. Not one of them had his sense of humor, warmth, intelligence, or good looks. Not one of them smelled like him, that subtle mix of his natural body odor—like leaves after rain—with the sharp scent of his favorite cologne. The green bottle of Brut still rested on our bedroom dresser. I sometimes opened it to breathe in a little bit of Nelson, but closed it quickly, afraid the cologne would evaporate, and I would forever lose the scent of my husband.

"Are you still there?" my mother asked.

"Yes, I am," I said. "And I'm also still grieving Nelson. Any other thoughts?"

"That was twelve years ago," she insisted. "And I know for a fact, this is not what he would want for you. Besides, you're still a relatively young widow. I don't know what you want, but you always do . . ."

She kept talking, but I was only half listening. In truth, I had stopped listening after her "relatively young widow" comment.

My mother was right, as much as her phrasing stung. I was no longer young, I was a "relatively young widow." If I was to change my life, the time was now.

Certain that I wouldn't be considered for a foreign assignment anymore—my old peers had retired, died, or moved on—I quit my job and negotiated a contract that would allow me to keep my byline in the paper but, essentially, as a freelancer. I would no longer have a full-time job, which was fine since I had no debts and Nelson's life insurance was more than enough to sustain us and pay for Dylan's schooling. I had been opposed to Nelson getting life insurance when Dylan was born. I told him that kind of preparation was unnecessary and maybe even would bring us bad luck. What I needed, what I wanted was life assurance, the guarantee, in writing, if possible, that he would live as long as I did, that his side of the bed would never be pristine and that my hand would always find his in the dark. He laughed off my fears and hugged my worries away. Now, of course, I'm grateful for his foresight.

Soon after, I sublet my apartment to a colleague, and I, too, flew the nest, taking with me only a few books, a suitcase full of practical mostly gray clothing, and a framed black-and-white photo of a lighthouse at dusk in Key Biscayne, an image Nelson had captured as a young photographer and that had always hung on the wall next to my bed.

As it turned out, I didn't go to Africa. But in ways I never could have imagined, Africa came to me.

Catalina

La Palma
1905–1913

WITH THREE HEALTHY DAUGHTERS and five wooden crosses in the garden, Catalina's parents had given up hope of ever conceiving a boy, but they were quite happy with their girls, who were tall and dark-eyed, like their mother, with the red hair and vitality of their father. From a young age they began helping in the fields and, especially, with the family business that had grown to include silkworms since Catalina was born.

As a birth gift, a neighbor had given them a box with fifteen silkworms inside. They interpreted the gesture and the coincidence of the number—the same as the number of the seeds they had once purchased—as a sign. At first, Inés María kept them in her apron, as if they were tiny pets, but it soon became evident that the worms needed a place of their own. Within a month, José Angel had built a shack for them not far from the house.

The small, agile hands of the three girls were perfectly suited to handle fragile caterpillars and delicate silk cocoons. Catalina, especially, excelled at patiently handfeeding even the most reluctant caterpillars. On her watch, they grew plump and content on their beds—wooden trays cushioned with mulberry leaves and stacked like drawers in the shack.

Throughout their small village of La Peña, in the only landlocked municipality in the center of La Palma, their farm eventually became known for providing the best mulberry leaves in the Canary Islands. Word got around that the silkworms fed with Quintana mulberry leaves laid more eggs than others, lived longer than eight weeks, and produced strong silk threads.

While the girls tended to the worms, their mother learned to weave silk. In the evenings when the housework was done, the entire family, including an ailing doña Elena, sat in the living room under the one light bulb José Angel had installed four years after electricity was introduced to the island. Doña Elena and the girls would embroider as the always gregarious José Angel talked about the trees, the farm, the weather, or the wind, and Inés María, still quiet even in her contentment, sat in front of her handloom and wove yard after yard of beautiful cloth.

She never wove the cloth to sell—it wouldn't have occurred to her—but to make dresses for her daughters, setting aside a few yards of ivory silk for their eventual weddings. Catalina's would be the first wedding dress she ever made, and the only one she would regret making.

Catalina met Juan Cruz Cruz when she was five years old, on her first day of school, and immediately felt a tug, almost like a pain she couldn't comprehend that made her want to be near him all the time. They were neighbors, but their paths hadn't crossed because he was about three years older. She knew he existed, the same way she was used to the presence of mules and cows in the barns nearby. He was the boy who lived in the only house she could see from her bedroom, but she had never really seen him until they sat in the same one-room school.

He walked in wearing shorts too small for his frame, no shoes, and an impish smile that declared to the world he paid no attention to what others thought. A girl, with features that matched his, and dark curly hair like him, held his hand fiercely. He whispered in her ear and gently pushed her toward the empty chair next to Catalina. When he sat behind them, Catalina turned around to have a closer look at him. His face was open, and his hazel eyes darted from face to face, as if he wanted to commit all the new students to memory or challenge them to speak up. At eight, he was his own person. He seemed to know what he wanted and how to get it. And what he most wanted from that day on was the little girl with the red hair and freckled cheeks who sat in front of him.

It was a happy coincidence that he didn't have to try hard. The teacher allowed his sister Ana to remain in the seat next to Catalina, who took an instant liking to her—this shy young girl who was as tall as her brother but only six. The two became inseparable. During recess, while Juan watched them from a distance, the girls sat on the dirt and played the first game they could think of: pretending they were mothers. And because they had no dolls, they swaddled some fallen twigs with discarded burlap and pressed them to their flat and narrow chests as if they were nursing their babies.

After school, they walked home together with Juan always a few steps behind them. At the dusty fork in the road in front of Catalina's house, she would veer right while the two siblings continued on to their smaller house, devoid of fruit trees but surrounded by wildflowers. From where she stood, Catalina couldn't even see any animals there. "What do they eat? Where do they get their milk?" she wondered aloud.

Though Catalina cherished Ana, it was Juan who captured her imagination.

She was thrilled and a little intimidated by the way he dealt with the world. He didn't pluck flowers, he whacked plants; he chased lizards, climbed trees, and tumbled down the hills. Every day he eagerly showed her fresh cuts or scrapes on his knees, elbows, or fingers. He was proud of his scars. After a few months of watching him, she tried to join Juan in his adventures, but it was impossible to keep up with him. It also became increasingly hard not to be near him during the long hours after school and the endless weekends. Every Sunday, she would look for him in church or the market, the only activities that brought nearly the entire village together, but Juan and Ana were never in church. At times it seemed to Catalina that they weren't real, and that maybe she had conjured them up to make school more bearable.

One weekend, as summer was approaching and, with it, the end of the school year, Catalina asked her mother if she could go to Ana's house to play. They were standing in the kitchen, where Inés María, with an apron tied to her thickening waist, was chopping vegetables while Catalina gathered the discards to make a broth as her grandmother had taught her. Her mother waited to finish her task before acknowledging the question. The wait seemed endless to Catalina.

Inés María moved her mouth as if to speak, but then changed her mind. When she finally spoke, she was gazing out the window and not at her daughter.

"Today is not a good day. Your grandmother isn't feeling well," she said. "Maybe another time."

With that she moved to the stove, and Catalina knew enough not to ask why her grandmother not feeling well meant that she couldn't visit her best friend. She tried again the next day. And the next. And she kept on asking until she became old enough to learn why she couldn't visit Ana, and why her mother would never explain it to her.

The Cruz family was shunned by most of the townspeople. It was said that the father—a man named Aureliano Cruz whom no one wanted to remember—was a drunk who had deserted his wife, Manuela Cruz, when the boys were toddlers. Without a man in her life, Manuela was a rarity in La Peña, a place bound by tradition, duty, and the fear of God. Without a man, she was also destitute but not entirely helpless. To survive, Manuela washed other people's clothes, spending hours in the river by herself, long after the other women had left to seek shelter from the midday sun. As soon as her sons were old enough to handle a machete or a sickle, they left school to work as farmhands, harvesting onions, digging potatoes out of the ground, and weeding endless rows of newly planted tobacco plants. The year he began wearing long pants, Tomás, the older of her sons, became a fisherman and the family situation improved somewhat. But, by then, Manuela had become the source of much gossip and scorn because, long after her husband disappeared, she had given birth to a daughter, Ana. Eventually the stigma of that fatherless birth faded, as memories do, but the ill repute clung to the family, and to Ana in particular, like molasses to fingers.

None of that could have thwarted Catalina's love for Juan. She wasn't sure when she had begun to love him. If forced to pick a day, she would have said it was the first day of summer the year she turned six. She was playing outside, alone, after milking the goat and helping her grandmother weed the herb garden. Suddenly, she heard a whistle coming from the trees on the side of her house. First, she thought it was a bird, and, though intrigued, ignored it. But the whistling continued. It seemed to be saying something sad and beautiful. Catalina had never heard any bird or person whistle like that.

She moved to the edge of the property where the pine forest began. Then the whistling stopped. When she started to walk back home, she heard it again. This time, she was sure it was human. It sounded like the tunes her father would sometimes sing. She turned around quickly, and as she did, she saw the unmistakable shape of a skinny dark-haired boy jumping down from a tree and running off. She knew it was Juan.

At that moment, her stomach dropped as if she had swallowed a stone. She sat down hard on the ground and watched him running all the way home. She couldn't have described what she was feeling. But from then on, whenever they weren't together, the days felt dull and endless, and it was hard for her to find a reason to smile.

Toward the end of the summer after Catalina's third year of school, her father announced that she wouldn't be going back to school. They needed her in the shack taking care of the worms, he said. Catalina protested.

"But Father, I'm learning numbers and words. I can help you better if I go to school," she said between sobs, even though a part of her was relieved she wouldn't have to sit all morning in a classroom pretending to pay attention to lessons she was not interested in.

It was difficult for José Angel to see his daughters cry, but especially Catalina, who, from the moment she could walk, had followed him around like a loving puppy. On family outings, she always insisted on sitting next to him as he rode his mule-driven cart to town. As soon as she began to recognize words and string sentences together, she read the newspaper aloud for his delight. If she stumbled over a word or mispronounced it, he ignored it. She had taught him to sign his name, and how to read basic words like *seeds* and *trees* and *cost*. When his knees hurt at night, it was Catalina who massaged his pain away with a salve of aloe from their kitchen garden. If a fence needed mending, Catalina was there with a mallet to help him. But he couldn't cave in. He needed his daughter to help with the business.

"You already know how to add and subtract, read and write," he said. "That's everything you need to learn in life from a teacher. The rest, you will one day learn from your husband."

That seemed to soothe Catalina who had already decided her husband could be no other than Juan. Catalina had been upset at her father's decision, mainly, because being in the house all day would make it even more difficult to see Juan and Ana, who she assumed would return to school in the fall. She was right about Ana, but not about Juan, who had decided on his own that it was time for him to leave school and begin working. Ana, despite her family's poverty, continued going to school for three more years. She had become a serious child, taking care of her often-sick mother as well as cooking, cleaning, and washing clothes for the entire family. Her small hands grew broad and raw, and her forehead developed two premature creases that arched over her eyebrows as if she were perpetually wondering what else could go wrong in her already bleak life. And yet her hazel eyes shone with a special light that, to Catalina at least, seemed strangely beautiful and soothing.

Ana carried books around like treasures she had found under rocks, and it wasn't unusual to find her reading, her back pressed against the trunk of a tree, after she was done with her chores. If anyone, even Catalina, approached and interrupted her, Ana would look up politely, eyes unfocused, and her index finger marking the sentence she was reading before the interruption. Gradually, the two girls drifted apart, Ana burdened by chores and lost in her books, and Catalina increasingly preoccupied with Juan.

When Catalina turned twelve, she finally shared her symptoms with her sister Simona, who was her closest confidant. Simona gave her malaise a name.

"I think you are in love," she said with a knowing smile. "But you shouldn't say anything to anyone, especially not Mother and Father. And make sure Juan doesn't find out either. It wouldn't be appropriate, and I have heard that boys don't like girls who like them."

Catalina promised. She relished the idea of having a secret, and she treasured her sister, who, though a year younger, was savvier than she was. Her brief conversation with Simona confirmed what she had already suspected. But Simona was wrong about one thing. Catalina was certain that Juan loved her too, even though he had never told her.

To see him, Catalina became deceitful. She knew lying was a sin, but she was certain she'd escape the wrath of God and all the saints her mother prayed to because her intentions were noble. Love, she thought, had to be understood even by God, perhaps especially by God. She knew that on Fridays Juan sold the fish his older brother, Tomás, caught during the week. With her sisters, Catalina always offered to go to the market to buy fish and bread and whatever else her mother needed. Her youngest sister Lucía thought nothing was amiss when

Catalina stood longer than necessary at the fish stall. She liked it, in fact, because she could play with some of the other children in the market. But Simona knew, and, from a prudent distance, kept an eye on her two sisters: the older one pining for her love; the younger one running about with her friends near the church.

"What would you like today, Catalina?" said Juan, reaching into the pocket of his ochre-colored cotton pants. He had a dirty half-apron tied around his waist and his once-white shirt was speckled with blood and sparkly scales. In the last year he had grown taller, and his shoulders had broadened. His hands, efficient and calloused from work, were out of proportion to his body, marking the transition from adolescence to manhood. Catalina loved those hands: the ridges and contours of his fingers; the rough palms, crisscrossed by scars from knives and fish bones; the way both pinkies were perpetually bent at an angle as if about to make a fist. She had once asked him about his crooked fingers, and he said he had inherited them from his father, like his whistling ability and reckless spirit.

"I'll have the usual today," she finally said, and waited expectantly as he carefully picked the most gorgeous *vieja* fish, a local favorite. He expertly chopped off the head and tail, knowing Catalina wouldn't eat any creature that seemed to look at her, even in death. She flinched at the whack of the knife against the wooden block and admired how swiftly he tossed aside the head and tail into a bucket he kept at his feet. Then he wrapped the gorgeous red and silver fish in brown paper and just before folding it closed, slipped in a note he'd pulled from his pocket.

Catalina was relieved, since this was the real reason she volunteered to come to the market. Juan always included a letter for her wrapped with the fish. In his childish handwriting, riddled with spelling errors, he would scrawl out a love poem copied from one of his sister's books.

One market day a year later, when Catalina was thirteen and Juan sixteen, the note inside the fish wrapping turned out to be not a poem but a plea: "Meet me by *La Roca* after sundown." *La Roca*, as everyone in town called it, was a giant stone protruding from the ground at the western edge of the Quintana property. When she was younger, she and her sisters had played a game where they'd race through the rows of mulberry trees and whoever touched the rock first would be the winner. Simona always won that game; Catalina always came in third.

Her heart started pounding when she read Juan's note. How could she manage to get away from her parents? But Juan knew something Catalina didn't. That evening there was a meeting in the church to welcome the new priest, Father Jacinto, since Father Manuel, who had baptized everyone and had married most of the couples in town, had passed away suddenly a week earlier.

When her parents left for the church after dinner, leaving her in charge of her sisters, Catalina told them to go to their room and close the door. She needed to feed the worms, she said. Her sisters obeyed and Catalina slipped out the back door but instead of going to the shack, she ran to *La Roca*. And it was there, against that massive boulder that Juan kissed her for the first time.

They had been sitting and talking with their backs pressed against the rock, when Juan suddenly took her hand and kissed it, keeping his eyes on her face.

"How much do you love me?" she had impulsively asked.

"Too much," he said, getting up and pulling her close.

"How much is that?"

"It can't be measured."

"Sure, it can," she said playfully. "Is your love as big my house?"

"Oh no, bigger," he said, circling her small waist and drawing her even closer to him.

"As big as *La Roca*?" she asked.

"Bigger," he said, and brushed his lips against her temples.

"Is it the size of the sky?" Her big brown eyes were feigning awe but showing desire. He lowered his lips to hers. She opened her mouth slightly and her sweet breath encouraged him to go on. He thrust his tongue inside her mouth, gently at first and then, meeting no resistance, ferociously, as if he had been walking in a desert for days and had encountered a spring. Catalina embraced him and let him mold her body against his own.

In her memory that kiss lasted an eternity. When he pulled away, he whispered in her ear, "My love for you is higher than the sky and deeper than the ocean." Catalina had never seen the ocean, but she knew it surrounded their island like a silk cocoon, keeping them both safe and trapped in its vastness. It was, in their minds, the most powerful metaphor for their young love.

Mara

Santander
July 2019

By the time the sun was beginning to peek over the mountains surrounding the city, I had showered and was dressed in my traveler's uniform—black pants and a gray T-shirt, loose enough to hide the extra ten pounds I was always trying but failing to lose. I threw a baby blue sweater over my shoulders, gathered my hair up in a messy ponytail, and put on my old leather work boots, practical and soft. The flight to Madrid was scheduled to leave at 8 a.m., but my apartment was minutes from the airport.

The city I live in, on the northern coast of Spain, has yet to be discovered by most tourists. I'm hoping they never do, which is why I haven't written a word about it for the travel section of my paper. Santander is only about four hours by train or car from Madrid, but it might as well be in another country. Tourists get as far north as the Guggenheim Museum in Bilbao, exactly an hour away from the door to my apartment, and then head back to Seville or Barcelona, raving about the beauty of the north, not realizing they have missed some of the best parts of this incredibly beautiful country. That suits me fine.

Twice a week a ferry comes from England carrying sun-starved tourists who think that, because they are going to Spain, they'll find sunny beaches. Many of them return home the same day, on the same ferry, slightly disappointed. Santander has the weather of Ireland: cool drizzly summers and cold misty winters. It's what makes it so appealing to me—so green and lush and clean and solitary. No matter what happened the day before, the morning rain washes it all away.

There's another reason why I chose to live here. I suffer from sudden panic attacks and sometimes I even faint when I go near deep water. When I told my doctor, he said I had "thalassophobia." I nodded because I was too proud to admit I had no idea what he was talking about and took the prescription he wrote for a pill I had no intention of taking. As soon as I left his office, I looked up the word on my phone. It sounded ominous, but *thalassophobia* is just a fancy word to diagnose an old affliction of mine: fear of the ocean.

Although I've lived with this fear for as long as I can remember, I finally decided to deal with it and started to see a therapist last year, once my son left for college. The therapist strongly advocated for a type of therapy called "exposure therapy," which meant I had to gradually expose myself to my fears. In Manhattan that would have been difficult. The rivers surrounding it hardly even registered as water for me anymore and since my world was very small then, I barely ever went near them.

After a few months looking at pictures of the sea and, later, videos and documentaries, as instructed, I decided to move to Spain, a country I've loved since I first visited it when I was dating Nelson, and learned he was a global citizen. He was Argentinian by birth, American by choice, and a Sephardic Jew by blood. My husband's ancestors were expelled from Spain sometime after 1492, as most Jews were. They fled to Italy, and, after more than four hundred years, some of their descendants made their way to Argentina, in South America. After they retired, Nelson's paternal grandparents decided to return to the land of their ancestors in the mountainous north of Spain, and bought an ocean-facing apartment in Santander in the late 1970s. When they died, they willed it to Nelson, who by then had reclaimed Spanish citizenship, through his ancient Sephardic lineage, and extended it to me as his wife. I was thrilled with my red passport and treasured it as only those who, like me, had once been stateless refugees can appreciate. We visited Santander every summer, a tradition I continued with Dylan even after Nelson's death when I inherited the apartment. I refused to rent it out the rest of the year. I couldn't allow other stories to dilute ours.

That apartment eventually became my home. Its front windows framed the rough but majestic Cantabrian Sea, as Spaniards call the area of the Bay of Biscay bordering northern Spain. On good days, the sea was serene, sparkling under the sun, its gentle waves carrying surfers up and down like a roller coaster in a real-life water park. On bad days, when the natives stepped outside and smelled the air, they'd shake their heads, muttering that the wind was blowing in from the south. Then everyone knew to avoid the promenade by the bay, or they could find themselves drenched by the waves.

The gradual exposure approach to tame my fear seemed to be working. I tried not to get too close to the beach when I walked in the city, but was able to admire the view of the ocean from my windows. At night the sound of the waves lulled me to sleep—Ibuprofen helped when I was in pain—and, in the mornings, the sun woke me up. Over the years the sun had bleached the arms of the old green couch that came with the living room, changing its hue in a way I found appealing. While I didn't particularly share my late in-laws' taste, when I moved here full-time I couldn't imagine throwing out all the furniture and paintings they had accumulated over the years or bringing my own from New York. Frankly, I didn't have the energy to change anything. For once, somebody else's skin suited me fine. Mine was too battered and frail, though I never would have admitted it to anyone.

Being busy and maintaining a predictable routine when not working kept me sane. I shopped at the fish market on Mondays, when the fishermen's wives sold their bounty in a plaza in the heart of the city. On Tuesdays and Thursdays, I took a yoga class and ran errands. Wednesdays, I visited museums or galleries. On Fridays I went to the movies, and on the weekends, I explored the quaint towns that dot this beautiful part of the world. I didn't have friends, but I wasn't trying very hard. Mostly, I kept to myself, working hard at repairing my soul and my heart, one uneventful day after the other. I got an average of two assignments a month and I also suggested ideas for stories that my editors usually liked. The bulk of my stories were about people on the move. I felt as if I was back on the immigration beat in New York; only here in Europe I was writing about open borders, and I used my French a lot more than my Spanish when interviewing new arrivals. But immigration stories, here and there, are all strikingly similar: a mixture of pain, hope, and fear that I was very familiar with.

My new assignment in the Canary Islands intrigued me, but it also frightened me. I wasn't certain what I feared, but my body had been on high alert ever since my editor called. It could have been the geography of the Canary Islands. The idea of such tiny pieces of land surrounded by so much water had always kept me from visiting, even though I always wanted to. But I couldn't stay away this time. It wasn't in my nature to turn down an assignment, even if I dreaded it.

I paused at the door of the bedroom for a moment. Which bag to take? The editor said it wasn't a big assignment, but he also said there may be more to it. On impulse, I grabbed the larger backpack, which would turn out to be a wise choice. And, as I always do before I leave on a trip, I muttered a prayer touching the mezuzah on the door frame. The mezuzah, too, came with the apartment. I'm not religious or Jewish, but I am Cuban and deeply superstitious.

Later that morning, after my flight had arrived in Madrid, I was looking for Nina in the airport when my phone began to chirp that unmistakable cricket sound I had assigned to my mother. I dug into my purse quickly and answered.

"How are you?" I asked reflexively.

"I'm fine now, but when I was talking to you earlier, I got that deep pain in my stomach I sometimes get. Didn't you notice how I hung up on you? I guess not, because you didn't call me back. Anyway, I could hardly breathe," she said without pausing to ask how or where I was, as usual.

My friend Nina entered my field of vision at that moment and flashed me one of her big smiles. She is petite, with short curly hair, and bony, like a sixteen-year-old boy, goofy like one, too, except she is sixty years old and fierce.

I mouthed the word "mother," and Nina frowned. She's known me long enough to leave me alone when my mother calls. Nina opened her big blue eyes wide, tiptoed around me and headed for the security line as I talked, or rather, listened to my mother.

"Do you want to hang up, rest some, and call back later?" I said patiently, aware that we'd had versions of this conversation before.

"No," she said, afraid to lose an audience. "I think I'm okay now."

But I wasn't. I had to get going and told her so.

"Oh, why didn't you say that before? I thought you were still at home. I have something I need to tell you."

"Well, yes, you already did this morning, remember?" I said, as Nina handed her passport and boarding pass to the officer. My boarding pass was on my phone. I needed to hang up.

"*Mima*, I need to go now."

As I pulled the phone from my burning ear I could hear my mother yelling, "Wait! This may be import—"

I handed my phone to the officer with an apologetic smile, and she clicked the call off with a long fake nail, before checking my ID and scanning my boarding pass. Nina was waiting on the other side, smiling the same way she had when she greeted me.

"Don't say a word," I warned her.

"Hello to you, too," she said, and stood on her tiptoes to kiss me on both cheeks.

My phone chirped again. I rolled my eyes at Nina, who shrugged while I picked up.

"As I was saying," my mother continued, relentless as ever.

"*Mima*, really. I'm at the airport!"

"I'll make it quick; I promise."

And for once she did.

"You asked me earlier if I remembered anything else about my grandmother, if I had a photo or anything like that, and I said no, but I did remember something, and I'm not sure if it helps. In fact, I'm sure it doesn't, and sometimes I think it may not even be true."

"*Mima*, you are talking in riddles. What is it?"

"A letter," she said, rushing her words now. "There was a letter I read once, a letter I wasn't supposed to read, and I'm almost certain it mentioned something about mulberry trees. Yes, it said the mulberry trees had grown back."

"Mulberry trees? And why weren't you supposed to read the letter?" I asked as I walked to the gate, but there was no response. I had lost the signal.

Catalina

La Palma
1914–1918

THE DAY HER FATHER BROUGHT HOME the news from town that the world was at war, in July 1914, Catalina's first thought was to find Juan and hold him tightly. She took advantage of the commotion in her house to run to Juan's. The sun was setting, but there was enough light for her to see where she was going. Lavender bushes lashed at her heels as she ran through a shortcut, but she paid no attention to those minor discomforts. Her heart was beating wildly. She placed one hand on her throat as if she could calm the beats with her fingers. With the other hand, she lifted her dress in a vain attempt to keep it clean and out of the way of her running feet. As she got closer, the wooden house seemed even smaller than it did from a distance: just a door and two windows at the front and a roof like a wide-legged letter A. Blue and white wildflowers dotted an otherwise barren patch of land.

As if she had conjured him up with her thoughts, Juan emerged from his house and lit a cigarette. Catalina saw the flame and slowed down to watch him. The light of the match illuminated his face for a moment, and she felt there was nothing or no one she loved more than this boy with mischievous eyes and warm hands. When he blew the match out, and his face grew faint in the twilight, Catalina felt a sudden sadness penetrate her body. She sensed that one day he would disappear like that dying light of the flame, leaving her alone. The thought was so unbearable, she gasped. It was then Juan saw her. Tossing the cigarette to the ground, he ran to her and took her in his arms.

"Catalina," he cried. "What are you doing here? What's happened?"

"War," was all she could blurt out before starting to cry, because it seemed easier to say that than to explain her sudden fear. "The world is at war."

Juan hadn't heard anything about it yet, but he tried to console her, explaining that Spain would likely not intervene, that they would be safe, that he would stay put and wouldn't have to leave. Gently, he wiped her tears away and, with his arm around her shoulder, steered her toward the path leading to *La Roca*.

Once there, Juan took a folded knife from his pocket and began scratching into the stone.

"See," he said when he was done. "That way we'll always be together."

In the growing darkness, she gazed at their initials side by side: *JC*. The *J* and the *C* were so close together that they seemed like the trunk of an uneven tree. That brought a smile to her face, and she let him kiss her. The war and her earlier premonition were soon forgotten.

The next four years were a blur for Catalina, who spent most of her waking hours helping her mother feed the family with very little food. They ate what they grew and not much else.

Though Juan had been right, and Spain kept its neutrality in the war, much of the country—and especially the islands—were deeply impoverished. Commerce had been severely curtailed as German ships and submarines hunted for prey at sea. Some days, when the adults slept after lunch, Catalina would escape to the rock hoping to find Juan there. With no way of communicating with him, all she could do was close her eyes and concentrate hard on her wish to see him. Often, it worked, and he would be waiting for her, as if he knew she was coming. At other times, when he wasn't there, she would caress the rock with their initials and dream of him. Sometimes, she would hear the longing sound of his whistle in the distance, and she would know that he was thinking of her. But it was not enough. It was never enough.

One day in the spring, when Catalina had just turned eighteen, Ana came to her door crying and told her that her oldest brother, Tomás, the fisherman, had died after catching a nasty cold at sea that settled in his lungs and killed him in a matter of days. As Catalina hugged her friend, she could not help but think of Juan and how the responsibility of his family would now surely fall on his shoulders. Ana left so quickly that, by the time Catalina's mother came to the door, she was already gone.

"What did that silly girl want?" Inés María demanded, barely hiding her distaste, but her features softened when Catalina explained what had happened and asked for permission to go to the burial with Ana.

"You may go, but with your grandmother and your sisters."

"Of course," Catalina quickly agreed, eager to be near Juan again.

Doña Elena accompanied the three girls, who looked older in their long black dresses. At the end of the ceremony, Catalina told her grandmother and sisters that she wanted to stay with Ana a little longer.

"With Ana?" Simona asked mockingly.

"Yes," Catalina said, her eyes pleading.

Simona relented, and the sisters took an exhausted doña Elena home. Soon Ana, too, left, holding on to her devastated mother.

When only Juan and Catalina remained at the cemetery, they sat under the shade of an almond tree. Certain nobody would see them, her hand resting in his, she leaned her head on his shoulder. It had been a clear day, but it was now rapidly changing. The clouds hurried across the sky as if the wind was chasing them, but there was no wind. The early fall air bore traces of lavender and molasses. Juan's hair was uncombed, as usual, and he was wearing his work clothes, ochre-colored pants, and a white cotton shirt that no longer seemed white. He smelled faintly of cow manure and onions, but Catalina didn't care. She was used to his smell.

"My parents say I'm too young to have feelings for a boy," she said, not sure how to tell him that her father had become suspicious of her constant outings and had hinted that she should keep away from "those people." He didn't have to say whom he was talking about. Ana had been a forbidden topic in their house for a long time, while Juan's name had barely been mentioned outside the bedroom Catalina shared with her sisters.

José Angel had always opposed Juan for reasons that to Catalina seemed absurd. It was true that Juan came from a damaged and extremely poor family, with barely any land or money, but, if anything, her father ought to respect a young man who had looked after his mother and sister while his older brother worked on a fishing boat. And yet, her father stubbornly clung to the idea that the Cruz family was cursed and that the boy, as he called Juan, bore his mother's shame and would one day repeat the sins of his father.

"You deserve better," José Angel had told her more than once. "I'm trying to protect you."

Catalina couldn't mention any of that to Juan. She didn't want to hurt his feelings or his pride. Without letting go of Catalina's hand, Juan grabbed a stick from the ground and began tracing their initials in the dirt.

"Would you say something, please?" she urged, squeezing his hand.

"That's not what they mean," he finally said. "What they are really saying is that they don't want you with me because of where I come from and because I have nothing to offer you. And they're right."

Catalina didn't know how to respond. It was true the war had brought hardships to all. Yet, she felt certain, it wasn't Juan's poverty that gave her father pause. After all, he, too, had once been poor and was no longer the prosperous man he had been before the war. For José Angel, the problem had always been Juan's family.

Juan looked at her tenderly, tugging at a curl on her forehead. He could sense her confusion and embarrassment. The clouds had halted their swift race in the sky and now loomed over them. "It's going to rain," he declared. "Go home, my love. I'll find a way to see you soon."

"How?" she asked, a little desperate. "It's getting harder to find an excuse to get out of the house."

"I'll whistle, and you'll know where to find me," he said, and extended his hand for her to take. But Catalina kept her hands firmly by her side, though she wasn't sure why, and regretted it the moment she saw Juan letting his hand drop slowly to the pocket of his pants.

"Go now," he urged her, thrusting his chin in the direction of her home. "You'll get soaked."

When she got home, the dark clouds had dispersed as quickly as they had gathered. Not a drop fell from the sky on the scorched soil. Over the years that followed, despite everything that happened or perhaps because of it, she sometimes castigated herself for not grasping the hand he had offered and running away with him that day.

Mara

Tenerife
July 2019

I WAS EXHAUSTED. After two days of working nonstop, I was having a hard time keeping my eyes open. But Nina was insistent. We were seated in a café and she kept pointing to the map on the table in front of us, telling me all the places we could visit in Tenerife on the one day we had left before returning to Madrid. She especially wanted us to visit the sanctuary of the patron saint of the islands, the Virgin of Candelaria, which was only twenty kilometers away.

"You like churches, don't you?" said Nina, who, despite her aversion to organized religion, shared my interest in old places of worship.

"It says here she first showed herself to the original inhabitants of these islands sometime between 1392 and 1401. What do you think?" she said, looking at me with the intelligent eyes of a person who remains curious despite having witnessed some of the worst of humanity through the lens of her camera.

"I think you sound like Dr. Seuss," I managed to say, adding and placing air quotes around, "Oh, the places you'll go!"

Nina groaned.

I yawned and signaled for the waiter. I needed another espresso. No matter how many I tried all over the world, they never compared to the strong and sugary, inky black cups of Cuban coffee from Miami.

I leaned my neck back, letting my hair hang over the back of the chair. I often used the tops of chairs to give myself an instant neck massage.

We were facing the port and I could see mountains in the distance. Beautifully dressed, well-behaved children were walking with their parents or riding scooters on a promenade dotted by date palm trees similar to the royal palms found in Cuba. A warm breeze from the ocean and the light from the sun, not as harsh as in Miami or Cuba, seemed to envelop everything in a gauzy filter. For a moment, it almost seemed as if the entire world was like this—soft and kind and beautiful.

I knew what Nina was trying to do by suggesting we take a trip and relax a little. I had been in a foul mood all morning. The work had been brutal. The days, endless.

On the first day, even before we found a hotel, we had interviewed and photographed the survivors of a shipwreck who'd been rescued by the Spanish authorities. With the aid of a local Akan translator, I was able to interview Akuba, a woman who said she thought she was about twenty-five, and was the mother of three children, ages five, three, and one. On the voyage from Ghana, she had lost the two youngest. She was still holding on to the body of the oldest one, a girl, when rescuers pried her daughter from her freezing fingers. By the time we arrived the bodies had been taken to the morgue. I insisted on seeing Akuba's daughter, though Nina didn't want to photograph a dead child. We knew a photo like that would not run in the paper anyway. But for some reason I needed to see that little girl, and I refused to think of her as "the body." Her mother told me she had named her Piesie Afua, because she was her firstborn child and because she was born on a Friday. Children born on Fridays are wanderers, the translator explained.

At the morgue, on a cold slab of stainless steel, I saw the child for the first and last time. Piesie Afua would no longer wander. She was wearing a green blouse and a beige skirt with ruffles.

Suddenly, a memory assaulted me: *For my own journey from Cuba four decades earlier, I had worn the red polyester bell-bottom pants my mother had made me, and my favorite red, white, and blue plaid blouse, buttoned in the front and festooned with navy blue ribbons around the neck. My mother had made that, too.* I had to push it away quickly or I wouldn't have been able to finish my job. Focus, I told myself, quickly returning to my notes. Tiny toenails painted frosted pink. Shoes? No. Of course not. She would have lost them at sea.

What shoes did I wear? I had no memory of the shoes I wore. That was so long ago. By the time Nina and I got to the hotel that first night, we were both so tired we couldn't begin to process everything we'd heard and seen. I went to my room to write and file my first article quickly. Then I sent Nina a copy. She would send off her photos separately. We hadn't talked about what we'd seen that day. Right before falling asleep, I got a text from her: "Hey, not sure if you are awake, but I just wanted to say what you did today was so important. This is why you are good at what you do. The details you included in the article humanized that girl for me. I mean, who wears ruffles for a journey like that?"

I, too, had wondered about the little girl's clothes. But the truth was I understood why she was wearing ruffles for her trip in a rickety old boat. My fingers hovered over the phone, but I didn't reply.

When I was fifteen, I wore my best clothes to leave Cuba. I didn't wear them to hop in a boat and spend endless hours at sea. I wore them to arrive in the United States. The clothes are aspirational, you see, I wanted to tell Nina. It's not about what you leave behind, but where you're hoping to arrive. It's about the dream. Only in this case, the family's dream had died in the ocean.

The next morning, when Nina and I went out to do a follow-up story, we found ourselves in the middle of a rescue operation. I was rigid with fear as we boarded the boat with the ominous words *Salvamento*

Marítimo on the side of its bow and hesitated for a moment when the rescuers placed an orange life jacket over my head. It was for a story, I told myself. It would all be okay. I kept hearing the words of my first editor in my head as we pulled away from the shore. "There are only three things that matter in journalism," he would say in his heavy Mississippi drawl, punctuating each word with a finger until he held up three fingers of his left hand and kept them aloft for effect while surveying the newsroom with his twinkling blue eyes. "Details, details, and details." This was now my cue to let go of my fears and begin taking notes of everything I could see, count, hear, smell, feel, or even taste.

After a few minutes, the captain got new coordinates over the radio and turned the boat around quickly. Suddenly we seemed to be almost on top of an overturned boat. It all happened so fast that it was hard to take notes while avoiding falling into the churning sea. The boat had been carrying sixteen immigrants. One by one they were lifted out of the water, shivering and afraid, but alive. The rescuers were jubilant, telling me they were sick of picking up dead bodies from the water. The whole point of a rescue operation was to save lives, not to collect bodies.

It was only on the way back, as the crew tried to keep the refugees warm with blankets, that I started feeling dizzy and disoriented at the sight of the waves leaping at the boat. I kept thinking of that other boat from long ago that had brought me and my family from Cuba to the states. My eyes were searching for my father but not finding him. I grabbed at Nina as if she were my mother and wouldn't let go. I was breathing fast, and everything was swirling around. Fast, too fast.

When I came to—Nina told me it was only about a minute later—I was in the arms of a young sailor who had no idea why a middle-aged woman had fainted in his rescue boat. If only he knew. I didn't faint, I later told Nina. It was a panic attack. I could tell because it had happened before. It was one of the reasons why I always tried to avoid reporting stories at sea and the main reason I'd never been on a cruise.

The sea terrified me, and not only because of my experience in leaving Cuba. It had always been that way. My mother, who was also afraid of the sea, was convinced I suffered from some inherited family trauma. She once visited a psychologist who told her that pain and trauma can be passed on from one generation to the other; it is coded in DNA, like hair color and certain mannerisms. I was intrigued by the thought but teased her about it. If that's so, I told her, how come I didn't get your fabulous curly red hair? She didn't know. And what, please tell me, was the original trauma? She had no answer for that either.

Whatever the reason, the fear was real.

And yet, here I was, sitting safely in a café on this beautiful island, the sun shining on my face, the ocean only half a block away. I ought to have felt grateful. But how did I actually feel? Restless, detached, tired. Ready to go home.

Not too long ago, I thought of every assignment as an opportunity to learn and explore. I'd talk to strangers in airplanes, strike up conversations with taxi drivers, sit at communal tables in restaurants, and chat with neighbors about the weather and even politics. When I traveled, which was often, I used every moment of my time in a new city as if I was never going to return.

But not anymore. I didn't seem to have the energy or curiosity necessary to go beyond what I needed to do to get by. I did my work, and my editors seemed satisfied, but I was hollowed out. The spark was gone. I worried about that sometimes, but not enough to bring it up with my therapist.

The waiter brought the coffee and lingered as if he was waiting for a tip. I realized I should probably pay and began riffling inside my brown leather bag looking for my wallet.

"No, there is no need to rush," he said with a sweet smile, and touched my arm for emphasis before he walked away.

Surprised at the touch, I started to think of something witty to say, but Nina beat me to it.

"He's been flirting with you the entire time and you didn't even notice. I swear the next man who comes into your life will have to show you a marriage certificate first and then, and only then, you might pay attention to him."

I started to reply, when suddenly I was startled by a thought.

"Wait, what day is it today?" I asked Nina.

"Monday," she said distractedly, looking down at the map again.

"No, what day of the month. I need a number."

"Oh, it's the 23rd. July 23, 2019. Why? Did you lose your memory, too?"

"No, I just realized it's the tenth anniversary of my father's death."

And right on cue, the phone rang with the distinctive cricket sound that even Nina recognized.

"Oh!" Nina said, folding up her map and mouthing a rushed "sorry-see-you-at-the-hotel" apology.

I picked up the phone from the table and signaled the waiter for another espresso, the third that morning, mimicking bringing a cup to my lips. This was going to be a long call.

My mother seemed subdued and asked how I was. I said fine. I didn't say anything about the story I was reporting, nor did I mention my panic attack or the nightmares I'd been having of the baby girl. No need to worry her, but she also didn't seem all that interested, taking my quick reply at face value and moving on to what she wanted to discuss. No surprise there.

She wanted to talk about my father, of how much she missed him, how much she needed him, of how different her life would now be if that awful cancer hadn't taken him at sixty-eight. She'd be in the Canary Islands with him taking care of business instead of asking me for a favor she was sure I had no time for and probably wouldn't even do.

"Did you?" she asked, interrupting her monologue that, somehow, in a roundabout way, had become another way to chastise me.

"Did I what?"

"Did you do what I asked, find my grandmother's birth certificate?"

Uh-oh, here we go. How to explain to my mother all I had done for the past forty-eight hours? How could I tell her about the little dead girl with the ruffles and the pink toenails, and the feelings their ordeal had stirred up in me? Had my mother been afraid when we crossed our own sea? Was our night in the Florida Straits as dark as the night in the sliver of ocean between Africa and the Canary Islands?

"No, *Mima*," I said instead. "I haven't had the time."

"I knew it," she said. "I'm always last on your to-do list."

"No, I mean, yes, but that's because I always save the best for last, like in the movies," I said, trying to change the subject. "I'll do it today, I promise."

That seemed to appease her, for the moment.

"I can still hear his whistle, you know," my mother said.

"Whose?" I asked though I knew well whom she meant.

"Your father's," she began, settling in for the story I knew by heart. "I'd be in the kitchen around two in the afternoon, preparing lunch, and every day, when he came home from work he'd whistle to let me know he had arrived."

I knew the whistle well. I, too, could still hear it. But I didn't say that, because if I had, I'd have to explain how I'd always heard his whistle, even before I had memories or words.

Catalina

La Palma
June 1918

THE FIRST TIME CATALINA HAD AN INKLING that her life was about to change drastically, it was a day like any other. In the morning, she milked the goats and fed the worms. She swept the floors of the house, helped her father with the trees, and then tried to read a little, but the letters blurred in front of her eyes. With the book open on her lap, her thoughts would turn to Juan and she imagined living with him in a small house, far from her parents, her sisters, even her sweet grandmother.

Later, she went for a walk with her sisters hoping to see Juan, even if from a distance. She hadn't seen him in about a month, since his brother's funeral. But despite walking as far as their parents allowed them to go, it wasn't to be. When they returned to the house two hours later, all the lights were on and there were vases with yellow and pink flowers from their garden on every surface.

The sisters looked at each other wondering if they had forgotten an important day, somebody's birthday, perhaps? Though Catalina had turned eighteen two months earlier, there had been no celebration. The scarcities of the war and a coughing disease that had crossed the sea to ravage the troops and wipe out entire families were a constant preoccupation. No one had been in the mood to celebrate. She hadn't minded.

Eighteen wasn't an important birthday—she was a young woman, but not yet capable of making her own decisions.

Their mother greeted them at the door and silently motioned for the younger girls to go upstairs, while she held Catalina's arm and whispered for her to follow. "We have a special guest tonight," she said, brushing Catalina's hair from her forehead and giving her a head-to-toe appraising look. "This will have to do," she said.

Before Catalina could protest, her mother dragged her to the living room.

Her father was sitting in his favorite chair, with his back to the chimney, and doña Elena looked pained as she waited silently on an old settee that nobody ever used. A stranger sat across from her father and grandmother. On the highly polished table between them was a tray with two glasses of homemade rum. Don José was wearing a white shirt with his formal dark suit, the one he donned for weddings, funerals, and important business meetings. His visitor, too, was dressed formally, and he kept his large hands resting heavily on the front of his brown pants, his fingers splayed flat.

Her father introduced her to the visitor, Antonio López, a man not as old as her father, but much older than she was. They shook hands, timidly, and she could feel in his warm touch the rough calluses of a working man. He was about her height, perhaps an inch taller, with thin arms but a strangely powerful torso, like a thick tree trunk with spindly branches. He had brown hair and piercing green eyes, and his beard was prematurely speckled gray. Catalina kept her eyes on the floor, but she could still feel the intensity of his gaze, searching eyes almost commanding her to look up. She refused to.

Antonio López. She had a vague recollection of hearing that name before. He was the friend of a relative, her father added helpfully, someone her family had known for a long time. Like many others from the Canary Islands, he had gone to Cuba a decade earlier in search of fortune. Now, about to turn thirty, and after years as a farmhand in the cane fields, he was the proud owner of a textile store in a thriving seaside village in central Cuba.

"A place not unlike this," he added, looking pointedly at Catalina, who failed to see what any of this had to do with her. But she listened with curiosity for she had never been anywhere outside her town.

Later, she would conclude that Antonio had chosen her because he must have mistaken her curiosity for interest. But that wasn't the case. Antonio had come expressly for her.

While Catalina listened, the men talked about how terrible it had been for Spain to lose Cuba to the United States two decades earlier.

"If those Americans hadn't intervened in 1898, we would have kept the jewel of the Caribbean. It's bad enough that we lost Puerto Rico and the Philippines, but Cuba? That was a disaster," Antonio said, punctuating his words with big pale hands that crisscrossed the air and came to rest on his thighs with a thud, like pigeons dropping from a tree.

"Do you know my wife was on her way to Cuba when I met her?" don José said, trying to change the subject because Antonio seemed agitated. "It's a good thing she wasn't there for the war with the Americans."

"Yes, I suppose so," said Antonio, somewhat deflated by the sudden turn of the conversation. "But I have to say that not much has changed. Spaniards continue to arrive each day from all corners of Spain and, though difficult at first, in the end they all prosper. Perhaps not as much as I have, or as quickly, but they do, eventually."

A silence ensued and don José hastened to fill it with topics he knew best: the dwindling silk business, the epidemic that had killed countless people, the extreme poverty brought about by the World War, and the hunger on the islands, where for the past few years basic staples, like sugar, flour, and oil, had been scarce.

The Quintanas had managed by living as frugally as possible and occasionally, more often than they thought prudent, thrusting an arm under their mattress to retrieve some of the money they had stashed away for uncertain times. But Catalina feared that if the war went on for much longer, they would have to start selling off pieces of their land, which would destroy her father. The thought made her shudder.

"Eighty ships!" Antonio exclaimed, jerking Catalina out of her thoughts. "German submarines have sunk twenty-five percent of the Spanish fleet, about 250,000 tons of merchandise lost. Lost! Feeding fishes in the bottom of the ocean, that's all, while people starve."

Antonio seemed angry, but he was a good conversationalist and, when he saw don José didn't share his sense of outrage at the cost of war, he deftly steered the conversation to safer ground. Mainly, the growing emigration of able young bodies to the Americas—not only to Cuba and Puerto Rico but also to Venezuela, Mexico, Argentina, even Louisiana and Texas.

Catalina's mind began to drift. She saw their mouths moving and tried to make her face seem interested while she observed them as an outsider would. Compared to the boastful Antonio, her father was measured, thoughtful, and kind. Why would he bring this small man into their lives? Catalina thought the meeting was not accidental. When her father was discussing business with another man, she had never been welcome. No, there must be something they wanted from her presence tonight, but she couldn't imagine what that was.

Antonio kept talking, somewhat nervously. Catalina tried to refocus her attention. Now he was explaining how the weather in Cuba was warm all year, with a few cold days during the mild winters. The soil was fertile. "You throw a seed in the ground and the next morning, you have a tree," he said, chuckling, and hit his thigh again with his open palm to emphasize the point.

"Do you grow mulberry trees?" Catalina asked, finally looking directly at him.

"Pardon me?" He looked startled at her interruption.

"Mulberry trees. You need them for the silkworms."

He laughed, the way an adult does at an imaginative child. Catalina disliked him immediately.

"No, it's too warm for mulberry trees and no one uses silk in Cuba. Such fine textures are alien to them," he said finally. "But we have other things," he added, and spoke in detail about his house, his garden, his store, his money, his friends, and his cattle. It sounded to Catalina as if he owned the entire island of Cuba. But then he said that he lacked something that he very much desired and that was the reason for his return to the islands.

Catalina hesitated momentarily before blurting out, "And what might that be?" She immediately regretted her imprudent question. Her father looked at her sharply, and Catalina lowered her eyes again, "If I might ask," she added, in a lower tone than she was accustomed to, her face bright red with embarrassment at her father's obvious displeasure.

But Antonio didn't seem to notice. His answer was quick and blunt, "A wife."

Catalina's blush deepened. She had found her answer, the motive she had been searching for. Almost as a plea, she turned her head, still lowered, to her mother, standing quietly nearby.

"Catalina, perhaps you and I should get dinner ready," her mother said. "Won't you stay for dinner, don Antonio?"

"I'd be delighted to accept your invitation," he said, this time smiling in a way that made Catalina flinch.

That night, after Antonio left and the house returned to its usual sounds and murmurs, Inés María went to her daughters' room and sat at the foot of Catalina's bed. Simona and Lucía were already asleep.

"Mother?"

"Catalina, child, I feel that we should have explained the impending visit of don Antonio to you before tonight, but we weren't sure when he would arrive."

"I understand, Mother," Catalina said cautiously.

"I don't think you do. But I think you'll understand if you let me explain."

"Please," said Catalina, who was now as alert as she had ever been.

"Don Antonio once had a wife who died giving birth to their first child," she said. "The little boy also died, minutes after his mother, and in his father's arms. In his grief, he decided that he didn't want to marry anyone from that island and that he would return home to find a new bride."

Don Antonio's first wife had not been like them. She had been born in Cuba, and he thought that made a difference, her mother explained. She wasn't strong enough; she didn't know the old ways. When she fell ill or sickly, she refused to allow healers to cure her with the old prayers and remedies that immigrants from the Canary Islands had brought to Cuba. Instead, she turned to a native woman everyone called "Enriqueta the witch," and drank her potions, falling under her strange spells. It was that woman who had killed her, don Antonio had told Inés María.

By the time her mother finished the story, Catalina was both horrified and fascinated by that faraway place where a woman could die from a witch's spell, a place where there were no volcanoes, no mulberry trees, no silkworms, and therefore no silk, and where the weather was consistently balmy and the land generous.

"We think you'll be happy there, child," Inés María said. "You'll see the world. And one day you'll come back as he has, and you may be able to help your sisters. Don't think of us. Think of them, and what's happening in this country. You know your father thinks the silk business is dying. If things don't improve soon, at least you'll be taken care of."

Tears were rolling down Catalina's face. She felt her mother's hand caress her cheeks and brush her unruly hair away from her forehead.

"But why me, Mother? He doesn't even know me!" Catalina protested.

"Ah, but he does, you just don't remember. A long time ago, he promised he would come back for you."

Catalina's body went cold as she recalled when she was about nine a distant cousin who was on his way to Cuba had visited them to deliver a letter from a relative. He brought along a friend who was also going on the trip and Catalina, always a curious child, peppered them with questions to which they had no answers. She realized now that the friend had been don Antonio, who had promised her that one day he would show her the island.

"It appears he is a man of his word," Inés María said.

"I was a child!" Catalina exclaimed, unable to contain her rage.

"Yes, but you are no longer a child. And we think he would be good for you."

Catalina immediately understood. They wanted don Antonio to take her away from Juan, from the only man she loved, the only one she would ever love.

"I don't want to go to Cuba!" Catalina cried out like a toddler at the beginning of a tantrum. Her sisters woke up, alarmed. Inés María closed her eyes and began to pray silently, no doubt asking for strength, as she did when her daughters tested her patience.

Awakened by the commotion, her father joined them in the room, and now he, too, stood at the foot of her bed. Catalina looked at her parents and understood they had accepted don Antonio's outrageous marriage proposal on her behalf.

"I won't do it," she told them, tossing the bedcovers aside and getting up.

They tried to hold her, to explain, but she ran downstairs and kept running as if she could escape their plans by leaving the house. She went to the place where she felt most comfortable in the world—the shack where the family kept their beloved silkworms.

In the darkness, she could hear her parents calling her, but she ignored them. She also heard her wise grandmother telling them to let her be. The two obeyed the older woman and retreated into the house. Doña Elena assured them she would sit in the living room and wait for Catalina to return. Then she would talk to her.

The door closed behind them, and there was suddenly silence, interrupted only by what sounded like approaching thunder.

At last, Catalina was alone. Only the worms could hear her sobs. "What am I going to do?" she kept repeating.

Thunder, sharp as the crack of a whip, interrupted her ruminations. She lit up a lump of coal and stood on her tiptoes to light a kerosene lamp that hung from a hook on one of the wooden beams. Her eyes clouded with fury toward her father. How could he love her so much and yet be so blind to her heart? How could he betray her?

Thunder, closer now, made Catalina jump and drop the lamp she had lit. It fell onto a clay jug, which shattered into dozens of pieces. Catalina stepped back, as the kerosene spread over the hay under the worm beds. A flame suddenly ignited, red and yellow and blue, beautiful in its own way.

Catalina was rooted in place. Her eyes kept darting up and down, right and left, paying attention to every little detail but incapable of movement. She tried to scream but couldn't find her voice. The flame jumped up from the pile of hay to the first worm bed; then, to the next, and, finally, it began engulfing the beams from the bottom. Pale pink smoke, like the inside of a seashell, began to coil upward, toward the rafters and the straw roof of the shack. The worms were piling one on top of another seeking shelter from the rising heat. Fingers of flame poked at Catalina's naked ankles.

She started coughing and tried to cover her nose and mouth with one hand as she gathered up the skirt of her nightgown and moved toward the door. Before leaving, she turned around and took a quick last look at the worms squirming on their beds a few steps away. Then, she cleared her throat and finally screamed for help. When she reached the house, yelling for her father, she turned back and saw that the shack was starting to collapse.

The wind, stronger now, picked up sparks from the shack, like falling stars in the sky, and blew them across the field, where they leapt from one mulberry tree to the other as if their branches were trampolines. The crowns of the trees looked like jewels dancing in the darkness. Everyone in the house woke up to Catalina's desperate cries. Her grandmother, who was still awake waiting for her, was the first to rush out, but her knees buckled and she fell to the ground before she could reach her granddaughter. Neighbors who could see black smoke curling up from the field came to help. To Catalina's disappointment, Juan was not among them. Water buckets were passed from hand to hand. No one worked harder or longer than don José.

By dawn, the fire had stopped on its own when it reached the harsh imposing surface of *La Roca*. There was nothing else green and lush to burn. The house was saved only because the wind was blowing in the opposite direction. Catalina's mother thought the Virgin of Candelaria had intervened to save them all. Only a saint that carried a baby in one arm and a candle in another could save her family from certain catastrophe. Only fire can fight fire.

"The trees will grow back," her father told her, as Catalina sobbed in his arms, asking for forgiveness. His hands were burned and bloodied and he reeked of smoke, yet he soothed her, caressing her hair and patting her back.

"It's not your fault," he continued. "As strong as you are, you can't unleash a storm and you can't create thunder."

"But you always say you are so lucky!" Catalina cried. "How can this happen to us, to you?"

"I am lucky," he said with emphasis, pulling her back from his body and holding her by the arms. "Look at me," he insisted, and held her by the chin. "We lost some trees and the worms, but we are all alive and unharmed, and the house is intact."

While they talked, Catalina's mother was sitting at the table, next to her own mother, who looked dazed and confused. The two women were surrounded by Simona and Lucía, both weeping quietly. Inés María's eyes were red and brimming with tears, and like the rest of the family she was covered in soot. Her long hair was untamed and dirty, and her clothes were ruined. The flames had burned the skirt of her white nightgown. Catalina approached and took her mother's face in her hands. In those eyes she could see the truth: no matter what her father said, the fire had sealed her fate. Her father may have been lucky, but she wasn't. The fire didn't happen to him. It happened to her. She would have to pay for it by acquiescing to her parents' wishes.

The following afternoon, when don Antonio came to visit, it was Catalina who greeted him at the door. He had learned about the fire in town and apologized for not being there earlier to help them—he had been to Tenerife that morning on business, he said. Since it wasn't customary for a young unmarried woman to open the door to a male visitor, Catalina felt the need to explain that her father wasn't feeling well; he was in bed with a cough. Antonio said it was probably from the smoke he had inhaled as he had battled the fire most of the night. By the end of his visit, Catalina and Antonio were taking a walk with her sisters at a prudent distance behind them.

Two days later, one of her sisters mentioned in passing at the dinner table that she had heard the priest say that Manuela, Juan's mother, had passed away from influenza on the night of the fire. Catalina felt the urge to leave the table and run to Juan's side, but she couldn't. She pressed her body harder against the chair, willing her face to remain a mask. When don José heard the news, he worried that he, too, would succumb, and called Catalina to his bedside. "Would you consider marrying soon? I'd like to walk you to the altar while I can," he said.

There was no longer any possibility that Catalina would refuse. With the ivory silk she had woven so many years ago for this occasion, Inés María made her daughter a dress. The priest set a date two weeks later, after discreetly consulting with the family's doctor about the graveness of don José's illness and the pristine state of Catalina's womb.

Mara

Tenerife
July 2019

A COOL BREEZE PLAYED WITH STRANDS OF HAIR that I had loosely pulled up with a pen when I left the café. The day no longer felt balmy, and the sun made my bare shoulders itch, a sure sign that unless I found shelter quickly, they would soon redden and burn. I forged on, ready to focus on my mother's request. On the next street corner, I asked Google where to get a birth certificate from the last century. It could be done online, it turns out, but only if one had more information than I did. I decided to walk over to *registro civil*, a sort of county clerk's office, and ask there. According to Siri, it was only a ten-minute walk.

Santa Cruz de Tenerife, the capital of this island, was a bustling city of not even a quarter of a million people. I had done some research at the airport in Madrid and learned that *The Guardian* newspaper once named it one of the five best places to live in the world. I could see why. The streets were clean and orderly. Palm trees swayed gently, and the never-far sea sparkled under the sun. The food was excellent, the people welcoming and warm, some architecturally interesting buildings broke the monotony of a beach town, and several striking pieces of sculptures dotted the downtown area, including one of a fish, typical of these waters, called *chicharro*.

It took me more than ten minutes to get to the office, and, by the time I arrived, I was sweaty and winded from the walk, but the clerk was helpful, though it was almost lunchtime, a sacred two- or three-hour period that splits the day in half for Spaniards. I provided her with my great-grandmother's name and two last names as well as a date of birth. Then she asked, "Are you sure the person you are looking for is from here?"

"You mean from Tenerife?" I wasn't sure where she was going with that question.

"Well, you said she was from Santa Cruz..."

"Yes," I interrupted her. "From here, Santa Cruz, the capital."

"Ah, but there is another Santa Cruz on the islands. Santa Cruz de La Palma, the capital of La Palma, which is another island. We call it *la isla bonita* because it's so pretty. Have you been there?"

This was all news to me. There was a serious lack of imagination here for names, I thought, confused. I could have kicked myself for being so unprepared.

"Wait," I said. "Can you repeat that slowly?"

The clerk, a not-so-young woman with spiky red hair, looked at me as if trying to guess my age and mental state. I decided to put her out of her misery and start at the beginning, as I should have done before I even arrived.

"Never mind," I said. "Do you have a map of the archipelago, please?"

"Certainly," she replied, and handed me one, exactly like the one Nina had tried to show me earlier and I had ignored.

"We are here," she said, pointing to the largest island on the map with a perfectly shaped unvarnished long nail. "And this one over here"—she pointed to another island to the west, shaped like a heart—"is La Palma."

I traced the outlines of the island with my fingers and placed my hand over the entire archipelago, half expecting it to pulsate with a message I could recognize as a sign of what to do, where to go, but the map lay disappointingly flat on the desk. I repeated the name under my breath, *La Palma*. I have always been drawn to palm trees because they remind me of Cuba. Why was the island named after a tree? I wanted to ask but didn't.

"Could you please search anyway and let me know? Here's my number." I scribbled down my information, taking care not to give her my business card. The name of the newspaper I work for always raises eyebrows and expectations and makes some people nervous. Besides, this was a personal matter.

I left with the map deep inside my bag and immediately called my mother. She picked up on the first ring.

"Exactly where was your grandmother from?"

"I told you already. Santa Cruz, in the Canary Islands," she said, taken aback by my tone. "Is this how you treat all your sources?"

I softened a little, but just a little, and told her about my foray into the clerk's office.

"Did you know there was more than one city called Santa Cruz?"

"No," she answered after a pause. "I didn't. So what are you going to do?"

"What am *I* going to do?!" I asked, elongating the first-person pronoun. Once again, she had turned one of her crises into my problem.

I looked up at the clouds, moving swiftly now. I had heard that weather changes here were common and dramatic. The wind was picking up and I could see people rushing to their cars or seeking shelter inside cafés. I was mesmerized by the scene but rooted in place. Details, details, details.

"I'm going to wait until I hear back from the nice clerk who's trying to help me," I told her, "and if she can't find it, then that's that."

But even as I was saying it, I knew I had to find this birth certificate. Not just for my mother, but for me as well. I couldn't explain why, but I had started to feel a sensation in the pit of my stomach I always felt when I was on the trail of a good story. There was no other way to describe it, and I hadn't had it in a long time: the sensation was one of curiosity.

"What other island?" my mother asked, but I ignored her question and instead asked my own.

"Is there anything else you remember about your grandmother, anything at all?"

I was shouting over the wind now. A piece of cardboard flew by, narrowly missing my face. I needed to find cover somewhere. I began to walk quickly toward the hotel.

"From her? Nothing," my mother said, oblivious to my mounting desperation. "She never talked about her life before Cuba."

Right at that moment, as my mother mentioned Cuba, I thought I caught a glance of a sign, more like a blur, that included the words *Cuba* and *centenary*. It was a sign on a city bus, but the bus passed quickly and I missed it. Lightning exploded in the sky, thick and strong, sending shards of light in all directions like the roots of an old tree.

"Sorry, sorry, can you repeat? I lost you for a moment. It's very windy here."

"Thunder, I hear thunder," said my mother who feared bad weather the way other people fear cancer, wars, or famine. "Santa Barbara *bendita*," she whispered, invoking the saint that protects devout Cubans from storms. Though I couldn't see her, I knew my mother had made the sign of the cross.

By now I was two blocks away from the hotel, and though I kept scrutinizing every city bus that passed, I didn't see the sign again. Did I dream that? Or had it been a poster flying in the wind?

I finally reached the hotel, panting from the failed effort to outrun the rain. The lobby smelled like the lilies in funeral homes. A statuette of the virgin that Nina had shown me at the café was mounted on an old wooden base that hung on a wall near the front door. The virgin was holding a baby in one hand and something else in the other. A staff? A candle? My senses were on high alert as if I was covering a protest or a revolution. I felt cold but was sweating. My mouth tasted like copper, and I realized I was chewing the inside of my cheek. I tried to bring my attention back to the phone now that I could finally hear my mother clearly.

"I was asking if you had found the place with the mulberry trees? I know what they are for," my mother was saying.

The trees! Yes, of course. I had forgotten to google them.

"And what are they for?" I asked impatiently. It seemed somehow important, though I wasn't sure why.

"They're the only food silkworms eat. Apparently, they used to weave silk on the islands. Maybe that's something to investigate, right?"

The answer both surprised and deflated me a little. Worms? Really? I was confused and my clothes were thoroughly drenched. Beyond the lobby windows, I could see the timid rays of the sun pushing through the dark clouds. The storm had passed as quickly as it had come. All was calm outside, but inside I felt strangely agitated.

Catalina

La Palma
July 1918

CATALINA STOOD ALONE before the old mirror that hung above the dresser in her parents' bedroom. The mirror had black and brown dots on the edges, like freckles framing her pretty face. The long curls of her reddish hair had been tamed and pulled into a severe chignon so tight that her scalp hurt almost as much as her feet, which were encased in old shoes, newly covered in ivory silk to match her wedding dress.

It was only fitting that she should be in pain today, she thought.

The dress her mother had made was long and simple, with a high boat neck and cinched at the waist by a bow that tied in the back. The silk enveloped her body as a cloud might, soft and airy. But there wouldn't be any more silk in her family now, Catalina thought, shaking her head. She didn't want to think about the fire. That would inevitably lead to Juan, and she couldn't think about him. Not today. But how could she not? Juan occupied all her thoughts, all her spaces. He was with her all the time.

Catalina sighed as she put on her mother's tiny pearl earrings—a gift from her father she was borrowing—and a dainty silver chain with a cross that had belonged to her grandmother. The thought of her grandmother made Catalina pause.

Shortly after the fire, doña Elena had suffered a heart attack and had died in her sleep. It hadn't been a great surprise, since she had been ailing for some time and always claimed that her heart had broken on the day her husband died thirty years earlier. She had gone on to live longer than anyone had thought possible. Still, Catalina missed her quiet presence in the house, her soft wrinkled hands, and the breakfasts of mashed ripe bananas with *gofio* she served them every day. It just didn't taste the same when her mother made it.

"Catalina, open the door!"

Simona sounded exasperated. She heard Lucía as well, whispering, and eager to get in.

"Catalina, are you well?" they both called out almost at the same time.

Catalina moved slowly toward the door and opened it. Her sisters burst in as if they had been leaning against the heavy old wooden door or attempting to push it in.

"I thought you were ill," Lucía said as she sat down on their parents' bed, which as always had been perfectly made, with a white bedspread knitted by their grandmother. Simona carelessly plopped herself down on the bed next to Lucía, who was playing with the delicate wedding veil. Catalina wanted to straighten the bed linens, rescue her veil from Lucía's fingers, and shoo her sisters out of the room. Instead, she remained frozen in front of the mirror.

"Mother is getting nervous," said Simona, who was so close to Catalina in temperament, looks, and age that people often thought they were twins.

Catalina's sisters had wanted to dress her on this special day, but she didn't let them. She thought she should be alone during her last few hours as a single woman and put on the dress herself. At least that she ought to be able to do, since so much of her life was out of her control.

"Let's not delay anymore," Simona said gently, putting an arm around Catalina's shoulders. She picked up the long veil and began affixing it at the crown of her sister's head with hairpins.

"You look so beautiful," Lucía said dreamily from the bed. She was not yet fifteen, but her eyes shone as if she were the one getting married. "You'll make Antonio very happy."

Catalina jerked her head at that, making Simona lose her balance and drop the pin on the floor. Tears began to pool in Catalina's dark eyes and Simona, who understood Catalina better than anyone in the family, pulled a handkerchief from the belt around her dress to dab at her sister's eyes.

"What did I do?" complained Lucía.

"You don't know anything," said Simona, who always enjoyed putting Lucía in her place. "You're just a child. Go tell Mother we'll be ready shortly."

Lucía looked around the room in bewilderment. Her sisters had once again turned against her. Wordlessly she got up from the bed and left the room, the heels of her hand-me-down shoes clacking on the hallway floor.

"Catalina, look at me," said Simona, grabbing her by the shoulders. "You don't have to do this."

"Oh, but I do," she said. "Father Jacinto is waiting at the church and Antonio has come all the way from Cuba for me. For me! Of course I'm doing this."

"Yes, but do you think you'll be able to be happy?" Simona insisted.

Catalina stared at her sister and reflected for a moment on what she could say. Should she tell her that this was the worst day of her life? At eighteen, she felt that her life was over. She was about to marry a stranger she didn't love, a man almost twelve years older than her whom she had met barely a month ago when he chose her as his bride. Why her?

Because she was special, her mother had told her when she asked. But then her mother always said Catalina was special.

"Yes," Catalina finally said, and Simona squinted, but said nothing. It was time to go.

A few minutes later, Catalina was standing in the living room in her wedding dress—no longer a girl, but not yet a woman—her arm nestled in her father's, her face dwarfed by a veil that seemed too big for her features, her eyes a little puffy from crying. Inés María, dressed in the deep black of mourning for her mother, made the sign of the cross and had to look away, for it suddenly seemed to her they were committing a sin.

Catalina's father patted her hand and bent a little to kiss her forehead. He looked feverish.

"You look beautiful, my darling girl," he said, suppressing a cough.

"Thank you, Father," she murmured, but couldn't look him in the eye. Instead, she looked at her mother. But Inés María once again avoided her gaze.

"Shall we leave?" said the ever-practical Lucía. "Father Jacinto must be worried."

Catalina smiled wanly and focused on her pained feet, taking one step after the other. Slowly and in almost total silence, they reached the church. Everyone in the small town had come to witness the wedding. Children stopped playing in the dirt and stood in awe of the beautiful bride. Couples walking in the dusty park smiled at her; some waved at the tight little procession because they knew the family.

Catalina searched the crowd looking for the familiar faces of Juan and Ana. To her chagrin, but also relief, they weren't there. Juan, Juan, Juan. Where could he be now?

At last, Catalina and her father reached the door of the small stone church, her mother and sisters behind them. Through the open door she could see Antonio, standing alone at the altar, waiting for her. He was wearing the same brown suit he had on the day he had come to the house to ask for her hand. His ample forehead shone with perspiration and his hands were trembling slightly.

For a moment Catalina considered untangling her arm from her father's, turning around, and rushing away from the church, Antonio, and her family to find Juan and elope with him. Others had done it; she had heard about such things. But she had also heard the scorn in the voices of relatives when they talked about "those girls." She understood the shame of running away with a man, and she knew the consequences for her unmarried sisters. She loved them too much and knew that one thoughtless act on her part would taint their reputation and condemn them to a life as spinsters. She couldn't do that. Simona was all but engaged to a local boy and Lucía, though still very young, would soon follow her path to the altar, she was sure of that. Above all, she would break her father's heart.

As if he had intuited her thoughts, don José tightened his hold on her arm and looked at her warmly. She thought she saw tears in his eyes and maybe a touch of regret. But the moment passed.

The priest welcomed them with a gesture, encouraging them to come in. But Catalina and her father didn't move from the threshold. Catalina felt a little push from behind and heard Simona whispering, "Go!" She glanced at her father, who looked ashen and uncertain. She squeezed his arm and smiled encouragingly at him. Don José began to walk, slowly leading his daughter to the altar.

The old organist played the first note of the wedding march, but Catalina didn't hear the music. She heard only her beating heart and a long sad whistle that seemed to come from the woods right outside the church. A familiar whistle everyone heard but only she recognized.

Mara

Tenerife
July 2019

I WAS SITTING ON MY HOTEL BED, my back propped up by puffy pillows as I googled images of mulberry trees, when the phone began vibrating. The caller ID made me smile. It was my creative, unpredictable son, Dylan, who, at nineteen, and after much soul searching, had decided to become an actor; he was taking summer classes at NYU to catch up on the credits he needed to graduate early. As always, he was rushing on to the next goal. I couldn't be more thrilled that he had finally found his calling and settled on a path. For now.

Before deciding that he wanted to be an actor after all, he had dabbled in journalism and filmmaking in high school. He had also toyed with the idea of studying political science so he could go to law school and, one day, become president of the United States. To every one of his ideas, I had always said yes, in part because I was swept up by his enthusiasm but also, if I'm honest with myself, because I knew they wouldn't last. As a child, he had tried swimming, diving, soccer, tap dancing, baseball, surfing, sailing, horseback riding, basketball, acting, guitar, drums, and football, even scouting. Nothing stuck. He would try them for a few weeks or months, even years, and then give up.

For a long time, I thought he had some sort of attention deficit disorder or an inability to commit. I fretted about how he would form attachments or develop relationships, but in time I came to see that he tried so many things because he was driven by curiosity. He didn't have to master any of them; he only had to try them. When he developed an interest in journalism, it all made sense. For what is journalism if not disciplined curiosity? Later, in his last year of high school, he took a course in music production and declared that was his future. But, in college, the talk turned to theater again, and that, too, made sense. After all, actors are always trying to get to the "emotional truth" of their characters, but not so much of their own. I once heard an actress say in an interview that she knew what books each of the characters she had played liked to read, but she wasn't sure anymore what books she herself enjoyed.

I could imagine my Dylan one day saying something like that. In fact, I could imagine him already saying it, which meant he had made the right call when he gave up on journalism. To be honest, I was relieved that he hadn't chosen journalism. He would never have to visit a morgue to see the body of a little girl or interview mothers who had lost their children.

I shook my head to try to get the images of the last few days out of my head and pressed the button to take the call. I put him on speaker and stretched out on the bed. A breeze from the ocean was swaying the gauzy window curtains. I breathed in deeply, detecting a whiff of jasmine from the garden.

"Mama? Are you there?"

"Yes, yes, of course."

"Are you alone?"

"Yes. I'm sorry, it's been a busy couple of days, and I'm tired, that's all. How are you?"

I was trying my best to sound like a mother should, always ready and available, and I wasn't sure why, but I didn't want to tell him yet about my mother's request and my search for the ghost of a woman, who, somehow, had always been part of my life. I couldn't broach that whole topic now with Dylan, so I decided to just let him speak.

"Tell me everything," I said, using a phrase I had used since he was a toddler to signal that, no matter what else was going on in my life and work, he always had my attention.

"Yes, well, that's why I'm calling. I have something to tell you."

Oh no, I thought, did I really want to hear everything? His tone was somewhat alarming, but I tried to stay neutral. Or as neutral as a Cuban mother can remain.

"What's happening? Are you ill?"

"No, no, nothing like that," he interrupted because he could hear the rising panic in my voice. "I've made a decision, and I wanted you to be the first to know about it."

That's a good sign, I thought. But was it? I wasn't sure.

"Okay," I said cautiously, slowly, drawing out the letters and holding my breath, because to be honest, I suspected what was coming, though I could never imagine the full extent of it.

"I've decided to join the Navy," he said.

My first thought was that it was a good sentence: short, declarative, complete. He always was a fantastic communicator. It was one of the things I loved about him.

My second thought was less charitable.

"Are you out of your mind?" I screamed, and held the phone tighter, as if I were grabbing my son by the shoulders and shaking him.

"Mama, Mama, calm down," he said. "It's not the end of the world. It's a good career move."

He went on to describe how, during career week at the end of the spring semester, he had met with a Navy recruiter who had convinced him that life at sea was much better than an uncertain life as an actor. He talked about benefits and how a military life would pay for his career and how he could become a lawyer after all and fulfill his old dream of becoming president of the United States one day.

"And wouldn't that be something? Your son, the son of a Cuban refugee, in the White House? You'd be so proud of me!"

"I'm already proud of you!" I found myself saying, conscious of the fragile ego of all men, particularly young men. "And tuition is not an issue. Your father made sure of that."

"Yes, but . . ." he said. "Let me explain."

And he did. By the end of the call, we were back to our old roles. I was the supportive mom/cheerleader telling him he'd make a great sailor and the Navy would be lucky to have someone like him, and he telling me how he'd be nowhere without me.

When we hung up, I felt depleted. All I could see in front of my eyes were waves, gigantic waves in the open sea swallowing up a ship. On the bow of the ship, dressed in white, like a ghost with a cap, was my son, my beautiful son, braving a storm. The ship had no name, but across its berth I could clearly read the words US Navy.

Tears clouded my vision. My son had always known that I don't have many fears in life, but the ones I have are deep and real. I fear mice, motorcycles, and mountain climbing, I had always told him. But, above all, I fear the sea. Yet so that he wouldn't grow up like me, so afraid that I never even learned to swim until I was an adult, I enrolled him in swimming lessons when he was still in diapers. He turned out to be a fantastic swimmer. Still, in beach outings, I implored him to swim parallel to shore, never in the deep.

"If your feet can't touch the bottom, you've gone too far," I used to tell him.

The problem was that my child had turned into a young man of six foot three, and he was heading for the deepest parts of the ocean, to places where I could never reach him or save him.

Catalina

La Palma
July 1918–April 1919

IN THE WEEKS THAT FOLLOWED THE WEDDING, Catalina didn't leave her father's bedside except to bathe and eat, though she ate very little those days. Her stomach was unsettled and, when she did manage to eat, she would throw up, so she started to avoid meals. There was no need to worry her mother more than she already was, so she didn't mention her poor digestion to anyone. The priority for all in the house then was to make sure José Angel's lungs cleared from the smoke so that he could resume his life as the head of a family that clearly adored him.

But he was wasting away. A wretched cough kept him up day and night, and his feverish body seemed to dwindle under the weight of the blankets his wife piled on top of him to keep him from shivering.

The sisters and their mother took turns kneeling down to pray to the virgin for his health. Even the priest, Father Jacinto, joined them on some evenings. The prayers seemed to work. One day José Angel improved slightly. He sat up in bed and asked for his favorite food: salty potatoes accompanied by goat stew. He wasn't strong enough to join his family at the table in the dining room, but they brought his food upstairs and accompanied him while he ate with gusto.

When the meal was over, Catalina made a move to pick up the tray and take it back to the kitchen to clean it, but her father held her arm in a surprisingly strong grip.

"You stay," he ordered. Catalina looked at her mother and sister, and they quietly nodded before leaving the two alone in the bedroom.

"Where is your husband?" he asked as soon as the door closed.

"He is out in the fields," Catalina said, and busied herself tucking the sheets and blankets around her father's emaciated body.

"Daughter, leave that alone for a moment. I want to speak with you. Sit, please," he said, gently this time.

Catalina went around the bed and sat in a chair, close to her father. He reached out and took his daughter's hands in his.

"I don't have much time," he began.

Catalina made a motion to protest, but he shushed it.

"Listen to me, please. There is no time," he started again, but a coughing spell forced him to stop.

Catalina's eyes filled with tears that rolled down her cheeks like pearls from a broken necklace. She sprang from the chair and started to pound on her father's back as if her palms could dislodge the disease that was wrecking his lungs.

Slowly, his cough abated, and she sat back down. This time, closer to him still, on the edge of the bed. She placed a cool hand on her father's forehead as his head lolled back onto the pillows and he caught his breath again.

"I want you to make me a promise. I want you to promise that no matter what happens, you will go to Cuba with your husband. You will not stay here."

Catalina held his hands in hers and interrupted him with a strangled sob. "I can't, Father, I can't. I won't leave you," she said, tightening her grip on his hands. But before she could go on, he halted her protests.

"Not now, I understand, but promise me that, when the time comes, you will go to Cuba with Antonio and stay there."

Catalina nodded, but he couldn't see her because his eyes were closed.

"Promise me," he repeated. "I want to hear you say it."

"I promise," Catalina said before dissolving into tears and running from the room.

Neither one of them could imagine then how that promise would one day alter the course of all their lives.

The next day, when José Angel took his last ragged breath, Catalina wasn't by his side. She was in town with Antonio getting her documents ready to travel to Cuba. Though Catalina had made it clear she would not leave while her father was ill, Antonio had convinced her that documents always took a long time and they had to start early.

As they returned to the house, they saw the doctor leaving furtively and quickly, like a thief, covering his face with a handkerchief. They tried to stop him, but he kept shaking his head and left before they could get close enough to talk to him. Catalina ran inside. Her mother and sisters were kneeling next to the bed where her father lay, eyes closed and finally at rest. It seemed impossible to Catalina that her father was dead.

That morning, before leaving with Antonio, she had served her father breakfast. How could he be dead? He had been lucid and hopeful; his legendary energy seemed to be coming back. She later learned from her sisters that shortly after she left, her father had asked for water. He sat up, took a sip, and leaned back again, closing his eyes. He never opened them again.

They had to send for the doctor to make sure he had stopped breathing. He had gone so gently they weren't sure if he was asleep. The doctor told them don José had died of "fulminant pneumonia," succumbing finally to his unrelenting cough, but everyone in the family blamed the fire.

It was her fault he was dead. Catalina was certain that her rage and unbridled anguish when she found out her father had promised her hand to Antonio had caused the fire that destroyed the mulberry farm. She was sure of it because when had there ever been such a thunderstorm without rain? It didn't rain that night; if it had, maybe not all would have been lost.

Before the doctor left, he instructed them to burn the body and the sheets. They burned the sheets but left the body intact. Don José was buried in the family plot, next to the church. His wife visited every day, but Catalina never did. It never seemed real to her that a patch of grass could contain the essence of her father. He remained forever in her heart, his death the first of many she mourned throughout her life.

Sometime in December she felt a fluttering in her stomach, like the wings of a trapped butterfly, and bowed her head in recognition of the miracle her body had created despite herself. It had been five months since the wedding and Catalina was carrying a child that she feared she would never love. She was resting her body against the side frame of the back window, looking out to the field behind the house where, not long ago, rows of mulberry trees, like lush green parasols, had lined up seemingly forever, stopping abruptly at the foot of *La Roca*.

Only the stumps remained of what used to be her father's pride and the family's main source of income. *La Roca* stood naked at its base, bereft of the intense green that had added a touch of life to its harsh grayness.

With a sigh, Catalina turned away from the window and looked at her surroundings as if for the first or last time. In the living room everything seemed both familiar and alien. The late afternoon light streaming from the window gave the room a yellowish tint. There was a framed photograph of her parents on the mantelpiece, taken on their wedding day. Her mother was unsmiling, as usual; her father, his hat resting on his thigh, was holding his wife's hand. He, too, was serious, but there was an air of triumph on his face, and his eyes shone with unmistakable joy.

Christmas was a mere two days away and the world was finally at peace. There were rumors that trade was reopening in Europe and the economy would soon bounce back, but Catalina doubted that those who had left for the Americas to escape the harrowing poverty of the war years would ever return. Practically every family she knew had lost a son or a daughter, not on the battlefields, but to America.

From where she stood, she could hear the chatter of Simona and Lucía in the kitchen as they made plans for the holidays. There was a feeling of buoyancy everywhere Catalina looked, except within herself. She missed her father.

Don José had been a happy man, a lucky man, he always told them. Lucky in love, lucky in business, lucky and blessed to have three healthy daughters. Catalina remembered how he had patiently taught them to work in the garden, weed the plants, remove any shriveled leaves, and keep the flowerbed moist and rich with nutrients.

"Happiness is like a garden," he often told them, plucking an unsightly worm from a half-eaten leaf. "You have to learn to cultivate it. You have to know what to keep and what to discard." But in the end, she hadn't been able to make him happy, despite her sacrifice. Catalina went over to the mantelpiece and cleaned the dust off the photo of her parents with a corner of her dress before putting it back. Almost absentmindedly, she caressed her protruding belly. Her mother had made her two new dresses, both black. The color was appropriate. She was mourning much more than the loss of her father and her grandmother. She was mourning the end of her family as she had always known it.

Her father's premature death had sent each member of the family reeling into their own separate worlds. Instead of bringing them together in their sadness, his death had split them apart like a butcher's knife cleaving through bone, bluntly and definitively.

Her mother had not left her room for most of the past five months. Simona, who had gotten engaged to her first love the day after Catalina's wedding, was preoccupied with the details of her wedding in the spring. Lucía, as ever, busied herself in the fields. They came together once a day for a meal usually prepared by Simona, since Catalina couldn't stand the smell of raw meat. One of them, usually Lucía, brought up a tray for their mother. Often, the tray came back with the food untouched.

When she looked at herself in the mirror—and she tried not to—Catalina saw a face she didn't recognize. The spray of freckles was still there, but her red hair had lost its luster and no longer seemed as wild as it did before the wedding. The doctor had told her to expect many changes. Perhaps this was one of them. Her ankles were thicker, but the rest of her body was trim. From behind, her sisters told her, she didn't look pregnant at all. She looked like her old self. How she wanted to believe that! But she didn't feel like her old self. It had been a long time since she had felt anything like the old Catalina.

She wondered what Juan would say if he saw her. She so feared his sadness or his scorn that she had barely left the house since the wedding. Antonio had returned to Cuba to take care of his business as soon as he learned of the pregnancy and promised he would return for her once the baby was born to escort them both to the island. From Cuba, she would be able to help her family much more than she could from here, he had assured her. Catalina couldn't imagine how that would be possible, but she had stopped questioning his pronouncements. She was surprised that, at first, she found herself missing him, the way one misses a pleasurable scent or a favorite dress that is too old to wear. But that didn't last long. For Antonio had managed to pleasure her body, but he had never touched her soul or burrowed into her heart. Her heart and her soul belonged to Juan.

Yet, she couldn't understand how her body had so willingly responded to her husband's caresses. How was it possible that loving Juan as much as she did, her body had yielded and warmed to Antonio's touch? And, how, above all else, could her body have opened like fertile ground and allowed him to plant a seed in her womb? Together, they had created a new life.

There it was again! The tiny butterfly in her stomach announcing herself. She was sure it was a girl, and that made her even sadder. How could she ever love a creature that wasn't Juan's? During confession, she had told the priest she was afraid of being an indifferent mother. It was as much as she could admit to Father Jacinto.

"The love will come," he reassured her. "All mothers love their children. It's unnatural not to."

But Catalina had felt even worse after their exchange. Praying the rosary hadn't helped. She felt like an unnatural woman, unable to love her own offspring.

"Catalina!"

Simona's cry made her jump back from her thoughts. Catalina realized she had been crying. "I've been calling you and calling you and you just ignore me," Simona said, sounding desperate.

"I'm so sorry, I didn't hear you," Catalina said, quickly drying her tears with the palm of her hands before turning around to face her sister.

"It's a letter from Antonio. It just arrived," Simona said tersely, and handed her a plain envelope without any stamps or a postmark. Her name was written across the envelope in a childish handwriting that she immediately recognized not as Antonio's, but Juan's. Her heart began beating fast and she swallowed to try to calm her nerves.

But before she could ask Simona where she had gotten the letter, her sister had left the living room and was already in the kitchen loudly moving pots around.

Catalina immediately hid the letter in the pocket of her dress and ran to her room to read it alone. She locked the door and sat on the edge of the bed that had once belonged to her grandmother and she now shared with Antonio.

"My love," it started, as she knew it would. Fat tears blurred her vision and she had to wipe them with the hem of her dress before she could continue reading. "It's been too long and so much has happened. My sister told me she heard one of your sisters in church say that you are soon leaving for Cuba. I won't let you. It doesn't matter to me that you are married. I told you once and I'll say it again, you'll always be mine and I'll always be yours. Meet me at midnight. You know where. Don't be afraid. All my love."

That was it. He had been passionate but careful. He hadn't signed his name, but Catalina had no doubt that Juan had written this letter, just as she had no doubt that, at midnight, she would leave her house, and head to their old hiding place by *La Roca*. She folded Juan's letter in two and placed it carefully back in her pocket, next to her heart.

The hours trickled by as she waited for darkness. She ate a plate of food her sisters had prepared and went to her mother's room to say good night. Inés María barely acknowledged her presence, but Catalina thought it was important to stick to routines and formalities to stave off the cruelties of this world. It didn't matter that her mother didn't seem to recognize her; she recognized her mother.

As she was leaving the room, Inés María suddenly spoke.

"He understood my nature better than anyone," she said.

"Who, Mother?" Catalina replied, startled by the confession.

"Your father, of course. He knew I would love him before I did," she said, and raised herself on one arm, her dark eyes boring into Catalina's. "Do you understand what I'm saying?"

"Yes, Mother," Catalina said, though she didn't. Not yet.

"One day you will. Certainty always precedes real love," Inés María said before reclining her head on the pillows again and turning away from her daughter.

* * *

It was dark in the pine forest as Catalina moved, guided only by the pale light of the moon. Then she heard it: a low whistle coming from the trees up ahead to her left. Anybody else would have thought it was an owl, but Catalina knew better. She breathed in and out. Slowly.

"Juan," she whispered.

A shadow stepped from behind a tree before she could get to *La Roca*. He seemed taller, thicker. His hair was longer. His shoulders, fuller. For a fleeting second, she thought she'd made a mistake, but he advanced, and she caught a whiff of his smell: sweat and soil and sun and onions.

"It's been so long," Catalina said before Juan sealed her mouth with a hungry kiss.

"Catalina!" he murmured, reclaiming her as if they had never been apart, as if she weren't married, as if her body still belonged to him and to him alone. For a long moment, she lost herself in that kiss. She threw her arms around his neck and breathed him in. He tried to bring her closer. Closer, closer still, but when he felt her rounded belly pushing against him, he recoiled. His hands left her face and brusquely patted her down in the darkness. They finally came to a rest on her stomach and pressed gently.

He didn't say anything, but he looked intently at her and cocked his head as if puzzled, as if he wanted to ask a question but had changed his mind. He understood now. He understood the silence, the distance, the quiet of his days, and the coldness of his nights. Now he knew why his whistles had gone unheeded, why the full moon no longer seemed as bright, and why the rooks had gone silent, their cries no longer splitting the quiet high up above the trees. Catalina was no longer his.

Catalina understood this, too, and began to cry. He turned away and started pacing. He's leaving, she thought, and felt the urge to beg him to let her explain that her pregnancy meant nothing, that she loved him more than she loved life, that she would never love anyone the way she loved him, that she had had no choice, that she had to obey her family, that Antonio was helping them with the farm, that she owed her marriage to her father after all she put him through because of their love.

But she didn't have to. She felt Juan's strong arms grabbing her waist from behind and turning her around to face him.

"Be mine," he whispered with a voice broken by desire.

She let him undress her for the first time. Not slowly, as Antonio patiently and teasingly did, but hungrily, desperately, as if he was afraid her body would evaporate from the tight circle of his arms.

That night she returned to her body. There was no flutter of butterflies alerting her to another heart beating inside her. She was present, herself, naked, without guilt, loving Juan and letting him love her as she had always dreamed, as she hadn't dared to hope.

She lost herself in his body, finding a home. It made her feel special and, at the same time, ordinary. At dawn, he woke her up and kissed her gently.

"No matter what you do or where you go, I will follow," he said, bringing her head toward him and touching her forehead with his. "I'll always be where you are."

Tears began to cloud Catalina's vision. The baby was awake now and kicking and Catalina felt a sharp pain stab her in the back. She doubled over.

"What's wrong?" Juan said, and drew her to him as if to steady her with his own body.

"I don't know," Catalina said, resting her head on his shoulder as the pain coursed through her. "It's probably nerves. I'm fine now."

Holding on to each other, they reached the edge of the pine forest.

"I'll find you," he said, and walked off toward his house before the sun was visible over the violet outline of the mountains.

Catalina watched Juan go and then rushed back home before the others awoke. Her thighs were sticky, but she thought it was sweat or the remnants of their lovemaking leaving her body. It wasn't until she stood in front of her mirror hoping to see the changes that she felt in her body and in her soul that she noticed her black dress was damp and there was a rivulet of blood running down each leg toward her feet.

She woke up in her mother's room, with her sisters and her mother around her. A white sheet covered her body, and her mother was talking to the doctor.

"Thank you, Doctor," she was saying. "I'll accompany you to the door."

Catalina kept her eyes closed. She didn't want to know the details. She remembered the blood. She remembered everything. The night with Juan, the pale half-moon, the prickly grass on her naked body. Oh no! Who undressed her? They must have seen it all. They must have noticed the changes. It must be obvious to all what she did. Somehow, she felt no guilt, only joy.

She opened her eyes.

"Thank God and all the saints, you're back," Simona said. "How do you feel?"

"Fine, I think," Catalina said. "Why is Mother up and talking? What's happened?"

"She was worried about you," Simona said. "We tried to force her to rest but she wouldn't hear about it."

"What's happened?" Catalina tried to get up.

"No, no, you mustn't," Lucía said, and with her strong arms grabbed her by the shoulders and pinned her back in bed. "The doctor said you have to be on bed rest for the rest of the pregnancy to save your baby."

"The baby?" Catalina said, realizing she had assumed she had lost the pregnancy and had been relieved at the thought.

Her sisters looked at each other and then at her as if she had lost her mind.

"Your baby, yes," the two of them seemed to say at the same time.

"Bed rest," Lucía repeated.

"For how long?" Catalina asked, wondering how long before she could see Juan again.

"Until the end of your pregnancy. With any luck, four more months. The baby is due in April, remember?" Simona said.

Catalina couldn't imagine not seeing Juan for four months. She desperately wanted to be alone.

"Are you hungry? Thirsty?" Lucía asked.

Catalina said yes, yes, so they would have something to do, so they would leave her alone with her memories, so she could plot a way to get out of that bed and run to the forest to be in Juan's arms once again.

Two weeks later, Antonio returned from Cuba. He said he had had a feeling, a premonition that he was needed, and he was right. It was Antonio who kept an almost constant watch over Catalina, attending to her needs as well as to the family business. Somehow, he seemed to accomplish it all with efficiency and without complaints. He read to her at night and helped her brush her hair in the mornings, but he also negotiated deals with vendors and hired workers to help him clear the lingering debris from the fire.

He set about understanding the family business. Antonio had heard all the stories about the mulberry trees and the worms and how proud don José had been of achieving his dreams, but Antonio wasn't a man to follow traditions. He said he had concluded that the silk business had moved on from the islands. The future, he said, was in bananas. He refused to rebuild the worms' shack or to spend a penny on mulberry seeds. Instead, he began to prepare the fields for banana trees, opening holes that were more than a foot wide and deep, and ripping out the roots of the mulberry trees.

Catalina's mother, who had returned to life the day Catalina had taken to bed to save her pregnancy, clung stubbornly to the past. "In a few months we can have at least one tree," she told her daughters in the kitchen one morning, showing them a cutting that she had managed to salvage from among the burned trees. And from the leaves of one mulberry tree a thousand worms can feed, they knew.

On April 20, 1919, Catalina woke up with a pain in her back, as sharp as the pain she had felt four months earlier in the forest with Juan. She opened her eyes and grabbed her husband's hand.

"Antonio!" she said. "It's time."

Four hours later, in her own bed, aided by her mother and a midwife, Catalina delivered a daughter, as she had envisioned. The baby had long legs and delicate fingers but almost no body fat. She had a small face that looked like a pumpkin. Her nose was flat, and her ears were tiny and translucent, like a mouse's. Catalina grabbed her baby and put her naked body against her chest. It was then that her daughter opened her eyes and looked intently at her mother for a long moment. Catalina had heard that all babies were born blind, but the way her daughter had looked at her she couldn't possibly be blind. The baby had also opened her fist and, for a moment, placed her palm, all fingers splayed like a starfish, on the center of her mother's chest.

Catalina took in a breath. She felt a strong wave of love rushing into her heart, with a force so pure and complete that it spread throughout her body, filling every part of her like a swollen river flooding the fields after heavy rain.

"Oh," she said. "There you are, my Carmen. Your name is Carmen."

She didn't say the rest out loud, but she knew her daughter could hear her: "Carmen Inés de la Candelaria López Quintana, I will always love you. I will protect you, and cherish you, and I will never abandon you."

Catalina was never certain why she made that promise to her daughter, but she would come to regret it. Those words would haunt her until the day she died.

Mara

Tenerife
July 2019

My worries about Dylan led me to my mother in that circuitous way thoughts work, bouncing around from one loved one to another and never returning to the starting point. I wondered again why my mother would want to claim citizenship in a country she barely knew. She had visited Spain twice, if I remembered correctly, and enjoyed it, but would she want to move here? Did she want to close the loop, in a sense, and return to the land of her ancestors? Was the pull of blood and history really that strong? And if so, is that why I had found my own way back to Spain? The truth is I had never really given my mother's family much thought, though my mother had mentioned her grandmother often, and I was certain I had never seen a picture of her.

My mother said her grandmother had an old-fashioned mistrust of machines and anything that required the use of technology, which she thought of as "black magic." Though there were families my mother knew who wore their best clothes to have their portrait taken by a professional photographer, her grandmother never allowed it. The whole thing seemed distasteful to her. A man hiding his face under a cloth was not to be trusted. Why leave an image behind if we are all going to disappear from the world? Why impose the burden of memory on those who come after us?

In the only picture I have of my mother before she met my father, she is sitting under a mango tree, bottle feeding a motherless baby goat. She is wearing a light-colored dress, which may have been white, with a high collar, and incredibly white sneakers. Incredibly white because the soil beyond the patch of grass where she was sitting looked very dark in the black-and-white image.

My mother must have been thirteen when this picture was taken. She is looking up at the camera with the beginning of a shy smile forming on the right side of her mouth, but the rest of her face didn't have a chance to catch up before the shutter clicked. She said she couldn't remember who had snapped that picture before her grandmother managed to intervene. In fact, on the left edge of the photograph there is a blurry image. That, my mother says, was her grandmother's hand attempting to come between her granddaughter and the lens of the camera.

Like so many old photos, it is now faded. My mother keeps it in her bedroom in a silver frame. That blurry image on the edge is the only image she has of the woman who raised her, the grandmother whose long-ago existence may now give my mother the opportunity to claim citizenship in a country where she has never lived, but must somehow carry in her bones, like the imprint of a lost love.

Getting up from the hotel bed where I'd been ensconced, I pulled out of my bag the maps and books I had purchased for research and took them to the small desk under the window. I had to tackle my mother's request seriously, as if it were an assignment, or else it would never get done. I dug into yet another book on the Canary Islands, learning more about the archipelago's geographical variety. More than thirty volcanoes pulsate under each island, like a cumulus of veins engorged by dust, fire, and ash. In the next book I selected, a sort of memoir written by a well-known Spanish journalist, I stumbled upon this: "The sea is our common point; it encloses us and defines us; it frightens us and warns us. It makes us the people we are."

It made me think of Cuba and my relationship to my own island. My being Cuban has always been an issue, beginning with my name. My first name is unusual for a Cuban, and my last name, Denis, does not telegraph my nationality. Though Denis is clearly not Spanish, I'm not aware of any English or French relatives. But beyond the name, it is not easy being Cuban, or rather, it is not easy being *in* Cuba, which I did for the first fifteen years of my life. Repression is so fierce and scarcities so vast that Cubans have come up with a short way of relating their woes, "*no es fácil*," which is an optimistic way of saying that life on the island is really, really hard. I no longer know what happens in Cuba. From my perch in Spain, I'm more interested in African refugees than in Cuban rafters. My mother tells me that the years we lived through in the late 1960s and 1970s are now considered to be the "good years," that it got worse, much worse, and that, currently, things are worse than ever.

I don't remember a time when I didn't know that we would one day leave Cuba. Growing up, it was hard to develop attachments when, in fact, everything was transitory. And yet, I did. I was a normal child, I suppose, if one can be "normal" in an environment of secrecy and fear. I was never to admit that we wanted to leave Cuba, because to do so would label me and my family as *gusanos* (worms), a word the government used to describe those who wanted to leave the country or who were not committed to the "revolutionary process."

At the first opportunity we had, my father arranged for a boat and we escaped.

Sailors say that in the total darkness of the sea you can see all the stars, but I don't remember seeing any stars. My mother and I were clinging to each other, resisting the maddening movement of the small boat while my father and others rowed after the ancient motor gave out. The stench of vomit and urine would have been unbearable if not for the waves that constantly washed over us and the entire boat, licking it clean. Miraculously, a US Coast Guard cutter rescued us in the early hours of the morning and took us to Key West.

I have told this story to several doctors and my therapist, who is convinced I have more than enough reasons to fear the sea. But I'm not convinced. My fear is primal and cultural. We Cubans are surrounded by water, yet we fear the rain. We run from sudden and frequent summer downpours—when the sky opens, and it seems as if the world will end in Biblical floods—as if our lives depended on getting to a dry patch under a roof. To hear our mothers and grandmothers tell it, it does. Tales of devastating hurricanes are passed down from one generation to another the way other cultures share folktales or recipes. We inherit tragedies and collect tales of misfortune the way others relish stories of happy times. We grow up fearing the worst but also expecting it with a measure of dread and excitement; and the worst often comes from nature.

In Cuba it's very easy to "catch a cold" from being exposed to the chilled air at dawn, or from getting wet in the rain, or swimming in the ocean in winter. Beach outings were a regular part of my life, but only in the summer when it was unbearably hot. Cubans seldom go to the sea from November to March when it would make more sense because the sun caresses the skin instead of torching it as it does in the summer months.

We are, in fact, islanders who live with our backs to the sea. Cubans sit on the famed seawall of Havana, not looking out to the water, but facing the city in its entire crumbling splendor. I've often wondered if that's because of a fear of the sea or a longing for it.

A knock on the door pulled me back from my ruminations.

It was Nina, and she was hungry. Though Nina couldn't possibly weigh more than a hundred pounds, she rarely allowed anything to interfere with her meal schedule. The woman was a serious eater.

"Ready?" she asked superfluously since she had already looked me up and down and determined that I was definitely not ready. I was still wearing the same clothes from the morning.

"Ready as I'll ever be," I said, tossing the book onto the bed and grabbing a rust-colored scarf from my backpack that had accompanied me on every trip since I became a reporter. There is little a properly placed scarf can't fix, and I have been told I have a flair for them. I pulled my hair up and picked up my increasingly heavy bag, slinging it over my shoulder.

"That shoulder of yours deserves a Pulitzer," Nina quipped, and I laughed, the first joyful sound I had made in a long time.

Because we were dining in the hotel, the choices were uninspiring. I opted for a salad and had to beg for ice in my water. In Spanish restaurants it's easier—and often cheaper—to drink the house wine than to get a glass of iced water.

"I'm not going back to Madrid," I told Nina when the plates were cleared and dessert was on its way.

She raised her right eyebrow in that way she had of inviting conversation without saying a word. So, I told her the clerk from *registro civil* had called and she hadn't been able to find anything with the information I had given her, suggesting instead that I try the other Santa Cruz, the capital of La Palma.

"And so, I've decided to stay and figure out where my great-grandmother came from. I need to get that birth certificate for my mother."

"You two deserve each other," Nina deadpanned, digging into the dessert that had been placed in front of her.

I narrowed my eyes and stabbed her dessert with my fork, confessing that I hadn't ordered my own *bienmesabe*—a sweet and gooey almond concoction that looked too good for her alone—because I was on a diet again. Nina snorted and gave me her dessert to finish while she went ahead and ordered another for herself. She never did like to share a plate of food.

The following day we took a cab to the airport. Nina flew back to Madrid, while I boarded a small plane to La Palma, one of the westernmost islands of the archipelago. A guidebook I'd read mentioned that La Palma wasn't well known among tourists, who flocked to the larger islands of Tenerife and Gran Canaria. However, the writer extolled La Palma's natural beauty, insisting that walking was the best way to get to know it, and, curiously, recommended a visit to a museum of silk. Coincidence? I wasn't sure. It wasn't much, but it was a start. Moreover, the guidebook said La Palma had an unusual law in the books. Commonly known as *el derecho al cielo* (right to the sky), the law unleashed a series of regulations to moderate artificial lighting on the island so that everyone could enjoy the stars. What a lovely idea! I thought, my interest in this land instantly heightened.

As the plane lifted off from the airport in Tenerife, I gazed out the window. From above, I felt no fear, only awe. Tenerife looked like Cuba—lush and green, with dry desert-like spots and tall mountains that seemed to jut out of the sea rather than the ground. That's the lure of the islands; there's a constant blurring of the boundaries between the ocean and the land that makes islanders feel in a perpetual state of flux. Are we coming or going? Are we leaving or arriving? There is no stability on an island; therein lies their charm and danger. I felt a tug in my heart and wondered, fleetingly, if the time had come to return to Cuba for a visit. After four decades away, these islands were making me think of my own native island, and of the pain of leaving the only place I had ever called home.

Before I could settle into the flight, the captain announced we were landing. At thirty minutes, this had to be the shortest flight of my life. I looked out and tried to focus on the features of the land that now loomed in the rectangle of my window. I could see why they called La Palma *la isla bonita*, for without a doubt it was a beautiful island, with rocky bluffs jutting out boldly from the shore like the fangs of a wolf and varying hues of green shimmering in the distance. I couldn't help but think of my mother, who, though her favorite color is cobalt blue, has always said the most intriguing color is green. "People think trees are all the same color, but look at them, just look at the leaves!" she often exclaimed. She was the first person who taught me to focus on details, even before my Southern editor drilled in the importance of observing things carefully. I was certainly looking now. Curvy roads crisscrossed the island like the veins on a tree leaf. When a pink cloud lifted to the right, I could see the tip of the famous *Roque de los Muchachos*, an astronomical observatory, where telescopes from all over Europe endeavor to decipher the mysteries of the universe.

I'd read that La Palma was the greenest of the eight main islands of this mysterious archipelago—so called because it seemed no one really knew much about the first inhabitants of these "fortunate islands," as some of the authors referred to them. There was wide consensus, however, that the earliest inhabitants were linked to the Berber people of North Africa, known locally as *Guanches*, with an interesting genetic mix and skin ranging from warm olive to the darkest brown.

I recalled how, a few years earlier, my son had sent me a gift membership to a genetics website. I dutifully spat on a tube, as required, and sent it to the address on the envelope. Though I had never thought about my lineage before, I was excited to open the email with my DNA report: 38 percent English (I wondered if that explained my last name), 42 percent from the Iberian Peninsula, and a whopping 12 percent from North Africa, with a few other percentages of Senegalese and Jewish blood thrown in the mix. I had interpreted the North African genetics as coming directly from my Spanish ancestry, since Muslims had ruled Spain for more than seven hundred years.

But this new information about the Canary Islands was making me rethink my gene pool. Perhaps my North African blood came via my great-grandmother, who, for all I knew, could have been a direct descendant of the original inhabitants of these islands.

Would this island reveal her to me? Or, perhaps more intriguing, would it reveal something about me? The truth was I had become more interested in unearthing my family's connection to these islands than in getting the birth certificate my mother so desired. But if I could accomplish both, that would be a bonus.

The more I read about the Canary Islands, the more I wondered what had made my great-grandmother Catalina leave these beautiful surroundings to move to an unknown place across the sea. Was it fear or hunger? Those were typical reasons to emigrate, in my experience. Or could she have been running toward the promise of something else? Love, perhaps? That would be interesting. Then I remembered that somewhere I had read a description of La Palma as having the shape of a heart with, at its center, "a pulsing core of fire."

Catalina

La Palma
August 1919

CATALINA STOOD QUIETLY, her back pressed against the kitchen wall. Her mother sat across from her, head inclined slightly to one side, the way she did when she was intently listening, her hands absentmindedly pulling threads from her worn black skirt. Catalina strained to hear the hushed conversation on the other side of the wall. From where she stood, she could make out only a few phrases here and there—land acreage, loans, the growing demand for bananas, and something about coffee beans—but not enough to understand anything. Still, it wasn't really necessary, for she knew Antonio and the other man, who was a businessman visiting from Cuba, were discussing her future, and it was to be a future away from her mother, her sisters, and her home, and, of course, from Juan. She took a deep breath, as her mother had taught her to do in times of distress, and looked out the kitchen window toward the barren field and the distant rock.

Despite the promise her father had forced from her on his deathbed, she didn't want to go to Cuba with Antonio, she was certain of that. Her young but bruised heart belonged to someone else. While she had briefly allowed Antonio to love her in the first few months of their marriage, after her one night with Juan in the forest nothing had been the same. She was not the same.

At first, the doctor had prescribed total bed rest to save the baby in her womb, so Antonio had not dared touch her except to caress her brow or her hand. Then, after Carmen was born healthy but thin and hungry, Catalina had been so focused on feeding and tending to her daughter that she had asked Antonio to trade bedrooms with her mother so that her mother could help her during the nights.

Wounded, but by nature optimistic, Antonio agreed; in part because it was clear that doña Inés was truly the only one who could help Catalina with the baby. Alone with her daughter and her mother beside her, Catalina allowed herself to think of Juan, to remember his body in the darkness and imagine tracing the curve of his back with her hands. His kisses were not like Antonio's, who was tentative in his touch, always checking to see if he was pleasing her. Antonio handled her with love and care, as if she were made of fine porcelain and could break in his rough hands. Juan, however, used his powerful hands and arms to make her feel desired. His urgency electrified her and made her want him more each day.

Some nights, as she was nursing the baby, she thought she could hear his whistle coming from their hiding place. Was it possible that he was waiting for her? He must have known she couldn't go to him now. She couldn't possibly leave her child.

When the man from Cuba left, Antonio came into the kitchen.

"It's been arranged," he said.

In response, Catalina raised her eyebrows encouraging him to go on.

"A magnificent ship is leaving August 21 from the port here, which means we don't even have to travel to another island."

Catalina felt her throat constrict and couldn't find her voice. What she wanted to say, had she been able to speak, she was certain Antonio didn't want to hear.

Her mother stepped in.

"So soon?" she said. "The baby is too young. Surely there will be another ship."

"The tickets have been purchased," he replied bluntly. Catalina could tell that addressing the question had been painful for him.

Doña Inés seemed flustered and left the kitchen quickly.

"Mother might be right," Catalina said after clearing her throat.

"Catalina, Carmen is almost four months old. That's enough time. As I said, the tickets have been purchased. Please be ready to go with our daughter in two weeks," he said, and looked her in the eyes in a way that Catalina had not yet seen.

"Less than two weeks," she dared reply, and, this time, she was the one who left the kitchen.

That Sunday evening, over dinner, Antonio shared his plans with the rest of the family and Simona's fiancé, a gentle young man named Ramiro Pérez whom everyone had known and liked since he was a child. Antonio announced they would be going to Cuba in a ship called *Valbanera*, named after the patron saint of La Rioja, the Virgin of Valvanera. It was scheduled to arrive in La Palma after stops in Málaga, Cádiz, and other ports of the islands. La Palma was the last stop on its way to Cuba.

"There is no doubt the *Valbanera* is the most comfortable ship in the Pinillos family fleet," Antonio said, opening his arms as if to encompass the entirety of his self-regard.

"The ship observes strict distinctions in its accommodations," he went on. "Even first class is subdivided into luxury, preferred, and first. I have booked two luxury rooms, one for us, and another, smaller room for the baby and the wet nurse who will accompany us on the voyage."

Catalina tried to speak, but she had suddenly lost her voice again. Her hands were unsteady, and her heart was thudding. She started to sweat. A nurse?

"Everything has been taken care of," Antonio said, reaching out to take Catalina's hand.

Simona and Lucía turned toward Catalina to see her reaction, while their mother stared fixedly at her food. A wet nurse? No one in this house would have ever considered such a thing. Inés María had nursed her babies herself, just like her mother had nursed her.

Oblivious to the discomfort he was causing around the table, Antonio went on to describe many of the ship's outstanding features, including the fact that it was built in a Scottish shipyard, and that, at almost 122 meters long, it could carry more than double its weight, or 12,500 tons of merchandise, plus 1,200 passengers.

Catalina's sisters seemed riveted by the details of the ship. But their mother was not as impressionable.

"Isn't the *Valbanera* the ship that killed all those people coming from Cuba?" she asked softly, her eyes downcast, focused on her untouched meal.

A silence descended in the room, as thick as the fog rolling down from the mountains outside.

But, after a pause, Antonio remained undeterred.

"Well, yes, but it wasn't the ship's fault. It was the captain's, and he has been replaced. And not just him. There will be an almost entirely new crew for our voyage," he said. "I'm certain of that."

"And how can you possibly be so certain?" Catalina asked, surprising herself with what she was sure her husband would interpret as an imprudent question.

"Pardon me?" Antonio replied.

Lucía interjected. "It was in the newspapers," she said, and went on to explain how the Pinillos family had launched a major public relations campaign to restore trust in the company after the *Valbanera* returned from Havana a month earlier full of sick people from the influenza pandemic. It had been carrying 1,600 passengers, 400 over the limit stipulated by law, and at least thirty people aboard had died from the virus, including five children of one woman whose sad story had made headlines everywhere in Spain. The living conditions in the ship had been atrocious, the surviving passengers had said. They were packed like matches in a box, and there hadn't been enough food for all.

Catalina listened gravely and thought of the terrible way her own father had died, as well as Juan's mother and brother. Could they have died of the flu as well? Was the virus on the islands and they didn't even know it?

"What happened to the bodies on the *Valbanera*?" Catalina asked Lucía.

"They were thrown overboard," Lucía replied.

At that, doña Inés, who had never discussed with her daughters how her own father's body had been disposed of at sea, pulled her chair back from the table and began clearing away the dishes. Her daughters followed her cue and rose to help, but Catalina remained seated next to Antonio, who seemed wounded by Lucía's outburst. Simona's fiancé, across from them, got up and lit a cigar, offering one to Antonio, who gladly accepted.

"I'm not feeling well," Catalina finally said, and rose to leave. The salty potatoes that she normally enjoyed so much sat like a rock in the pit of her stomach. She hadn't even touched the meat, which remained cold and bloodied on her plate, the grease congealed around the two strands she had managed to cut up with her knife. She felt a wave of nausea and excused herself quickly.

Antonio pulled back his chair and made a motion to follow her, but Catalina stopped him with a firm hand. "It is not necessary," she said, and ran upstairs.

In the commode of her room, she splashed water on her face, and sat on the bed, looking at Carmen, who was peacefully sleeping in a basket atop the bed, sucking her thumb. Catalina rested her forehead against the bed's headboard and closed her eyes.

Simona knocked lightly, afraid to wake the baby, and walked in. She sat next to Catalina and put an arm around her.

"Don't mind Lucía. The ship will be fine. Antonio is a careful man," she said.

But Catalina wasn't worried about the ship's ill reputation. She was more concerned about the wet nurse.

"I'm sure his intention is to spend more time with you, and it may be good for you as well," Simona said, conciliatory as ever.

"In what way can it be good to be away from my child?" Catalina retorted, wounded. "But it seems I have no choice."

Lucía came in at that moment, her eyes downcast, a little sad that she had spoiled the Sunday meal with her stories of disasters and death. She wrapped her arms around Catalina's waist and rested her head against her back.

"Everyone knows you're leaving," she said quietly.

Catalina stiffened her back for she understood the intention of the message immediately.

"Everyone?" she asked rhetorically.

"Yes," Simona chimed in. "In church this morning everyone was talking about it. Father Jacinto wants to see you before you go."

"He does?" Catalina asked, surprised.

"He wants to see the baby, too. He hasn't seen her in months," Simona said pointedly.

Lucía made a sound, as if clearing her throat. "Since the baptism, Simona means," she said hurriedly.

The exchange was quick but meaningful.

"And when does Father Jacinto want to see me?" Catalina asked tentatively, hoping she had understood the message her sisters were trying to convey.

"Tomorrow after morning mass," they said in unison.

"I see," said Catalina. "Tell Father Jacinto I'll be there, please."

"And the baby," said Lucía. "Don't forget Carmen."

As if on cue, Carmen woke up and began wailing with hunger.

"Oh, I almost forgot," Lucía said. "The ship can't be named after the virgin from La Rioja."

"Why not?" Simona retorted, and immediately regretted her curiosity. She didn't want the conversation to go back to the ship that she feared was cursed.

"The spelling is wrong," Lucía responded. "The virgin's name is spelled with two *v*'s. The ship's name is with one *v* and one *b*. It's wrong, you see."

"I see," said Catalina, holding the crying child to her breast with one hand and, with the other, trying to insert her dark engorged nipple into the tiny mouth. "And does that matter?"

"It doesn't," Lucía said breezily, "unless you are superstitious."

Simona pushed her out of the room and closed the door behind them. From the bed, Catalina heard them arguing in the hallway. Well, yes, she thought, she was superstitious.

In the morning, Catalina dressed carefully, wearing one of her black dresses, and swaddled Carmen's tiny body in warm blankets. Though it was summer, the weather was so unpredictable on the island, it was best to be prepared for anything. When she came downstairs, she was relieved to see Antonio had already gone into town for one of his business meetings.

"Where are you going?" Doña Inés asked from the kitchen.

"To church, Mother. Father Jacinto wants to see me and the baby before I go."

"Yes, I heard. Your sisters told me," her mother said, as she came into the living room drying her hands on her apron. "Do you want me to go with you?"

"Oh no, no, no," Catalina said a little too quickly and emphatically.

Her mother cocked her head and began untying her apron. Catalina had to think fast.

"What I mean is, there is no need, and I really must get used to doing things on my own. Soon I'll be far from you and what would I do then?"

Her mother had already taken off her apron and was standing stiffly in front of Catalina.

"All right," she said. "I'll walk to the church with you, anyway. I must get a few things in the market, and I haven't visited your father today."

There was nothing Catalina could say to that.

Mother and daughter left the house together, shutting the door behind them.

The day was spectacular. Though it would surely get much warmer later, the sun was hiding behind a cloudy sky, its rays barely visible among the enormous clouds, making them glow at the edges as if a distant fire were burning behind them. It had rained the night before, and the air was fresh and new, with a breeze that rustled the branches of the pine trees high up in the mountains before wafting down to their small valley. Yellow, blue, and white wildflowers dotted the fields as far as the eye could see, and, behind everything, anchoring not only their property but also their entire world, *La Roca* stood, as immovable and as quiet as ever. Birds serenaded each other in the trees and the gravel made a pleasant crunching sound under their feet as they walked the slight incline up to the church.

Inés María broke the silence.

"Are you worried about the voyage?" she asked.

"A little," Catalina admitted. "But excited, too."

"Your father would have wanted to take you to the ship himself, to see you take the first steps toward your new life," Inés María said, holding back the tears that filled her eyes every time she mentioned her dead husband.

Catalina tried to change the subject.

"How does it feel to be at sea, do you remember?" she asked, shifting her sleeping baby to her other arm to relieve her aching right arm.

"Oh, I do, of course. It's vast. So big and endless, you can't imagine. And the water is cold, even in the summer, and salty and transparent, but only up close. From a distance, it can seem blue, green, or even gray or black, depending on the weather," said Inés María, describing the sea of her native Cantabria, not the one that surrounded them.

"Here we are," Catalina interrupted her, abruptly stopping in front of the stone church.

Inés María looked at her daughter with inquiring eyes, but her lips remained pressed together. She bent down and lightly caressed her granddaughter's forehead, keeping her eyes on her daughter. "Yes, we are," she said pointedly. "I'll see you at home later." She squeezed her daughter's hand and walked away.

Catalina closed her eyes and tried to focus on the moment. If she had understood her sisters' message, behind those doors of the church the man she loved was waiting for her.

She pushed the heavy door in; as always, it was unlocked, and she stepped over the wooden threshold. Inside it was cool and dark, and an intense mixture of scents—sweat, incense, and withered gladiolus—invaded her nostrils. She waited a few seconds while her eyes adjusted to the darkness. There were a few women praying near the altar, their heads bowed and covered with mantillas. Catalina had brought her own, but it was tricky putting it on with a sleeping baby in her arms. She took a few tentative steps inside, not sure where to go. She was halfway down the nave when she heard it: a low, almost imperceptible whistle coming from behind her and to her right, in the direction of a small chapel.

Catalina spun on her heels, and it took all the force of will in her body not to run toward Juan. She walked fast; the clickety-clack sound of her footsteps amplified by the empty cavernous space.

She didn't even have to open the door. He opened it the moment she approached and pulled her to his body, hugging her tightly, so tightly the baby woke up and began to cry. Juan released Catalina without letting go of her forearms, and gazed at the baby between them. His eyes shone with tears. Catalina reached out and touched his cheek, looking carefully at him. She noticed he looked sadder and more unkempt than usual. His black hair was messy, his eyes looked tired and feverish, but his hands were warm.

"I always thought I would carry your child one day," she said, and stopped because it seemed imprudent to give in to her yearnings now that her fate had been decided.

But Juan was unperturbed.

"And you will," he said, reaching out and caressing Carmen's head. "She's so beautiful, just like you."

Carmen stopped crying and fixed her eyes on Juan, as if committing his features to memory. Catalina and Juan both smiled.

"She likes you," Catalina said.

"That's good," said Juan, "because very soon we will be together, and I will be the only father she will know."

Catalina's heart began to beat furiously in her chest.

"What do you mean, Juan? What are you planning? Please tell me."

"I'm going to Cuba with you," he said calmly.

Catalina reeled back as if she had been struck with a red-hot poker.

"But you can't!"

"I can't live without you, and I can't force you to stay here. I told you before, I'll always be with you, Catalina."

"But, Juan, you can't leave your sister alone. Besides, I'm a married woman and a mother now. What are we going to tell Antonio? What if he sees you? What if . . ."

He didn't let her finish. Instead of an answer, he drew her to him again, and began caressing her curls, breathing in her scent deeply.

"Ana has given me her blessing. She is going to move in with a distant relative who needs help. And, don't forget, I will be able to send money from Cuba once I start working. As for the rest, don't worry. I know how to take care of myself."

He pulled her even closer and kissed her deeply, hungrily. Catalina kissed him, too, with the desire she had been holding in for months. His hands moved from her hair to her back, feeling the curve of her hips through the linen of her summer dress. She was beginning to feel dizzy with pleasure, but the baby stirred in her arms.

"I have to go, Juan," she said, pulling away from the embrace. "I have to feed her, and my mother will wonder what's taking so long. Also, I'm supposed to see Father Jacinto."

"May I?" Juan asked, pointing to the baby.

"You want to hold her?"

He nodded, and Catalina gently deposited the baby in his arms. A wide smile spread over his face and his eyes crinkled with joy. It had been a long time since Catalina had seen the impish face of the boy she fell in love with.

"She is so light!" That was all he said, but Catalina could see he was struggling with emotions. She, too, felt rattled. She tried to look away but couldn't stop gazing at her daughter in Juan's arms. Oh, how she wanted this to be her family!

"I will always love her as if she were mine, you know," he said hoarsely, looking down at the baby. It seemed he was making the promise to Carmen, not to Catalina. "Because she comes from you," he added, this time looking straight at Catalina.

Tears fell on her bosom as she took the baby from Juan. She dried her face with a handkerchief and tried to flatten out the wrinkles of the skirt with the palms of her hands. She tried to speak, but her throat was painfully constricted with so many emotions that she didn't dare open her mouth. She took a long look at Juan, trying to record every single detail of him: the way his black curls fell over his eyes, the way his eyes became smaller when he smiled, his perfectly delineated nose and shapely lips. His forehead, ample and prematurely marked by two deep wrinkles that added character to an otherwise boyish face. His chest, hard and strong, just like his arms, where so many times she had found comfort and warmth.

Her eyes filled with tears again as she turned around to leave. But Juan grabbed her by the shoulder and made her face him again. "This is not goodbye, Catalina. I will see you aboard the ship in a few days," he said.

Catalina wanted to say he was crazy or imprudent or that he shouldn't do it, but she didn't want those words to be the last words she ever said to him. Instead, she ran from him, certain that she would never see him again, but hoping that she was wrong.

* * *

The next few days were a blur as Catalina packed and fretted about the trip. Her sisters came and went; her mother busied herself in the kitchen making elaborate dishes and her specialty dessert, *buñuelos de gofio*. The entire house smelled of sugar, cinnamon, and toasted almonds, but also of tears, sadness, and despair. Lucía busied herself tending to the farm, while Simona was occupied with making preparations for her wedding to Ramiro. There was a last meal together, but Catalina was mostly away from the table tending to Carmen, who wouldn't settle during the day or night; all she did was cry as if she too could sense she was being uprooted.

The final night, as she lay in her bed for the last time, Catalina was unable to sleep. In a few hours, she would be leaving the only home she had ever known, perhaps forever. Her body ached from trying to stay still when, with all her might, she wanted to leap out of the bed and run, run, run. As she had been doing since Carmen was born, her mother slept next to her, with an arm covering her face. Catalina looked at her tenderly. She wanted to touch her but didn't want to disturb her sleep. Will I ever see her again? she wondered, and quickly looked away. The thought was too painful.

She was worried about the journey, about what awaited her in Cuba, that mythical island she had heard so many stories about. She worried, too, about her life with Antonio, who seemed to be not as patient with her as he had been before Carmen was born. She wondered how he would behave once they were alone in a different country and far from her family. And she worried, above all, about Juan's ill-conceived plan to join them on the ship. How would he do that? How could he afford to buy a ticket and how would he manage to be undetected by Antonio?

It was then Catalina realized Antonio didn't know Juan. That could certainly make it easier for Juan to move about the ship, but what of her? How would she react if she found herself face-to-face with him? Catalina shook her head as if trying to pry her thoughts loose from her brain.

She peered into the basket next to her and smiled. Her daughter had finally stopped fussing and was now sleeping soundly, the way babies do when they are exhausted from crying. It was hard to imagine now how she had once thought she could never love Antonio's child. She didn't think of Carmen as his child at all. Her daughter was hers, a piece of her flesh, of her body and heart and soul. She fed her and tended to her every need. Those plump cheeks and pudgy wrists were her doing. She, alone, was responsible for this child's survival, and she intended to do everything in her power to keep it that way.

Yet, for the last two weeks, her daughter had refused her breasts. And the less the baby suckled, the less milk she produced. The less she produced, the hungrier the baby became. It was an endless cycle she didn't know how to break. Her mother had started feeding Carmen with a rag dipped in goat's milk. But it was a laborious process. First, she boiled the rag to make sure it was perfectly clean. Then, she dipped it in milk and, drop by drop, squeezed it in the baby's mouth, as if she were a bird. Carmen was now too big and too hungry for that sort of feeding. She wanted more and she wanted it urgently. So, they had resorted to feeding her mashed bananas with goat's milk fortified with *gofio*. She seemed to like that. Catalina had no intention of using the wet nurse at all, but she admitted begrudgingly to herself, she may have to. And, who knows, perhaps she would need help with other things once they arrived in Cuba.

She sighed. She was going to miss her sisters even more than her mother. Her sisters were her confidants and the keepers of her memories. When she looked at them, she could see her life unspooling before her. She remembered the day she had fallen into the ditch, and no one could see her or hear her, but Simona said that her nose had found her, and from that day on, the family joked that Catalina's stinky feet had saved her life. And, further back, she recalled the first day of school when Juan entered the room with his sister, Ana. But more precious than any of those other memories was the day Juan had kissed her for the first time.

Catalina shuddered. No matter what she was thinking about, her thoughts always began and ended with Juan. Her mother stirred next to her. Inés María woke up the way she always did, ready to face the day. "Is it time yet? What time is it?"

"No, Mother," Catalina said. "It's the middle of the night. Rest your head and your thoughts and go back to sleep."

Her mother reached up for her and pulled her into an embrace so warm and intimate Catalina couldn't remember the last time her mother had hugged her like that.

"I know you don't want to go," her mother whispered. "But you are a married woman now, and he is a good man. You'll have a nice life, a better life than your sisters have here, with the farm in disarray and your father gone. One day soon you'll come back to visit and, who knows, I may even be able to visit sometime."

Inés María was a woman of few words, who spoke only when necessary. Her mother's outburst and warmth caught Catalina off guard and broke the dam of her feelings. In her mother's arms, Catalina wept for a long time. The last thing she heard before dozing off was the sound of her mother's soothing voice urging her to be brave and assuring her that God and the Virgin of Candelaria would always protect her. Then she felt her mother's always warm hand on her forehead before she fell into a deep sleep.

The crow of a distant rooster stirred her, then their own rooster responded. Finally, she heard the goats bleating, and the unmistakable tin-tin and the whoosh of the milk as it streamed into the bucket. Her sister Lucía must be milking the goat. Every day of her life she had risen to these sounds in the morning, but today they seemed amplified and more precious. She stilled herself for more. She wanted to take it all in, every single detail, so she would never forget where she came from and where, she hoped, she would one day return.

The faintest whiff of coffee and warm bread reached her nose, and she realized she was hungry. She looked to the other side of the bed, but her mother had already gotten up. Carmen began fussing in the basket and Catalina reached for her to feed her. She opened her nightgown and placed a nipple in her daughter's hungry mouth, but the baby wouldn't latch on as she used to. There's something wrong with my milk, she thought. It was no use. Carmen wouldn't take the breast. With resignation and a little sadness, Catalina tucked her breasts inside her gown, kissed her daughter's forehead, and headed downstairs to boil the goat's milk.

The bags were packed and by the door. Antonio had begged her to pack lightly. He promised she could have as many dresses as she wanted in Caibarién, their destination in Cuba. She liked the name of the village. It meant nothing to her, but Antonio had described it with such love and in such detail that, despite her lack of enthusiasm for the trip, she was looking forward to the house, which he said was wide and sunny and right next to the church and near the town square. She imagined a life by the sea, and that was somehow exciting even if that life would be lived with Antonio and not Juan.

She was nervous at the thought of Juan all over again. It was wonderful to be so loved and to love so deeply in return, but, at the same time, it terrified her, for she didn't know what Juan was capable of. He had nothing to lose. She, on the other hand, had much to lose. But what if she didn't lose anything and instead gained? What if it meant she could live in Cuba with him and Carmen and be happy forever?

Her thoughts were interrupted by Simona and Lucía who had come to help her with the baby so that she could get ready. But Catalina was ready, or, at least, she was dressed for the journey. At that moment, Antonio came into the kitchen with a yellow hibiscus flower he had picked from the garden.

"I want you to wear it in your hair," he said. "It'd look pretty on you."

Catalina blushed and thanked him. Despite his occasional outbursts, he was a gentle man. Why couldn't she love him? He was wearing the same brown suit he wore the day he came to the house to ask for her hand in marriage and on their wedding day. His fingers played with the rim of his hat nervously. He reached for her, bending a little and kissed her brow.

"Did you sleep well?"

She didn't answer because what could she say? She was beginning to learn silence was sometimes a better option than a disagreeable word.

The whole family came together for a farewell breakfast. It should have been a sad occasion, but Catalina's sisters made sure it was not. They kept the conversation light and playful. When the time came to say goodbye, it was almost a relief. Once she left, she would no longer have to pretend not to be dying a little inside.

Catalina quickly hugged them all. Though she hugged Simona the tightest, she was unable to say a word to her closest sister. To Catalina's surprise, her mother's cheeks were wet with tears. She had seen her mother cry only once before, when her husband had died. Inés María made the sign of the cross on Catalina's forehead and then she tried to do the same for Carmen, but the baby squirmed away. "May God and all the saints protect and guide you," she said to both, nonetheless. "Take care of Mother," Catalina whispered to Lucía, who would soon be the only one left in the house with Inés María. Catalina tucked behind Lucía's ear the flower Antonio had given her earlier. Then, she turned around and boarded the mule-drawn cart where Antonio awaited. He had hired a local man to take them to the port.

Her sisters waved goodbye for a long time, but her mother stood still, her face a mask of sadness and apprehension. Catalina kept looking back at her family, at the fields once so full of life, at the spot where the shack had stood behind the house, and, far in the distance, the forest where she had known love. They passed the schoolhouse where she had seen Juan for the first time, and the church where she had seen him the last time, and, finally, the shady spot in the town cemetery where the body of her father forever rested under a birch tree. She looked back again, and now her family was but a dot in the distance. Beyond them she could see through her tears the road that led to Juan's tiny family house, dwarfed by the imposing presence of *La Roca*.

Mara

Santa Cruz, La Palma
July 2019

I STEPPED OUT OF THE PLANE and into a terminal teeming with sunburned European tourists. Since I had only my backpack, within minutes I had left them all behind. Of course, no one was waiting for me at the airport. I should have been used to that by now, but I wasn't. When the doors open and I see all those expectant people, I always scan the faces in the crowd, wanting one of them to recognize me and move forward happily to greet me. But that only happens when I've had the foresight to arrange for a driver to pick me up and there is a lone man—it is usually a man—with a sign that says Ms. Denis or Mr. Dennis or any variation of my gender and last name waiting for me. They pretend to be happy to see me, but I know it is just business. In this instance, I hadn't even called ahead for a driver.

Looking at the many eager faces around me, I wondered what were the odds that one of them could be related to me somehow. They all seemed vaguely familiar, using their hands to make a point and speaking the way Cubans do, with the same smooth cadence that makes us aspirate rather than pronounce every letter of a word. They were boisterous and loud and joyful. Even their features seemed somehow to resemble Cubans I knew in the States or that I had grown up with in Cuba. Middle-aged women like me were wearing sleeveless summer dresses, unapologetically showing their saggy arms. I couldn't remember the last time I had dared to go outside without sleeves or a shawl to cover up my less-than-toned arms. But these women didn't seem to care. Men had potbellies but moved fast, like men half their ages did back in Miami, or even New York. There were some quick embraces as people greeted each other and then others came forward for hugs and kisses. I was mesmerized, and I wasn't sure why. It was a scene I had seen hundreds of times before, but never in Europe.

I blinked and, to my surprise, a tear fell down my cheek. Oh no! This was too much. I had to get it together. Grabbing my backpack, which I'd placed on the floor to give my back a rest, I swiftly left the terminal in search of a taxi. And, there, on the other side of the doors, was the sea, as if the airport were a fancy resort. I quickly shifted my gaze and jumped in the first taxi on the line.

To my chagrin, the driver was playing loud music, and the car smelled like Christmas and stale cigarettes, with a cardboard pine tree hanging from the rearview mirror—a failed attempt to mask his habit. Suddenly I felt very tired and reclined my head against the back of the seat, closing my eyes.

"Do you want to sleep?" the driver asked, jolting me.

He told me we were about sixteen minutes away from the hotel, and kindly lowered the volume of the radio.

I may have thanked him, I don't remember. The last things I registered before dozing off were a flash of aquamarine as we came to a tight curve outside the airport and a feeling of apprehension as I wondered if I would be able to escape the sea on this island. Best to keep my eyes shut, I thought.

In the morning, I felt refreshed and rested. I wore my last clean gray T-shirt (I own ten; gray is a great color for travel) and gave all my dirty laundry to a very nice woman at the bed-and-breakfast where I was staying. She told me she'd have everything ready by evening. I was so grateful, I wanted to kiss her. Instead, I made a mental note to tip well. I already knew that tipping wasn't customary in Spain, but in some areas of my life I was decidedly American.

I needed to get my thoughts in order, but, first, breakfast. The whole point of staying in a B&B isn't the bed but the breakfast and this one did not disappoint. The night before the woman at the reception desk had asked me at what time I was coming down for breakfast. When I said I wasn't sure, she said, "When you do, let us know, so we can start boiling the eggs to your specific requirements." I had chosen well. I hadn't had eggs for breakfast since the last time I was in America.

A French couple, Gladys and Claude, who had moved to La Palma to enjoy their teachers' pensions while still young, owned the home where I would be staying for two nights, and lived in an apartment off the kitchen. After a few years of early retirement, they'd gotten restless and turned their home into an oasis for travelers. The entire house smelled of strawberries. Somehow, they'd managed to grow berries in this climate and were in the process of making their own jam that evening as guests started to trickle back from their excursions and settle in for the night.

At breakfast I enjoyed the fruits of their labor in the garden, surrounded by clay pots overflowing with flowers. Crusty bread and a tall glass of freshly squeezed orange juice complemented the eggs, the Iberian ham, and the jam. Behind me, the two-story home stood cozy and welcoming. For a moment, I felt I could live here. Yes, I could. Why not? This was always the first sign that I truly felt comfortable in a place: if I could imagine myself living there, then I could certainly enjoy a vacation, though, technically, I had my mother's quest to deal with. Gladys approached and served me more *café con leche*. I took the opportunity to ask about the house. It wasn't very old, she said, in that way Europeans have of dismissing anything that wasn't built before the Renaissance.

"It was built two hundred years ago, but it was one of the first private homes in La Palma to have indoor electricity, in the late nineteenth century," she said proudly.

That surprised me. I tried to imagine what it must have been like for my great-grandmother, going from electricity and paved streets in La Palma to life in rural Cuba. Electricity had not yet reached my grandfather's house by the time I left in 1979, almost a century after the arrival of the *isleños*, as those from the Canary Islands were called in Cuba.

I glanced at my watch. It was close to noon already. If I didn't get to a government office before lunch, the workday was effectively over.

The day was clear and sunny, so I decided to walk. As I began, a little alarm went off in my brain and I pulled out my phone to check if the newspaper had run my story on the refugees rescued off the coast of Tenerife. I found it on page five. Copy editors had trimmed about four paragraphs of it, but it wasn't a dramatic cut, and I was used to it. What I could never get used to were the wrenching stories of immigrants and refugees, and I was glad. What kind of a reporter would I be if that little girl in the morgue didn't stay with me? I suppose it's like being a doctor in the ER. You move on to the next patient because you have to, but that doesn't mean you forget the one you couldn't save.

The first time I wrote an immigration story, in 1987, I wasn't looking for one. I was, in fact, walking around on an early Friday morning, bulk trash day, looking for discards. In my old Miami neighborhood, people threw away all kinds of things. I was young, newly married, and poor. Nelson and I made $42,000 between us, not enough to splurge on new furniture for our first apartment, small but charming, and I desperately needed a desk. Because I was looking down, I noticed words on a cracked portion of the sidewalk, where the concrete had been partially lifted by the roots of the giant oak tree that loomed over the street. The inscription read, "*Te quiero Alicia 1957.*" Who was Alicia? And who had loved her so much as to leave his feelings in writing for all to see? I looked up at the house standing directly in front of the sign and wondered if Alicia still lived there. There was only one way to find out. I knocked on the door. An elegant woman opened it. She looked to be about fifty. Black hair framed her still youthful face and she wore creased dark blue jeans and a starched white poplin long sleeve blouse. She looked like a model in a Carolina Herrera ad. "Yes?" she said, opening the door a crack.

"Are you Alicia?" I asked with the boldness that comes from carrying a reporter's ID and a pad, which I never left at home.

She was indeed Alicia, and, when I asked about the words on the sidewalk, she invited me in and told me the story of her life. She had come from Cuba with her parents when she was twenty years old in 1957, because her parents feared that the revolution brewing in the mountains would end up taking possession of the government and installing a Communist dictatorship, which is exactly what happened. They also wanted to keep her away from a certain long-haired young man whom they viewed as too radical for their daughter. But the man, whose name was Carlos, followed her to Miami and tried to convince her to return to Cuba with him. She was tempted, she said, but, in the end, stayed home with her parents, refusing to open the door to him despite his pleas.

The day after he finally left, Alicia went outside and found his love letter inscribed in the freshly poured cement of the new sidewalks. Her parents wanted to erase it, but were afraid to destroy city property, so the message stayed. She never heard from Carlos again, but every day, when she walked outside her house, she was reminded of his love and of her cowardice. She had never married.

Ever since then, I've been bearing witness to the tragedies and the triumphs of the world's oldest story, older than history, older than language: the human drive to migrate to survive. And here I was again, chasing another immigration story, but this time, the subject was a lot closer to my heart, because my mother had managed to keep alive in me a memory of a great-grandmother I never knew. Her whimsical phrases were sprinkled in my mother's vocabulary, which was now mine, too, and her fears and torments formed part of my mother's DNA, and, therefore, mine.

* * *

Claude, from the hotel, had given me precise directions. I had to walk only a fewblocks. Take Avenida Marítima, at the restaurant La Placeta, make a left; at the end of the alley, a right and the Juzgados building would be on my left. Once inside, the civil registry office would also be on my left. Easy enough.

It was a perfect day for a walk, even one that took me to a wide avenue facing the sea. I kept my gaze averted from the black-sand beach and focused on the avenue, which was dotted with exquisite old houses with hanging wooden balconies, a type of architecture unlike anything I had seen in the rest of Spain.

In no time, I was standing in a short line in the lobby of a nondescript white building, wedged between a store with a 50 percent off sale sign and a two-story private home with an ornate top that resembled frosting on a wedding cake.

When my turn came, I was strangely tongue-tied. It seemed somewhat absurd to be searching for a birth certificate that was more than a hundred years old. All I had was a name, a date, and a vague idea of a place of birth. Pulling out my reporter's notebook, I pretended to review my notes. The simple act of having that narrow notebook in my hands immediately made me feel stronger and gave me a sense of purpose, but it was short-lived.

The woman behind the counter started shaking her head the moment she heard my query. Finally, she pushed back the piece of paper I had given her bearing my great-grandmother's name and date of birth, and told me that it wasn't possible because the date went too far back.

Few things embolden me more than being told something can't be done. I become obsessed with the need to prove them wrong. My mother calls it my "contrarian gene." I call it my "having-lived-under-Communism-and-being-pissed-off-all-the-time gene."

"Is there someone else I can speak with?" I asked, giving her my best smile.

Without answering, she looked over her shoulder and called out to a man, younger than her, who approached the counter quickly. I could tell my query intrigued him, but I also realized he didn't want to embarrass his coworker.

"I have to think about this," he said cautiously. "Could you come back in an hour?"

I could wait here, I thought, but it didn't seem prudent to argue. I took his name and walked outside into a postage-sized shady plaza, where I chose a bench and finally opened the local newspaper I had been carrying in my bag.

A headline on the front page, on the bottom right, stopped me. I saw something I thought I had seen before or perhaps had dreamed of. It wasn't a very imaginative headline, but it did the job: "REMEMBER THE *VALBANERA*," it read in bold letters. And then, this below the headline: "On the 100th anniversary of the ship's sinking off the coast of Cuba, join us tonight as we remember the hundreds of souls lost to that tragedy." There was an address and more details about an exhibit, but my mind was racing. Where had I seen that name before? I don't have a good memory for anything, except words. I tried to focus and think back, almost as if I was going through an old Rolodex, quickly scanning my most recent stories to try to locate the place where, I was certain, I had not only seen the name of the ship but also read about it. And then, I had it!

A few months earlier during a weekend stay in a rural house in a hamlet in Asturias, I visited a museum of migration called Indiano Archive Foundation. Each floor was dedicated to a country or a region where Spaniards had migrated. Cuba and Tampa were on the first floor. The pictures of the ships and the thousands of people boarding them mesmerized me. The hope and sadness on those faces was not unlike the hope and sadness I found every time I reported a story on immigration. It was also the same expression I had found in the pictures hanging on the wall at Ellis Island—a mixture of fear, nostalgia, and excitement. The next floors were dedicated to immigration to Mexico, Chile, and Argentina.

On the top floor of the building, a sort of tower overlooking the town there was a special exhibit focused on wreckages and migration.

That was where I first encountered the name *Valbanera*. I couldn't recall the details now, but I knew the ship had sunk near Havana, or was it Key West? And I thought I remembered there was a mystery associated with it because hundreds of people had died, but no bodies were ever found. I recalled standing in front of the glass displays for a long time looking at the pictures of the survivors and some of the pictures of those who had died. It struck me that I had never heard about that story before, though I had visited Key West dozens of times, and even honeymooned there with Nelson.

Then I moved on and forgot about it. Until now. This must be what I saw in Tenerife as well, that flash of text and color on the bus while I battled the wind. It had been quick, but I knew it included the word *shipwreck*. A chill ran through me, and I had the fleeting impulse to call my son and beg him to reconsider his decision to join the Navy. But I didn't. I remembered all the times he had started a project with great enthusiasm only to drop it a few weeks or months later. The same would happen now, I was sure of that. I simply couldn't imagine him in the military. And I'm sure Nelson, if he were alive, would have tried to dissuade him.

A warm breeze rustled the newspaper in my hand, and I went back to reading, putting thoughts of Nelson in the place where he lived, the back of my mind and the center of my heart.

There were all kinds of events planned throughout the islands for the centenary of the *Valbanera*'s sinking: concerts, a play, a reading, a conference, and an exhibit that evening with actual pieces from the ship. Intrigued, I ripped out that section of the paper, folded it, and put it in my purse. I would go to the opening of the exhibit tonight. Hopefully, I could get what I needed for my mother in a matter of minutes, take the rest of the day off, and return to Madrid and Santander tomorrow. Back to my life and my routine. On to the next story. I needed to come up with stories that took me out of this endless circle of dreams quashed by an angry sea. Let someone else cover the tragedy of immigration for a while.

The sun was beginning to creep up on my back. It was time to move. Then my phone began to ring with that horrible chirping sound.

"Hello," I said neutrally, though I was eager to tell my mother about La Palma and some of the things I had already seen.

"Do you have the certificate yet?"

"Good morning to you, too. I'm well, thank you, and you?" I said, knowing that I was doing to her what she had done to me in the past.

Without apologizing, she went on to say something about a fast-approaching deadline. The deadline to apply for Spanish citizenship was in six months. Plenty of time, but I didn't say that to my mother. Instead, I told her how pretty La Palma was and how well I was eating and how, as a matter of fact, I was standing right outside the office where I hoped to have her grandmother's birth certificate by 2 p.m. today. She was thrilled to hear that and went on to tell me about her various ailments and other general complaints. At that point I interrupted.

"I want to tell you about these dreams I've been having," I said.

"What?"

"Nightmares," I yelled.

"Don't yell!" she raised her voice.

"I thought you couldn't hear me," I said. "I've been having nightmares."

I told her about how, in my dreams, I'm always searching for a baby girl, a daughter, it seems.

There was a long silence after that.

"I used to have dreams like that, too," my mother finally said, quietly, as if talking to herself.

"You did? You never told me."

Another pause. "Maybe it's like any other phobia," she said thoughtfully.

"What do you mean?"

"Maybe I passed it on, like skin tone or good teeth or my fear of the water."

Another pause. I thought of a phrase I had heard somewhere, an Armenian poet who told an interviewer that he braided together "filaments of trauma" to feed his muse. Was this one of my inherited traumas?

"I was always afraid of losing you," my mother said.

Tears immediately rimmed my eyes and I swallowed hard. My mother hadn't always known how to express her love, but when she did, it was powerful. Her hand on my forehead always lowered my childhood fevers, and her soothing voice had often allayed my fears.

"Losing me? But I'm still here," I said with a small laugh to lighten the mood.

"Yes, I know," she said in a voice so low it seemed as if she were talking to herself. I pressed the phone to my ear and closed my eyes to focus on her words. "But I've lived with that fear for a long time."

Catalina

Aboard the *Valbanera*
August 1919

CATALINA WAS SHAKING AS SHE WALKED toward the ship with Carmen in her arms. Her eyes darted everywhere. She was searching for Juan and keeping an eye on the luggage, while trying to catch a glimpse of the ocean, but it was nearly impossible. The ship was so large, it occupied her entire field of vision. And there were so many people moving about, she began to feel dizzy. Antonio held her by the elbow.

"Are you looking for the nurse?" he asked. "She is already on board. You'll meet her soon enough."

Catalina realized Antonio was more perceptive than she had thought. She would need to be careful.

"No, no. I'm just looking at everything. It's all so new to me," she said, and leaned into him.

Before they stepped on the gangplank, a photographer hired by the shipping company asked them to pose for a picture. Catalina, the baby in her arms, stood next to Antonio, who held her by the elbow. She was wearing a black dress with a lace bodice her mother had made especially for the trip. Catalina cocked her head to the right, as her mother sometimes did, because the sun was shining directly in her eyes. Carmen woke up and raised a fist out of her white knitted blanket. Antonio, holding his brown wool hat at chest level, looked down and noticed that the yellow hibiscus was no longer in Catalina's hair. He was leaning in to ask her about it, and Catalina turned to respond when they both heard the loud click of the camera shutter. Behind them, in red bold letters over a white background, the photographer had made sure to capture the name of the vessel: *VALBANERA*.

For years, her father had promised her he would one day take her to the sea, which was so close to their home that Catalina could smell the crisp salt air when the morning fog lifted, and the wind blew a certain way off the mountains that blocked her view of the ocean. But the work on the farm was so intense and never-ending—caring for the silkworms, pruning the trees, weeding the vegetable garden, tending to the animals—that the trip always got postponed.

But here she was now, aboard a ship, surrounded by more people than she had ever seen together in one place, and about to embark on a journey that would take her away from everyone and everything she had ever known and loved. Not everyone, she thought, and held her daughter tighter.

If it weren't for her daughter, Catalina was sure, she would have turned around, run from the ship, and jumped on the cart pulled by mules that had brought them to the port of Santa Cruz. But her precious daughter asleep in her arms, her lovely, sweet Carmen, with her big blue eyes and dark hair, deserved to grow up with her father and feel his love, just as Catalina herself had when she was growing up.

She had no doubt that Antonio loved their daughter deeply. She still remembered how, shortly after the birth, she had walked into their room to check on the baby and had found her husband bent over the basket next to their bed caressing Carmen's little feet. When he heard Catalina's steps on the hardwood floor, Antonio placed the baby's feet in the palm of one hand and looked up at his wife.

"Isn't it amazing?" he had asked.

Catalina shrugged and furrowed her brow, puzzled.

"Her feet," he said quietly. "I'm marveling at her feet, how tiny they are and how, one day soon she'll be wearing shoes and then later maybe have feet larger than mine."

Catalina had laughed at the strange comment, and she smiled now as she remembered it. Antonio noticed, and seemed to interpret her smile as a sign of joy.

"I knew you'd be impressed," he said, and placed a gentle kiss on her forehead. "Wait until you see our room. I picked the best one for us. I'm certain you'll like it."

Catalina didn't reply, for what could she say? She was never sure what to say when Antonio made such displays of wealth and status. Or was it love? With him, it was hard to tell. Or perhaps it was hard for her to accept that a man who wasn't Juan loved her even if she didn't love him. She knew he wanted to please her, but in the end, his comments were always meant to show how much more than others he had. At times, it had been embarrassing, as when he regaled her sisters and Simona's fiancé after supper one evening with stories about his store in Cuba and his large house in the center of a prosperous town.

"Like ours?" Lucía had asked, gesturing toward their own home.

Antonio had cleared his throat and blushed slightly, taking Catalina's hand and playing with her fingers for a moment, as he searched for an adequate response. Finally, he had said, "There is no comparison, really. The styles are so different." And he let it go at that. Her sisters had looked at her with a mixture of embarrassment and pity.

Now, on this large ship, Catalina felt suddenly very alone. She could no longer turn to her family for support. All she could do was smile and follow a butler who was leading them to their luxury class cabin down a richly ornamented hall, leaving behind the noise of the bustling port. The walls were covered with a floral wallpaper in pale pink and yellow tones that made her think of home. But she pushed the thoughts from her mind and kept walking, her feet practically gliding on the gleaming wooden floor.

When the butler finally came to a halt outside one of the doors, Antonio took her hand and gave it a gentle squeeze. As soon as the butler opened the door and stood aside, Catalina could see that Antonio had not exaggerated. The room was larger than her bedroom had been at home. A thick dark blue carpet cushioned her feet, and a glass chandelier hung from the ceiling, bathing the space in a golden glow. Two beds with wooden headboards framed a pretty cabinet with a marble sink. An armchair and a mirrored vanity table with a plush banquette made the room feel both elegant and efficient, with everything in its place, including a wicker bassinet that had been placed on one end. On the far wall, opposite the door, velvet drapes of the same shade as the carpet had been drawn over the windows to block out the sun.

Antonio nudged her in. Their luggage had already been placed on a low table beside a cedar wardrobe. He strode over to the windows, opened the drapes, and sunlight streamed in, blinding Catalina momentarily.

When her eyes adjusted, she could see only green. In the distance, there was a line where the sea and the sky came together. Her father had told her it was called the horizon and that it was only an illusion. Later, when the ship reached that line that seemed so far away and forbidden, another would appear and another. The possibility of an ever-expanding horizon seemed to her a good omen. She remembered Juan's words, "My love for you is higher than the sky, deeper than the ocean," and felt a pain stab her heart so sharply she had to fight the urge to lie down. Was he on the ship, as he had promised? She hoped not, but also, she desperately wanted him near her.

The sound of a horn startled her, and Antonio, solicitous as ever, embraced her, kissing her temple.

"It just means we are leaving soon," he said. "You'll like it here, I promise."

Before they could unpack, there was a soft knock on the door.

"That must be María," Antonio said, and reached for the doorknob.

It was indeed María, the wet nurse Antonio had hired to feed Carmen and relieve Catalina from the constant care of her daughter during the journey. María was petite, with bright dark eyes and a mane of golden-brown hair she kept pinned away from her face. She had a mischievous smirk that sat at one corner of her mouth and never quite developed into a warm smile. She stood there in her white dress, looking at one and then the other. No one knew what to say after the introductions.

"Is it time to feed the baby, doña Catalina?" María finally asked.

It was, in fact, a good time since Carmen had started to fuss, turning her mouth looking for a nipple, and Catalina's breasts felt empty and useless. Antonio excused himself to see the captain and discreetly left the cabin. Catalina disentangled the baby from her aching arms and handed her to María; she watched, fascinated, as her daughter latched to a breast she had never known before and began hungrily suckling. She had thought it would be difficult for her to see her daughter feed from the breasts of another woman, but it wasn't. If anything, Catalina felt relief that her daughter's life was not completely and solely dependent on her.

While the baby fed, Catalina set about opening the luggage and organizing the room. It was so freeing to have another woman taking care of her baby that she felt almost happy. She was leaving all she knew behind, but her new life was calling to her. What would it be like? As if the captain could hear her thoughts, Catalina felt the ship begin to separate from its berth with a thud.

She hurried out of the room to the deck to take a last look at her island. As the ship pulled out of port, the city of Santa Cruz de La Palma appeared as though it were lying on a sloping green incline, its flat-roofed white houses clustered at the foot of the mountain. When the ship had retreated from the coast, the houses gradually became white dots in the distance, but the green of the view remained, like an impenetrable curtain enveloping the island. Catalina began to fear that she would never return to her native land.

She felt a wave of nausea seize her insides and held on to the railing of the ship with her head lowered, waiting for her stomach to settle. The movement of the ship was maddening. From the window of the room, the sea had seemed so calm and flat that it hadn't occurred to her to fear it in any way. Now, she felt as if everything around her were moving in endless circles and she couldn't stop any of them. She was desperately trying to assert some control over her body, but her limbs felt liquid and slippery, as she slid down the rail toward the deck.

A man picked her up before her body reached the ground, and holding her by the arms, brought her back inside to the corridor, where she directed him to her cabin. After thanking him, she walked into the room and immediately threw up on the carpet. Though ashamed, there was nothing she could do. Everything was spinning around and around, and all she wanted was to lie down.

For two days and two nights, Catalina lost track of time and of herself. She knew María was taking care of her and of baby Carmen, but she could barely eat or stand straight. Her husband's face came in and out of focus several times, but she couldn't understand what he was saying. A doctor came to see her and gave her some powdered medicine to mix with boiled water and drink. On the third day, she woke up with the sun and knew immediately that the worst had passed. She raised her head from the pillow carefully and tried to focus her eyes, but it was too soon, and she felt queasy again. Blindly, she reached for the bassinet, and found it empty. Where was Carmen?

Just then, someone opened the door. It was María, with Carmen in her arms.

Catalina felt a wave of gratitude. What would have happened if María hadn't been traveling with them? Who would have taken care of Carmen?

"Where is Antonio?" she asked.

"Antonio? You kept asking for someone else," María said with a smirk, her eyes fixed on Catalina's.

* * *

That night Catalina was well enough to don her best dress—a black silk dress with ruffles at the waist and a lace bodice—and joined Antonio at the captain's table for dinner. The table was at the center of a grand, carpeted room with high ceilings. Tall, paneled windows encircled the first-class dining area like a crown. Under the chandeliers, cutlery and wineglasses shimmered like jewels. The meal was splendid—roasted venison, Italian pasta, and *fabada*, accompanied by warm crusty bread and exquisite wines, and followed by a cheese tray, tea and coffee, and a delectable chocolate tart topped by a white sail made of almond cream. Catalina was ravenous with hunger after almost seventy-two hours without eating.

The captain, new to the ship, was regaling his guests with facts about the *Valbanera*—its size, its power, its elegance, its provenance—even though he admitted at one point that it was essentially a mixed-use ship that carried not only people but merchandise to and from the Americas.

To Catalina it all seemed irrelevant, but the others were impressed with the young captain's stories. Antonio was distant and preoccupied. Catalina felt mortified. If she had really called for Juan in her delirium, as María had said, she could imagine that Antonio would surely be upset and perhaps even suspicious. She wasn't sure what to do or say. The wise words of her mother rescued her from her misery: sometimes, the best thing to do is to do nothing at all. It was one of her mother's favorite sayings. Catalina thought this was one of those times. Perhaps it was best if she pretended María hadn't said anything. Antonio would soon forget it, she told herself. After all, how long could he stay angry at her, and would it matter in the end?

She tried to make conversation with others at the table: a doctor from Madrid who was traveling to Cuba with his wife to visit their daughter who had just given birth to their first grandchild, and a couple from Tenerife who had six children; one of them, the oldest, sat quietly and politely at the table as if he were a pint-sized adult. When the conversation petered out and Catalina delicately yawned once or twice behind her strategically placed hand, Antonio got up and announced an early retreat. The men complained loudly, for they were getting ready to light up cigars and wished for Antonio to join them.

Promising he would return, he walked his wife to their cabin without a word, kissed her on the temple, as was his habit, and told her he would be back later. She nodded, grateful to be alone, and went inside the empty room. María was probably feeding the baby in her own room. Resting her back against the door she considered what to do. They had been on the ship for three or four days, she had lost count already, and she still had no idea if Juan was on board. She thought he wasn't, for if he was, if he was this close to her, breathing the same air, Catalina was certain she would have felt his presence by now. But she had felt nothing except relentless nausea that, thankfully, the doctor had cured, or perhaps her stomach had gotten used to the motion of the ship.

It was time to look for Juan. Slowly, as if she were afraid to wake someone, she opened the door of the cabin and stepped into the corridor. Which way should she go, left or right? She decided to walk in the opposite direction from the dining room. At the end of the hall, she found what seemed a narrow, abandoned stairwell. She peered down and saw that the steps led to a lower level. She started to climb down, carefully, holding the rail. Almost immediately, she heard steps rapidly climbing toward her. Her heart began to beat furiously. The stairs were dark. She could hear the distant sounds of the orchestra playing a waltz and something else, something she thought she recognized.

Catalina stopped, uncertain, but then she heard it again: a low whistle. Was it her imagination? She heard it again, closer this time. Where was it coming from? Catalina started to turn around, confused, but before she could turn her head, a hand grabbed hers in the dark.

Mara

Santa Cruz, La Palma
July 2019

I WAS SPEECHLESS and didn't have the time to psychoanalyze my mother's fears about losing a daughter. I disentangled myself from the call quickly after that and went back to the building. The courteous man from before was waiting for me outside, his head anxiously swiveling from side to side.

"Ms. Denis, I've been waiting for you," he said, bowing slightly, and introduced himself. "Fernando Suárez Jiménez, at your service."

Oh, oh, he must have googled my name.

"Pleased to meet you," I said, meeting his firm handshake with mine and looking him in the eye, as my father had taught me so many years ago.

"Won't you come inside please? We can talk in my office," he said, and swept his arm in a gallant arc, opening a path for me.

I thanked him but let him lead the way, debating silently at what point I should tell him my question was related to a personal issue having nothing to do with my job or the newspaper I worked for. I decided I'd let him speak first. When we reached his office, he pulled up a chair for me and seated himself behind an imposing wooden desk. He told me it was an honor to have me in La Palma, his dark eyes blinking rapidly under long lashes while he tapped his desk with a pen as if sending a message in Morse code.

I tried to put him at ease.

"May I have some water, please?"

"Certainly," he said, and sprang from the cushioned chair behind the desk. "And would you like some coffee as well?"

I almost said no, but then I realized that, yes, I wanted coffee. In fact, I was hungry, but coffee would do for now.

"Yes, please, with a little milk, if possible."

"*Un cortado*, then," he said.

He came back almost immediately, then settled in.

"I have to tell you I'm a fan of your work," he said, the pen back in his hand, but, mercifully, not tapping now. "I read your paper as often as I can to practice my English."

"Thank you, that's wonderful to hear and very nice of you to say, but—"

He cut me off before I could tell him I wasn't there for work.

"And I want to do anything in my power to help you, so I've found what you were looking for and more, if you'll allow me," he said, and slid toward me a white mid-sized envelope.

Intrigued, I opened it. Inside, I found a plastic sleeve protecting a frayed yellowed document: my great-grandmother's birth certificate. At last! Her full name was Catalina de la Candelaria Quintana Cabazas, as I already knew, but her birth had been recorded on May 29, 1900, a month after the date my mother had given me, in a hamlet called La Peña in El Paso, a municipality of La Palma.

The clerk mentioned as a curiosity that El Paso was the island's only municipality without access to the sea.

"Though I'm sure you can smell it from there," he added. I looked at him, not really understanding what he was talking about.

He cleared his throat and went on, "Well, it is said this island is so small you can see the sea from everywhere, no matter how remote or how far from it you are. And if you can't, you can at least smell it."

Mr. Suárez kept talking, but I wasn't listening anymore. My hands were trembling as I regarded the yellowed document. This record of the birth of a woman insignificant to history, but not to my family, was almost 120 years old.

"Thank you so much for taking good care of it and for finding it so quickly," I said, my throat constricting. I had a sudden urge to leave and be alone with my thoughts.

Something was thrashing about in my mind, looking for a place to settle. *She had lived far from the sea.* It was like trying to fit a piece of a puzzle somewhere in the unfinished picture in front of me. But a picture of what? I made a move to stand up.

"You are very welcome, Ms. Denis, but look at the other paper we found," he said just as I was getting up.

I sat back down and reached into the envelope again. At first, I didn't understand what I was looking at. He must have sensed my confusion.

"It's a marriage license," he said with barely concealed excitement. "We've been registering marriages here for a little over a hundred years. Hers was one of the first."

"Her marriage?" I asked, and my heart sank, because I realized he had made a mistake. No wonder the birth dates didn't match. He couldn't possibly have a record of her marriage here. I was certain she had met and married my great-grandfather in Cuba.

He got up from his chair, came around the desk and, with his index finger, pointed to the rectangular box on the license listing the name of the groom. "There!" he said triumphantly. "His name was Antonio López González."

I wanted to explain how that was impossible, but I didn't think it was prudent to reveal too much about my personal quest to this man I didn't know. Instead, I asked why he was so sure the documents recorded the life I was interested in, given the different dates of birth.

"It was a common occurrence back then, because people often waited a while to record births and weren't always diligent in checking what a clerk had written down," he explained with the tone of someone who'd had to explain this many times before. "Now, if I might ask, why is this woman so important to your paper after so many years?"

It was too late to clarify anything, so I deflected his question. I got up quickly and asked him if I could make copies of these documents. Of course, of course, he replied, and handed me the copies he had already made for me. I shoved them in my cavernous bag, shook his hand, and left the building before he could see my confusion and embarrassment. I was mortified. I should have told him from the beginning that Catalina de la Candelaria Quintana Cabazas was indeed a very important person, but only because she was my great-grandmother.

I called my mother the moment I was back in the park, across from the building.

"I got it!"

"You got it?"

"I did, yes! But I'm confused. The birthdates don't match and . . ." I hesitated a moment and my mother noticed.

"What, what is it?" she asked impatiently.

"And they also gave me a marriage license. Apparently, she married a man named Antonio when she was eighteen. Antonio López. It says here she got married in a town called La Peña, not far from here, I think."

"Married? No, that can't be. They got the wrong person. My grandmother was married in Cuba," my mother said. "Who do they say she was married to?"

"A man named Antonio López González," I repeated slowly. I could sense she was disappointed and upset.

"Who is that?"

"I have no idea, *Mima*," I said.

"You know what? You're the reporter. Go find out."

And she hung up. Or we lost the connection. With my mother it was hard to tell.

I didn't know what to make of this new information, but I decided not to dwell on it too much. I had what I'd come for, and I could now go home. Or at least relax a little.

Buoyed by the progress I had made in half a day, I treated myself to an early lunch and a little shopping. In a beautiful shop called Berlin, I bought a dress, something I hadn't done in years. Nothing fancy, just a simple linen dress in a bottle green shade, loose and soft, to match all the lush greenness that surrounded me. I paired it with gold sandals and an orange scarf. Then, just because I had nothing better to do and, also, because I badly needed a haircut, I crossed the street and went to a salon. Two hours later, I felt like a new woman: same hair color, with my gray intact, but a new cut and styling that made me feel younger and lighter. I'd even gotten a manicure and pedicure. Should I take a selfie and send it to Nina? I wondered. No! I'd never live that one down!

That evening I went to the opening of the *Valbanera* exhibit, similar to the one I had already seen in Asturias, but more detailed. It felt wonderful to be in an art gallery with my new dress and haircut without having to think about work or my mother's request.

I'd always loved the feeling of being alone in a new place where no one knew me. I could observe, without being observed. There were no expectations or demands. No one was waiting for me. That thought, which terrified so many of my married friends, was strangely liberating for me. I could get lost in the crowd. I could be myself or someone else; the fact is I never felt alone. Because I had lost so much early in life—my home, my friends, my country, my husband, my father—I was able to carry everything I needed inside. My anchors were internal. My shelter was ever changing and almost irrelevant, but my home and my loves I always kept with me.

They were here with me now, walking in this impossibly white gallery, where dozens of men and women, dressed for summer on an island, gathered around pictures I had already seen in a faraway place in completely different weather not even six months ago. What are the chances, I thought, that I'd find the same exhibit in two so radically different places?

At the entrance I had read that the events around the centenary of the *Valbanera* shipwreck had really started a few months earlier in Las Palmas de Gran Canaria, the first stop the ship made to pick up passengers on the Canary Islands. Then, it went to Tenerife, the second stop, and, finally, it came to Santa Cruz de La Palma, the last stop of the ship on its way to Cuba. All told, there were 1,142 passengers and eighty-eight crewmembers when the ship sailed the 21st of August 1919, toward Puerto Rico, Cuba, and Louisiana.

At the end of one wall, there was a group of people reading a list intently with a magnifying glass.

"What is it?" I asked a woman who was leaving the group.

"Oh, it's the list of those poor souls who went down with the ship," she said. "All four hundred and eighty-eight of them."

"But the letters are so tiny!" I complained.

"No, no you don't have to do it like I did. I just wanted to read it in the original format. You can also scroll down this way," she said, showing me a smart contraption that rolled the names on a computer screen. "What name are you looking for?"

"Nobody," I said. "I'm just curious."

"Well, there you go. They are in alphabetical order," she said, and left me alone with the names.

The computer screen didn't appeal to me after all, so I took a magnifying glass that hung from a chord attached to the wall and began looking at the facsimile of the old newspaper pages as the others were doing. Up and down, I moved the magnifying glass, like a detective in the comics. Suddenly, a name jumped out at me: Antonio López González.

It couldn't be. But, I reasoned, Antonio is a common name and so are López and González, so I dismissed the coincidence. Then, as in a trance, I dropped the magnifying glass, and moved to the computer. I kept scrolling down until I found the letter *Q*. I clicked, and I kept clicking. The *u*, the *i*, the *n* . . . and there it was: Catalina Quintana Cabazas. My great-grandmother's name among the dead.

Catalina

Aboard the *Valbanera*
August 24–September 5, 1919

CATALINA CLOSED HER EYES and breathed in the familiar scent of onions, sweat, lavender, and pine needles that seemed to emanate from every pore of Juan's body. She reclined her head against his chest as he began kissing her neck, her hair, her shoulders. He let go of her hand and encircled her waist. She held his beautiful face and kissed him deeply on the mouth. It felt like it was the first time they had ever kissed. It had been so long, and she had been so afraid that he had stayed behind.

Without a word, Juan took her hand and began climbing down the stairs. Quietly, she followed. She would have followed him anywhere. But for now, he took her to a dark corner where, finally, he whispered her name.

When she got back to her room, flushed and worried, Catalina was happy to see the baby asleep and María nodding off in the armchair beside her. Gently, Catalina touched her on the arm and told her she could go back to her room.

She was glad Antonio had not yet returned. Carmen was sleeping soundly in her basinet, and María was gone. Just as well. She wanted to be alone with her thoughts and her memories as she readied for bed. Finding Juan in such a large ship had been a stroke of luck, she thought, but he explained to her that luck had nothing to do with it. He had managed to slip in the ship at the port and, so far, had remained undetected among those who had paid seventy-five pesetas for the lowest possible class accommodations, the "emigrant category," a cramped storage space without ventilation or privacy where the poorest of the passengers slept in metal-framed cots. Catalina had been horrified. "What if you get caught?" she had asked him. "I won't," he had replied with a confidence she sensed he didn't feel. Juan also told her that, with the little money he had managed to save, he had bribed a low-rank young officer who checked the passengers list and told him where in the ship he was likely to find Catalina. "The back stairs," he said. "No one ever goes there after sunset. Too dark and narrow."

And so, every night since the day they left Santa Cruz, he had paced those stairs up and down, whistling for her until, finally, tonight, she had come to him. Catalina could still feel Juan's hands and mouth on her, his ragged breathing as he entered her body and told her repeatedly how much he loved her and how they would always be together. She hadn't dared ask him how exactly he was planning that, but she was certain he would tell her soon. They had made plans to meet the following night if Antonio went out again.

That night Catalina slept soundly in the soft bed of the cabin for the first time since they had departed, the waves of the sea gently rocking her to sleep. In her dreams, she was back at home, with her mother and sisters collecting leaves from the mulberry trees for the worms. She was just a girl, and her sisters were young, too. Her father was alive, and they all worked under the sun. Her mother sang, but she couldn't make out the words. A baby was crying somewhere.

It was her daughter's hunger cries that woke her up. She automatically placed her baby on her breast to try to go back to sleep, and then she remembered her breasts were already empty. With a pang, she got up to find María, and that's when she noticed Antonio's bed was still perfectly made. He hadn't been in the room yet. A quick glance at the clock on the nightstand revealed the time: 5 a.m. Too early for him to be already up, she thought. She sniffed the air as a dog would. Her nose had rarely failed her. But Antonio had not been in the room. His pungent odor, a mixture of tobacco and cologne, was hard to miss. Catalina bundled the baby and went to María's room. As she did, she saw Antonio stumbling down the hall toward her. His tie was skewed, and he wasn't wearing any shoes. His jacket hung over his left arm, and he was looking for something in the pocket of his pants.

She was embarrassed to see him like this, and quickly knocked on María's door, who must have been waiting for Carmen, because she extended her arms for the baby the moment she saw them standing at the threshold. "I'm sorry," she said. "I should have brought her with me so you could rest." Catalina dismissed the apology and waited a few prudent moments before she tiptoed back to her cabin. Antonio was already snoring in his bed; an arm reaching all the way down to the floor, as if caressing the carpet with his index and middle fingers. In the odor that emanated from his body Catalina detected whiskey—his preferred drink—and something else, something acrid and revolting that she couldn't quite place.

That morning, she whiled away the hours walking on deck, chatting with a few people she had met at the captain's table, including the couple who had six children. They were trying to soothe one of their daughters, who must have been around six or seven years old. The little girl was crying and repeating over and over, "The ship is going to sink, the ship is going to sink, the ship is going to sink." Her parents, clearly embarrassed, looked around with an apologetic smile, but, except for Catalina, no one seemed to have heard the girl's cries.

Catalina turned away quickly and went back to her room. Could that have been a premonition or a warning? She wasn't hungry anymore, so she skipped lunch. Later, as Antonio was dressing for dinner, she claimed to have a headache to stay behind. The headache was real, though. The words of the girl were pulsating in her temples as if trying to push their way out of her mind. Catalina opened her mouth to let the words out, to share her fear with Antonio, but she closed it quickly and swallowed instead. She didn't want to seem superstitious or gullible. Antonio had told her many times the ship was safe.

"As you wish," Antonio said, knotting his tie, his face turning away from her. "If you feel better, you know where I'll be," he said, and left, closing the door gently behind him. Catalina understood then that the new odor that she had detected on her husband was the smell of shame.

"Antonio knows," Catalina said to Juan when the two were alone again, hiding under the stairs.

"How do you know?" Juan asked, cupping her face.

"He doesn't look me in the eyes anymore, and last night he didn't come to bed. I saw him before dawn, and he was drunk."

In response, Juan held her tighter and told her she need not worry about Antonio anymore. The moment they arrived in Cuba, they would abscond from him with Carmen, and he would never be able to find them.

"It's a big island," he said. "It's not like home. I heard there are cities everywhere, a lot of places to work and they are looking for men like me, young and strong."

Catalina rested her head on his chest. How would they get away from Antonio? There was no way. They were all trapped in the same ship.

"There is a way," Juan said as if he were reading her thoughts.

To encourage him to keep talking, Catalina didn't say anything.

Juan went on. He had written a letter to Ramón Fernández, his best friend from childhood. Catalina remembered him from the time she had attended school. Ramón had left for Cuba a few years before in a ship not unlike the *Valbanera* and was working for a friend of his uncle's in a bar in a town near the sea. The pay wasn't great, but he was sure he could get Juan a job with him or on a nearby tobacco plantation.

In his letter, Juan had asked Ramón to wait for him and Catalina on the 5th of September in Santiago de Cuba, the first stop the *Valbanera* would be making in Cuba.

"But I'm not going to Santiago," Catalina interrupted. "We are going to Havana."

The ship was scheduled to continue its journey to Havana, which was where Catalina and Antonio were headed, because Antonio wanted Catalina to experience a great capital city like Havana, with its wide avenues and elegant stores, modern buildings, and stately homes, before they settled at home in the center of the island.

Juan barely acknowledged Catalina's interruption. His plan, he explained, was to disembark in the port of Santiago de Cuba with Catalina and Carmen, leaving Antonio behind.

"Don't you see? He'll never find us," Juan said excitedly.

Catalina thought the plan was weak; she was certain Antonio would be able to track them down. But, more than anything, she couldn't see how they would be able to escape without Antonio noticing what was happening.

"Leave that to me," Juan told her, and began kissing her with such passion that Catalina's worries subsided.

Life on the ship assumed a predictable routine from that point on. Each morning, accompanied by María, Catalina would take a stroll on deck to get some fresh air. During one of these walks Catalina learned that María had left her own four-year-old son behind to take this job on the ship. This was her third trip to Cuba accompanying a family. Sometimes, she stayed on the island for a few months to make additional money. But this time, she said, she had promised her son she would be back soon. He was getting too old to be left in the care of his grandmother. She said she was grateful to Antonio for buying her a ticket in first class. By custom and ship policy, maids were supposed to be in third class, but Antonio did not consider her a maid; neither did Catalina, who had never had a maid, or met anyone who had one until now.

In the afternoons Catalina would either play cards with other women she had met during their meals or try to read, but she found reading as boring and difficult as always and wished she had thought to bring needles and thread to embroider. With very little to do on the ship until she met Juan in the dark, she took long naps and wrote letters to her family that she hoped to send once they arrived in Cuba. The days seemed endless.

In the evenings Catalina had dinner with her husband, always at the captain's table and then, when he invariably left to join other men at the bar, she would slip away and meet Juan in their hideaway under the back stairs. One night toward the end of the journey, Antonio was in the room when she returned from seeing Juan. His drunken absences had emboldened her, and Catalina no longer bothered to fix her hair before returning to their cabin.

As usual, the lights were off when she entered the room. When she turned on the chandelier, Catalina saw Antonio sitting in the armchair, a glass of whiskey in his hand. His hair was disheveled, and his shirt was partly untucked, but the bow tie around his neck remained in place, though a little skewed. This time he didn't avoid her gaze, as he had been doing. He simply asked where she had been.

"Taking a walk," she said, and self-consciously started pinning her unruly red curls back.

"No," he said. "Leave them. It suits you."

Antonio got up from the chair and approached her. He took a lock of her hair, curled it around his index finger and pulled it a little. Catalina flinched. Antonio stood very close to her. She could feel his body heat and that strange odor emanating from his body. She could feel him almost vibrate—from desire? Ire? It was impossible to tell, but she knew she wanted to get away from him. Catalina tried to move but he kept her in place, still holding her long hair. He placed his lips near her neck. She thought he was going to kiss her. Instead, he whispered, "Be careful who you mingle with. There are all kinds of people on this ship." Then, he gently placed the lock of hair behind her ear and kissed her on the temple as he was fond of doing.

"I'm going to bed," he said casually.

Behind him, on his nightstand, Catalina saw the shiny black muzzle of his gun.

For the last two nights of the voyage Catalina couldn't see Juan. Antonio did not leave her side. She hadn't been able to alert Juan that Antonio had a gun. She couldn't imagine how he managed to bring it on board. In a pamphlet she read before boarding, it was clear that all weapons had to be entrusted to the captain, but it was also clear that Antonio and the captain were friends.

As she packed their suitcases the night before arriving in Cuba, Catalina tried to think of a way to see Juan. His plan had failed. He was going to have to leave on his own and she was going to follow her husband after all. They'd have to find each other in Cuba somehow. Or, they'd have to forget about their love. But how could that possibly be? Their love remained the only constant in Catalina's life. Now that her father was dead and her sisters and mother were far away, who was she without those who had loved and known her all her life? Her daughter would perhaps one day love her like that, but even then, her own daughter would only know a piece of her, the Catalina she was as a mother, not the child she had once been, the adolescent she became, the young woman she grew into—all those selves only Juan knew intimately. Giving him up would be impossible, like tossing a piece of herself into the sea. Without him, she would have to become somebody else, someone who had never known joy or love. Someone she would never want to be.

Catalina closed the last suitcase with a force she didn't know she possessed and stood back from the bed. She walked to the window and looked outside. Suddenly, she felt sad and very tired. She wondered again why her father, whom she had loved so much, had so stubbornly tried to separate her from Juan. It was his decision to force her to marry Antonio that had unleashed the series of calamities that had destroyed the farm, the family, and his own life. And now it endangered her life as well as the life of her daughter and of the man she loved.

A full moon peeked from behind the clouds, sending its stream of light down to the black ocean. Small waves with foamy white peaks crashed repeatedly against the side of the ship as Catalina stood there pondering what to do.

She had to go looking for Juan. She simply couldn't wait for fate to happen to them; she had to meet fate halfway. She changed into the dress she had set aside to wear the next day. It had to be a dress Antonio had never seen on her, so he wouldn't recognize her as she left the ship. Because he had seldom seen her wear anything but black since her father's death, Catalina chose a gauzy mauve-colored dress her mother had made for Cuba's tropical climate. It fit her perfectly, bringing out the golden strands in her red hair. She wore black comfortable shoes and took care to tuck inside her bodice the green silk handkerchief embroidered with her sisters' names that her mother had given her as a parting gift. Inside it were three mulberry seeds.

Antonio had told her he would be playing bridge for a while, and Carmen was next door with María for the night. She had originally arranged it that way so she would have an excuse in the morning to leave the cabin to get her daughter. She hoped that would give her enough time to escape with Juan; hopefully, without raising Antonio's suspicions.

Catalina left the cabin and quickly made a right. She wanted to run toward the stairs at the end of the hall but forced herself to walk. She could hear her own heart thumping against her chest, forcing her to swallow hard. What if she was too late? What if Antonio had already reached Juan and the two had fought? What if Antonio shared his suspicions with the captain and Juan was detained or imprisoned somewhere in the ship? Was the gun still in the room? She couldn't be certain. Catalina closed her eyes hard to squeeze the images out of her mind. Finally, a little out of breath, she reached the stairs and looked down. A shadow lurked right under. Juan! She ran down the steps and, as she was about to throw herself into his arms, the clouds parted, and the light of the moon shone brightly on Antonio's face.

Catalina staggered back, but Antonio held her by the arm.

"What are you doing here?" she asked, stammering.

And the moment she asked, she knew she had made a mistake.

"I was about to smoke my cigar. And you? What are you doing here? Or were you looking for me?"

Catalina nodded and tried in vain to free her arm from his grip.

"I thought so. Well, you found me. We should go back," said Antonio, and he began climbing the steps, holding Catalina's arm as if she were a misbehaving child. As the two walked in silence, Catalina thought she heard the faint sound of a whistle coming from the floor below.

Too late, my love, she thought, and closed her eyes, letting Antonio guide her to their cabin. She couldn't sleep that night, and she was certain that Antonio wasn't sleeping either, but they both remained quiet, each in their bed, until sometime in midmorning, when they felt the thud of the ship as it reached its berth in the port of Santiago de Cuba. It was the 5th of September 1919.

Almost immediately, Catalina began hearing noises outside the door of their cabin.

"What's going on?" she asked Antonio.

"People are disembarking," he answered dryly. He hadn't said a word since their encounter the night before.

"Why so many?" Catalina insisted. "I thought most passengers were going to Havana, like us."

Antonio sat on the edge of the bed. Like her, he was still fully clothed, and seemed to consider her comment.

"I don't know," he said. "I'd better find out. Perhaps something's happened."

He got up, washed his face, and carefully combed his hair, taking care to part it on the side as he always did. Then he grabbed his hat at the door and, without a glance at her, left the room.

Catalina was certain that Juan was among the passengers who were getting ready to disembark. She had to join him. But, first, she needed to get her daughter from María's room. She hadn't seen Carmen in hours.

As she stepped outside her room, she immediately felt she was in a different place. The air felt heavy and charged. Driven by curiosity, she made her way toward the nearby deck and peered outside. The sun was blanketing a good swath of the deck. On the docks, a crowd had gathered to welcome the passengers, who were just beginning to trickle out. Birds were chirping, and there were dozens of palm trees near and far. A hazy yellow light Catalina had never seen before seemed to envelop everything like a warm blanket while in the distance tall green mountains pushed against a blue sky, just like on her own island, only there was no fog here. The edges of everything were slightly blurred by the heat that seemed to emanate from the ground.

Reluctantly, she admitted to herself that Antonio was right. She could be happy here, if only . . .

Someone grabbed her by the arm. Hard.

"What are you still doing here?"

It was Juan. Juan!

Catalina could hardly believe her eyes. Juan was alive and well and had come for her. Relieved and overjoyed, she forgot all precautions and fear and threw her arms around his neck to embrace him. Juan responded briefly but disentangled himself to urge her to hurry up.

"Come with me now!" he ordered, and began pulling her toward him, toward the gangway, crowded now with joyful families leaving the ship.

Catalina pulled back.

"No, Juan, I can't go without Carmen."

"Where is she?"

"With María. I was on my way to get her now."

"Then we should not delay," he said, and moved away from her to go back inside the ship.

"No, I'll go," she said, already running toward the cabin.

"Catalina, wait!" Juan exclaimed, and in two long strides he was, once again, by her side. "The boat is going to leave soon. If we don't go now, we'll miss the opportunity. Go down and wait for me. I'll be quicker, and I'll bring Carmen to you."

"Juan, be careful," Catalina said, and, remembering the gun, hastily added, "Antonio has a gun."

For an answer, Juan pressed his lips to hers.

"What if the boat leaves before you can get out?" Catalina whispered, her words tumbling together like weeds in the wind, and her hands holding on to his rough peasant shirt, not wanting to let go.

"If that happens, don't worry. I'll find my way back to you. Find Ramón. He's waiting for both of us. Find him."

He hugged her fiercely and pushed her away toward the gangplank at the other end of the ship. Catalina saw him turn a corner and disappear, but he was going to the right, the wrong way. She yelled and went after him, but he was gone.

Catalina ran to María's cabin. The door was locked and there was no answer. She searched her own room, but María wasn't there either. The baby's bassinet was empty. Where was her daughter? Antonio must have her, to punish her. She was beginning to feel desperate. They were running out of time, she knew. She willed her body to remain still and breathed deeply to calm herself. What was the plan? Think, she urged herself. She would wait for Antonio and, if she had to, she would wrest her daughter from his arms.

In the silence that surrounded her, every sound was amplified. She could hear the creaking of the wood as the passengers made their way down the corridor. Someone was yelling orders, someone else responded in anger. A little girl cried for her doll and her mother shushed her. The old man across from their cabin was laughing affably, as always, his laughter echoing in the hall. The constant ticking of the clock on the dresser was a reminder that the seconds were turning into minutes.

Suddenly, she realized her plan was absurd. She could never overpower her husband, not even counting on the element of surprise. She held a hand to her chest to still her heart. The need for her baby was stronger than anything she had ever felt. Stronger even than her forbidden love. Without her baby, her arms felt useless by her side, like the oars of an empty boat. Find her, find her, find her, she heard herself whispering, and, opening the door carefully, she leapt out of the cabin like a leopard hunting prey.

She ran through the now-deserted narrow hallways, arms outstretched, fighting the urge to scream. Where were they? She felt the polished floors under her feet and realized she had left her shoes behind. Turning corners and more corners, out of breath, she was quickly back to the point where she began. She opened the door to their room and peered inside again. Nothing. She rattled a few doorknobs, including the doors of the other luxury suite and the first-class cabins, but all the doors were locked. On this most exclusive deck, it seemed, everyone had disembarked.

She thought about returning to the cabin and grabbing her suitcase, or at least getting her shoes, but, at that moment, she felt a movement under her feet and realized they were pulling away from the harbor! Wait! She screamed and rushed down the hall toward the bow of the ship, found the plank to the docks, breathless, and ran out just before a deckhand started to lift it from the concrete platform of the port.

The glare of the sun blinded her, and the heat burned the soles of her feet as she searched for the familiar contours of her husband's face, but she couldn't see him. People moved hurriedly around her, tugging children and luggage, as they formed a long line to go through Customs.

The cry of a baby stabbed at her heart, and she lunged to pry the baby from the man's hands only to see, at the last moment, that it wasn't her Carmen after all. She felt like crying but tried not to. No one would help her if she lost her composure. She began to walk back toward the ship slowly, breathing deep and steady as her mother had taught her, counting to ten, to ground herself, to avoid going mad. It was hot and sticky on this island. At home, the weather would be turning by now. Here, she was beginning to feel the sweat pooling under her arms and under her breasts. The stale air reeked of rotten fish and spoiled food. Street vendors were yelling incomprehensible words to hawk their wares. Loud music was playing somewhere. Too loud. It suddenly seemed impossible that she ever imagined she could live here, that she could be happy here.

She looked up at the ship and saw its bow turning slowly toward the open sea. Men and women on deck were waving white handkerchiefs and the sound of the ship's horn was loud in her ears. A little girl in a green coat tossed white and pink roses into the oily water of the port; they bobbed in the frothy wake of the ship as if chasing it. Catalina called out her lover's name, then her husband's, until her throat was raw, and her breath left her. She didn't call out her daughter's name, because in her heart she knew she had already lost her.

Her cries had attracted the attention of passengers and at least one guard. Catalina turned around looking for a way out. She had no intention of crossing the threshold into this new country without her daughter. Turning a corner, away from prying eyes, she held on to a wall to stave off a wave of nausea. A hungry, solitary dog sniffed at her naked feet but kept going. Her body no longer followed her commands or her will. The last sound she heard was the languorous horn of the ship as it left the wide-mouthed bay. A vein pulsed on her temple, and she collapsed on the ground, spent, her gauzy mauve dress pooling around her like the petals of a flower.

It was there that Ramón found her. By then, dusk had closed in, and a pale full moon was hanging low over the harbor of Santiago de Cuba.

Part II

We die with the dying:
See, they depart, and we go with them.
We are born with the dead:
See, they return, and bring us with them.
—T.S. Eliot, *"Little Gidding"* (1942)

Catalina

Santiago de Cuba
September 1919

She woke up in the arms of a man she thought she recognized. He was calling her name when she opened her eyes.

"Thank God. Can you stand, Catalina?"

Catalina focused on the man's face. He had kind eyes, a long nose, and curly light brown hair.

"Ramón Fernández Cueto, Juan's best friend," he said. "Don't you remember me?"

Though they had gone to the same school as children, she hadn't seen him in a long time. The last time she saw him, she was taller than he was, but now he was taller than Juan, with a thick beard and a hardened face that bore little resemblance to the sweet boy she remembered. The unforgiving sun had darkened his skin and a deep crease was visible over the bridge of his nose, making him look years older than he was. But his dark blue eyes retained their playful light, and she trusted him instantly.

He saw the recognition in her eyes and squeezed her hand.

"Ramón," she whispered, smiling faintly.

"Yes." He nodded and, inexplicably, blushed at the sound of his name from her lips. "How are you feeling?"

Catalina looked around in the semi-darkness as if gathering her things, searching for someone or something. She was disoriented, infirm, and thirsty. Water, she needed water. And then she remembered what had happened and what she was looking for.

"Carmen!" she yelled, her voice cracking at first but then clear and loud. "My daughter! Where is my daughter?"

Ramón looked puzzled.

"The ship! Where is the ship? I must have fallen asleep," she said urgently, grabbing the lapel of his worn brown jacket.

"The ship is gone," Ramón replied. "It left hours ago. But please tell me what's happened, and where is Juan? I've been waiting for him for a long time."

"Juan didn't come off the ship?" she asked, swallowing hard. Her throat was so dry.

"I haven't seen him, no."

"Are you sure?" Catalina insisted, still holding on to his jacket.

"I'm sure. I've been standing right here. I couldn't have missed him," he said. "Unless he left before I arrived."

"Left? What do you mean?" Catalina asked, puzzled.

"I was a little late," Ramón said, blushing again before hastening to add, "but only a little, and I haven't moved from here. I saw you on the ground but thought you were . . ." Ramón stopped before he continued. He had thought the lump of a dress on the floor was one of the women who trolled the port hoping to catch the eye of a sailor.

"What I mean is I didn't realize it was you until I decided to look more closely," he continued. "You were moaning in your sleep."

"We have to find him!" Catalina yelled, and started to get up. "Please take me to him and my daughter. My daughter is on that ship!"

"Your daughter? You and Juan have a daughter? But—"

"I'll explain later," Catalina said, interrupting him. "But no, we don't. It's not his daughter. It's too difficult to explain now. Please, let's go to them."

And she began sobbing

"What's happened, Catalina?" he asked as he helped her get up.

Between sobs Catalina told him that she thought Juan was still on the ship along with her daughter and Antonio, her husband. At the mention of her husband, Ramón lowered his eyes as if embarrassed by her and for her. Catalina was so caught up in the moment that she lost sight of the impropriety of her affair with Juan, but Ramón's clear discomfort made her feel suddenly ashamed. She pulled away from his arms brusquely and tried to think for herself.

Ramón was a step ahead of her.

"What do you want to do, Catalina?"

The question took her by surprise. It had been such a long time since someone had asked her what she wanted to do. Not even Juan had asked that when he'd come up with his outrageous plan to leave the ship together. Her parents had never asked her if she wanted to marry Antonio. Only the priest had asked during her wedding, but that was just a formality and what could she possibly have said then?

Right now, however, she had only one desire: "I want to find them, wherever they are."

Ramón held Catalina by her arms and looked intently at her face. Her eyes were moist with tears, her red curls had become undone, and her features were twisted in agony.

"Listen, Catalina," he began. "The ship is on its way to Havana. They are expected to arrive in a few days, I think—"

"Then we must go there," Catalina interrupted again, already pulling away from him. "Please take me or help me get there."

Ramón looked around for her luggage but found none. He looked at her dirty feet, felt the weight of the few pesos he had in his pocket, and quickly reached the conclusion that this was a bad idea, but couldn't say no.

"All right," he said, "but, first, we must find you some shoes."

Ramón didn't tell her that if he bought her a pair of shoes, he wouldn't have enough money to buy two train tickets to Havana. He barely had enough to pay for a hotel for the night. He'd have to think of a way, but he had no doubt that he would. In Cuba, there was always a way.

Catalina saw two young boys, shoeless, like her, selling bottled drinks. She had forgotten for a moment how thirsty she was.

"May I have some water please?" she pleaded, with a voice that seemed raw and unused, unnatural for her. But the boys didn't have any water. They only had some colorful homemade concoction that Ramón forbade her to drink. He looked around and told her he'd go find water, but she needed to stay put. He didn't want to lose her in such a busy port.

No danger of that, she thought. She was so tired she couldn't go anywhere even if she wanted to. Catalina sat down on the ground with her back against the dirty wall. She felt so utterly spent that she couldn't imagine ever moving from there. Her eyelids were beginning to droop closed again when Ramón came back with a tin cup dripping cool water.

"Here, drink this," he said, kneeling next to her.

She drained it.

"It's so hot," she said. "Is it always like this?"

He smiled and cocked his head in a way that, years later, Catalina would come to find endearing. Now, though, he seemed to be mocking her, as if her question had been too childish.

"In this part of the island, it's worse sometimes, much worse," he finally said.

Ramón offered to fan her with his straw hat, but she waved away the gesture. His face turned serious as he told her he had asked and there were no trains leaving that night to Havana, and all the shops were already closed. They'd have to wait until the morning to get her shoes and buy the tickets. But there were hotels nearby, and they should try to find a room before they closed for the night, he told her. Also, they had to go through Customs.

"No!" Catalina said intuitively. "I'm not here, not without Carmen."

Ramón thrusted his hand inside his pants pocket and took out a bill.

"Fine, follow me," he said, taking her by the arm to the first officer he encountered.

"I'm taking her home," he said, sounding like an exasperated husband. He handed the money to the guard, who waved them in.

And that's how Catalina spent her first night in Cuba, anonymously, in a small hotel near Santiago harbor, sharing a room with a man who was neither her husband nor her lover but who, at the moment, was the only person on the island who knew who she was.

The sounds of the city stirring woke them up before dawn. Ramón had slept on a folded blanket on the floor and Catalina had spent a restless night on a narrow metal-framed bed pushed against the wall, as far as she could physically get from him.

During the night, as Ramón snored softly and the light of the moon shone through their open window, Catalina had had hours to think of her situation. She went over the events of the previous day in her mind countless times and still couldn't understand why she hadn't been able to find Carmen at the last minute. She guessed Antonio had somehow intuited her plan and set out to thwart it knowing she would never leave her daughter behind. But in the end, she had. Hadn't she?

That was the fact Catalina couldn't comprehend. She kept coming back to it, like an itchy wound one can't stop scratching and won't allow it to scab over. She thought her suffering, her torturing herself with the incessant questions could somehow make her pay for what she had done and allow God and the saints to take pity on her, and let her daughter be returned to her.

It had been only a day or so since she'd seen her, but it seemed like a lifetime. In the four months since Carmen was born the two had not been separated before the trip to Cuba and the arrival of María. Back home, even when Carmen slept, Catalina often watched her, afraid she would stop breathing as punishment for her once thinking she wouldn't love this baby. How could she have been so careless with her thoughts? Words mattered a great deal, even thoughts, she knew that. The priest said it, her father always said it, too. "Have good thoughts, always," he used to admonish them all the time, because your thoughts become reality.

But Catalina had been oh so careless with her thoughts! It wasn't until she had seen her daughter, until she held her in her arms and the baby unfurled her tiny hand over her chest, that Catalina's heart felt a sudden surge of emotion. When she opened her mouth to say her daughter's name for the first time and to promise to love her and to protect her forever, her empty heart was flooded by a love so profound that at times it hurt. Times like this when Catalina had to physically hold her chest, swallow, and whisper to her galloping heart to return to its usual rhythm, because to her it felt as if it might escape from her throat, like a sob.

Calmer now, Catalina let her eyes roam around the sparsely furnished room. The walls were painted avocado green. There was a washstand with a mirror and a porcelain bowl, a small table with a wooden chair, and several wall pegs for hanging clothes or hats. On the wall opposite her bed was a picture of the Sacred Heart, with Jesus pointing to the center of his chest where his heart was encircled by thorns and flames. This is exactly how she felt: her wounded heart burning her chest but, somehow, protected by hope. At that moment she made a promise to God: "Please bring my daughter back to me, and I will always keep this picture of you in my home, no matter where I end up, and I will glorify you with flowers and candles and my eternal gratitude."

She did not expect any response, knowing well that miracles, if they happen, do not always manifest themselves right away. The only sound she heard was the stirring of Ramón on the floor, trying to shield his eyes from a timid ray of sunlight filtering in through the window slats.

Waking up together was awkward for both, but Catalina was beyond formalities. She had a mission to accomplish, and Ramón was the only person she knew on the entire island. She had no money, no luggage, and no shoes. All she had was the dress she was wearing.

"Good morning," she said, and Ramón muttered a reply. She was sitting on the edge of the bed like a broken doll. Ramón washed his face in the basin and hurriedly smoothed down his hair. He reached the door without looking at her.

"I'll be back soon, with shoes, breakfast, and travel tickets," he called out as he gently closed the door behind him.

Catalina remained alone in the room, which was getting hotter by the minute. She opened a window and a breeze from the harbor wafted in. Now, with the light of the sun mercilessly bearing down on the city, she could finally begin to comprehend how far she was from home.

The small hotel where they were staying was situated in what appeared to be a main street in a bustling commercial district. From her window on the second floor, she could see a cathedral looming over the streets like a mantle, offering a shady respite to nearby workers walking beside loaded mules, oxcarts with families, men and even women and children on horseback. Further up the hilly street, she spotted a few shiny automobiles, something she had never seen in La Palma, and a small train that she later learned was an electric tram. The streets were noisy and smelly. Sniffing the air, she searched in vain for the smell of pine, or lavender or even onions with the hint of sea breeze she was so used to. Here, the stench of waste was overpowering, mixed in with something else, something greasy and garlicky.

Catalina felt her stomach turn and remembered she hadn't had anything to eat in more than a day, but she wasn't hungry. She remained at the window. The buildings on the street, built of stucco, were adorned with columns and cornices. A few had porticos where people of all colors sought out the shade. She was so immersed in her thoughts that she didn't hear Ramón knocking on the door. Finally, he called out her name.

Catalina opened the door, and Ramón stood there with a pair of black leather shoes in his hands. The shoes had a velvet buckle on the side and Catalina thought they were the finest she had ever had. They were more appropriate for a ball than for a trek across the country, but they fit her well enough to wear.

It would have been better for her to accompany Ramón to the store to try on the shoes herself, but they both knew it wasn't a good idea to walk the streets of Santiago de Cuba in bare feet. So he had borrowed a pencil and a sheet of paper from the hotel manager the night before, and she had stood on the piece of paper, holding the hem of her dress above her ankles, as he knelt before her and traced the contour of her feet in an oddly intimate act that made them both blush.

Catalina felt better prepared to face the day with her new shoes, and immediately turned to Ramón to ask him about the tickets. Instead of answering, he lowered his eyes and suggested they eat first. But Catalina was still not hungry. She had no idea how far Havana was from Santiago, and she felt they had already wasted enough time waiting for daybreak and getting her shoes. When Juan came off the ship with her daughter, she wanted to be there, waiting.

"The thing is, Catalina, I don't have enough money for that," Ramón finally said, nervously gripping the brim of his straw hat as if it were the harness of a wild horse.

Catalina felt faint and took a step back. Ramón saw it and grabbed her hand. Words poured out of him; she barely heard them.

"No, but listen, please. I promise I will. I've asked my aunt to wire me some money. It should be here this afternoon. I managed to send a message this morning from the post office. We just have to be a little patient."

Patient. Catalina caught that word. She didn't know if she could be patient, but she could try. At least there was hope.

The two spent the day walking aimlessly in the dirty streets of Santiago. Ramón tried to distract her by pointing out something colorful or pretty, but Catalina showed no interest. She focused on the distance, where she could see the lush green mountains, and that made her think of home, everything she had left behind, and all the wrong turns her life had taken. She felt tired and queasy, as if she were still on the ship.

Her mind raced frantically from one scenario to the other. She imagined Juan had found Antonio and had snatched the baby from him. But why hadn't he disembarked then? Or, she thought, perhaps the ship had left before Juan had a chance to get to the gangplank. And, if so, what was now happening between the two men as the ship made its way to Havana? Was Juan hiding again? Had Antonio chased him away with the gun? At the thought of the gun, Catalina doubled over, suddenly nauseous. Her stomach was empty, and she vomited up bile.

"We must stop somewhere for food. You need to get something down or you'll get sick," Ramón said solicitously, leading Catalina across the street to a gleaming white hotel with a restaurant in its lobby. As they entered the Casa Granda, its dark interior of polished wood and resplendent chandeliers reminded Catalina of the ship and she started to cry so hard that the maître d' approached and asked them to leave. Dejected, the two stood outside, under the shade of an awning until Catalina's sobbing subsided. All Ramón could do was hold her and pat her back as if she were a child.

At exactly 4 p.m., they walked to the post office. Ramón went inside while Catalina waited in a park across the way, under the most magnificent tree she had ever seen, which she would later learn was called a *ceiba*, a sacred tree on the island. No one could ever cut it, which is why the base of the trunk was as big as a house. Under it, Catalina felt protected, and was beginning to breathe easier until Ramón came back with a worried look.

"You didn't get the money?" she asked, holding her breath.

"Yes, yes, I did, but I've got some worrisome news, too," he said, looking up at the sky. The sun was hiding behind bruised clouds that were gathering above them, creating a golden halo that gave everything a strange yellow tint.

"What's happening?" Catalina asked, suddenly aware that people were running from the park while those in the streets were retreating into their homes and shops and closing windows and doors.

"A hurricane is approaching," Ramón said.

"Here?"

Ramón nodded and made a humming noise at the back of his throat, a habit she found irritating. She knew that meant yes.

Catalina remembered the ship was on its way to Havana. She didn't know how far the capital was from this port city, but she knew it was far. She supposed they could make their way to the capital and wait for Juan there, which is what she desperately wanted to do. Or she could do what Juan had asked her to do. He had said that if they got separated somehow, she should go with Ramón and trust him. Juan had also said he would find his way to her with Carmen. Catalina needed to believe him. He would bring her daughter to her. She wasn't sure how he was going to accomplish this, but Juan had never failed her. She looked at Ramón, who stood quietly in front of her.

"Then we wait," she said. "Juan will find us."

Just then a fat drop of rain fell on Catalina's right shoulder. It felt like a frog had landed on her, wet and solid. Catalina instantly recoiled and looked up at the sky; the sun had completely retreated behind pregnant dark clouds. Another drop fell. Then another.

"We better run," Ramón said, grabbing her by the arm.

Catalina turned slightly away from Ramón so he wouldn't notice her fear. She made the sign of the cross and ran off with him into the rain. Behind them, sheets of rain began streaming down from the branches of the giant tree, forming a curtain of water that seemed impenetrable.

Mara

Santa Cruz and El Paso, La Palma
July 2019

THE NIGHT WAS CHILLY as I left the gallery, not really knowing which direction I was going but moving quickly so that I could gain some distance and think. Clearly, my great-grandmother hadn't died aboard the *Valbanera*, or I wouldn't be here chasing her ghost. But then why was her name on the list of the dead? Not only her name, but also her husband's? And who was that man she had married before she left La Palma?

This quest was no longer about getting a birth certificate. I had that already, but did I have the right one? Could there be two people with the same name born in the same year? It was possible. The year and day were correct, but not the month. Any delay in registering a birth could cause that, and delays were common a century ago, as the helpful clerk had explained. But how common is it to have two Catalina Quintana Cabazas on the same small island? That didn't seem likely.

There was only one way to find out, and, unfortunately, it did not involve Google. I had already tried that. I had to stay until I found out where the thread led. I had begun tugging at it, almost accidentally. Now, I felt the need to pull, hard and fast.

I went to a bar, ordered a glass of the house wine, and called Felicia Garrison, the travel desk editor in New York. I had written a few pieces for her from different European cities, so I felt confident she would remember my name.

She answered on the first ring.

Selling a travel editor on an idea is harder than it seems. When I said I wanted to write a travel piece on the Canary Islands, she replied, "Been there, done that," citing a story on Tenerife, which I'd read as part of my research. I gently reminded her that Tenerife was but one of the islands, and that the Tenerife story had run five years ago. It was time for another take.

Before we hung up, she had agreed to a story and a sidebar, but not right away. She had more stories than she could use. In two months then? I asked timidly. Make it three, she said, adding that I'd get $3,000 plus expenses, which was great, but not why I had proposed the story. The real reason was the way my mind operates: now I had an assignment to justify my stay in La Palma. I was no longer just chasing ghosts.

I woke up flailing in bed, as if I were trying to swim out of the mattress. My heart was thumping in my throat and my mouth tasted sour, like the morning after a bottle of cheap wine. I checked the time: just five minutes after eight. I lay there, smoothing the old T-shirt I'd worn to bed and trying to breathe through the anxiety of my nightmare, which wasn't a nightmare at all, but a repressed memory that had returned to torture me.

I've tried not to think of the day I last swam in the ocean, and, mostly, I've succeeded. I hadn't told the story to my son. Not yet. I figured he had inherited enough trauma from me, why add to that mix a memory that wasn't even his, though it certainly pertained to him.

I learned to swim in my late teens. Nelson taught me, in fact. When we met, I was mortified I could never go in the water with him and enjoy the beach as other girls my age did with their boyfriends. Nelson was a loving and patient teacher who, because he knew I would never take lessons in front of others, would get up at dawn and take me to the beach at a time when only the very old swim in Miami Beach. In a few months I felt confident enough to do it on my own, but I never let go of the fear of the deep. I always swam parallel to shore and went in only as far as where I could safely plant the soles of my feet on the sandy bottom.

But that day, I had been swimming alone near a sandbar while Nelson went to the car to get me the cooler with some sandwiches we had packed. I was nine months pregnant and hungry all the time. When I reached the end of the sandbar, I was literally out of my depth. Somehow, I surfaced, though disoriented and crying, and managed to focus on the sun. I knew the sun set behind the trees on the shore. I couldn't trust myself to do breast strokes anymore, so I turned around and began using backstrokes, kicking furiously with my legs until my fingers touched land. I lay there like a beached whale in my tiny black bikini, water slushing from my glistening giant belly, until Nelson found me. I don't know how much time passed, but it was enough for my body to get cold and my nose stuffy from all the crying.

"I'm never getting back in the water," I said, hiccupping as he held me and caressed my matted hair.

When we got home that night, I felt the first contractions. Our son was born the next day. Nelson wanted to name him Neptune, because he had come into the world through the power of water. I refused, but I liked Nelson's idea of naming him after the sea, as my parents had named me. *Mar* is ocean in Spanish. My mother added an *a* at the last minute to make it less obvious and to compromise with my father who wasn't keen on naming his daughter after a body of water.

Nelson and I compromised as well. Dylan is Welsh for "son of the sea" or "born from the ocean." At the time, we couldn't have known our son would one day join the US Navy. Dylan was in a pool by the time he was seven months old. He swam before he could talk and kept swimming competitively on and off until he left for college. After Nelson's death, it fell on me to take him to swim practices and meets. I could not close my eyes, as I wanted to do, when he dived in the pool from the highest board because he would always look at me before jumping and flash me a smile. I had to smile back.

The smell of coffee wafting in from the garden brought me back to the present and helped clear my mind. I needed to get going. I had big plans for the day.

After another delicious breakfast, I rented a car. Soon I left the city behind and began a roller coaster of a drive zigzagging through tight curves around seemingly endless mountains. Thirty-five minutes later, I was standing in the pretty town square of the municipality of El Paso. If the birth certificate was correct, my search had to begin here.

I looked around the square and tried to situate myself. There was a church up an incline—there is always a church—along with an official-looking building where government business was probably conducted, a couple of grand houses that had been nicely restored, and a few stores. The place was quiet. If I were reporting a story, I'd go inside the church and ask, but for what? I supposed I could ask if someone knew the Quintana family. Though Catalina Quintana had lived somewhere near here more than a century ago, I knew that time was measured differently in Europe. People lived in houses that were hundreds of years old and kept their cows in fields dotted with the ancient ruins of Roman buildings or bridges. Someone in the church was bound to know somebody who knew someone else. I had to start somewhere.

Across the street I noticed a two-story building with beautiful drawings of worms and wide green leaves on its walls: the silk museum I had read about in the guidebook! I quickly glanced at it, but it was closed. Better, I was eager to go inside the church.

The nave of the church was pitch black as my eyes adjusted to the contrast between the brightness of the day outside and the muted and musty feel inside the building. The smell of incense and calla lilies lingered in the air. I walked toward the altar, simple and small, covered with a white cloth. On the wall behind it, inside a blood-red niche, the image of a virgin glowed golden and inviting. The inside of the church seemed to be very old, older than the façade, which was renovated and exquisitely painted a chalky, sandy white. One modest stained-glass window to the right let in the only light, creating rivulets of pink and magenta on the worn stone steps leading to the altar.

A small, quavering voice startled me.

"May I help you?"

I spun around to face a tiny old lady, who seemed as ancient as the walls of the church. A black mantilla was draped over her hunched shoulders, and she had lifted her face up with some difficulty to look at me. But she held her ground, demanding an answer.

"Yes, I'm sure you can," I said with a smile, grateful that my parents had never allowed me to forget my first language. I told the old woman I was looking for anyone who might be related to Catalina Quintana Cabazas. She thought about it for a moment.

"I don't recognize that name," she said, and I could feel the air escaping my lungs. I must have been holding my breath and didn't even know it.

"However," she went on. "The Quintana family is well-known here. They are a large clan. There once were three sisters, I hear. I knew one of them. The last of them died about ten years ago, maybe more. I don't know . . ."

She stopped talking and looked away.

"And where are they?" I asked, eager for her to go on.

"Who?" she said, as if surprised by the question.

"The Quintanas. You said they are a large family."

"Oh, yes, I'm so sorry. One of them, a son, or a grandson, has a bar around here, I think. The name is Bar Alegre, or Bar Alegría, something like that. It's just around the corner. His name is Julián. You can't miss it . . . or him."

Then she went quiet again and looked away, but she had said enough. I thanked her profusely before leaving and when I had reached the door, I turned to see her kneeling in front of the altar, her head bowed.

Outside, the brightness was unbearable. The concrete benches of the park seemed to radiate with the heat of the day. This was the time when people were heading home to have lunch and take a *siesta*. With any luck, the bar would be open for lunch.

I googled "Bar Alegre" on my phone and there it was: exactly 250 feet away to my right, around the corner, just as the woman had said. Sooner than I expected I stood in front of an old-fashioned-looking bar. I pushed the heavy wooden door in and walked into a place that seemed to live up to its happy name, with colorful tiled floors that reminded me of Cuba and yellow and red walls bearing framed pictures of cheerful-looking people who were either dancing or hugging each other or both. A fair number of them seemed to have red hair and freckles; some had light-colored eyes. Clearly, they were all related.

I was certain I was in the right place. But there was no one here.

Through a door at the back, I could see an interior courtyard and headed there. An ancient tree with a thick trunk was planted in the middle of the patio, and there were potted plants and flowers all around. Dozens of birds in cages were chattering simultaneously to one another, and a water fountain off in one corner added the final notes to this spot that was surely someone's idea of paradise. I heard a voice from behind a door, but it seemed like a private phone conversation, and I began to retreat, a little embarrassed that I had advanced so far into what I now realized was a private home.

Just as I was retracing my steps, a door behind me opened, and a man called out, *"¿Quién eres?"*

Who was I? That was an interesting question. But I knew enough about the Spanish character to know that what he really meant with such a frank and direct question was to ask me what I wanted and what I was doing in his courtyard.

I turned around to face him and was surprised to find that his manner wasn't brusque or aggressive. He was merely curious, as intrigued by my presence as I was by his.

"I'm looking for Julián," I said, though I was certain I had found him.

He took two long steps toward me keeping his eyes on my face. I could see him clearly now. He was tall and built, not from years lifting weights but from working outside, possibly in the fields, certainly with his hands. He wore a sky-blue cotton short-sleeve shirt and white shorts. It was easy to see his hair had once been brown and wavy, now it was salt and pepper and receding, but there were stubborn curls clinging to his large ears and near his neckline, where tufts of chest hair pushed up, refusing to be contained. A deep vertical line creased his left cheek in two when he smiled, and his eyes were surrounded by a web of tiny wrinkles that made him look older than he probably was. By the way he walked and the twinkle in his eyes, I guessed he wasn't even fifty-five.

"If you had red hair, you could be one of my cousins," he said, extending his hand. "I'm Julián Martínez."

I'm not very good at quick comebacks. I usually come up with witty retorts a day or two after the fact, but, for some reason, I was ready for Julián.

"That would be my mother, the red-haired one, but I think we may be cousins."

I was certain I hadn't been this giddy and this overwhelmed since my wedding day a lifetime ago. Or, as my son liked to point out, "last century." Indeed, Nelson and I had gotten married in May of 1987, a few days after graduating together from the University of Miami.

But unlike today, the day of our wedding had been highly anticipated and choreographed. Joy was expected. This was something else entirely: a complete surprise, after a dubious quest undertaken to please my mother. Who could have guessed that it would lead to this? Surrounded by a large and ever-growing family in a bar called "happiness" in a town most people couldn't place on a map and that I didn't even know existed until I happened to find my great-grandmother's birth certificate.

I'd been sitting with Julián for hours as he kept calling relatives with endearing nicknames like Cachita, Chucha, and Coca, who, as if by magic, appeared at the door holding children or accompanying old people with canes who claimed that, somehow, they were related to me. It was all very confusing. But grabbing at the strands of so many revelations coming to me at once and from all sides, I was beginning to get to the trunk of the family tree I happened to find that glorious afternoon.

I discovered that Catalina had been the eldest of three sisters. Everyone thought she had died on her way to Cuba, along with her husband Antonio and their only child, Carmen. As far as they knew, she left no survivors. That part wasn't true, because, clearly, there I was. The other two sisters, however, had more than made up for the stubborn line of only one child per generation on Catalina's branch. Simona had six children, while Lucía, the youngest, had nine. One of those children was Clara Martínez, the mother of Julián, the owner of Bar Alegre. Lucía had outlived her sisters and, sadly, two of her own sons. I was surrounded by the descendants of those two women, the Quintana girls, as they were called in their village, who were known for their longevity, their beauty, their spunk, and, I was told, their flaming hair.

I showed them pictures of my own very small family. My mother, Lila; my son, Dylan; and a black-and-white picture I took of my Nelson two days before he died. They grew a little quiet when they saw his picture. They changed the topic and told me they saw the family resemblance in my mother and complimented my son's looks, but I could see they didn't really understand how I managed to live in the world with such tenuous connections. They questioned my living so far from my mother and from the place where I was born. And they were intrigued to learn that I didn't speak to my son daily and that I wasn't even certain where in the world he was at the moment, since he had already left New York for training with the Navy.

Their idea of Cuba was outdated and romantic. They dreamed of visiting the island but hadn't been able to. They seemed to have so many things to do, so many events to attend. They said the years went by so quickly—punctuated by weddings, baptisms, graduations, anniversaries, birthday celebrations, and Christmas parties—that it was impossible to plan anything. Also, they wouldn't want to go alone. Either they all went, or none did. I pictured them all on a cruise headed to Cuba and thought to myself that I wouldn't miss it for the world. I'd want to be there the first time one of them encountered a swarm of flies in an outdoor restaurant or a shortage of wine. But then I realized they probably would never run out of wine in Cuba. They'd be traveling as tourists, of course. Do tourists encounter pesky flies around their food in Cuba? I wasn't sure.

I tried to change my train of thought as I could feel my mind beginning to wander. It was getting late, and I was tired. I couldn't possibly meet any more people or toast to happy encounters again. This crowd was just a little too joyful for me. I needed, no, I craved some solitude to put my thoughts in order and understand what had happened. It really was too much for a day that began, simply enough, with a breakfast of eggs, bread, jam, and a glass of orange juice at Gladys and Claude's. That now seemed like a world away, another life.

As if he could sense my discomfort, Julián looked at his watch and told them all it was time to leave. That was it. No apologies or excuses. Off you go, basically. She is tired. I'm tired. And I have a business to run, go, go. And they went. Quickly. No one seemed angry.

I was depleted and relieved.

"Where are you staying?" Julián asked, breaking the sudden silence in the empty bar.

The truth was it was quite late and I didn't know I was staying. My plan had been to go back to Santa Cruz. I didn't have anything with me, except my purse and my sunglasses.

"Then it's settled," Julián said. "You stay here, in the back. We have plenty of room."

"We?"

I don't know why I had asked the question in such a pointed way. It seemed probing and intrusive. Dozens of people had just left. This was clearly a large family. "We" could mean anybody.

"In a manner of speaking. It's just me. Me and the birds," he clarified with a smirk.

I could have pushed on and gotten more answers, but I was so tired, all I really wanted was a shower and a clean bed.

"In that case, thank you, I'll stay," I said, grateful that I always traveled with an emergency toothbrush and a bottle of Ibuprofen in my purse. In my line of work, you never know where the night might find you.

In the strange ways the brain works, a thought came to me unbidden as I closed my eyes: how did they know about Carmen? My grandmother, I was sure, was born in Cuba. Confused and weary, I let the thought go until the morning.

Catalina

Las Villas, Cuba
September 1919

Two days after Ramón had found her, Catalina had settled in a small yellow house on the outskirts of a coastal town, in the central province of Cuba, Las Villas—halfway between Santiago and Havana. Ramón thought it would be better for her to stay with his aunt, doña Emilia, while she waited for Juan and Carmen to join them.

Discreet and tested by the vicissitudes of life, doña Emilia was, at fifty, a childless widow. She had married Ramón's uncle, Timoteo Fernández, when she was practically a child, at fifteen, and he had brought her to Cuba from Tenerife. After twenty-seven years of gentle harmony, marred only by the lack of a child, Timoteo's horse tripped and fell one moonless night, after a long day working in the fields. Someone found him the next morning, his neck broken. The horse, its legs shattered, was still, and, like its owner, beyond help. The man who found them shot the horse, hauled Timoteo's body onto his own mare, and walked it all the way back to town. When Emilia saw the horse approaching from the window of her kitchen, she knew immediately that the bulge over the saddle was her husband and that he was dead. She quickly closed the window, trying to keep the news from reaching her, and got on her knees to pray for a miracle.

Doña Emilia probably would have succumbed to her sadness if fate hadn't intervened. Shortly after her husband's death, his nephew Ramón arrived from La Palma bearing only a sack with two pairs of pants and three shirts. Ramón was fourteen years old and was disconsolate when he heard his uncle had died. His pockets were empty and so was his stomach. But he was hungry for work and hopeful that Cuba would help him become a prosperous man. Doña Emilia saw his dark blue eyes, exactly like her husband's, and without any questions took the boy into her care. Such were the ways in which families were reassembled from one island to the other—older parents lost their adolescent boys to the lure of Cuba and understanding relatives helped them settle into a life of hard work while everyone, on both archipelagos, yearned to be together again under the same sky.

Ramón immediately found a job in a nearby sugar mill but continued to live with Emilia until he was able to move to his own home, a small *bohío* that he built out of the trunk of palm trees with the help of other new arrivals. Eventually, he left the sugar mill and got a less taxing job, sweeping the floors of a bar owned by another Spaniard, a family friend. The island was flush with money because the price of sugar had shot up during the war, and there was an insatiable demand for workers to harvest sugar cane. Many of those workers were strong young *isleños*, like Ramón. Though he was paid a pittance at the bar, he wasn't given to complaints. Cuba was his future and, no matter how poor he was, it never occurred to Ramón to return to the Canary Islands where he had known not only penury but also fear. Fear of God, the various virgins and saints, the evil eye, the threat of volcanoes and sandstorms. On this island, no one seemed to fear God's wrath. People were happy, without having a reason to be. The feeling was intoxicating, and Ramón felt lulled and protected by the childish optimism of the Cubans.

When Ramón brought Catalina to his aunt's house, doña Emilia recognized the sadness that enveloped the young woman and didn't ask any questions. Instead, she focused all her energies on creating a space for all the grief that seemed to emanate from Catalina. She helped her out of her mauve dress, now dirty and sweaty after days on her body, and prepared a tin with scalding hot water for her to wash away the stench of her travels and to lighten her soul. She tried to get her to eat the Cuban meals she had learned to make—white rice, black beans, a pork stew, fried plantains—but Catalina left the food untouched. Then, she tried some old recipes she remembered from home, but that didn't seem to work either. Catalina seemed to survive on milk, bread, and water.

At first, Ramón told Catalina it would be a matter of days before the *Valbanera* reached the port of Havana. He had learned that, for some reason, more than seven hundred people had disembarked in Santiago, but there were still passengers on board, perhaps five hundred more.

Catalina and Ramón had checked and rechecked the train schedules and followed the weather reports. A hurricane had swept into Havana's northern coast. That wasn't all that alarming. As the largest island in the Caribbean standing as a sentinel at the entrance of the Gulf of Mexico, Cuba was always at the mercy of tropical disturbances. Cubans were used to floods and torrential rains, Ramón explained, not unlike La Palma, but without the devilish winds and sandstorms from the Sahara Desert.

Still, this hurricane packed a peculiar punch. Windswept waves topped the famed Havana seawall; extensive flooding had reached as far inland as six blocks. The newspapers carried pictures of homes and monuments under water as well as stories about the evacuation of homes at risk. Transportation to and from Havana had been halted, which would make it impossible for them to travel to the capital and for Juan to reach her, even if the *Valbanera* had managed to reach the port before the storm.

There were reports of boats and larger vessels lost at sea, but Ramón assured Catalina those were small boats. The *Valbanera* was a large ship, capable of weathering any storm. Besides, he told her, ships couldn't possibly flood since they were already on the water. They'd just bob along until the wind calmed down and the ship could find its way back to the harbor.

Catalina wasn't so sure. She remembered how proudly the captain had told them at one of the dinners aboard the ship that this was his first time at the helm of the *Valbanera*. He had never commanded a vessel of that size. But there was no need for worry, he had added with a reassuring smile. In the intimacy of their cabin, Catalina had commented that she was indeed worried about the captain's inexperience, but Antonio had argued that a shipping company like that of Pinillos wouldn't trust one of their best ships to just anyone.

She desperately wanted to believe him now, but then she remembered something that happened as they were about to leave the harbor in La Palma. At the last minute, one of the anchors had gotten trapped in the muddy bottom of the sea and wouldn't budge. The chain attaching it to the ship broke and the ship had to sail on without one of its anchors. She had overheard one of the crew members calling it bad luck. Also, there was the misspelling in the ship's name that Lucía had mentioned the day they had discussed the trip to Cuba. And of course, how could she forget the little girl who kept crying because she was certain the ship would sink.

Catalina punished herself trying to remember the last time she had held or kissed her daughter and just couldn't recall. Her last days at sea had been so consumed by Juan and his absurd plans to escape and begin a new life that she hadn't focused on her daughter, letting María take over her mothering role. Why had she allowed Antonio to bring María along? She had completely delegated her responsibilities as a mother to a woman she hardly knew. The more she thought about it, the more horrified she felt with herself.

Then, she had a thought. What if María or Antonio or Juan had managed to leave the ship with Carmen in Santiago and were wandering the streets looking for her? This was certainly possible because Ramón had been late, hadn't he? He couldn't possibly know, with any certainty, that Juan had not come off the ship. But even if he had been on time, he didn't know María or Antonio and he would have missed their arrival, focused as he was on finding his friend and Catalina. Terror and hope seized her heart for hours until she was able to relay her thoughts to Ramón, who assured her he had already thought of that and had made sure to check around before they left the harbor. No one had reported seeing a woman or a man alone with a baby, and their names had not been registered by Customs. But Catalina's name was not registered either, and she was very much in Cuba. Catalina couldn't shake the feeling that her daughter was out there somewhere, waiting for her.

Catalina lit candles, prayed to the *Virgen de la Candelaria*, though she couldn't find an image of the virgin anywhere in the town Ramón had taken her to. Instead, she lit a candle to the virgin Cubans revered, Our Lady of Charity, who, as the story went, had saved three poor sailors from a storm in the same bay where she had last seen the *Valbanera*. Catalina couldn't think of anyone better to help her than one with the power to evade storms at sea.

She accompanied doña Emilia to church every day, and on her knees, had confessed all her sins. She wanted to be pure for her daughter; she wanted to deserve her. Above all, she wanted her daughter back. She wanted her old life back. And for that, she'd do anything; she'd even give up Juan forever, she told herself. Her love for him now felt infantile, dangerous, impulsive. How had she put her daughter's life at risk for a possible future with Juan when she had already sworn, before God, that she would forever be faithful to her husband? There was only one way to think about this. God was punishing her. But she pleaded, oh how she pleaded, for one more chance.

At times, if she closed her eyes, she could almost imagine her family was intact and she was back home with them. But nothing here reminded her of home. The air in these parts smelled of grass and manure, baked by the relentless sun, and a hint of something like lilac from the wildflowers that dotted the field behind the house. Gusts of wind from the cyclone still brewing somewhere at sea brought in the smell of the ocean, salty and slightly putrid from all the dead fish the fishermen left behind.

She was homesick for her family, for her trees, her garden, and the large boulder that loomed over all of it. She used to think of *La Roca* as so limiting; now, she understood it had always anchored them. It was where she belonged. She craved the order and security of knowing her territory, of knowing where she was from, of understanding the silent codes of a culture—the meaning of a glance, a sign, a whistle. In Cuba, food tasted bland to her palate, flowers seemed colorless, and oh how she missed the stars of La Palma! At home they seemed so close that you wanted to stand on your toes, stretch your hand and touch them. Everything seemed possible in a place with easy access to the stars, but here they seemed too far away and not as bright.

She thought of writing a letter to her mother, or her sisters. But what could she say? How could she explain that she had arrived in Cuba without her daughter? Her mother would never understand that. Nor would she ever be able to forgive her. Still, she couldn't help herself and, in the afternoons, when there was nothing else to do in doña Emilia's house and she was too restless to nap, Catalina sat down at the dining table and wrote long letters to her mother describing the details of her days, her regrets, and her hopes for a future back home—a new life with them and Carmen, without Antonio and without Juan. All she needed, she told herself, was her daughter. Her daughter and her family. But she didn't send the letters. The moment she finished writing them, she would carry them outside, throw them in a pit behind the house, light a match and burn them, making sure not one of her desperate thoughts escaped the licking of the flames.

Mara

El Paso, La Palma
July 2019

I WOKE UP TO THE SMELL OF COFFEE and the chirping of the caged birds in the courtyard. I had slept in an old T-shirt Julián had given me. It was soft and white, with the image of the yellow sun bursting from behind a mountain. It said BAR ALEGRE in red bold letters. It was a bit too much, so I quickly changed into the same clothes I had worn the day before. I'd washed my underwear and top in the shower and they had dried overnight. Nothing like the heat of summer to dry clothes fast.

"Good morning," I said, striding into the kitchen, where Julián was making what looked like meatballs, but, in fact, were *gofio* balls, a local food made with a cereal I remembered from my Cuban childhood. *Gofio* with milk and a little sugar, indeed. These were made with honey and almond. Delicious.

He turned around and gave me a sheepish smile. "Eggs OK?"

"Sure," I said, a little uncertain in this warm but not-mine kitchen.

"Myself, I prefer eggs at dinnertime, but you Americans have weird customs," he said, cracking the eggs over the hot oil.

"Beautiful day, no?" I said, trying to make us both more comfortable. Not twenty-four hours before I didn't know this man existed, and now, it turned out, he was my mother's second cousin, and I was staying in his house.

"Well now, yes. You missed the fog earlier. It was dense, but now it's gone," he said.

I looked at my wristwatch. It was 9 a.m. I had overslept. "I must have been really tired," I said.

Julián spun around with the pan in one hand and a worn-down wooden spatula in the other. He was wearing an apron around his potbelly and looked the part of the Spanish chef, with reading glasses hanging from a red cord over his chest. With the ease that comes from practice, he lifted from the pan two perfectly fried eggs—with crispy whites and yolks trembling slightly—and set them on a plate before me.

"Sit," he commanded. "Eat."

On the bare wooden kitchen table, he had already placed ham, cheese, a loaf of bread he told me he had made earlier, freshly squeezed orange juice, and a steaming mug of *café con leche*, just the way I liked it—dark and with plenty of sugar. I sat and I ate. I was hungry and everything was delicious. Julián sat across from me, and we both ate in silence, breaking off pieces of bread and dipping them in the egg yolk. I felt restored and content, but also directionless. What now? I'm used to having at least one goal a day: finish a story, call New York, pay bills, do some shopping. I wasn't sure what the next step was now.

"I want to show you something," Julian said, pushing an envelope from the corner of the table. "I wanted to show it to you last night, but it didn't seem like the right time."

From the envelope, he pulled a photo. He pushed up his reading glasses, looked at the picture and placed it in front of me. I reached for my own reading glasses, which I mostly wore as a hair band, and lowered them onto my nose with a swift movement.

"This was Catalina the day she left for Cuba. You can see the name of the boat behind them, see?" he said, leaning in to point to a tall and fierce-looking woman. "This is Antonio Lopez, her husband, and the baby in her arms is Carmen, their daughter. She must have been four or five months old when they left. That's what Grandma Lucía always told us, and she had an impressive memory."

I almost couldn't hear him. I was focused on the baby. Who was this baby? Certainly, my grandmother's name was Carmen, but I could have sworn Mima had always told me her mother was born in Cuba. If that hadn't been the case, I could have looked for Carmen's birth certificate instead of Catalina's to try to get my mother's citizenship. Certainly, the ties would have been closer from mother to daughter, rather than from grandmother to granddaughter.

I stood up abruptly. Julián looked at me puzzled.

"This makes no sense," I said.

"What?"

Instead of answering his question, I asked what he was doing that morning.

Julián had to go to Santa Cruz to meet with a wine supplier for his bar, he said as he got up with his hands full of dirty dishes. I followed him to the dishwasher and helped him clean up. He asked if I wanted to come along, and I jumped at the chance. My day was beginning to take shape, and that included an urgent call to my mother. Among other things, I was thinking with pleasure, how I was going to tell her that I had come all the way to this island to find my past in more ways than one: I'd had *gofio* for breakfast once again.

While Julián held his business meeting, I walked over to the art gallery where I had initially seen the list of the people who perished in the shipwreck of the *Valbanera*. The gallery was closed, a sign attached to the glass said so, but the door was ajar.

"Hello," I called out. No one replied. I pushed the door slightly, wide enough to get in without attracting too much attention, and entered the place, which was empty of visitors. I felt a chill run through me as I gazed at the pictures of the ship on the wall. Alone in the gallery, the pictures seemed more menacing than I remembered. I had seen them before, of course, but at that time I hadn't been aware of my connection to the

Valbanera. Now I knew that my great-grandmother had traveled on that ship. She may have died on it, too. I shook my head at the thought. That couldn't be. I had met the descendants of her sisters and the resemblance to my mother was impossible to miss. Catalina had been on the boat, but somehow she had survived. The question was how. And the bigger question: Why had she never let her family know she'd survived?

In the semi-darkness of the gallery, I walked to the far wall, where I had found her name and that of her husband, Antonio, among the dead. With my index finger I traced the laminated poster, and quickly located their names again. Then I looked for Carmen Fernández Quintana, my grandmother, but, as I expected, her name was not on the list of the dead. Then I tried Carmen López Quintana. Nothing. But her name wouldn't be, I reasoned. After all, she was my mother's mother. Without Carmen, I wouldn't have my mother.

I heard the click-clack of high heels approaching on the highly polished tiled floor and turned around to face the tallest woman I'd ever seen. She wore a yellow dress that engulfed her like a tulip and red-framed round glasses that matched her shoes. The yellow and red combination made me think of the Spanish flag and I smiled a little condescendingly. But she quickly put me in my place, introducing herself as Gertrude Siller, the German-born owner of the gallery and curator of the exhibit. Though she spoke almost perfect Spanish, we switched to English once I realized it was a more comfortable language for her. Gertrude was not happy that I was in her space.

"We are closed," she said, pushing her glasses up her nose with the middle finger of her left hand. A large gold and onyx ring hugged the finger as if it had been implanted. "How did you get in?"

I told her the truth, that the door was open. She frowned.

"Since you are here, how can I help you?" she asked, in a sudden change of tone.

I explained who I was and what I was doing, strategically mentioning that I was a reporter, but that this was not part of an assignment.

This was personal. Still, Gertrude's mood changed almost magically, as I knew it would.

She invited me to sit in her office upstairs, a small and completely white place. Gertrude was the only touch of color in her environment. The effect was jarring, but it made me think of an anecdote I had read about the French writer Guy de Maupassant who supposedly ate lunch every day at the base of the Torre Eiffel because it was the only place in Paris from which he couldn't see the tower. I was certain Gertrude had an aversion to colors.

"Can the list be wrong?" I asked, dismissing the formalities that Spaniards are used to but that, I knew from experience, were unnecessary with Germans.

"Absolutely," she said, immediately understanding what list I was referring to. She gave me some details that sent my thoughts reeling in a million different directions.

Gertrude said the list was based, initially, on the record of tickets purchased to Havana and those kept by Customs in Cuba, though, she admitted, both were unreliable. Since the *Valbanera* had never made it to that harbor and sank off the coast of Key West, it was assumed only those ticket holders traveling to Havana had perished. However, more passengers than expected had disembarked at the first port of call on the island, in Santiago de Cuba. Unless those who were originally bound for Havana had reported their survival, they would have been counted as dead. She emphasized that no one who was aboard the *Valbanera* after the 5th of September, the day it left the harbor of Santiago, had survived.

"That you know of," I said, though I regretted my comment.

Gertrude's face changed, clearly peeved at the interruption.

Still, she agreed. "That we know of, yes," she said. "But there is no record that the ship stopped anywhere else or that anyone escaped the shipwreck."

Clearly, then, Catalina must have disembarked in Santiago, despite holding a ticket to Havana. But why? And, more crucially,

I kept going back to the same unanswered question: Why had she broken all ties to her family? Why not tell them she was alive? Gertrude had no answers for that, of course, but she did say that some passengers disembarked earlier because they were seasick or had had a premonition or were simply tired of being on a ship for so long. She said there was a famous case of a girl who cried as she boarded in Barcelona and remained upset for the entire trip because she feared the ship would sink. When they arrived in Cuba, her family finally relented to her pleas to get off the ship. That decision saved their lives.

I could imagine Catalina having a premonition. After all, if superstition was passed down from generation to generation, like my fear of the water, it would explain why I continued to avoid black cats, opening an umbrella inside a house, or placing a box on top of a bed. There were so many things my mother had asked me not to do in order to appease the gods of superstition, that it was a wonder I was still able to get on a plane without fear.

Lastly, Gertrude said, stowaways wouldn't appear on any list because, technically, they were not on board, and young children who didn't need tickets would not be counted among the dead unless someone added the name to their list. Some families had; certainly, there were children listed among the dead, but Carmen was not one of them.

"I haven't come across that name," she said, after asking me to repeat it. "I'm sure there are no records of it in the archives, but I'd be happy to look into it if you are ready to report her as one of the dead."

I said no, of course. I wasn't about to report my grandmother as "dead" one hundred years later. For all I knew, Carmen had survived and was my mother's mother, under a different last name.

I must have looked a little ill when Gertrude finished her explanation because she got up and offered me a glass of water. It was only then I realized my lips were parched and that I was gripping the arms of the white leather office chair where I sat. My hands trembled a little while I sipped the water under the red-rimmed eyes of Gertrude.

And yet, I wanted to know more. I wanted to know everything.

"Do you have records of the shipwreck itself?" I asked.

"What do you mean?"

"I want to know what happened."

"Oh, well. As you know there were no survivors, but historians and meteorologists and expert seamen have helped us piece together a narrative of how it could have happened."

"Where can I find that? May I read it?" Suddenly, I wasn't trembling anymore. I needed to read this narrative.

"Yes, you may, but we also have a video, a re-creation of the shipwreck, imagined by a variety of experts, and, as I said, I want to emphasize that we don't really know . . ."

"It doesn't matter," I said rather brusquely. "I'd like to see it."

"Very well. It is downstairs. Follow me," said Gertrude, getting up.

I followed her downstairs and into a small rectangular room with backless benches and a large screen dominating the back wall. Gertrude switched off the lights and, with a remote, turned on the video. Immediately, an image of an angry sea under heavy skies flooded the screen. It looked so real that for a moment I thought the water would spill over into the room. I recoiled. Gertrude placed the remote in my hands.

"I'll return in twenty minutes," she said, and closed the door behind her, leaving me alone in the darkness, facing my biggest fear: the roaring ocean.

Catalina

Las Villas, Cuba
September 1919

She was helping doña Emilia set the table for lunch when Ramón rushed in from the street, hatless and out of breath, sweat dripping from his face down to the stiff neck of his starched white *guayabera*.

"Have you heard?" he asked, grabbing the frame of the door for support.

"No, what? What happened?" doña Emilia said, nearly dropping the platter she was about to set down.

Catalina knew that whatever the news was, she didn't want to hear it. She took a step back, and thought about hiding from Ramón. She feared that what he was about to say would shatter her life. She looked at Ramón, almost willing him to leave, to go back to the bar and let her be at peace with her fears.

For days dread had lodged in her heart. No matter what she told herself or how she tried to soothe her soul, it would not budge. She tried praying, walking in the fields, and sleeping. Ultimately, working her body to exhaustion all day until she could no longer feel her feet was the only way she could tamp down her anxiety.

Mornings usually found her in a chair, waiting for the sun to rise so she could go outside and begin the tasks that kept her busy: milking the cow, feeding the chickens, collecting the eggs, making breakfast, cleaning an already immaculate house, killing a hen, preparing lunch, doing some laundry in a pail under the trees, hanging the clothes on the line, tending to the animals, sweeping the floors again, working in the garden, making dinner, doing the dishes, mending some of Ramón's old clothes, ironing the laundry, even the sheets and doña Emilia's underwear. And the same thing over again the next day.

Nights were the worst. Fear, pure and intact, found her in her bed every night. It coiled around her heart like a vine and wouldn't let go, pulling her down into such darkness she thought she'd never see the light of day again.

But fear was better than grief. Fear implied a measure of hope. Grief was darkness, punishing and solitary.

On September 20, 1919, the day Ramón brought the news home that the *Valbanera* had never made it to the port of Havana, her fear finally left her for good. And where her fear used to be, grief took residence. It was a space in her heart that she could physically feel as tender.

Years later, she would be able to recall that moment in detail, down to the taste of blood in her mouth from biting down on her lip with such force. How would her body cope after being hobbled by a terminal wound? How could she live with a hole in her heart? Until the day she died, Catalina would place her hand over that spot to connect with her anguish, the way one visits an old friend. She eventually grew accustomed to her grief, but on those rare occasions when she felt levity or joy and the pain seemed to dissipate, she made sure to summon it back, rubbing her fingers over her heart until she evinced that familiar ache of despair. There, I'm whole again, she would tell herself. But that came later, much later in life.

Ramón told them that the hurricane winds had pounded the ship, sending it far from Cuba until it finally sank in the shallow waters off the coast of Florida. He heard that afterward only the foremast could be seen above water; the rest of the ship remained buried in the sandy bottom of the ocean.

The Americans had sent a rescue boat, but there were no survivors, and no bodies had been found.

Doña Emilia made the sign of the cross and instinctively moved toward Catalina, who remained standing, though slightly shaking.

"Where are the bodies?" she asked.

Ramón grimaced painfully and lowered his head.

"Where?" Catalina insisted, searching in vain for Ramón's downcast eyes. Now she wanted to know. Grief, unlike fear, was morbidly curious.

"No one can say. My guess is they are deep, deep in the ocean, deeper maybe," he finally said, looking into her eyes. His were brimming with tears; hers were dry, taking in the enormity of his comment.

Catalina felt it then: a little squeeze in her heart, as if a hand had reached in there and poked it or pinched it. The air left her lungs, her knees buckled, and all went black as she remembered Juan's words, "My love for you is higher than the sky, deeper than the ocean."

Mara

Santa Cruz, La Palma
July 2019

There was a narrator in this short film, a scientist identified as the foremost expert on the tragedy. The film opened with his voice, rich but raspy, as if he were an old survivor of the *Valbanera*. "There is no longer a horizon, no ocean or sky," he began, his voice barely audible over the sounds of angry nature re-created in a studio somewhere in Spain.

Water, a turbulent grayish white, occupied all the corners of the screen. Here and there, a portion of the ship could be seen, shaken by the waves. A huge wave, perhaps twenty feet high, seemed to lift the ship from the ocean itself and then drop it, as if a giant hand were playing with a boat made of Legos. On the bridge, thirteen men protected by heavy raincoats struggled mightily to regain control. The narrator explained they were struggling to get out of a low muddy area where, the crew understood, a vessel of this size could be sucked in like a shoe in quicksand. Suddenly, the bow of the ship disappeared under the sea.

The *Valbanera* vibrated, and a sound like a coffin being dragged over gravel took over the narration of the film. The ship continued its way down, angling itself like a fishing rod pulling against a large fish. The lights went out. The screen was black. But the sounds continued: screams, metal scraping against metal, thunder, and water.

The overwhelming roar of the ocean was everywhere as it swallowed the *Valbanera*. The last image, after the total darkness of the screen, was of a mast poking from a calm sea—the only evidence of the ordeal that took almost five hundred lives, but, not, it seemed, the life of my great-grandmother.

I left the gallery shaking but determined not to cry. Though the film was only a reenactment of the disaster, it moved me deeply. So deeply that I thought if I gave in to my emotions, I wouldn't be able to stop.

Julián was still where I left him, at the bar of the wine supplier he had come to see. The meeting was over, and he was nursing a beer. His eyes were unfocused and he seemed lost in thought, with a trace of a smile on his face and his hands were relaxed around the beer bottle. There was no way I could tell him what I had just seen. I tried to wipe the horror from my face as I walked up to him. He didn't see me until I collapsed in the chair opposite his.

"No wonder you've all stayed on this island. You are all afraid to leave," I said, half in jest, but Julián seemed serious.

"That bad, huh?" was all he said, the half-smile still on his lips. He must have seen me going into the gallery earlier.

I nodded and motioned for the waiter to bring me a drink—a gin and tonic to calm my nerves.

"Do you still have the picture you showed me earlier?" I asked.

He nodded and pulled it from the pocket of his shirt, no longer inside the envelope.

I looked at the photo, lovingly kept after all these years. The borders were a little discolored and it had the typical yellow tint of older photos, but it was remarkably well preserved. Catalina looked impossibly young. Too young to be married and holding a baby. The man, Antonio, was holding her elbow in a proprietary way and leaning over as if caught in the act of saying something to his wife. They both wore dark clothing, though his seemed lighter than hers. His could have been brown or gray, while hers was probably black or navy blue. She didn't look particularly happy. In fact, she looked sad.

I could relate to that look. Though almost forty years had passed, I still remembered vividly the moment I took one last look at my country. It was dawn, the outlines of trees and shrubs were beginning to take shape in the receding darkness as we rowed away from shore, the motor quieted so as not to alert the Cuban Coast Guard. All I could see were patches of green, a flag flapping in the wind, and a small white structure on top of a distant hill. Where were the palm trees, the beautiful buildings of Havana, and the wide avenues dotted with poinciana trees? The shore seemed barren and unwelcoming, more yellow than brown as I leaned on my mother's arms and began to cry.

Julián's voice rescued me from the tears that always flowed when I got to this point in my buried memories. Now he was showing me a small ochre-colored envelope. I looked inside, and saw pieces of what looked like dust or ashes. Perplexed and a little afraid, I gave it back to him.

"My grandmother always kept it," he said. "It was a yellow hibiscus Catalina placed in her hair before she left. She kept it because it was the last thing her sister touched."

At that, I couldn't hold my tears any longer. Julián ignored me, thankfully, and went on with his story. He said that for a long time the family had hoped that Catalina had survived the catastrophe and a letter would arrive announcing that she was safe in Cuba, with her husband and baby daughter. Back then, he explained, the newspapers were full of stories of people who were thought to have died, but had, in fact, survived because they disembarked, either by mistake or premonition, in Santiago de Cuba instead of continuing on their way to Havana. Catalina's sisters, but especially Lucía, clung to the idea that perhaps Catalina had been one of those.

Other survivors of the *Valbanera* had been lost to their relatives for a long time or forever because they were illiterate or had no money to send a telegram, he said. There was an often-repeated story of a woman who had been waiting for her husband and two children in Havana. When she heard the ship was lost in the hurricane, she went mad, not knowing that her husband and children had disembarked earlier, in Santiago, where they remained with no way to communicate with her. Years later, one of her now adult children went to Havana on business. As he was getting his shoes shined, a beggar approached him. The young man listened as she mumbled to herself the story of her terrible loss. "She always does that, talks to herself and repeats the same story," the shoeshine man said, without looking up from his task. "No one knows if it's true." But the young man realized that the crazed and destitute woman in front of him was his mother. He didn't tell her right away for fear of injuring her fragile psyche even more. Instead, he offered to take her home with him and give her shelter and food. Eventually, he and his brother were able to tell her they were her long-lost boys.

Julián took a break to let that story sink in. He was a gifted raconteur, and I was mesmerized by both his voice—deep and growly—and the stories. If true, the tragedy of the *Valbanera* had been even worse than I had thought possible. I couldn't imagine being separated from my son during his entire childhood. I shuddered at the idea and looked up at Julián, waiting for more.

He said they were certain that something like that couldn't have happened to Catalina, who was married to a wealthy man. Though she had gone to school for only three or four years, which was more than most girls had been able to accomplish at that time, she was smart, and she could read and write. But, above all, she never would have allowed her family to go on suffering thinking she was dead when she was alive.

"The question, then, is why did she?" I mused out loud.

Julián didn't seem to hear me, but he went on to say there was a story in the family that Catalina was in love with someone else, a local boy named Juan Cruz, who disappeared around the same time

Catalina and Antonio left on the *Valbanera*. "He may have followed her there," Julián said. "But we'll never know."

The thought was intriguing. I looked at the picture in my hands again, trying to read her features. I had once taken a tour of the Metropolitan Museum of Art in New York with a woman who specialized in teaching professionals, such as physicians, reporters, and detectives, to look closely at art. The idea was that being trained to search for telling details would make you a better doctor, journalist, or cop, able to find clues in mannerisms, clothing, and facial expressions that others might miss. I tried to do that with my great-grandmother's photo, but all I saw was a couple and a child in front of a ship. Then, after looking more closely, I noticed how her upper body was slightly bent back, as if unconsciously rejecting her husband's advance. Or was my reading of the picture influenced by what I had just learned about her loving someone else?

But what really captured my imagination was the baby. Who was this baby?

"Where was this baby born?" I asked.

"Who? Carmen?"

I nodded.

"Here, of course," Julián said. "Well, not here, but where the original family house was. Still is, but no one lives there anymore."

"Where is that?"

"In a little place called La Peña, in the middle of nowhere."

"But if I wanted to find Carmen's birth certificate, where would I find it?" I asked.

"I'm not sure. I think you'd have to do that here, where the main government offices are. Why? What are you thinking?" Julián asked, eyeing me over his reading glasses in the same way that countless people had looked at me all my life, a look that says, "Here comes trouble." I was so used to it, most times I didn't see it anymore. It certainly had never stopped me.

I explained to Julián why I had to find the certificate. The most important reason was that, though I never knew Catalina, I had known her husband, the man who raised my mother as a father. To me, he was a grandfather, and his name was not Antonio López.

"It makes no sense," he said. "Why would they make everyone believe that the baby was born in Cuba?"

I shrugged, but what I thought, and didn't say, was that perhaps they had had immigration reasons. It was a wild theory, but I was wondering if at a certain point it had been easier for immigrants from Spain to pretend to be Cubans. I know my life would have been easier in the US if I could have pretended to be American-born and hide every trace of my Cuban accent.

Twenty minutes later Julián and I arrived in the same government office I had visited two days earlier. We had a name: Carmen López Quintana, and even a date of birth because Julián's grandmother had kept a family album recording every birth, baptism, wedding, and death. Baby Carmen was born April 20, 1919, almost exactly nineteen years after her mother.

I couldn't understand how this baby was connected to my grandmother, whose full name was Carmen Fernández Quintana. Were they the same child under different names? The *Valbanera* was no longer a mystery to me, but my grandmother was becoming one. I thought about calling my mother again, but I resisted. I didn't want to add to her confusion. I preferred to wait until I was able to unravel the story and call her with something more concrete.

Julián went inside to talk to some people he knew and about half an hour later handed me an envelope. Inside, folded in half, there was a pristine piece of paper, still warm from the copy machine: the birth certificate of a Carmen Inés de la Candelaria López Quintana.

"And this proves exactly what?" he asked.

"I'm not sure," I said, tossing the envelope in my bag with a lightness I didn't feel.

Catalina

Las Villas, Cuba
October 1919

SHE NEVER KNEW EXACTLY HOW LONG she remained in bed. At some point she asked doña Emilia to close all the windows, please. She couldn't stand the smell of the sea, or the briny breeze that on some days drifted inland, rustling the fronds of the royal palms and seeping into the house through windows and doors. It seemed to be calling to her, almost demanding that she rejoin the living. But Catalina had no strength or desire to do anything. Doña Emilia cooked for her and fed her in bed, as one would a sick child. She kept Catalina's body clean, dipping a sponge in warm water and gently wiping her face, her arms, and her legs as a mother would. All Catalina could do was to murmur her gratitude.

When she managed to sleep, nightmares overwhelmed her. She dreamed of a darkened boat and bodies floating, trapped in the ocean under the overturned hull. She saw herself among the dead, her red hair floating away, as if separate from her body. Her arms could feel the heaviness of her daughter's tiny but bloated body, and she could see small silver fishes crawling out of her eyes.

The nightmare was always the same and, invariably, Catalina woke up screaming. Doña Emilia would come to her aid, carrying a *tilo* infusion. She would place a hand on Catalina's forehead and wipe the sweat away. Then, she would help her sit up and urge her to sip just a little. Catalina obeyed. She no longer had the willpower or strength to do anything. Her mind had disconnected from her body, and she allowed doña Emilia to arrange her limbs on the bed, as efficiently as she performed her other household chores, but with great tenderness. In those intimate moments in the middle of the night, Emilia never said a word or asked how she was feeling. Catalina was always grateful for that.

There was a reason Emilia didn't ask. Though she was not a mother, she thought she understood Catalina's pain. The loss of her baby was unimaginable, but Emilia also knew, though no one had told her, that Catalina must have been mourning the love of her life. Emilia hoped that the shock of the last few weeks had made her forget the man she must have loved. This was important because, pious as she was, every night before bed, she prayed that Catalina and Ramón would fall in love. She wasn't sure if Catalina had feelings for her nephew, but she was certain he had feelings for her. The way he looked at her when Catalina wasn't aware of his gaze said it all. At twenty-two, Ramón was old enough to experience love and to have a woman in his life.

Catalina felt nauseous, the way she had felt the first few days on the ship, when she couldn't eat anything or get out of bed. Concerned that she was getting worse with each passing day, Ramón went to find the town's doctor. Two days later, the doctor came and examined her carefully. It had been a month since Catalina had received the awful news, and Ramón thought she seemed like a different person. She was extremely emaciated and there were patches of baldness on her scalp. Her cheeks were hollow, her brow had creased, and her lips were cracked, despite doña Emilia's aloe potions. Her nails had become ragged, as if she picked at them in her stupor. To give her privacy with the doctor, Ramón left the bedroom and waited outside the door with his aunt.

Catalina was asleep for most of the examination, but she woke up with a jolt when the stethoscope reached her heart. The doctor jerked back, then smiled and patted her hand as her father used to do.

"I hear you've lost a lot of weight and you can't keep anything down," he said.

Catalina nodded.

"I don't like the sound of your heart," he went on.

Catalina was almost surprised to learn her heart was still beating.

"For now, I'm going to ask doña Emilia to prepare you a beverage of rue, lemon balm, and a little ginger. That should help with the nausea and the appetite, but you must make an effort, too," he said, getting up to open the window curtains before turning back to her. "We have to get some light and fresh air into this room, and you have to eat."

In response, Catalina just gazed at him, puzzled that this man couldn't or wouldn't comprehend the extent of her damage. Hadn't he listened to her heart? Hadn't he already detected her wound? She would have to tell him, to make it clear there was nothing he could do for her. She cleared her throat; then, she asked the doctor how it felt to drown. He looked at her, puzzled.

"Why? Are you feeling short of breath?"

"No, but I need to know. Please tell me," she pleaded.

"I see. In that case, I can tell you that, like all deaths, it's a mystery only experienced by those unfortunate enough to go through it."

He pulled a chair close to Catalina's bed and grabbed the edges of the seat with his hands as if to anchor himself before he spoke.

"Death by drowning is one of the worst ways to die," he began. "When a person goes underwater, he automatically stops breathing to prevent water from filling the lungs. In essence, the brain concludes that it's better not to breathe than to breathe water."

Catalina swallowed hard, and hoped the doctor, seeing her distress, would stop. At the same time, though, she wanted him to go on. There was something exquisite about her pain, and she wanted to feel the full intensity of it. Only then, she intuited, could she understand her daughter's ordeal.

"However," the doctor continued, "eventually, the body's oxygen is so low that an involuntary reflex forces the drowning person to inhale. That's the end."

"How long does that take?" Catalina heard herself asking, not sure how she had been able to formulate words.

The doctor had begun putting his instruments back in his black leather bag, but resumed speaking in his professorial tone. "It is believed that the moment is reached in less than ninety seconds. Without oxygen, the brain succumbs to darkness, and despair. Few die gracefully, as the body rebels against the inevitable, the abyss."

Catalina gasped and covered her face with her hands.

The doctor sat back in the chair next to her bed and gently pulled her hands away from her face. He looked at her with compassion before he spoke again.

"I suspect you've suffered a great loss, Señora, but at the moment it is of utmost importance that you be strong for your baby," he said, regarding her meaningfully.

She tried to comprehend what he had said. A child? It couldn't be. It couldn't possibly be. But then she remembered her frenzied nights on the ship with Juan. How could she bring another child into the world without a father? How could her heart ever mend enough to offer fresh love to an innocent baby?

"Now then, I'll go and speak to your husband," the doctor said, startling Catalina who had forgotten he was seated next to her.

Before Catalina could react, he got up, took his bag, reached the door, and closed it behind him without another glance at her. She licked her dry lips and grabbed another pillow, propping it under her head. From this semi-seated position, she looked down at her body, which seemed to stubbornly cling to life. Another child.

Ramón knocked on the door and called her name, but he didn't wait for a reply to come in. Gently, as if fearful to wrinkle the sheets, he sat on the edge of the bed, his back to her, and looked away, toward the field behind the house. The smell of grass wafted in through the open window, and a small white butterfly flitted near the wooden frame. The insistent barking of a dog interrupted their silence.

"You don't have to do this alone," he said.

Catalina raised her arms from the bed where they had been lying flat against the sheets. She placed one hand on her belly. All this time, while she was mourning, life had been quietly stirring inside her. She thought of her father.

She could almost hear him now, the lessons he imparted as they gardened together. "You plant a seed and then watch it grow and see how it goes. If it likes where it is, you let it be. If not, move it a little, add more water perhaps? More sun? A shadier spot?" But how do you grow new leaves and new roots when the trunk has been damaged? How do you get rid of so many weeds that threaten the only beauty you've ever known? Life isn't like a garden after all. It's much crueler than that. But still it is life. She felt her sorrow recede a little, like water in low tide.

Catalina kept one of her hands on her flat belly, tentatively caressing the idea of another child. The other hand, she pressed hard against Ramón's strong back.

Mara

El Paso, La Palma
August 2019

"I think Antonio must have died and she remarried and changed her daughter's last name," Julián said. He was wearing the half-apron he favored, the kind only serious cooks dare to wear, and chopping onions, while I peeled potatoes for the omelet that he had promised to make me since we met. A Spanish omelet is a full meal of potatoes, onions, and eggs, and only a few can make a good one. Julián was one of them.

We were in his kitchen, back at the house. The bar was closed, and Julián seemed relaxed. I, on the other hand, was as tense as a sailor's rope. I kept feeling that tingling in my stomach that usually indicates I'm close to a good story but can't quite grasp it yet.

What Julián had just said seemed plausible, until I remembered that, technically, she had died, too.

"According to the records, they both died on the ship," I said. "I feel like there is a piece missing. I should check the records of the *Valbanera* again to see what else I can find."

"Yes, but not tonight," Julián said.

I arched my eyebrow in response.

"We are going to a concert tonight."

"A concert?" Music was the furthest thing from my mind.

Julián explained it was an open-air concert, one of the local events commemorating the centenary of the tragedy of the *Valbanera*. Immediately, I thought of Nelson, who adored music, classical above all. For him, there was always a good reason to attend a concert. In times of sadness or happiness, he sought music, the same way I found solace in literature. It took me a long time to understand how central music was to his understanding of the world and to the processing of his emotions. But, once I did, it deepened my love for him. For how can one not love a man who used melodies to express all his emotions, even anger?

"Did you hear what I said? Where are you?" Julián asked with a smile so wide I could see all his perfectly white teeth. He must be one of the few Spanish men of his generation who had never smoked cigarettes.

He set the omelet on the table and opened a bottle of red wine. Then, he cut a triangular slice of the omelet and placed it on my plate, poured wine for each of us, and sat down across for me, making a sound somewhere between relief and pain that made me realize how much time he must spend on his feet every day. His brow was sweaty, and he wiped it with the corner of his apron.

"I'm so sorry. I'm here, yes, the concert, I'll go. I'd love to," I said in a rush, trying to escape intrusive thoughts of my dead husband.

That night, I borrowed a white dress from one of the cousins who lived nearby. It was a little loose and I wondered if I had lost weight. That would be a welcome outcome of my family search. I complemented the look with a red scarf and pulled back my hair because I didn't have time to wash and style it, something my mother was always harping about, but she was not here, so it didn't matter.

The concert was on a beach about forty-five minutes away, on a raised platform on the sand. The night was glorious and balmy. There were paper lanterns along the path so the audience could find their seats, and the musicians had tiny lights above their music sheets, but the rest was dark. Small waves rippled onto the rocks of the shore making a sweet low sound as if they were planting thousands of tiny kisses on the rocks. It reminded me of the way my father used to kiss my mother at night. I often went to sleep in our Havana apartment listening to the sound of those tiny kisses. I tried to focus on that memory and not the proximity of water, though, for some reason I wasn't as anxious as I normally was near the ocean.

The splendid starry sky of La Palma shone above us, a show unto itself, as the orchestra began tuning up. There were maybe fifty people in the audience, which made the concert feel intimate and special. Uncharacteristically, no one gave a speech explaining the significance of the concert. The conductor arrived and the music began. The first note seemed familiar. When I recognized the melody, I felt my breath catch. It was Debussy's La Mer, one of Nelson's favorite pieces of classical music. He had delighted in explaining to me how the composer evoked the fury of the sea and the power of the waves in the third movement of what it's widely believed to be his masterpiece.

I looked up at the sky and searched for the brightest light: Venus. There was my Nelson, looking down at me and laughing at how improbable the whole thing was. Our own "son of the waves" in the Navy, and me, sitting here with a distant cousin, investigating the life of someone who had left this island long ago never to return. A woman who had reinvented herself on another island, the country of my birth—a place I, too, had left never to return, and that I was now certain I would go back to because of her.

I closed my eyes, scared at my own thoughts. It almost felt like the curse of exiles: to return to the forbidden place, to be always searching for that elusive home. I remembered a line from a memoir of a Syrian writer: "What do you do when you can't stay, and you can't go back?"

My heart ached for my lost country in a way I hadn't felt in a long time. It ached, too, for Catalina and her frustrated love story, for I was certain that if Juan had loved her so much that he followed her to Cuba, Catalina had loved him with an equal intensity. What had happened to their love story? What happens to any love story when the protagonists were no longer there? I knew that my own love for Nelson still burned bright and strong, but what about Nelson's? Did he take it with him? Or had he left it behind, scattering it in the wind like stardust so that it would find me and comfort me in my loneliness?

The musicians were now playing the second movement of the piece, called Play of Waves. It was easy to feel the rocking motion of the waves, undulating gently, and then the sudden shift of the current as the music punctured the thick darkness of an otherwise soundless night. The sea, a mere few feet away, cooperated, and remained as silent as it could. Occasionally, you could hear an actual wave breaking on the shore and its sound competed with that of the orchestra. When that happened, it was a delight. The real thing amplified by dozens of violins attempting to imitate the inimitable.

My eyes began tearing up, but I didn't care. I let my tears run, like a sudden Caribbean downpour, and made no attempt to hide them. Julián covered my hand with his, large and marred by cooking cuts and burns. I put my other hand on top of his. It felt good to have his hand trapped in mine like a bird.

When the music ended, Julián kept his hand in mine while everybody else applauded. After the ovation died down, a young woman dressed in a long white dress went up on the stage and read a poem about a shipwreck. It ended with these words:

> Familiar as the taste of tears to me,
> As on my lips, insistent, I discern
> The salt and bitter kisses of the sea.

I cried and cried and cried.

Catalina

Las Villas
December 1919

It took great effort to get Catalina up from the bed, where she had entombed herself since the day she heard about the sinking of the *Valbanera*. She finally got up about two weeks after the doctor's visit. When she found the courage to look at herself in the mirror, she didn't recognize herself.

Her hair was an ashy shade of copper, and her curls had lost their luster and spring. Her freckles had all but vanished and her face had set into the full-moon shape that would accompany her for the rest of her life: broad and white with thin lips, a small nose and a strong jaw line that never really sagged with age or fat. Her hands and feet had grown with the first pregnancy and seemed larger now that she had lost so much weight. She couldn't be sure, but she thought she had grown as well; she thought she was as tall as her father, perhaps more. While her soul had shriveled, her body had expanded.

In the days to come, she began to occupy more space and demand more attention by her sheer presence, but she remained quiet, speaking only when necessary and revealing so little of herself that even people who saw her every day in the market or at church were hard pressed to recall her name. That's how she wanted it, for Catalina longed to erase her old self and become someone without a past, without mistakes, and without memories that dragged her down into a well of misery so deep she felt she might never resurface again.

It didn't help that wherever she went everyone was still talking about the "tragedy of the *Valbanera*." Even if she didn't go anywhere, the news came to her. For months after the hurricane there were stories about the shipwreck on the front page of every newspaper. Doña Emilia hid them the moment Catalina came into a room where she was reading, but inevitably Catalina would find them while dusting or cleaning. The headlines jarred her and yet she couldn't help but read the articles: "Steamer *Valbanera* sinks with possible loss of 450 lives," "Divers find vessel in forty feet of water with only the mast protruding," "No trace of either passengers or crew has been found."

She was puzzled by that last headline. How could that be? She forced herself to think of different scenarios in which hundreds of bodies could disappear, leaving behind only the sorrow of those who had loved them. Some days, she had the urge to get up and walk, and to keep walking toward something that as yet remained shapeless and ineffable, but that she hoped would reveal itself in the process. She knew she needed to get away from this yellow house and this village by the sea where she had known pain as she never had before, where her heart had broken into a million little pieces and somehow reassembled itself to keep ticking for this other life she was carrying, where she had shed her old skin like the silkworms that she used to care for with such devotion. She knew that when worms shed their chrysalis and turned into moths, the cycle was complete, and metamorphosis had occurred. But she also knew that, after centuries of domestication, adult silk moths couldn't fly; their wings were small and useless. Catalina hoped her own wings had not yet become useless.

When she shared her thoughts with Ramón, he looked befuddled. He didn't understand her comparison to moths or worms. Instead, he was more pragmatic, wanting to know where they could possibly go in her "condition." He disliked the idea of leaving his job and his elderly aunt behind, but Ramón was a man of honor, a man of his word, and he had promised Juan that, if anything were to happen to him, he would take care of Catalina. Besides, from the moment he found her at the port, disheveled and in agony, Ramón had felt the desire not only to protect her but to please her. It was the closest feeling to love he had ever felt.

He paid close attention to her face to decipher her moods and tried to keep her distracted with the minutiae of life to steer her thoughts away from the tragedy. After work, they took walks together, always in the direction of the town center, away from the coast. He wondered if Juan had had a premonition that he was going to die or if he had simply extracted that promise from him in a thoughtless way, as people do before they embark on a long voyage. Juan's trip across the ocean had been his first, and, as it turned out, his last. He must have been worried or perhaps, when he sent him the letter from Canarias asking for help, he wasn't even certain that he would be able to travel in the *Valbanera* with Catalina. In fact, when the newspapers had published the list of names of those who had died in the shipwreck, Ramón was surprised Juan's name wasn't among them. He hadn't told Catalina and he hadn't shown her the list because he didn't want her to know that, among the dead, he had found her own name and that of her husband, though not her daughter's or Juan's.

And thus, Ramón agreed with Catalina's idea to leave the yellow house and even began to feel excited about their adventure. The only risk he had ever taken in his life was leaving La Palma and coming to Cuba, but that was a measured risk, because he had relatives and a job waiting for him. This was different. Now he was about to be a married man, expecting a child that wasn't his but that he would learn to love as his own. And, of course, he would have to learn to love Catalina as well. There was something about her inner strength facing so much pain that gave him an interior fire he didn't know he possessed. It wasn't that he desired her. He did not. He had not yet touched her beyond a gentle caress on her face to brush her hair back or to hold her hand. And yet, despite her strength, he felt tenderness toward this pregnant, sad woman who was alone in the world and depended solely on him.

He supposed it was because she needed him. No one had ever needed him before, and that made him feel like a grown man. In time, perhaps, these feelings of dependency and admiration and need could grow into love, he hoped. Certainly, life would be easier if that were the case, but he knew life was not easy. For now, he was sure all they had was respect and a mutual dependency that felt safe and comfortable for both.

Catalina and Ramón wed in a civil ceremony on a sunny afternoon the day after Christmas. She wore a rose-colored dress with lace around the high neck that doña Emilia had kept from her youth, but fit Catalina perfectly since she had gained some weight with the pregnancy. Ramón wore a white linen *guayabera* and dark pants.

The only witness to their union was Emilia, who gave them a black cow and a sack of rice as a wedding present. That evening, when they returned to her yellow house, Emilia insisted on cooking a special meal for them. They had kept the pregnancy from her, as well as Catalina's love story with Juan, telling her only that they wanted to marry so that they would remain together through life. Emilia was surprised neither had mentioned the word *love* and couldn't believe she had misinterpreted her nephew's looks in Catalina's presence. Now she could see that they behaved more like survivors of a wreck clinging to each other for support than young people in love. After their vows they hadn't even kissed, not even at the urging of the priest, who seemed perplexed when Ramón stood still and gently shook his head no.

She couldn't understand why they had made the decision to marry so hastily, but it was better this way. She hoped that they would find comfort and companionship in their marriage. That, after all, was sometimes better than love, especially after living through such an ordeal, she reasoned.

The day after the wedding, Catalina prepared a bundle of clothes she had collected for the two of them. After a hearty breakfast, they grabbed their belongings and mounted Ramón's mare, and left the village, the yellow house, and doña Emilia, who waved at them until they were a blurry speck on the horizon, the black cow trailing them.

At the edge of town, Ramón leaned back and asked Catalina, "Where to?"

"As far from here as possible. Find us a place where I'll never again have to see the ocean or even smell it," she said, and rested her head on his back.

Ramón thought for a moment, made up his mind, and kicked his mare hard and low in the belly. They headed south toward the interior of the island where the land was moist, red as clay and known to be very fertile. Ramón was very much hoping that was true. All he had in the world was seventeen pesos in his pocket, a black cow, a sack of rice, and a pregnant woman leaning against him on a dappled stubborn mare named Panchita.

Mara

El Paso, La Palma
August 2019

THE FOLLOWING DAY I DROVE BACK to Gladys and Claude's to settle the bill and get my backpack. There was no point staying there any longer when I had an extended family that claimed me and wanted me near them. Also, Julián had enticed me to stay with the promise of showing me the house where Catalina and her sisters had been born. And where Carmen, my grandmother, had also been born. Or so it seemed.

After returning to Bar Alegre and dropping off my backpack, I went outside to join Julián by the car. I could see that he had prepared a picnic basket, which he had carefully placed on the back seat. A blue-checkered napkin peeked from the top wrapped around the neck of a wine bottle. Though I didn't say anything, he must have registered my surprise and delight.

"Just in case we get hungry or thirsty," he said a little sheepishly, like a boy caught in an act of kindness. "It's so pretty there and I'm always looking for an excuse to go, but everyone is always too busy. Since Grandma died, it's usually just me."

His words petered out and he looked away, as if embarrassed by his explanations.

"Well," I said. "You found a perfect excuse today. I can't wait to see it, and I'm always hungry, so picnic baskets are my best friends."

Julián grinned and we got into his car, an old Peugeot the color of ripe tomatoes. He revved up the engine and we set off for La Peña, leaving behind all the houses and businesses in the center of town. Before us a road appeared, like a black ribbon unfurling around the mountains. On this part of the island, the soil was dry and had a dull grayish color, unlike the rich brown and explosive greens I had seen in the capital. Julián explained that this was volcanic ash.

No other place that I had visited changed as precipitously as La Palma. In half an hour or so, one could go from a beautiful crowded beach to a dry lonely stretch of road skirting towering peaks, and ancient monoliths. Turn a bend and suddenly there would be a rushing stream, a cascade, or a lush pine forest. Laurel bushes and wildflowers hugged the curving roads like multi-hued crowns, and capricious rock formations and impossibly steep hills formed a seemingly endless barrier between the road and the rest of the world on the other side.

It must have felt both glorious and claustrophobic to grow up here, surrounded by these peaks. My frames of reference were quite different, wide open or open-ended, like the sea. The barriers I grew up with were not imposed by nature but by men. Those are easier to conquer—you can either topple them or get out of the way. We got out of the way, and left Cuba. But mountains such as these? I couldn't decide if they were limiting or inspiring. In the end, though, Catalina too had left. Perhaps these peaks had been too much for her. Perhaps she, too, had sought the wide vistas of another island, and I hoped she had found in Cuba what she had been looking for. I hoped that whatever choices she made and however she chose to live her life she never missed these mountains as much as I missed my own island.

It was strange. No matter where my train of thoughts started, lately, they seemed to always take me back to Cuba. It had been so long since I'd stopped obsessing over Cuba, but I was feeling vulnerable and tired, away from home and missing my son.

I reached down to lower the window the old-fashioned way, by cranking the handle, and took a deep breath. I detected the scent of laurel, pine, and lavender, but something was missing, and I couldn't quite figure out what it was. My nose felt dry and wanting, trying in vain to breathe in that odor so peculiar to the other parts of the island I had visited.

"You won't smell it here," said Julián, reading my thoughts.

I had to laugh out loud. "What is *it*?" I finally asked.

"The sea," he said. "You can't see it and you can't smell it from up here, but you can from the old house. You'll see. It's a little lower, a little closer to shore."

I kept the window down to look at the mountains without the filter of a glass. It was a warm day, and I was wearing my regular outfit: black pants, gray T-shirt; a two-tone green scarf added some color and—I hoped—a bit of glamor to an otherwise drab look on day three of my visit.

We drove the rest of the way in silence. For all his joviality and forced happiness—not everyone owned a place called Bar Alegre—Julián was the quiet type. I sensed he was so used to noise that he relished silence. That suited me perfectly. And yet, I was full of questions. I wanted to know more about his life, and the lives of every member of this extended family that had suddenly embraced me as their own just because I showed up and claimed to be the great-granddaughter of a relative of theirs who was long dead.

A hard stop brought me out of my thoughts.

"Here we are," Julián said, and grinned, as if contemplating the house for the first time.

I looked at it through the windshield and my hand immediately went for the door handle. I opened it as if in a trance.

Before me was an almost exact replica of the house where I'd spent all my childhood summers in Cuba. My nose flared and my throat constricted with that familiar feeling of unbidden tears. A shiver ran through me as I realized without a doubt that I had found my mother's clan, and therefore my own.

Catalina

Sabanilla, Las Villas
1919–1923

AFTER THREE HOURS OF RIDING, Ramón pulled the reins of his mare on a plot of land deep in the country that seemed perfect to him. It was far from the sea, as Catalina had requested, and far from roads, stores, people, and trains, but close enough to town so that he could visit his aunt. At first, Catalina thought the silence was complete, but she soon realized she was surrounded by sound: buzzing mosquitoes, mooing cows, thunder rolling in the distance, crowing roosters, hooves approaching from the embankment, someone chopping wood—the thwack sound of the machete against a trunk echoing in the valley.

Later, she learned that town was called Sabanilla, but Catalina never knew why, and, to her, it never really seemed like a town anyway but a scattering of houses, not visible to one another in a vast land with no visible borders.

Within a few days, Ramón had negotiated a lease on a shack in exchange for work. Catalina had never worked as hard in her life. She thought she knew hard work, but this was different. From the moment she got up in the morning to the moment she rested her head on the pillow at night she and Ramón wrestled with the elements for survival.

Their new house was a typical *bohío* made of wood with a thatched roof of palm fronds. When it rained, water poured in from everywhere.

They had to place buckets in every room of the house, or they'd be living in the mud. At night, when she finished cooking, they spread the ashes from the stove on the floor to try to keep it dry. A thankless task, for no matter how much Catalina cleaned and wiped, the house was always dirty. They were always dirty. Dirt got on their clothes, under their nails, in their hair, even inside their mouths, forming a gritty film over their front teeth. They had no running water, no electricity, and no bathrooms until Ramón built an outhouse a few steps from the shack. That night they celebrated with a special meal: Catalina made *ropa vieja*, a Canarian dish of meat and potatoes that had already become part of the Cuban diet.

She grew to love her *bohío*, all of it: the sounds, the quirkiness, the way the light of the sun seemed to infiltrate every inch of every room unless they closed and latched the wooden panels of the windows, and the almost constant smell of ripe mangoes in the summers. But it took time, and it was never home.

A few months after they had settled, Ramón went to visit his aunt and found the yellow house shuttered. Worried and confounded, he went to the church where the priest gave him the sad news that doña Emilia had died in her sleep. The priest, surprised not to see her in church on Sunday, had checked on her and found her in bed, fully clothed, her fingers braided atop her chest as if she had been awaiting death. By the time Ramón learned of his aunt's death, she had already been buried. Catalina prayed for her but felt no need to go to the cemetery to pay her respects. Everything doña Emilia had meant for her in the brief time they lived together, she carried in her heart, and she had no compulsion to share it with anyone. She had never visited doña Emilia since she left. In fact, she had not left Sabanilla since she arrived, in fear of being recognized by a newly arrived immigrant from La Palma.

After a brief respite immediately following the tragedy of the *Valbanera*, ships had continued to arrive in Cuba loaded with immigrants eager to find work in the booming sugar and tobacco industries. The harvest of 1919–1920 had brought in more money to the island than ever before, with the price of sugar at an all-time high. And where there was work and money, there were immigrants who wanted to partake of the bounty.

Catalina shuddered to think what would happen if someone from El Paso recognized her as the lost Quintana girl. Or, worse, as the widow of Antonio López. She knew that her family and everyone back home would think she was buried with Antonio and their daughter in the muddy waters off Florida. Catalina thought it best to let it be so. It wasn't a conscious decision, but as the days turned to weeks and then months, she realized it was easier that way.

Ramón inherited doña Emilia's tiny yellow house, but he never contemplated going back. Instead, he sold it. With the money, he bought the plot of land they had been renting. The day he signed the papers on his new property, Ramón brought Catalina flowers he picked from the fields and asked her to share a drink with him. She obliged. Catalina could tell Ramón wanted to make her happy. She, too, wanted to be, if not happy, resigned, and productive. But her suffering was so brutal that it left her depleted most days. Often, she looked at her growing belly and wondered how her daughter was still there for she was certain she was carrying a girl. Only a woman would cling to life with such tenacity.

On June 2, 1920, six months after they had moved to Sabanilla, Catalina was alone in her improvised kitchen feeding logs to the fire to cook breakfast when her water broke. It wasn't a complete surprise. The night before she had had a dream that a white dove came out of her distended belly and hovered over her before taking flight through the open window. She woke up in pain and, certain that the birth was imminent, she asked Ramón to kill a hen for later. He did, wringing the neck of his best hen, the one they called *colorá* for its brightly colored plumage. But the early morning passed, and the baby had shown no desire to free herself from her mother's body. Until now.

Catalina's eyes watered from the smoke, as they always did, and she was momentarily paralyzed, half blinded and wet, not daring to hold on to anything for fear of burning her hands. She knew excruciating pain would come soon, she remembered it well from her last pregnancy, but that birth had been so different. Just over a year ago, she had been surrounded by her sisters and her mother, in her home, in her own bed; the town's midwife had been staying with them since the day before she was due. That birth had been easy.

This one would not be, and yet Catalina was not afraid. She no longer feared things beyond her control. Ramón was not in the house, but he was just outside. She wiped her eyes with the corner of her apron and decided to go find him.

Just then, a sudden wave of pain hit her with such force that she sank to her knees on the dirt floor of her kitchen. She felt her belly drop and a pressure gather momentum between her legs. No-no-no-no, she repeated out loud, moaning. She held her legs closed and begged her child not to come now. "Not now, please, not now."

She called out to Ramón, but it was a waste of time. She was sure he wouldn't hear her. Catalina looked around in horror. She couldn't possibly bring a child into the world on a dirt floor. Placing her hands on the wall, she forced herself up and, walking between contractions, made her way outside. From where she stood, she could see Ramón, his back to her, milking the black cow they had yet to name.

Before she could call out to him, he turned around as if he could sense her. He took one look at Catalina and ran, dropping the bucket with the milk. The startled cow jerked its massive body away from him and ambled away.

Wordlessly and white as the milk he had just spilled, Ramón lifted Catalina in his arms and took her to their bed. She was moaning, biting down on her pressed lips so she wouldn't scream. Her hands were making fists on the white sheets.

"I'm going to go get the midwife," Ramón mumbled.

"There is no time," Catalina yelled between contractions. "Bring me a towel."

He did as she asked and placed it under her body. Catalina twisted in pain.

"I think I should go anyway," he said, already at the door.

"Please don't leave me alone," she yelled out, but it was too late. Through her agony, Catalina heard the sound of Panchita's hooves piercing the morning stillness as Ramón sped away. Catalina began praying to the Virgin of Candelaria under her breath.

Forty-five minutes later, when Ramón returned with Pepa, as everyone called the midwife, a baby girl lay cold and bloody between Catalina's legs. Catalina hovered over her, eyes clouded by tears, her brow sweaty and her hands trembling. A purple cord, thick like a rope and pulsating with life, still connected the baby's belly to her mother's body.

Catalina looked up, in despair. Her face was soft and drained of blood. Her eyes were dark and feverish. Pepa didn't waste any time. Muttering a prayer in a language Catalina couldn't understand, Pepa cut the cord with a knife she carried in the pocket of an apron, ordered Catalina out of the way, grabbed the baby, turned her upside down and hit her once on the back. The baby coughed and let out a piercing cry that to Catalina seemed like the sweetest sound she had ever heard.

"Oh! Thank God and the virgins and all the saints, oh thank you, thank you, thank you!" Catalina cried and took the baby that Pepa was offering her, like a prize.

She was small but beautiful, with alabaster skin just like Catalina's, and jet-black hair that curled at the ends. Her eyes were tightly closed, and so were her fists, which looked like ripe figs ready to be plucked from a tree. Catalina held her naked baby wrapped in an old blue towel against her chest. She sniffed her hair and breathed in her scent, wet and coppery from the blood and something else, something briny and stormy, like the sea. She closed her eyes and thought of her Carmen. This time she made no promises; she simply held on.

"Take care of her," Pepa said. "This one is a gift from the saints."

All Catalina heard was the word *gift* and she nodded furiously. Yes, a gift. Her precious daughter was a gift. When Pepa went to the kitchen to make a chicken broth for the mother, as was customary, Ramón walked in. She looked at him with such relief and gratitude that he bent down and kissed her deeply and hungrily on the mouth for the first time in their lives.

She felt the center of her body open to him like a morning flower. He sensed her acquiesce and his body tensed with desire, but instead of holding her close after that kiss, he reached for the baby, who was bundled in her mother's arms. Gently, he placed his large and calloused hand on the baby's head, lowered himself to her tiny ear and whispered the words he couldn't have known Catalina was reluctant to promise again: "I will always love you and protect you."

The infant was sleeping, her chest rising fast with each breath as if in a hurry to take in every gulp of air that had been denied in the first harrowing moments after her difficult birth. But Catalina was wide awake and heard every word. She felt her heart expand with love and, leaning her head on his shoulder, she whispered, "Thank you, Ramón." In response, he kissed her again, but this time softly, on her cheek. That was the closest they ever got to a declaration of love, but it was all they ever needed.

She decided to name her daughter Carmen C. Fernández Quintana. Carmen, to honor her dead daughter. The middle initial, *C*, would forever be a secret. To everyone who asked, she explained her devotion to the Virgin of Candelaria, but only she knew that her daughter's middle initial stood for Cruz, the last name she should have had if her father had lived. Fernández was a given. In the eyes of the law and of everyone who knew them, Carmen was always Ramón's daughter.

Ramón remained true to his word until there wasn't anyone to love or protect anymore.

When Carmen was three years old, Ramón came home one day with a letter. Every month or so he still visited the town where he used to live with his aunt to collect his mail and gather news from home and from Cuba. Isolated, as they were, they knew very little about what went on in the country besides fluctuations in the price of sugar and variations in the weather—both topics that directly affected them.

This letter had come addressed to both Juan Cruz and to Ramón Fernández, and it had been mailed to the old yellow house. The post office had saved it for Ramón, as it saved all his mail since he sold the house. The name on the envelope was vaguely familiar but Ramón wasn't sure who had sent it, so he decided not to open it until he got home.

The letter was from Ana, Juan's sister and the childhood friend Catalina remembered as sweet and loyal to her brother and supportive of their forbidden love. Catalina ripped open the envelope with trembling hands. It was the first communication she had received from La Palma, even though it wasn't for her.

August 5 of 1923

Dear brother,
I've written so many letters, and you never write back. I don't know why but I'm convinced my letters don't reach you wherever you are. I know you are alive. My heart tells me you are alive.

Over the years some ill-intentioned people have tried to convince me of how you must be dead, but I think I'd know if you were. I know you told me you were going to follow Catalina to Cuba on the Valbanera, *and I know that ship sank, my dear brother. How you must have suffered when you learned of her death.*

Her family here still mourns for her and for her child and husband. I have checked the list of the dead passengers and your name isn't on the list. I have hope that you are alive and somehow can't or won't get in touch with me. I can't imagine why. Unlike others who can't put words on paper, I know you can. Are you ashamed of something? Afraid? You don't have to tell me, just know that I remain your faithful sister.

I'm writing now to tell you I have a plan. I have saved enough money to go to Cuba and I intend to go to look for you. I will find you.

Much love always from your sister who never forgets you,

Ana

PS: I wish you and Catalina could see her family's farm now. It's as beautiful as it used to be, maybe more. The mulberry trees have grown back.

Catalina pressed Ana's letter to her chest and swayed a little. Her heart began to beat wildly. She heard Ramón ask what the letter said, but she couldn't answer; her heart was like a trapped bird, batting its wings to escape its cage. She feared it would fly away the moment she opened her mouth.

Ramón had seen her go through episodes like this in the past and ran to get her a glass of water. He led her to a chair and fanned her with his hat. Then, he took the letter from her hands and read it. The contents of the letter were not news to him, but they were to Catalina.

For it was then that she learned that she was dead, while Juan might still be alive. And if he was alive, could her daughter be with him?

Hope, Catalina understood in that moment, could be even crueler than grief.

Mara

La Peña, La Palma
August 2019

Julián had moved ahead and was already opening the front door with a key he carried on his keychain. For a moment I envied him. He probably didn't know how lucky he was to be able to carry in his pocket the key to his family's ancestral home.

When we left our own home in Havana, my father had taken the key with him, only to lose it at sea. I can still feel the specific weight of it in my hand, the softness of the leather cord it hung from, its faded copper color and the worn ridges that always fit perfectly in our front door. Of all the keys I've known, in all the houses and apartments I've either rented or owned, I've never had a key like that—one that didn't need a "trick," that wasn't temperamental or capricious, that simply did the one job it was created to do and did it efficiently, day after day, year after year. I have yearned for that key on nights when I've wondered exactly where my place was in the world. After seventeen moves in forty years of exile, where was home?

Julián waited for me at the door, but he had the good sense not to rush me. I decided not to go in just yet. The house was old, no doubt about that, but it was also clear that a century ago, it had been a good house, perhaps even a great one. It still was.

The walls were thick and made of stone. The front door, a slab of dark wood, was rotting at the bottom, but someone had recently painted it in a shade of blue that was my mother's favorite: azure. Two windows stood like sentinels on each side of the door. As I looked, Julián opened one. White linen curtains fluttered in the breeze. I could see the darkness inside and was drawn to it. I imagined it would be cool and peaceful, as the house where my mother grew up used to be even on the hottest days of my Cuban summers. There was a garden of wildflowers in front, where white and black pigeons assembled expectantly. I understood why when I saw Julián dropping breadcrumbs from a window.

I kept walking in a circle around the house, not really daring to go in yet. I found a washing sink made of smooth stone under a myrtle tree, and a clothesline tied from that tree to a pole. A dry fountain that seemed to have been used to irrigate the garden before modern plumbing stood near the kitchen, next to a gate leading to a corral where, I'm sure, animals used to be kept. A low wall made of rough stones surrounded the entire perimeter of the land, and five old crosses were crowded in a corner under some bushes. I leaned over to straighten one that had fallen. I wondered what they represented. A pet cemetery?

It was quiet here. A few noises came from inside as Julián moved about, opening windows and, it seemed, straightening furniture. A field of lush trees was behind the house, extending all the way to a large boulder, where, suddenly, the view ended. There was no way to see anything else beyond that massive rock. The only way to look was up. I could imagine how the stars must look from here at night with no pollution and, seemingly, no other houses around, though I thought I saw a small cottage not too far from the road on our way in. It looked very old and abandoned. Further, to my left, there was a pine forest. I had never seen pines as formidable as these.

Julián had opened a back door and I finally went in. A musty scent, typical of uninhabited houses, assaulted my nose, but it was quickly mitigated by the smell of coffee Julián was brewing on a stand-alone ancient-looking stove with elegant, curved legs. The stove was the only old appliance in the kitchen. The floor, too, was old, made of polished stones. The rest had been updated not too long ago. There was a gleaming refrigerator and a built-in microwave, and the cabinets and the counter were solid blond wood. Throughout the room were touches of green in various shades, like the leaves of the trees outside the window. It was clear that a serious cook used this space.

Julián looked pensive, as always.

"What are you thinking?" he asked me, without looking up.

"Funny you should ask," I said. "That's what I was just going to ask you."

He smiled a little.

"I was thinking this is all very strange," he said. "I still can't believe that Catalina didn't go down in that ship. It makes no sense. You've seen the picture. They boarded that ship."

I nodded, not knowing what to say. I had so many conflicted emotions. On one hand, I desperately wanted to know the real story of my great-grandmother. On the other hand, I felt protective of her. If she had a secret, who was I to try to expose it? But then, why not? It had been so long. Who could it possibly hurt? My mother, my son, and myself were, after all, her only real descendants. The other branches of the family knew exactly where they came from.

My mother and I had been previously exiled from family, country, and home. Now, it seemed, we were also exiled by secrets. If we could unearth some of this history, perhaps we could find a part of what we had lost along the way.

But I didn't say any of that to Julián.

Instead, I pointed at the stove and said, "I can't believe that old thing still works."

"I take good care of it," Julián said, wiping a spot of coffee from its clean black surface. "I learned to cook here, with Grandma Lucía."

Julián handed me the coffee in a white IKEA mug that somehow seemed to fit well in this kitchen. He went on to tell me how, as a boy, he and his brothers used to spend summers here with their grandmother, who lived in the house until her death. That came as a surprise. I assumed the house had stood empty for a century, as if Catalina's leaving had robbed it of its soul. But why would that be the case?

"Until the day she died, Grandma Lucía held out hope that Catalina would one day return," Julián said, once again reading my thoughts. "She always insisted on leaving the outside light on, so Catalina could find her way back."

Since there wasn't a body or a burial, she never believed her sister was truly dead.

"Now we know she was right," he said.

Julián stopped then and looked me in the eye.

"Because now I'm here," I said, and he nodded.

I thought about how cruel it was that Lucía didn't get her wish. If only my mother had asked for the birth certificate a few years earlier, I probably would have met her during one of our summer vacations. No, it wouldn't have been Catalina, but at least Lucía would have gotten some closure. An awkward silence descended on the kitchen like a mantle and Julián got up to get more coffee.

"What are those trees behind the house?" I asked as Julián refilled my mug.

"Those are mulberry trees. They used to run—"

"The mulberry trees have grown back," I interrupted him.

"What?"

"Never mind," I said, already pulling the phone from my pocket. "I have to make a call."

I walked outside to call my mother, but the line was busy. My mother refuses to get call waiting on her landline and she never picks up her cell phone. Frustrated, I went back in, but the kitchen was empty.

"Julián!" I called out, somewhat frantically. For a moment I felt as if I had dreamt the whole thing.

"Over here!" he yelled from somewhere above my head.

I followed his voice upstairs. The dark wooden steps creaked as I climbed, and I had to watch my head. There was no doubt that a century ago people used to be shorter.

"When was this house built?"

"We couldn't find any records," Julián answered, coming out of a room, "but possibly in 1888, when Inés María and José Angel married. They were the parents of the three girls. Here's their picture, look," he said, pointing to several pictures hanging on the walls of the hallway that led to the three bedrooms. There was a wedding picture, yellowing but intact, of Inés María and José Angel, as well as one picture of the girls together. There was another picture of Catalina with Antonio on their wedding day.

The rooms were bare, except for an iron bed in two of them. The larger room had a double bed, with a carved wooden headboard. The bed was perfectly made with white sheets, a pillow, and a clean white duvet.

"I stay here sometimes," Julián said, adding, "alone" as an afterthought or a clarification.

At the end of the hallway, there were dozens of marks on a wall, reminding me of the way I used to mark my son's growth every year on his birthday. Before I could ask, Julián explained the marks belonged to each grandchild. Lucía measured every one of her twenty grandchildren, but most of her notations next to the marks had faded with time and now no one knew what mark belonged to whom. The house had been painted several times since they were all kids, but Julián was too sentimental to paint over the marks, so they stayed. I asked Julián to pose in front of them and I took a picture, but it was too dark, and it seemed a bad idea anyway.

Going downstairs, I saw the part of the house I had overlooked on my way to find Julián. A small space with comfortable armchairs centered around the fireplace leading to a larger room, a dining room next to the kitchen. There was another room that Julián called the sewing room because that's what Lucía called it. In one corner, I found a strange wooden contraption. It looked like a handloom for weaving. That's what it was, Julián said. His grandmother had told him that the family had once kept silkworms in a shack outside the house until a fire, and, later, changing times, ended their lucrative business. Worms? I chuckled.

"What's so funny?" Julián asked. But I couldn't explain to him the significance of that word in my life. I caressed the worn wood of the loom, choosing to think of my great-grandmother and her mother in this room, spending evenings by a fire while weaving silk.

"Nothing," I said, and walked toward the books and family pictures on the shelves. I felt I could spend hours here decoding faces, stories, making connections, and trying to understand this large family I had inherited.

The furniture in the living room was not as old as I had hoped it would be. It looked to be mid-century, but Julián pointed to a center table. He said it was French, but it had come from Cuba from a relative. I wasn't so sure that the table was French, but then again I'm no expert on furniture. What was important was they treasured the piece because it had occupied the same spot for more than a century. And then he showed me another piece of furniture that had already caught my eye. It was like an old wooden radio atop a locked box. But instead of knobs for dials it had binoculars to look through.

"What's this?" I said, leaning over to look through the visor.

I gasped in delight. On the other side, there was a perfectly preserved photo of three girls dressed in identical light-colored dresses with pleated skirts, and wide silk ribbons holding manes of curls back.

The girls were holding the same pose, legs crossed, their arms around each other, their faces open and their chins defiantly thrust up toward the camera.

"They are Catalina, Simona, and Lucía," Julián said.

In that picture, which Julián said Lucía always kept there because it was her favorite, the girls must have been six, five, and three. Julián said the photo box, too, had come from France. His grandfather had bought it as a gift for his wife Lucía on a wedding anniversary. The pictures were preserved inside a glass framed in wood. There was no way to take the picture out without damaging it, so this was, in fact, the only "family album" they had, and it was treasured. Preserved like that, those pictures could last forever. It was, in a way, an earlier version of the cloud.

I was overcome by emotions and torn between the desire to record everything I was seeing and simply allowing myself to be in the moment. Be present, I told myself. I was aware this experience was special and magical, and that history was unfolding before my eyes in a way that no book or newspaper story could ever reveal.

"I want to show you something else," Julián said. "I think you'll find it interesting."

He took me by the hand and walked me through the living room, the kitchen, and out the back door to the mulberry field. I didn't protest, because it was a sweet gesture, warm and friendly, not sexual, or intrusive.

We trudged through the stony, weedy terrain until we reached that massive rock I had seen earlier. He let go of my hand and began examining the rock closely, as if he were an archaeologist, his hands feeling along the contours of that imposing ancient monolith as if searching for a button or a lever that would lead to a secret passage.

"What are you looking for?"

"You'll see," he said. "It's a love story."

Oh, he had me there. Julián was a very smart man after all.

"Here, I found it. Look!"

He pointed to a carving on the rock, barely visible. I could make out a *C*, but Julián insisted that the letter *C* wasn't alone. There was a *J* before, but so close to it, it almost seemed like a mirror image of the *C*. Once he explained it, I could see it: *JC*. "What does it mean?"

"Remember I told you there was a boy here who was very much in love with Catalina? Grandma Lucía told us he carved both names, or maybe just his initials on this rock for her, for Catalina."

"What was his name again?'

"Juan. Juan Cruz Cruz," Julián said with a laugh, "perhaps the most common name on the islands."

That was true. I had heard the name Cruz many times since I had first landed in Tenerife a few weeks earlier. Some people, like this Juan obviously did, even had the same last names from both sides of the family: Cruz Cruz. It was almost as confusing as the names of the islands and their capitals.

"Was she in love with him?"

"I don't know," Julián said after a pause, cocking his head. "I don't think we ever asked Grandma Lucía that question. We only knew of his love for Catalina."

"And what happened to him?"

Not only had he disappeared around the time Catalina left for Cuba, as Julián had already told me, but also, a few years after the tragedy of the ship, Juan's sister had gone to Cuba to look for him, and no one had heard from her since.

"Did the Cruz family by any chance live in that cottage that was on the way here, on the road?" I asked, though, for some reason I couldn't explain even to myself, I already knew the answer to my own question.

"Yes!" Julián exclaimed. "I'm surprised you even noticed. Most people don't. Farmers use it now and then to rest or get some shade when they are working here. That family was very poor. The father abandoned them, and the oldest son and the mother died of the flu epidemic around 1918 or later."

"Really?"

"That's the story Grandma Lucía told us, anyway. Who knows, right? It was so long ago."

"What was the sister's name?" I asked, not sure why.

"What sister?"

"The sister who went to Cuba after Juan."

"Oh, I think it was Ana, but I'm not sure."

On the way back to the house, I let Julián walk ahead. I wanted to be alone to call my mother again. This time, she picked up on the first ring, and tried to do what she always does: make me feel guilty for not calling her every day. But I didn't let her. Instead, I took over the conversation and told her what I'd learned about the *Valbanera* and about meeting all the cousins, ending with the mulberry trees in the back. When I finished my mother was quiet for a moment.

"Say something," I commanded, because I was beginning to worry. It's not like her not to have a ready answer to everything.

"I'm in shock, to tell you the truth," she muttered.

Though she had always known her grandmother had arrived in Cuba on a ship, she had never known any more than that, and never thought to ask.

"It was just something people didn't do in those days," my mother said. "There was always too much that needed to be done, and memories just got in the way."

But the fact that her grandmother might have survived a shipwreck and the reality that she had been married to another man before she left for Cuba were simply too outrageous for my mother to comprehend. The people in her world lived orderly lives; they didn't reinvent themselves or cut ties with their families just because they switched countries.

I remembered how, when we arrived in the US bearing nothing, not even birth certificates or any other official identification, immigration officials asked us our names. Before we could answer, a man who spoke Spanish flawlessly told us we didn't even have to give our real names, just any name. "You are starting a new life," he stated. "You get to be whoever you want to be here." My father gazed first at the man, then at us, and then back at the man and told him our full names, spelling them out for him, just in case he didn't know how.

"We are keeping our names," he told the man. "That's all we have. Our names and our memories."

Catalina had apparently not felt the same way. Though she kept her name, she seemed to have erased her memories, or, at the very least, her family, and she had changed her daughter's last name.

"I just can't believe that the person whose birth certificate you found can be the same person, because I know my mother was born in Cuba," my mother insisted. "There is only one Carmen Fernández Quintana, and that's my mother, born in Sabanilla, in the old province of Las Villas, in the same place, and the same bed where I was born."

In fact, my mother went on, she had been told her mother's birth story multiple times, how she almost died, how a quick-thinking midwife saved her life, how their favorite hen was sacrificed to make a broth. That story, my mother insisted on the phone, couldn't possibly be a lie.

"I used to have my mother's birth certificate, but it was left behind with everything else, so I don't know. I don't understand," she said, finally pausing for breath. Still, there was a measure of uncertainty in her tone. I kept the phone pressed to my ear, my fingers aching but reluctant to let her go. I could sense she was wrestling with her memories, questioning her own identity and that of her mother. I felt sad for her and a little protective. The call wasn't going the way I had hoped. I had wanted to give her the good news of the extended family I had encountered here. Instead, I had somehow converted that happy ending into an unsettling story of confused identities.

Then I remembered the love story. Certain she would at least find it appealing, I told her about Juan Cruz and his love for Catalina.

"That was the name on the envelope!" my mother interrupted me.

"What envelope?" I asked, confused.

"Remember I told you I had found a letter?"

"Yes, of course, the letter where the mulberry trees were mentioned."

"It was addressed to my grandfather Ramón and to a Juan Cruz. I remember because I had never heard that name before," my mother said.

"Really? Why would your grandmother have a letter addressed to Juan Cruz in Cuba if he lived here in La Palma?"

"I thought you said he followed her," my mother said sensibly.

"True," I said, more confused than ever.

Julián had started to close the windows when I reached the house, and I helped him finish. The sun was hiding right behind that huge rock in the mulberry field. The rock's edges seemed to shimmer in the late afternoon sky, and the leaves of the trees undulated like waves under a golden light. I closed the window and locked it with a metal rod, the old-fashioned way. When I turned around to face him, I said the first thing that came to my mind.

"I've made a decision. Catalina's story is no longer in this house. It's in Cuba, and I'm going there to try to find it."

Part III

Had the pain not been so precise
I would have asked to which of my sorrows should I yield.
—Hisham Matar, *The Return: Fathers, Sons,*
and the Land in Between (2016)

Catalina

Sabanilla, Las Villas
1924

Satiated, Ramón released her and turned on his side to sleep. In the darkness, Catalina groped in the sheets for her nightgown, then sat up and slipped it on. Ramón grabbed her arm and muttered something she couldn't understand.

"I'm just going to get some water," she said. He let go and grunted his assent.

He was asleep already. For her, however, sleep was elusive. So was pleasure. Ramón desired her in a way that to her seemed unnatural. No matter how tired he was, he reached for her every night they were together, as if afraid she would leave, as if afraid she had already left, and he was intent on bringing her soul back to her body one thrust and one kiss at a time. She let him, and sometimes, like tonight, she feigned that she was present and that he was pleasuring her, though she wasn't there. She was never there.

For years, she felt her soul had remained somewhere at sea, trying to reach her, but failing every time. No amount of love or fierce lovemaking could make Catalina forgive herself. She was hobbled by guilt and lost love but rescued from the abyss of her own mind night after night by a man who, like her father, never gave up.

In the darkness, Catalina made her way to the kitchen, where she found the matches and lit a kerosene lamp. It was raining outside. And rain always made her feel anxious. She checked on her daughter, sleeping peacefully in her own bed. Then she went through the entire house room by room looking for leaks. She found one and placed a bucket under it. The toc-toc of the drops interrupted the silence of the night until gradually the bucket began to fill up and the sound faded.

During the past five years, Catalina had grown to love Ramón, although not the way she had once loved Juan. That had been an immature and reckless passion that had almost destroyed her. What she felt for Ramón was not like that at all. She couldn't compare him to Antonio either, because she had never had any feelings for Antonio; she had simply allowed him to love her, and he had been her first lover. But Ramón was something else. Ramón was her partner, her husband, her guide in this new country, a true father to Carmen and, she hoped, the father of other children they would one day have. Ramón was everything to her.

She wasn't sure how that had happened. Catalina couldn't recall Ramón ever declaring his love for her, and she was certain she had never told him she loved him either, but she remembered in detail the moment she knew theirs would be an enduring love.

It happened shortly after Carmen was born. The baby, who fed regularly and slept most of the day, began wailing every evening after dinner. The cries of her daughter, so similar to those of the baby she abandoned to the sea, repelled her. Instead of tending to her daughter's needs, as she forced herself to do every day, this one time, Catalina covered her ears, looked at Ramón pleadingly and ran from the house so she wouldn't have to hear what, to her mind, sounded like a cry for help from her lost child.

Ramón thought of stopping her but didn't. Instead, he took the disconsolate baby, cradled her in his arms and let her suck on his pinkie until she settled herself back to sleep, hiding her tiny face in the nook of his arm. Holding her, he reached the window and searched for Catalina in the darkness. He couldn't see her, but he heard her quiet sobs and tears came to his own eyes before he walked back to their bedroom.

When Catalina returned to the house about thirty minutes later, all was quiet. She tiptoed into the room holding a lamp and found the baby resting on top of Ramón's naked chest, sucking on her thumb, content with the cushion of love her father was providing. Ramón was awake and, when their eyes met, she took his hand in hers and kissed it. That night, the three slept together in a loving embrace—Carmen between them, keeping them apart but also pulling them together.

Their romance had flourished after that.

Catalina returned to the kitchen and dipped the tin cup inside the *tinajón* where the drinking water from the well was kept cool and clean in a clay pot. She poured the water in a mug and drank hurriedly, rivulets of water running down the corners of her mouth and coming to rest as fresh blossoms on her white nightgown.

She licked her lips dry and looked around the open kitchen. On the dining room table there was a pile of corn. Tomorrow, in a few hours, she was planning to shuck the corn, a tedious task she performed at least once a week because corn had become a staple of their diet, and Ramón enjoyed the fritters she had learned to make with his aunt. Instead of returning to bed, Catalina sat on a *taburete*, put a pail between her feet, and gathered her gown above her knees. By the light of the lantern, she removed the husks along with the silky threads that so stubbornly clung to the grains. Enough, she thought to herself. In the morning, she would shell the kernels, grind them, and turn them into corn grits.

After wiping away the debris from the table, she swept the dirt floor with a new broom Ramón had just made from palm fronds. Catalina sighed, suddenly, feeling very tired. But what was the point of going to bed now?

* * *

Catalina's life took an unexpected turn the day she learned she had a gift for healing. It happened accidentally, after a neighbor named Teresa knocked at her door on Catalina's twenty-fourth birthday and complained of an *empacho.*

"Do you know of a remedy for that?" Teresa asked, her face twisted in agony. "I've tried everything I know to do."

Catalina looked around her improvised apothecary. There were tinctures for headaches, ingrown nails, stuffy noses, lice, and parasites, but she didn't see anything that would help stomach pain. And yet, she felt the need to tend to this woman, as if by helping her, she would be helping herself. She remembered how her grandmother Elena had cured all her childhood ailments with a prayer to the saint after which she had been named: Saint Catalina of Siena.

"Why don't you lie down?" Catalina asked Teresa, untying her dirty apron, and leading her to a bedroom. "I may be able to help."

Teresa, who could hardly speak from the pain, did as Catalina asked and lifted her shirt, showing her distended abdomen.

"I'll be right back," Catalina said, and went back to the kitchen. She took a tub of pork fat, a candle, and matches and returned to the bedroom. Teresa was holding on to the sheets with closed fists.

Catalina lit the candle, dipped her hands in the fat, and rubbed her palms until they were warm and sleek. Placing them on the woman's pale stomach, she began to mutter the words she remembered doña Elena reciting in times of trouble.

My power hasn't weakened, nor can it be weakened, because my power comes from the almighty. I can, I want, I know how to help those who need me. I can, I want, I know. I'm powerful yet humble. I implore you to guide my hands so that I can do your work. I can, I want, I know.

Keeping her eyes closed and her focus on her hands, Catalina began gently rubbing the woman's skin. Teresa moaned in pain, but Catalina continued, pressing more firmly and repeating the words in a louder voice. She wasn't really thinking anymore; she tried to allow the prayer to move through her body and manifest its miracle through her hands.

Wanting to remedy so many ailments, God has given us a bridge. Cross the bridge, Teresa, so you don't drown in the river or the tempestuous sea that is our tenebrous life.

"Stop!" Teresa yelled before she twisted her body off the bed and ran to the open window. Leaning over the railing, she threw up.

When she had finished and sat back down on the bed, Catalina was waiting with a towel and a glass of water.

"Thank you, my dear friend," Teresa said, pulling her blouse down over her stomach. "I feel better now."

But Catalina told her to stay in the bed for as long as she wanted and went to make an infusion of cloves and oregano leaves, plucked from her herb garden. When she delivered the steaming mug a few minutes later, Teresa was asleep, her knees folded almost to her chest, and snoring gently. Catalina left the tea on the night table, tiptoed away, and went to tend to Carmen, who from the doorway had been silently witnessing her mother's transformation into a healer. Three hours later, Teresa, a mother of six, restored from the nap and grateful for the cure, hugged Catalina and proclaimed that she had the "gift."

Teresa visited often and brought others with her, including her oldest daughter who had painful menses. For that, Catalina used a mixture of chamomile and ginger. For muscle pains and spasms, she used rue and lavender. To prevent colds from settling into the lungs, she used a tincture of oregano and honey. The more combinations she tried, the stronger she felt. Her herb garden flourished, and so did she. It seemed that a dark cloud was lifting away from her at last.

While Ramón worked miles away from home during the sugar harvest from June to December, Catalina gradually became known as the town's healer. She could cure pains—especially stomachaches—and she could rescue even those afflicted with the evil eye. With an overturned glass of water on top of a feverish head, she took care of heatstroke. A special prayer made skin rashes disappear, and a glass of water blessed by her and placed under the bed kept nightmares and insomnia away. For the evil eye she used a prayer that no one ever heard.

But those cures often reduced her to tears, for it seemed as if she took on herself all the afflictions of those who had been wished ill. Her crying left her spent and frightened Carmen, who hung on to her as if by sheer force of will she could help her mother return to her own self—the doting, though mostly unsmiling, mother she so loved. On those occasions, only Carmen's own tears saved Catalina from the darkness.

Though Catalina wouldn't accept payment, most people paid her what they could. They brought her chickens, a piglet, a sack of rice, or a quintal of beans from their fields; once, someone brought her a chocolate-colored mule that Carmen quickly claimed for herself, calling it Nieve for the white of its legs.

Sometimes Catalina wondered what her mother and sisters would say if they could see her now. She was sure her mother would have been appalled at the harshness of her environment but pleased she had found her calling. Often when she bent down to do work her mother and even her grandmother would have labeled "a man's job," Catalina would break into a faint smile. This, she was sure, was not what her father had in mind when he assured her life in Cuba would be better for her.

There was always so much to do, and there were so many inconveniences to overcome: mosquitoes, rain, mud, unbearable heat, sudden thunderstorms, and torrential summer rains.

In the mornings, when the sun was not yet shining over the hills that surrounded her home, she would feed the chickens, moving her arm in a semicircular motion, spreading a shower of corn kernels and stale breadcrumbs on the ground outside her kitchen door. Then she'd turn over a pail and sit down to milk the cow so that she could serve her daughter fresh milk in bed. She'd then go back outside to feed the pigs scraps of food from the evening's leftovers and move the cows and the goats to a fresher patch of grass, pulling on a rope that dangled from their necks. After breakfast, she would begin preparing for the day's meals, often pulling potatoes and yams from the dirt and slaughtering chickens or goats by herself. Before lunch, she weeded the garden with Carmen by her side. Carmen's small hands were ideal for plucking smaller leaves, and she worked with pride and delicacy, just like Catalina had done when she was a child and was in charge of feeding the silkworms.

The afternoons were for those who came to her door asking for help, as word spread of her miraculous hands and of her talent with herbs. If she had no visitors, she'd observe Carmen playing in the garden or trapping butterflies with a glass jar, while she worked on her sewing or embroidery. She was only idle in the evenings, after dinner and cleaning the kitchen, when she'd sit by the light of a lamp with Carmen curled on her lap and tell her stories. The more fantastic, the better.

It was a hard life, but she welcomed the punishment. Her back ached in a way that balanced her heartache. Her legs were swollen and bore the scars of mosquito bites, animal scratches, and mishaps from the sharp fence of the *potrero*, where the cattle were kept, and her hands had become calloused and strong from all the work. All of it she accepted as a blessing. Her expanding body would tolerate it all. She felt strong and powerful.

There was something else, too: she had a secret that was starting to illuminate her days like the soft glow of a candle in the darkness. She wanted to keep that warmth and light all to herself for as long as she could before telling Ramón.

All she asked was that in this new life she had created, her Carmen would be spared.

Mara

Sabanilla, Cuba
October 2019

I HAD NEVER SEEN HAVANA from above. I had seen many other cities countless times, especially New York, but I still felt a jolt of excitement every time the contours of a place I loved began to appear in the plane window, growing closer and closer as we approached landing until it disappeared and all that was left was the runway and, depending on where I was, a fence, trees, distant mountains, or something so stripped of a distinct character that the actual landing was always a bit of a letdown.

But not this time. I should have known that everything about this trip, my first since I had left some forty years before, would be different. From above, Cuba looked like a patchwork quilt of green and brown surrounded by different shades of blue. But once we landed, I felt a pleasant tug inside my body as if everything was being realigned in a more comfortable way. And it seemed I wasn't the only one. The passengers, mostly Cubans traveling from Spain to visit relatives on the island, jumped from their seats, ignoring the pleas of the flight attendants, and applauded in jubilation—a tradition I normally despised, but this time made me smile. Yes, I understood the joy. They weren't applauding the pilot for a smooth landing. They were applauding themselves. We were home. My joy, though, was short-lived.

The moment I left the plane, all the complexities of Cuba hit me with great force. The airport was disorganized and understaffed. The immigration officer inspecting my passport and visa took forever to let me in, wanting to verify that I was there as a private citizen and not as a reporter. Also, he wanted to make sure I understood that, even if I traveled with my US passport, I was still a Cuban citizen in their eyes and always would be. In other words, if anything happened to me in Cuba, the US government would have no jurisdiction.

I had returned to the mouth of the wolf.

This was the main reason I hadn't told my mother I was going to Cuba. I wanted to spare her the worries and spare myself the guilt. Cuba was the one place I knew that would have upset my father to know I had visited. He never explicitly banned me from going to Cuba, because he understood I had to go where the story was. As it happened, reporting had never taken me to the island of my birth. But my family finally had. I was here on a personal quest, and I hoped that, were he still alive, my father would have acknowledged that this was even more important than work.

Returning to Cuba had not been an easy task. Leaving Julián, the cousins, but, especially, the house in La Peña behind, had been wrenching, more than I could ever have imagined. I went back to the house with Julián every day for a week, the time I thought I needed to report the story I had promised the editor in New York, and then I flew back to Santander, to my life and routines while applying for a visa and securing a Cuban passport, as all Cuban-born citizens must do, even if they are citizens, as I am, of other countries. It took nearly two months, more than enough time to do laundry, write, and file my travel piece, get cash, since US credit cards are not accepted in Cuba, and recharge my batteries. I knew my stay in Cuba would be emotionally draining, so I needed to prepare. I ate well, slept deeply and long, and tried unsuccessfully to put all thoughts of Catalina and the *Valbanera* out of my mind. But that now seemed like a lifetime ago. That was in Spain. This was Cuba.

By the time I was behind the wheel of my rental car and headed for the room I had rented in a mansion in Miramar, I was angry and having a mental conversation with my father, wherever he was, thanking him for getting us out of Cuba so many years ago. I wish I had thanked him in person, so that he had understood how much I appreciated his foresight and sacrifices.

It was hard to focus on the driving when my roving eyes were trying to capture every detail of a city I never really knew. I missed a turn at *Plaza de la Revolución* and kept driving straight. I was lost but didn't care. I was so eager to see everything, to understand the country I had left behind. While I lived in Cuba, I was too young to venture on my own outside my neighborhood and my parents were very protective of me. Now, at fifty-five and with plenty of experience as a traveler in my arsenal, I was looking at this city with fresh eyes. It was true that Havana was a well-designed city with a plethora of architectural styles, not just arches and porticos as so many pictures have depicted it. In just a few blocks, there were Art Deco and Art Nouveau jewels standing next to nondescript mid-century bungalows or imposing neoclassical buildings.

Some of the houses were so well kept and in such an array of pastel colors they looked like *petits fours* trapped under glass in a French bakery. But others, the majority, were but ruins of their former selves. Sixty years of inefficiency had turned this grand city into a pile of rubble. Patches of green broke through the façade of formerly beautiful homes. Cracks ran down many walls like dry rivers, and roofs had caved in in so many places that certain blocks looked like a mouth with rotten teeth. Abandoned dogs roamed the streets and there were mounds of dog excrement everywhere.

People didn't fare much better than the streets. Some young students in uniform chased each other as kids do everywhere near the famed seawall, *Malecón*, but others I saw that night were visibly burdened by life. Men and women wearing tattered shoes and mismatched clothes walked with hunched shoulders and sour faces. It seemed they had been squashed by the travails of daily life. Most—men and women—carried bags in their hands as if hoping to encounter something along the way to sell or to eat. Anything. Others, very young women and men, were selling themselves, languorously reclining against walls and wearing clothes that would not have required a lot of effort to pull down or up for a hasty encounter.

Stopping at a light, I saw an old man riding a bicycle with what looked like a wedding cake in one hand while the other held the handlebar. I swerved to stay as far away from him as possible. At the mouth of Miramar, before entering the tunnel that would deliver me to the neighborhood where I would be staying, there was a man sitting on a patch of grass, looking lost. It would have been a perfectly normal sight if it weren't for the stuffed bags that he kept near him, protectively.

I looked away in frustration. I knew what I'd find upon my return to Cuba, or, rather, I thought I did. What I was encountering, though, was cataclysmic, as if a bomb had razed the city, leaving behind a dazed and emaciated population. I batted away my tears when I realized I was probably nearing the house. I had memorized the instructions I had received via email when I made the arrangements through Airbnb from Santander. Fingers crossed, the room would be as clean and beautiful as it looked in my laptop. I needed a refuge to escape the black hole Havana had become. No amount of research or emotional work could have buttressed me against what I was seeing. I almost preferred it, though. The horror show on the other side of the car's windshield was distracting me from the thoughts that had invaded my waking hours and even my dreams since I had arrived in La Palma more than two months ago.

There was practically no traffic in Havana, and I arrived at the house without complications. The room I had rented faced the ocean. It wasn't a surprise, but it was a coincidence. I hadn't been looking to continue my "exposure therapy" in Cuba. I figured there was no need to add a phobia to the emotions of a return after so many years, but when the owner told me, "You are in luck. The only bedroom I have left is the one with the best view," I felt it was destiny and I took it.

The owner—his name was Alberto, but called himself "Al," as in "Al Pacino," he clarified in Spanish—talked nonstop as he showed me his beautiful home. It was a typical Miramar mansion built in the 1940s, a period of great architectural creativity in Cuba. Al said he had inherited his house from his mother who had received it as a gift from Celia Sánchez, one of the founders of the movement that led to the triumph of the Cuban revolution and long rumored to be Fidel Castro's paramour. I didn't ask Al how exactly his mother had compromised her soul to receive the gift of such a house. It seemed imprudent as I only planned to stay there two nights.

The house was unusual in that most of the great houses of Miramar were on Fifth Avenue, not on First, as Al's was, backing into the sea. The outside walls were painted a blush pink with white trims around the windows and near the roof, as pretty and ornamented as if it were a layered pastry topped by merengue. It had six bedrooms—four upstairs and two downstairs—and seven bathrooms. The floors were fitted throughout with handmade concrete tiles now very much in vogue but so typical of Cuba that I never noticed them when they were under my own feet. But I did now. The tiles here were square and matte with light blue arabesques, and they were simply stunning. High ceilings with shiny hanging lamps that sparkled like diamond tears complemented the look. Al said his cousin was an architect, as if explaining why his house was so pristine while the rest of the country was crumbling.

I didn't believe a word he said that night or ever, but it didn't matter. Al clearly lived in an alternative reality, and I was digging for mine. In that way, we were both lost to the present. I never saw any of the other guests, and, later, much later, as I tried to piece together the details of my stay in Cuba, I sometimes wondered if Al and his house had been real after all.

The night I arrived, I was enchanted but exhausted. Normally I would have appreciated a tour with a lengthy explanation of each nook and crevice. I love old houses and I'm always ready to listen to a good story, but I was tired and overwhelmed and the roar of the ocean in the darkness of the backyard had me on edge. My head hurt, and all I wanted was a shower and a glass of wine, alone, with my feet up or soaking in Epsom salt. I could sense the beginning of my back pain, the tingling sensation I always felt on my upper neck, right at my hairline. My hands went automatically to my neck and held it, creating a flesh and blood scaffolding around my head. Al noticed.

"What's the matter?" he asked.

"Oh, nothing, just a pain I get," I said.

Al thought for a moment, looked me up and down for the first time and came close to my face, closer than I was comfortable with. Finally, he pulled back and said my problem was most likely Yemayá, the deity that represents the sea in Afro-Cuban religion.

"You must have done something to anger her," he said, arching an eyebrow that had been fastidiously plucked.

I laughed and said, "No, it's probably age."

Nonetheless, he approached again.

"May I?" he asked, and before I could answer, he had placed a cold hand on my forehead and another on my neck, right over my hand. His hand was soft and smelled of fried plantains; his breath smelled of black beans. He must have just finished eating. He whispered a prayer that I couldn't follow, but I know it ended with "cleanse me, nurture me, sustain me." His words seemed harmless enough, so I didn't object. That and a glass of wine ought to do it.

"You must have angered her," he repeated.

"Me? I doubt it. If anything, I should be angry at her," I said, thinking of my fear of the sea, my mother's own fears, and Catalina's fate.

But once finally alone, before I went to sleep, I thought of my son Dylan, and I remembered that it had been almost three weeks since we spoke last, and just in case Yemayá could possibly be angry with me, I got on my knees and prayed, something I hadn't done in many years. For good measure, I ended with the words I remembered from Al, "cleanse me, nurture me, sustain me."

In the morning, the sea looked calm and glorious from my open window. Gone was the roar I had heard in the evening. Under the morning sun, the water shimmered like endless yards of silver *lamé*. My neck no longer hurt, and my body felt strong and alert, just as I had felt in the airplane the minute we landed, ready to tackle the mission that had, at last, brought me home: unraveling the life story of Catalina, a woman who was only real because my mother existed, because I did, too. For everyone but my mother, Catalina was nothing but a distant memory, or a ghost.

I made my way to the pool, in the back garden, where Al had promised breakfast would be waiting until 11. It was 10 a.m. I had overslept, but I wish I could say I had had a restful night. For part of the night, I had been plagued by nightmares, most of which I didn't remember, but one stood out so vividly that I wrote it down when I awoke.

Once again I dreamed I was searching for my daughter, a little girl. I was in a tunnel, or a hallway. I couldn't tell, but it was dark, and I was running. I finally found her, but she was stuck in a hole in the wall. Her legs were dangling out and the rest of the body, which I couldn't see, was on the other side of the wall. I began pulling her toward me, and the little girl started to scream. Someone was pulling from the other side. The harder I pulled, the harder someone whom I couldn't see pulled in the other direction. Finally, I stopped, aware that, if I didn't, we were going to kill her. The pain of letting her go was so deep, so devastating, that it woke me up. I sat up in bed, crying for a long time.

On nights like these, I really missed my husband. If he had been with me last night, he would have taken me in his arms and would have soothed me back to sleep. It's a fallacy that we don't need people in our lives to be complete. We can love ourselves, and I do, but I can't wrap my arms around myself when I'm shaking with fear.

Breakfast was waiting for me on a magnificent patio that led to a pool and, beyond, the ocean. I caught a whiff of the rose garden to my left as I made my way to a wrought iron table festooned with a white tablecloth. Al himself served the healthy breakfast he promised: green juice, eggs, ham, a scrumptious brioche, and tropical fruits. With all the scarcities and limitations in Cuba, I couldn't imagine where he got his bounty, and I didn't ask. He probably would have said he had a cousin who was a chef. Also, the coffee was excellent. I wondered where . . . No, I wasn't going there. Just enjoy it, I told myself. The whole time I was facing the house, with my back to the water.

My phone dinged with a text message, and, hopeful that it would be Dylan, I quickly picked it up. It was Dylan! He had sent me the briefest text possible, one that immediately brought a smile to my face and peace to my soul. He sent me a number one. In our mother-son shorthand, developed when I started to trust him to go out alone in New York City when he was in middle school, it meant that all was well, but he couldn't talk. Though I wasn't a believer, at that moment I chose to believe Dylan's message had been Yemayá's gift to me, a peace offering of sorts. That's all I needed.

After breakfast, I got in the car and went to visit my old neighborhood of Santos Suárez, where I had lived with my parents in a one-bedroom apartment for fifteen years until I left Cuba. I had no idea who was there now, but I was hoping they'd let me go in to see it. I yearned to touch those walls and stand on the balcony where I'd spent a good portion of my childhood dreaming of being somewhere else.

I got lost several times in the narrow one-way streets of Havana before I finally got to the cul-de-sac where I grew up. I almost didn't recognize it. The asphalt in some side streets had broken apart like a jagged flesh wound, releasing clouds of dust that made the air hazy and dull brown in the twilight. The sidewalk was shattered in so many pieces it was like walking on crushed glass. Most of the trees, bushes, and flowerbeds that we had planted as a community in 1976, were gone. The few trees that were left were dry, brittle, and bare. Houses and buildings were unpainted, or the paint was peeling, some had chunks of plaster falling off or holes in the walls exposing the innards of buildings. A permanent cloud of dust settled on everything.

Some people were walking around me, but I didn't recognize any of the faces. I felt trapped in a nightmare. How could it be? I had just spent the night in a beautiful home, meticulously renovated and, in the span of forty minutes, maybe less, I was in another world, a completely abandoned neighborhood. I walked around in a daze for hours. I looked for the movie theater where I had learned to love films but couldn't find it. The building had collapsed, someone told me. The school, too, was gone. The fish store was permanently closed. José, who had once owned a bodega and continued to work there as an employee after the government took it from him, was dead. Most of the neighbors I once knew had left the country; some to Spain, others to Miami. A girl I went to school with was a medical doctor working in Venezuela, as part of an exchange program between governments that traded doctors for oil and other goods. The markers of my childhood had disappeared. It was devastating.

Finally, I knocked on the door of the apartment where we used to live. An old, frail woman opened the door. She said her name was Rita and seemed to recognize me immediately, though I could tell that she was blind. Both her eyes were covered by a white film, erasing all color from the irises. I had to look away.

"I knew you'd come back someday," she said, explaining she knew I came from *el exterior* because of the smell. I asked her what that smell was like. "Clean," she said. "Fresh, like a winter day."

After assuring Rita I didn't want anything from her or the house, I asked to come in. I just wanted to see the place where I grew up. She was very welcoming and offered me coffee, which I declined. Three cups in one morning was my new limit. To my surprise, the apartment had been well preserved, much like I remembered it. Above the couch there was a painting of white and yellow hibiscus that my mother's cousin had given her as a wedding present in 1962. Since I left the crib in my parents' room at three, I had slept on the living room couch under that painting. It was the first thing I saw when I opened my eyes in the morning and the last before closing my eyes at night. I had memorized it, down to the weird angle of the letter *W* in his signature, Wilfredo.

"Do you like the painting?" the woman asked, intuiting where I was standing.

"Very much, yes," I said, choking back tears.

"My son painted it for me before he left."

I was speechless. Clearly, we couldn't be talking about the same painting.

"Your son?" I managed to ask.

"Yes, he left in a raft years ago, for Miami."

I asked a few more questions, enough to understand the woman had lost her mind. Her son had indeed left in 1994 in a raft, and she had never heard from him again. He had been seventeen at the time and an aspiring artist. Like me, he used to sleep on that couch. Probably like me, he used to look at the painting and perhaps mentioned to her that one day he was going to paint one like that for her and send it from Miami. Maybe.

Suddenly, I realized I couldn't be in this apartment any longer. I didn't even want to see the kitchen or the tiny patio with its concrete wash basin or my parents' bedroom or the bathroom where I used to lock myself in for hours to read, so many hours that my father took the lock away once and never had the chance to put it back.

I left a one-hundred-dollar bill on top of the dining table, under the water glass she had been using, and said a rushed goodbye to that poor blind woman as if I didn't want to get contaminated by her sadness and despair. I got in the car and drove away fast, my body tense with a mixture of sadness, fury, and regret. Cones of muted orange lights from poles standing on every street corner of Havana guided my way back to the house in Miramar.

Early the next day I wrote Al a note thanking him and left without saying goodbye. The reality of the island was getting under my skin, and I didn't want to deal with someone like Al, frivolous, privileged, and politically dubious, after meeting the sad and destitute Rita.

It was the first day of October and the weather had turned. The morning was damp, parallel bands of clouds hung low over the horizon, almost kissing the roiling sea. As I drove on Malecón, along the famous seawall of Havana, a huge wave catapulted over the wall and crashed in the middle of the avenue, licking the asphalt with its foamy tongue before retreating to the ocean. I saw the looming wave and stopped the car quickly, my heart thumping wildly inside my chest. I began to sweat and hyperventilate; the cars behind me started honking. I was paralyzed. My hands were shaking, and I couldn't breathe. I was having a panic attack.

Somehow, the other cars realized I wasn't going to move no matter how much they honked, and they began to swerve around me. I tried to focus on a good image, as my psychiatrist had counseled, an image that brought me peace, not related to water, of course. Most people think of the ocean when they want to relax. I think of rolling hills, or my son's face, or the light of a candle. Water, even drinking water when I'm having a panic attack, can make it worse. I chose to focus on my son, his beautiful face with his wild, curly hair—by now surely cut very short. I was thinking of him as he was, or used to be, not in uniform, not in the Navy, not in danger, not near water, but as a teenager, making music in our Upper West Side apartment, playing the old upright piano in cold winter afternoons while I read. Slowly, slowly, my grip softened on the wheel, and I could feel my breath returning to normal.

I felt well enough to keep driving, but I made sure not to look to the left. I had seen enough water to last me for weeks. Clearly, the exposure therapy worked well if I was only looking at it. If water came after me, as it had just happened, I was not ready to face it. Not yet.

Soon enough, I was entering the Havana Tunnel. Before I landed in Cuba, I had mapped out the route I had to take eastward to get to Sabanilla. The tunnel was unavoidable; the idea of it terrified me.

I cranked the windows up and pressed down harder on the accelerator. If I could have closed my eyes, I would have. I remembered an old Paul Newman movie where he tells a boy that, when he was a child, his grandfather told him that to keep fear at bay he had to be brave for just one minute. Then, if needed, two. I had remembered that line on many other occasions when I needed to summon up courage. This time, I hoped to only need to be brave for about thirty seconds.

When I emerged from the tunnel, my knuckles white from holding on to the wheel so tightly, I had left most of the city behind. A smattering of ugly buildings appeared and then, on the left, the vista quickly opened to the beaches where I used to go with my parents as a child. I thought of stopping but kept going past Santa María, Guanabo, and, finally, Cojímar. Suddenly, to the right, royal palm trees appeared. Tall and regal, like sentinels of the fields, they brought tears to my eyes. This was the landscape I always envisioned when I dreamed about Cuba, lush endless vistas dotted with thick-trunked palm trees and low rounded hills.

My thoughts drifted, as they often did in recent days, to the tragedy of the *Valbanera*. I had been reading about shipwrecks, hurricanes, and the way ships interact with waves and wind. It was depressing homework, but fascinating at the same time. In a book about the history of shipwrecks, I learned that the first large ship to sink near Cuba was the *Santa María*, one of the three under Christopher Columbus's command when he stumbled upon the islands of the Caribbean in 1492. Soon afterward, with an increasing number of ships journeying to the Americas in the wake of Columbus's voyages, shipwrecks became commonplace in an area of the world battered by hurricanes and unpredictable weather. I discovered that hundreds of sunken ships surrounded Cuba, like a string of pearls.

I drove for hours, unburdened by traffic. Here and there, a cow crossed my path, but I managed to brake in time, aware that I was entering their territory, not the other way around. I purposely didn't play music or use the AC. Instead, I kept the windows open, wanting to hear and to smell Cuba. The sounds were muted: kids running somewhere behind a dog, a truck passing, a man whistling, a boy selling cheese, an old man peddling onions, a woman hawking paper fans, the wheels of a distant train over the rails. I could smell raw milk, garlic, and the lingering traces of cow manure as I continued, and though I was tempted to stop to take it all in, I kept going.

By late afternoon, I arrived in Central Ramona, the town where I thought I would park the car to begin the trek on horseback to my mother's childhood house, as we used to do every summer when we lived in Cuba. We'd ride in a bus from Havana; then, board a rickety old train that everyone called *el tren lechero*, or the milk train. Eventually, not even the train could penetrate the jungle that led to my grandpa's house. At that point, we either walked or rode horses; often, someone waited for us with a machete to open stubborn paths if the shortcut was impassable because the river was swollen.

To my surprise, there was now a bus station in the town and the few people I asked told me there was no longer any need to walk to Sabanilla; I could drive to it. There was a road, not a good one, but a road nonetheless. I had driven in worse conditions, I thought, remembering a trip on the back of a truck to a mountaintop shrine in Ecuador that had me peeing blood for a day. How bad could this be?

"Are you going to the old Fernández farm?" asked one of the men I consulted about the roads. I said yes, somewhat surprised; I hadn't realized it was so well known. He said his parents had met there at a dance, many years ago. "But that house is empty. Everybody is dead."

His bluntness hit me like a blow, and I swallowed hard. I said I knew, but I wanted to visit anyway.

"There is a caretaker, though. He may still be around," he said. "That is, if he hasn't died and we just haven't heard," he added with a wink. I wanted to ask who the caretaker was, but the man's bus had arrived and he was already boarding. I checked the time. It would be getting dark soon.

As I had been warned, the road was treacherous—full of watery holes, ropy roots as thick as tree branches, rocks jutting out at odd angles, and dead animals littering the way. But it was passable, and I was eager to get to the house before nightfall.

After about twenty minutes, I began to recognize certain things. The ground changed color. The soil was no longer an earthy brown but more like reddish clay. The trees grew closer together, forming a barrier against sound and light. Cumulus clouds moved swiftly as if gathering for rain or some other atmospheric event. It was quiet and gray, just as I remembered it in the early mornings when fog seemed to rise from the ground on certain days and a mist clung to the tree leaves, causing them to sparkle like stars when the sun finally made its appearance.

Then I heard a voice, as clear as thunder, calling out from the bushes to my right: "*Azabache! Villanueva!*" followed by the sound of giant rubber wheels crunching in the dry rocky soil as a wooden cart pulled by two enormous beasts crossed my path. One of the oxen, the one closest to me, was stark black, with sharp horns that must have been a foot long each; the other was light brown, like butterscotch, with shorter horns. I stopped the car and slowly got out, my arm resting over the open door for balance and support, not daring to move.

The liquid black eye of *Azabache* focused on me. I looked back to that vortex of an eye, weary and ancient. Could it be? How long had it been? Forty years? It couldn't be. These couldn't possibly be my grandfather's oxen, even though they had the same names. The cart came to a full stop, and two barrels of water clanked in the back, spilling some. The man with the reins seemed as surprised to see me standing there as I was to see him. He wore an old straw hat, no shirt, brown pants with a faded leather belt, and old work boots without shoelaces. He smiled a toothless smile and said the last thing I expected to hear.

"You look just like your mother."

Catalina

Sabanilla, Las Villas
1924

CATALINA WAS DOING THE LAUNDRY under the mango tree so heavy with flowers that she had to scoop them out of the wash bucket, but she liked the shade here and the way the field spread endlessly before her. A bucket of soapy hot water at her feet contained the dirtiest of Ramón's work shirts. He had come home the night before from the cane fields, but only briefly, to drop off his dirty laundry and to kiss his girls, as he called them. He had left again before dawn. Together, they had walked, their arms around each other and Carmen holding her father's hand, to the edge of the property, until he couldn't linger anymore. He promised he'd be back soon and kissed Catalina behind the ear, a place he found particularly tender and had claimed as his. Right before he pulled away, Catalina was tempted to whisper her secret, but something held her back.

"What is it, woman?" Ramón asked, holding her by the waist.

In response, Catalina just kissed him. "Be safe," she said, disentangling her body from his. "And come home soon."

Ramón's work was grueling, cutting and hauling cane stalks to the mill where they were turned into precious grains of sugar, but the pay was good and it was helping them make improvements on their house, one room at a time, as the money from doña Emilia had run out soon after the purchase of the land. In the last few months, the palm fronds had been replaced on the roof and there were no longer any leaks. Concrete, polished to a shine, now covered the dirt floor and they had even managed to reinforce the walls with the strong wood from the trunks of palm trees. They had built partitions for the three bedrooms and a large pantry to hang the cured meats and preserved fruits Catalina prepared, as well as to store sacks of rice and beans from their own land.

Still, Catalina wished there were a better way for Ramón to make a living. Though he came home every fifteen days or so for a day or two, he was so tired when he arrived, his body so burned by the sun and battered by gashes from the cane stalks' blades that his presence was yet another chore for her. Catalina tended to his cuts and pains, cooled his body with an aloe ointment she had concocted, fed him his favorite foods from the islands, and lay with him. But the visits were too infrequent, and Catalina was lonely without him.

She was thinking about the sweetness of his brief stay when she heard the dogs barking furiously, signaling someone was coming. Catalina's fists froze over the shirt she was pounding clean on the wooden washboard. Carmen was playing with a kitten at her feet, but she, too, looked up with concern. No one but strangers ever came from that road. Catalina's neighbors and those who sought her healing hands approached from the back of the house, not the front. Catalina pricked her ears and craned her neck toward the road. In the distance, she saw a lone figure approaching. She dropped the shirt in the bucket and clutched her heart with her wet hands, but she dared not to hope.

She took a few steps forward, with Carmen holding on to her skirt. But as she focused her eyes on the distant figure, she realized she was looking, not at a young man, but at a woman, who wore a dark blue dress and a small hat that didn't quite cover her abundant hair. She held a burgundy leather suitcase in her hand, and she walked slowly and tentatively, as if she weren't sure where she was or whether she wanted to be there at all.

Catalina hastily dried her hands on her dress and began walking toward this woman who seemed somehow familiar. She was tall and lithe, with black hair, just like . . .

Catalina walked faster and then took off running toward the visitor, who dropped her suitcase and started running as well, her arms open wide. In no time, the two women covered the distance between them, raising a cloud of dust. They met in a tight embrace and sobbed on each other's shoulders.

"You are alive! You are alive!" Ana shrieked between sobs. "You are here!"

But Catalina, holding her old friend by the shoulders, just kept shaking her head.

"No, no, I'm not here," she said. "I'm somebody else."

Ana wasn't sure she understood. She was just glad her trip all the way from the Canary Islands had not been in vain. She had come looking for her brother, and had unexpectedly found Catalina, whom, like everybody else back home, she had given up for dead years ago. It seemed unreal, but now that she had found Catalina, Juan would surely be there as well.

"How did you find me?" Catalina asked, but Ana waved her off.

"Where is Juan?" she asked, wiping her tears with the back of her hand. Before Catalina could answer, Ana noticed Carmen, who had been hiding behind her mother while the two women hugged. The little girl was clinging to her mother's leg, looking up at this strange woman with her enormous hazel-colored eyes that, under the right light, took on the color of wheat, just like her own, just like Juan's.

Ana knelt in front of her.

"Oh, there you are," she said, and held out her arms to the child who walked into them as if she had known this woman all her life.

"I'm your Tía Ana," she said, caressing Carmen's black curls.

At first Catalina flinched at the word *aunt*, but let it pass. Carmen was too young to understand what it meant, and how could it harm such a lonely girl to have someone else love her as family? Besides, Ana was truly her aunt, even if Catalina had vowed never to reveal to her daughter the true circumstances of how she came to be in the world. Catalina had never told Carmen that she hadn't been her firstborn, or that her own name had briefly belonged to another child, who had been lost. In fact, she never told Carmen anything at all about her life before Cuba. As far as Carmen knew, her mother had come from Spain in a ship and met her husband in a yellow house by the coast. As far as Carmen knew, there had never been a man named Juan in her mother's life. Ramón was her father.

Carmen's brow furrowed as she tested out the new words. She tried to say Tía Ana, but what she actually said was Liana. Ana chuckled. "I like it," she said. "Liana it is."

Looking at Catalina from the ground, Ana repeated her question behind Carmen's back. "Where is Juan?" she mouthed. She looked so anguished and so hopeful at the same time that Catalina felt her heart would break if she had to explain the truth at that precise moment. Instead, she touched her heart and whispered, "Here, always here." Then, she reached down, grabbed her daughter, and sat her on her hip; Carmen's long legs dangled all the way to Catalina's knees. With her other hand she picked up Ana's suitcase from the dirt and urged her to follow them home.

"How did you find us?" Catalina repeated her question.

"It wasn't easy," Ana said, explaining that her brother had left her the address of where Ramón lived in Cuba. She went there and found a barren lot, but helpful neighbors had given directions to Sabanilla and Ramón. She figured, if nothing else, he would know where her brother was. Catalina just nodded, reflecting. Despite all her precautions, she was not as invisible and unreachable as she had thought.

As they walked, Carmen stretched out her small hand and Ana, brokenhearted but hopeful, took it and held it close to her lips until they reached the house.

Mara

Sabanilla
October 2019

"I reckon you are Lila's daughter, Marita."

At the sound of my childhood nickname, I remembered who he was. This old man was my mother's cousin, Linito, the son of her dear Liana, the blond boy she had loved like an older brother, the one who had never left, and the one person my mother wished she could still visit, if she could only summon up the courage to make the journey I had just undertaken for the two of us.

"Yes, yes," I said, sobbing.

The oxen huffed and paced but Linito reined them back and looked away while I cried alone next to my car and the sun exploded in a riotous display of purple, pink, orange, and yellow in its slow descent behind the low hills of Sabanilla.

Linito walked with a limp into what was left of his home. It was a shack now. Half of the house had fallen into such ruin that it was no longer usable. He lived mostly in two rooms. In one he cooked and ate; in another, he slept. I couldn't tell where the bathroom was and didn't think it prudent to ask. I was appalled by the poverty. Was it always like this and I hadn't noticed? I had no memories of being inside his house, but I must have been, and I was sure he had lived in better conditions.

He looked old but was still strong. I knew he was only a few years older than my mother, but he seemed to be in pain. A nerve in his left leg was bothering him, he explained.

"What brings you here after all this time?" he asked, sitting down with a groan on a *taburete*, a handmade chair covered in cow skin, which he expertly reclined against the wall by pulling his head back hard.

I couldn't possibly tell him why I was here, not yet, but I didn't want to lie to my mother's cousin.

"I came to see the old house," I said. "What's left of it."

"I try to take care of it, even though it's been empty for a long time."

I knew that.

"It turns out those *isleños* knew what they were doing when they built a house of stones," he went on. "Those last forever."

I said nothing, not knowing what else to add or what to do with my body. He had offered me a seat, but I was too wired to sit down.

"We should go outside now, before it gets too dark," he said, getting up from the chair. "I'll get a flashlight. We still don't have electricity in these parts."

I wasn't surprised. I remembered my summers here and how dark it got after sundown; so dark you couldn't see your own hands. In bed at night, I used to become so disoriented that I once woke up my father to ask him which way was "the right way" to sleep, not certain which way my body was positioned. The darkness was total.

Linito went into the bedroom, and I stayed at the threshold, with one foot in the living area and another outside. I decided to step inside. The room was clean, albeit small. On the wall next to the open door that led to the bedroom there was a framed black-and-white photograph of a tall black-haired woman with light eyes and an easy smile; she wore a button-down summer dress with short sleeves, and held a book in her hands, as if she had been caught by the camera while reading. Under the frame there was a vase with yellow plastic flowers.

I felt something vibrate like a bell inside my chest wall, which usually happens when I smell a story. I approached the picture slowly.

Linito came back and found me staring at the picture.

"Who is that?" I asked softly, managing to keep the excitement out of my voice, because even before he said it, I knew the answer.

"Oh, that's my mother," he said, his voice softening. "But you never met her. Her name was Ana. Ana Cruz Cruz."

I pulled a *taburete* from the table and took it outside, planting it firmly next to Linito's. I wanted to hear all he had to say. The house could wait.

Catalina

Sabanilla, Las Villas
1924–1934

WHEN ANA ARRIVED, almost exactly five years after the shipwreck of the *Valbanera*, Catalina understood the hurt she must have caused her family for not telling them she had survived. But even then, she couldn't reach out to them, in part because she was convinced the person she had been had truly died at sea. Someone else, someone stronger, wiser, and physically altered had taken her place. To return home now, even to visit, or to write a letter to her sisters or her mother would be to reopen a wound. It was probably better for them to accept that Catalina had died with her daughter and her husband than to learn she had survived only because she had left her daughter behind, trusting her lover to find her when she had failed. No, Catalina was certain the woman who had been capable of such recklessness was buried deep in the ocean, with the other victims of the shipwreck.

It was easy to fold Ana into her life. The two women, united by their shared history and similar character, went about their lives together as if that had always been the plan. When Ana did the wash, Catalina swept the floors. Together, they collected mangoes in buckets to make marmalade. Whenever Catalina was cooking or tending to the sickly people who came to her door, Ana would take care of Carmen, who always referred to her as "Liana," the name she'd given her on the day they met and the one Ana had adopted as her own.

Ana watched Catalina carefully for signs of sadness, but she saw only a stoicism and strength that left her in awe of her friend. "Do you not miss La Palma? Do you not miss your people?" she asked her one day while the two were peeling potatoes for dinner.

"I miss my sisters," Catalina said quietly. "And my mother."

Ana simply nodded.

Catalina didn't say anything else. There was no need, really, to tell Ana how much she missed her family. She thought of her mother all the time: when she was peeling garlic, when she trimmed the leaves of a bush, when the songs of birds awakened her in the morning, and when the weather shifted. Her mother had had an uncanny ability to detect the first signs of a change in seasons, particularly fall and spring. She could detect a whiff of autumn in the air even in the midst of a late summer heat wave, and she always got agitated when the Lenten winds began swirling above the mountains that surrounded their house.

Catalina thought of her mother, too, when she was embroidering a dress for Carmen, hemming Ramón's pants, or picking flowers, when she added condensed milk to a banana, when she had *gofio* with milk in the mornings and, before bed, when she refused to pray as she had been taught, and felt the desperate need to tell her mother she was alive but knew she couldn't.

On one of those evenings when Ramón was away working and Carmen was asleep in her bed, the two women were embroidering by the light of a lantern when Ana surprised Catalina with a question she had asked herself thousands of times but had long ago given up trying to find an answer to.

"What do you think happened to them?"

Catalina knew exactly what Ana was asking. For Catalina, the pain of not knowing was so old that she had grown used to it, while for Ana it was still a fresh wound. All these years she had believed her brother was alive. To bury him in her mind, without a body to pray over, was a difficult thing to process, Catalina knew.

She dropped the blanket she was embroidering on the table and stood up, walking toward the window as if the darkness might reveal the answers they both craved. Catalina was starting to show—her thin body filling out around the waist—but she still had not found the right time to share the news of her pregnancy with Ramón. She suspected Ana knew her secret, though she had not mentioned anything. The cool night air of early spring brought in the fragrance of the gardenias she had planted the summer before. They had finally bloomed.

"I don't know," she said, her back to Ana, who had stood as well, expectantly. "But I have an idea."

Catalina came back to the table and sat down again, hitching the hem of her dress above her knees for comfort. Then, she grabbed her friend's hands as she tried to put into words, for the first and last time, how she imagined the end had come for Juan and Antonio, and, above all, for her baby daughter.

"I have gone over everything many times these past years, and this is what I think," she began slowly, as if it was difficult to form the words. "Antonio knew or intuited what we were planning. I felt it in the way he looked at me the last time he kissed me. I was supposed to meet Juan under the stairs, but, instead, Antonio was waiting for me. I think the wet nurse he hired for the trip must have told him. They may have been involved, I'm not sure. I was too young, too naïve, but I've come to believe that his insistence that we travel with a nurse was his way of making sure they could be together on the ship. I imagine that, had he lived, she would have come to the house and stayed with us, and their relationship would have continued. She had a son. He may have been Antonio's, but I can't be certain, and I never will."

Ana squeezed Catalina's hands encouraging her to continue.

"More than anybody else, she knew my routine. She was precise and vigilant about time with the baby, supposedly because she was disciplined about the baby's feeding schedule, but I don't believe that anymore. I had my suspicions then, but I was more concerned with Antonio's drinking and his gambling habit. He played every night. I think he had gotten heavily into debt but kept playing to try to earn some money back."

Catalina paused for a moment, letting go of Ana's hands to take a sip of water from her glass on the table. She had never told anyone of her suspicions about Antonio's character. It felt wrong, somehow, but also, a release to finally confide in someone the doubts she had been holding on to for so long.

Ana didn't dare move. She had waited years to ask this question, to know the details, that she could wait a little longer until Catalina summoned the strength to continue.

"I think the morning we arrived in Santiago, Antonio ordered María to hide somewhere with the baby so that I would not be able to leave. He never imagined I would leave without my daughter. Neither did I."

Catalina stood up again and went back to the window. It was like looking at a black rectangle. The moon wasn't out yet, or, if it was, it was hiding behind a cloud. She could hear the animals stirring as they searched for a comfortable spot to spend the night, but she couldn't see a thing. A cool breeze wafted in, chilling them both. Catalina closed the window and returned to the table.

"I imagine that, at some point after the ship left the harbor, María returned to the room with the baby. Or maybe Antonio returned from wherever he was. Or perhaps they had been hiding together. They were hoping I'd be in the room, looking for them. Instead, I'm sure they found Juan. There must have been a confrontation, a fight. I'm not sure, but my guess is Antonio shot Juan and either killed him or wounded him. Antonio had a gun with him on the boat, even though he was supposed to leave it with the captain when we boarded, but he never did."

At this point in the story, Ana started to cry softly, covering her mouth with one of her hands, but Catalina didn't notice. Her gaze was fixed on a point far beyond the living room.

"They must have been trying to figure out what to do with the body when they felt the first gusts of wind. I read afterward that the wind was sudden and cruel. The waves were enormous, as tall as buildings. They couldn't even approach Havana's harbor. The last time the ship was seen it was near here, off the coast of a town called Caibarién, where I was going to make a home with Antonio when we arrived. And the last anyone heard from the ship was on the evening of September 9. They were communicating with a lamp, in code, saying they would go out to sea to wait out the hurricane. The authorities said other ships saw the *Valbanera* turn slowly, tossed about in the waves like a toy."

Ana shrank in her chair, hugging herself to stave off the merciless narration. Each detail felt like a fresh assault on her.

Catalina sighed and continued.

"It was, we later learned, an unusually devastating hurricane. Other ships were lost as well. There are reports that, on the 12th of September, someone from the ship tried to communicate, but the communication was immediately lost. I don't know what to believe. What's certain is that when it was safe to go out to look for the ship, the Americans looked for days and, at first, they couldn't find it. Eventually, they saw the mast protruding from the sea, near Florida, far from Havana's harbor. They tried to search for survivors, but there were none. There were no bodies, either. None. It was as if the ship had been traveling without passengers, or without a crew."

"Like a ghost ship," Ana said quietly.

"Like a ghost ship," Catalina repeated. The weak light in the glass lamp flickered as the wick burned off and the two women were immersed in darkness. It was better this way, Catalina thought. She didn't want to face Ana tonight, not after she had unburdened her soul with her deepest fears and her deepest regrets to this woman who could have been her sister-in-law.

Ana was glad for the darkness as well. She was no longer crying. When Catalina finished her story all she could cling to was the hope that Catalina was right, that Juan had been dead by the time the sea swallowed the ship, so that he never knew he had died in a place so deep and dark that no one had been able to find him. Better that way, Ana thought. And then she got up, found the matches and a candle, and led Catalina to her bedroom. She tucked her in, like one would a child or an ailing mother. Then she kissed Catalina on the forehead and placed a hand on her bulging middle. "We must go on," she said. "And we never have to speak of it again."

Once Ana learned what had happened to her brother, she knew she would never be able to return to La Palma and leave her niece behind. Catalina never told her Carmen had been conceived aboard the *Valbanera*, but she didn't have to. This little girl reminded Ana so much of her brother and she already loved her so much that it was clear she had found her place in the world. Carmen was tall for her age, with unruly black hair and an impish face that made her seem older and more mischievous than she was. In fact, Carmen was a docile little girl, who spent her days playing with a glass bottle swaddled in an old towel that she pretended was a baby, just like Catalina and Ana used to do in La Palma. Wherever Ana went, Carmen followed, as Ana used to do to Juan.

When Catalina started bleeding and had to stay in bed during the fourth month of a pregnancy that she never had the opportunity to announce to her husband, Ana took over the household and the care of Carmen. It was Ana who helped Catalina deliver her dead twin boys. And it was Ana who named them—Maríano and Mario—because, as she told Catalina, every soul needs a name to be recognized and remembered. She put away the baby clothes they had made and buried the tiny bodies, wrapped in white linen, behind the house, in a shaded spot where the animals were never allowed. Yellow and white wildflowers covered the graves in less than a week.

Ana helped Catalina get out of bed, and, shoring her up with her own body, she took her outside for a bit of sun and fresh air, taking care to steer her away from the graves. Slowly but forcefully, she rescued Catalina from her sadness with warm broths and the promise that life would go on. This happened again and again, as Catalina, like her mother before her, went on to lose three more pregnancies in less than two years until her body, exhausted by pain and disappointment, dried up. She stopped bleeding monthly before her thirtieth birthday. Ramón never knew any of it.

Ramón and Catalina were grateful for Ana's presence. It made them more of a family. She was both a link to their shared past and a bright light for their future. With her in their midst, they were no longer afraid of what would happen to Carmen if anything might befall them. In Ana, she would always have a mother, they knew.

During those years, and with Ana's help, they focused on improving their lives. Slowly and prudently, they bought more animals, increased their crops, and started to build the house of Catalina's dreams: a stone house just like the one where she used to live, but with only one floor and no chimney because money was tight, and, besides, who needed a chimney in Cuba? In the absence of mulberry trees, Catalina focused on planting guava trees. When they had first arrived in Sabanilla, one lonely and rather small guava tree grew at the edge of their land. Now, rows of mature trees stood in line in the *guayabal*, just like the mulberry trees had stood at home. At harvest time, in July and August, the fruits hung from their trees like Christmas ornaments—yellow, red, and green, shiny, and plentiful. Some afternoons, when all the important tasks were done, Catalina, Ana, and Carmen played hide-and-seek in the *guayabal* and returned home with pockets full of fruit to turn into delicious desserts.

A peaceful contentment began to fill Catalina.

* * *

The year Carmen turned thirteen, the country was thrown into chaos. Overnight, workers lost their jobs and many sugar mills closed. The price of sugar plunged and the president, a despot named Gerardo Machado, had to escape the country in his pajamas one night. In Havana and other places, people took to the street calling for revolution. Stores were sacked and homes were destroyed. But, for Catalina and her family, these were distant events. What mattered was the harvest, the weather, and the health of the animals. It mattered if it rained enough for the rice to grow, if the animals had parasites, if the milk was fresh and the roof was tight and sealed against the elements.

And in Sabanilla life went on, as Ana had predicted. The chickens were multiplying, and the cows were producing milk. Despite the sugar crisis, Ramón managed to hold on to his job at first, and also worked on their land to expand their rice and bean production beyond what they could consume. While the rest of the island convulsed in the throes of revolution, in Sabanilla, their biggest concern was how to become self-sufficient so they would never have to depend on the capriciousness of sugar cane prices.

Then, Catalina had an idea. What if they opened a bodega in the back of the house? There were no such places in Sabanilla. If one wanted to buy anything, the only option was to get on a horse and ride two hours into town. It was cumbersome and complicated. Most folks around them cultivated their own land and had enough to eat from their animals and their gardens, but there were other needs. One couldn't live on rice, pork, potatoes, and chicken alone.

Ana immediately took to the idea. She rode a horse to town with Carmen's old mule, Nieve, in tow to help her carry her provisions back to the house. She bought flour, crackers, cookies, cola, paper, pencils, notebooks, sugar, salt, spices, matches, candles, and soap. While she was out on her errands, Catalina cleared out part of the pantry and placed a high table outside, under a window and flushed against the wall, creating a makeshift counter. Soon after, the two women walked for miles to farms throughout the area to inform their neighbors that they were open for business. The first day they made fifty *centavos*, certainly not enough to justify all the work they had put into it. So they thought about how to attract more customers. They decided to make beef empanadas, pairing them with sodas and selling them for twenty *centavos* each.

Within a week, they had recovered the cost of their initial expenses. By the end of the month, they had made twenty *pesos* and were sending a neighborhood boy to town for more groceries. By the time Ramón returned a few weeks later, after the sugar mill he worked at closed, too, the women had a thriving business, and put him to work in the front of the store with Carmen while they cooked empanadas, molded croquettes, and stuffed potatoes with *picadillo*. The smell and sound of sizzling oil permeated their days and before long their arms and hands and even their torsos bore the marks of a life spent in a hot kitchen.

But Catalina and Ana didn't stop there.

One night, as the two were seasoning ground beef for the next day's empanadas and stuffed potatoes, Catalina remembered her home. She didn't often think of La Palma anymore, but this night she did, perhaps because the light of their lantern was particularly weak, and Catalina longed for bright light. At home, she recalled, her father had installed electricity as soon as it became available on the island, years before she was born. "Did you know that?" she asked Ana, as if the other woman had been able to read her thoughts.

"No, but tell me," she said, a little surprised that Catalina had punctured her usual silence in the evenings.

"La Palma was the first of the islands to have electricity," Catalina said.

"Is that right?"

"Yes, my father used to say that all the time. I remember how proud he was of that."

"Your father used to say a lot of things," Ana said dismissively.

"Yes," Catalina said thoughtfully, and because that night she felt something close to happiness, she told Ana how her father had always compared the state of happiness to a garden.

"How so?" Ana asked, raising an eyebrow.

"Well, you have to work at it, that's all," she said.

"Yes, you do," said Ana encouragingly, because she could tell Catalina was mulling something over in her mind.

And she was right. Catalina told her she had been thinking of expanding the business and opening a dance saloon in the terrace adjacent to their bodega. They would call it *El salón de la alegría*. Catalina's eyes shone with purpose as she explained her plan and Ana had to agree that the idea was good, and that happiness, indeed, was what they needed. If it hadn't come to them naturally, why not create it themselves?

In two days, they had designed a flyer announcing opening night. Ana took it to a printer in town and then paid a young neighbor to distribute the flyers all around the valley. Meanwhile, they swept and cleaned the terrace until it shone under the sun, the polished concrete sparkling like water under their feet. They also devised a menu. To their usual items, they added a creamy *arroz con pollo* and fried green plantains, which were tricky because they had to be fried as the orders came in or they would harden as they cooled.

Opening night arrived and some neighbors came but few danced. There were more men than women, more children and old people than young couples. It was not at all what Catalina and Ana had envisioned. Some of the men didn't even bother to dismount their horses. It was embarrassing and a little sad, the opposite of happiness.

The following week, when Ramón returned from another failed attempt to find work harvesting cane, the women told him what they had done. At first, he was miffed that they had embarked on such a venture without him, but Catalina sat him down and explained the business opportunity. If it went well, she said, he could finally stop looking for work in the punishing harvest, and he could stay home and focus on the farm. They were both getting older, and she couldn't continue taking care of the animals anymore if she had to run a bodega and a dancing saloon on the weekends.

Ramón, who had been eager to leave the cane fields for years, thought about it and finally gave his blessing along with some ideas. To do it right, they needed to bring girls. Young men would come and spend their money only if they knew they could dance with girls. There were no places where men and women could meet and dance in the countryside. *El salón de la alegría* would offer that outlet in a family atmosphere, Ramón insisted. It needed to be decent and clean. No drunks in his home.

And that's how it happened that, at thirty-four, Catalina became the hostess of her own dance hall. Her daughter, at fourteen, made the prettiest sight twirling alone on the dance floor in new white shoes and a yellow dress with embroidered white flowers that Catalina had made for her. But she wasn't dancing alone for too long. From up on his horse, an eighteen-year-old farmhand with a broken nose from a horse's hoof, had noticed her moves and was watching her. Before the night was over, he had added his name to her dance card for fifty *centavos*. His name was Orlando Martín, he told her, but everyone called him Macho. After she saw his hooded gray eyes and full mouth, Carmen put the card away and didn't dance with anyone else that night, or ever again.

Mara

Sabanilla, Las Villas
October 2019

AT FIRST, THE BUZZING MOSQUITOES OUTSIDE Linito's house bothered me as we sat there, and I kept swatting at them. But, after a while, I no longer heard them or felt their sting. Wrapping my arms around myself, I leaned forward the way I do when I really want to listen, and all I felt, all I heard, were Linito's words.

I was fascinated by the cadence of his speech, which was rushed and loud. He swallowed the ending of some words and mispronounced others, in the speech pattern typical of a peasant, or *guajiro*. But I soon discovered that Linito was a gifted raconteur, with a life full of remarkable experiences that to him were mundane, yet to me seemed magical and revelatory.

At some point during his narration, I began to realize that what he was telling me would radically alter the way I viewed my family and, therefore, how I saw myself. At times I almost wanted him to stop, but of course I didn't. If anything, I didn't dare move or interrupt him for fear that he might change his mind and clam up instead.

When he finished speaking, we both fell quiet for a long while. I had sat so still on the *taburete* for so long I could no longer feel my legs, and my mind felt numb as well after so many revelations. By then I knew that the kindly Ramón I had known as my grandfather all my life, wasn't my grandfather at all, not even my great-grandfather. My real grandfather was a man nicknamed Macho, lost to the family and to history. And my great-grandfather was, unsurprisingly after what I'd learned from Julián, Juan Cruz Cruz, a man who never even knew he had sired a child with the only woman he had loved.

"My mother always told me everything. I was so quiet when I was a boy, and she said I was the perfect listener," Linito said, looking a little sheepish. "But she also wrote everything down. She had good penmanship. In another life, she could have been an educated woman, maybe even a writer."

He got up from his *taburete*, went into the bedroom and returned with an oversized plastic bag from *El Corte Inglés*, the Macy's of Spain. In the bag, which he clearly treasured, because one of his daughters had brought it with a gift from Spain, there were dozens of old notebooks.

"I haven't read them, but you should," he said, handing it to me. I took it with both hands, as if it were a basket full of eggs.

"And you never told anyone any of this?" I asked.

"Not all of it, no. No one ever asked," he simply said. "I didn't think it was a secret. But it was something we just didn't talk about. What was the point?"

I could think of many answers to that question. The point was to always speak the truth, I wanted to say. But was it? I wasn't so sure anymore. My grandmother Carmen's time on earth had been relatively brief, and what would she have gained by learning who her real father was? And would my mother's affection for Ramón, the man who raised her like a father as well as a grandfather, have changed if she had known that he wasn't the one who had planted the seed, so to speak? He had done everything else. He had been there from the beginning, even before her birth. He had taken care of a pregnant young widow who, in a matter of hours, had lost not only her husband and the man she had loved since childhood, but, more crucially, her firstborn baby daughter. How broken she must have been! How hard she must have worked to put all the pieces of her life together again, or, come to think of it, to discard that life and begin a new one, away from everyone who knew and loved her.

A shudder went through my body. I was tired and my neck was cramping. I rested my head against the edge of the *taburete* to give myself an instant and rough massage. That always seemed to work, and the pain eased instantly, but the cloud over my head did not dissipate.

As always when I'm reporting a story, I needed distance to process things before proceeding. It probably wasn't fair to Linito, or to the rest of the family, that I was framing my search as a reporter's assignment, but it was the only way I knew to operate. If I maintained a certain detachment, I could think more clearly. If I was too close to the "story," I would be too emotional, and that wouldn't be helpful to anyone. I was almost at the end of my quest, anyway, and had found what I had come for. And now I had a bagful of notebooks which, I hoped, would reveal even more information about Catalina as well as Ana Cruz, a woman I never met, but had always heard my mother refer to as Liana, the wife of *el gallego* who was notorious for being the only communist in a family of *gusanos*. It had never occurred to me that Liana was not her real name, and that she had grown up with Grandma Catalina in the Canary Islands. I'm sure my mother didn't know that either.

It was too late to return to town to spend the night. I craned my neck and, in the darkness, saw the silhouette of my grandfather's house looming ahead, separated from this shack by a stone path that used to be bordered by a lovingly kept herb garden. Now, weeds had taken over the garden, but the path was still there.

I had always thought of that house as my grandfather's house, as if no one else had ever lived there. Grandpa Ramón, who died six months after we left Cuba, had already been living alone in that house for a long time when I was a child. Somehow, he had been enough for me. I didn't feel that way anymore. I wanted all my ghosts back.

"Is there a bed in the house?" I heard myself ask, and realized that I was planning to stay there after all.

"Yes," Linito replied. "I've always kept a bed ready. My mother asked me to, in case someone from the other side returned."

I thought of that phrase for a moment. "The other side." Cubans live with such fear of the all-powerful government that sometimes they speak in riddles to avoid being reported to the authorities as counter-revolutionaries. It was hard to know what he meant. Did he mean La Palma? Miami? Or "the other side," as in heaven? I didn't want to ask.

Linito walked me to the house with a flashlight, bringing along a lantern and a glass of water. He showed me to the bedroom where I'd be staying and quickly left. I was tempted to take up the lantern and explore the place in the darkness—it had been so long since I was last here—but I decided against it. My mother always said everything looks better in the morning, and I wanted my first encounter with the house after four decades to be a pleasant one. I sat down on the bed and watched as the lantern's tenuous flame cast giant amorphous shadows on the opposite wall.

The last time we were here was the summer of 1978. My parents were not yet forty, and I must have been fourteen, because it was a year before we left Cuba. This was the room my parents usually occupied. I remembered the full-sized bed I was now sitting on, with its iron frame and blue chenille bedspread. On the wall above, there was an image of the Virgin Mary. On another wall, a calendar page from September 1983. I wondered who the last person was who had stayed here. The room smelled musty, but it was clean. A green glass vase with dried roses stood atop a dark wood dresser, with a naked doll seated beside it who was missing an eye. I picked it up and put it in a drawer.

I knew I wasn't going to be able to sleep, so I kicked off my boots and propped myself up against the pillows, pulling the cover over my legs. Reaching inside the plastic bag, I took out one of the notebooks and began to read.

Catalina

Sabanilla
1936–1953

DURING ONE OF THE DANCES at *El salón de la alegría,* Ana met a robust blond *gallego* named Aquilino Canal, seven years younger than she was. Like Ramón, he was a seasonal worker in the sugar harvest. The rest of the time, he was a carpenter, he said, pointing to the cuts and scrapes of his calloused hands. Even the hair of his strong arms was golden, like the sun; his face was freckled, and his blue eyes twinkled like stars. He had recently escaped from Spain after several members of his family had been killed in the Civil War. He, too, had fought and had the wounds to prove it—a long jagged scar snaked along the side of his right leg and made him walk with a pronounced limp. Aquilino had managed to escape certain death by hiding in a tunnel that he and his brothers had dug under the house before the war started. Ana was fascinated by Aquilino's story and charmed by his limp. It made him seem vulnerable, and it was in her nature to take care of others.

Aquilino called himself a Communist, but that had no meaning for Ana. What she cared about he possessed: a broad chest, warm hands, and a way of kissing her that melted her to the core. Within a month, they announced they were getting married because, as Ana said bluntly to her family, she had waited long enough for her wedding night. Ana was thirty-six and pretty, with long shapely legs, a tiny waist, and melancholic hazel eyes framed by dark lashes. But, before meeting Aquilino, she knew men had already started to look at her—if they looked her way at all—as an old maid.

The wedding took place on a Saturday night, at *El salón de la alegría*. The couple left early for their honeymoon in *Playa Panchita*, a small beach town, riding a reddish-brown horse named Candela for its color and hot temper—a wedding gift from Ramón and Catalina. The party went on without them and when it was over, when the last guest had left, Catalina realized it was the first time that, for about eighteen hours, she had not thought of the loss of her baby daughter and of the man she had once loved. She didn't know if this was a sign of healing or a curse. Just in case, before she went to bed at that darkest of hours before daybreak, she got on her knees and prayed, her hand rubbing the spot above her left breast where her pain hid from the world but not from her. It helped to keep her always vigilant, always afraid.

Nine months after the wedding, Ana gave birth to a long skinny blond boy who cried from the moment he was born until he was nearly a year old. When he turned one, several things happened at once: he stopped nursing, he started to speak and walk, and he developed such a jovial personality that he rarely cried again and didn't know how to react when others cried in front of him. He was named Aquilino, just like his father, but to the family he was always "Linito."

Ana and Aquilino built a small wooden house next to Catalina and Ramón because Ana couldn't imagine leaving them behind nor did they want her to leave. Catalina had grown used to her presence, her laughter, and her cooking, particularly the loving way she made her specialty from home: warm *gofio* with milk and bananas. To her, Ana was no longer a reminder of all she had lost, but a sister that filled in the huge space once occupied by the family she had left behind.

It was the best time of Catalina's life. She and Ana worked harder than ever before on the houses, the animals, the farm, the garden, the bodega, and the saloon, all at the same time and without complaining.

Carmen helped, but reluctantly. She preferred to spend her time reading under the trees in the guava grove, dreaming of being someplace else. She wasn't sure where. It didn't matter, as long as it wasn't home. When she was little, Carmen used to tell her mother she was certain the stork had made a mistake and had dropped her in the wrong place. When she understood where babies really came from, Carmen still believed that a profound mistake had been made and decided to rectify it as soon as she could. Catalina blamed herself. Perhaps if she hadn't made up so many tales of lives elsewhere—in castles surrounded by snow, in cities where sophisticated women wore hats and gloves, in far-away places where flowers grew wild, and volcanoes brewed under the surface—Carmen would have been more accepting of her circumstances.

But that was not the case. At sixteen, Carmen had blossomed into a beautiful young woman. Her once jet-black hair had lightened into a soft copper, and, under a certain light, one could see shades of red. She was tall and carried herself like a queen; from Juan, she had inherited a wild streak that Catalina fought hard to trample but failed.

When she was younger, twelve or thirteen, she had begged her parents to let her go to school beyond sixth grade, which would mean moving to a town with another family, but Catalina couldn't imagine not having her daughter near her. Now, she wished she had, for it was clear to her that Carmen was besotted with Macho from the day they met. He came to the salon every weekend to dance with her, and Catalina tried not to criticize Carmen's choice, remembering her own forbidden love story with Juan, but there was something about this boy-man that repelled her. She was certain that her daughter had not chosen wisely.

And she was right.

One morning, when Carmen failed to appear in the kitchen for breakfast, Catalina knew something was wrong. She went to her daughter's bedroom and was shocked to see the bed made, just as she had left it the day before.

"Carmen!" she called out, even though she knew her daughter could no longer hear her. Still, she searched the house and then rushed outside, shading her eyes with her hand as she scanned the terrain as far as her eyes could see. There was no sight of Carmen so she hurried over to Ana's house.

"Have you seen Carmen?" she asked urgently. Ana, who had come to the door at the sound of Catalina's steps, was quiet and lowered her eyes.

"Have you? Please tell me, tell me!" Catalina demanded.

"No," she said finally. "I have not, but please calm down. You are going to make yourself sick."

"Don't worry about me. Tell me the truth. You know something you are not telling me."

"Candela is gone," Ana said.

"Your horse? What does that have to do with Carmen?"

"I don't know, but I think she took it," Ana replied, and, from her apron, pulled something small that she placed in Catalina's hand. "This was next to the house, where we keep the horse saddled for Aquilino in the morning. When he left for work today, he found it on the ground."

Catalina looked at her open palm. It was a small brown barrette that Carmen loved. Ramón had made it for her from the horn of a bull.

"Oh my God and all the virgins!" Catalina exclaimed, making a tight fist. The barrette poked her hand, but she felt no pain. The real pain was in her heart. She felt lightheaded and nauseous.

Ana noticed and ran inside to get her some water. When she brought it outside, Catalina was sitting on a *taburete*, her head down between her legs.

"She is only sixteen," Catalina muttered, almost to herself.

Ana knelt beside her.

"You married young, too, remember," she said, but wished right away that she hadn't.

"Yes, I did," replied Catalina furiously, whipping her head up from her knees and staring Ana down. "I was married. She left with the first man who looked her way."

"Maybe it's love, real love," Ana said stubbornly. She felt sad for Catalina, but she also felt protective of her niece.

Catalina let that sink in before she replied, "We'll see. But I doubt it. I give them a month."

It took much longer than a month, but Carmen eventually returned, alone and five months' pregnant, riding Candela. Macho didn't want a baby, she told them, and, it turns out, he didn't want her either. And that was the last thing she said about the man she had loved so passionately.

She had a bruised shoulder and a sad demeanor, but otherwise she was whole. Theirs was a story often repeated in the countryside, but one Catalina had hoped her own daughter would avoid. Two months later, on the 21st of October, 1939, a tiny premature girl was born. The midwife thought the baby would not survive the night, but Catalina was a stubborn woman and she decided to wrest this child away from death. She fought day and night for her granddaughter, warming the baby with her own body and feeding her like one would a bird when Carmen, devastated by her loneliness and the difficult pregnancy, couldn't produce enough milk. Catalina remembered how her own mother had done the same for her first baby daughter. The circle, she felt, was now complete. This was her redemption. This was her opportunity to pay back the miracle she had been granted twice with motherhood. That's all she wanted—a life for a life.

Catalina decided to shut out the world to focus on her own private battle against fate. A month earlier she had been worried about a distant war, remembering the bleak days of her youth when everyone she knew suffered because of the Great War. But now nothing except this child seemed to matter. She declared *El salón de la alegría* temporarily closed. Day and night, she redirected all her energies and prayers to her tiny granddaughter, carrying her on her body until her chest began to feel full, as if her breast were readying to produce milk for a child that didn't come from her own womb.

Six weeks later, it was clear Catalina had won the battle. The baby was beginning to gain weight and she seemed strong and willful. Carmen decided it was time to name her daughter, but Catalina had already done it, for how can you nurture what you don't name?

"Her name is Lila," Catalina told Carmen, who liked the sound of it. But because her daughter's life had been a surprise and a miracle, she added a middle name, Milagro. As for the last name, there was no choice. She would take her mother's last name. The baby looked just like her mother, except for one imperfection that would accompany her for her whole life: the pinkie of her left hand was bent almost at a right angle, just like the pinkies of the grandfather she never knew. Carmen always wondered about her daughter's deformed finger, but the rest of the family understood that Juan was making his presence known through this child.

Lila's birth made a woman of Carmen. She had held out her affections at first. In part, because she was so weak after the delivery, but also because she wasn't sure that little thing that clung to her mother's chest like a bat could possibly thrive.

The day Lila turned one, Ana baked her a cake and Catalina made her a dress from a piece of bright yellow lace she had saved. As Carmen held her daughter to blow out the one candle for her, the baby reached up with her pudgy little hand and caressed her mother's face. "Mama," she said, and Carmen held her breath. The others around the cake applauded in delight, calling Lila the smartest baby in the world. But Carmen knew her daughter had recognized her wound and was trying to heal her. She loved her fiercely at that moment and until the day she died. The love was mutual, for Lila was devoted to her mother even beyond death.

Side by side, the Fernández and the Canal families raised their children together—two Spanish families away from home, rearing Cuban children on their own fertile plot of land and augmenting their income with the bodega and the reopened dancing saloon. Between the seven of them, they had all they needed.

Catalina, who had never visited the graves Ana had dug for her dead babies, planted roses where headstones should have been. This was her private refuge; the place she visited to tend to her grief—gently but purposefully. But it was also the place where Catalina went to be thankful. Lila and Linito brought so much joy to her life, to all their lives, that it was hard to remember all that had happened before them. The graves kept her grounded and alert.

When they were five and seven, Lila and Linito walked to a one-room school where children from Sabanilla learned to read, recite poetry, and do basic math until the sixth grade if they were lucky. Lila was lucky. Linito left in third grade, claiming he just didn't have a head for words or an interest in numbers higher than those he could count with his fingers and toes.

The two cousins spent endless afternoon hours chasing after chickens and dogs, searching for frogs in the banana trees, or reading, their naked bellies flat against the cool concrete of the porch on hot summer afternoons. Lila read books; Linito perused the comics.

The two households—linked by the unspoken memories of their shared past and by a path made of river stones bordered by oregano and *ají cachucha* plants—existed as in a vacuum from the rest of the world. Outside, governments, presidents, *caudillos*, and revolts came and went, but to these families it all had little relevance. As long as it rained periodically, and the plants grew and the pigs fattened, they were content in their isolation and disconnect from the rest of the island.

But that relative peace would not be long lasting. It all began to change on July 26, 1953, on the day of the feast of Saint Ana, the mother of the Virgin Mary, and the day Ana turned fifty-four.

"Turn on the radio!" Ana cried out the moment she stepped into Catalina's kitchen, panting from the short run from her house.

"Armed men have revolted against the government and are attacking Santiago."

Catalina turned away from the stove where she was boiling milk and frying pieces of bread for breakfast. She wiped her hands on her apron and stood in front of Ana, not knowing what to do or how to process the information. The only word she focused on was *Santiago*, the city where, thirty-four years earlier, her first life had ended.

Ana marched in and went to the corner of the living room where the large battery radio sat, practically unused, since Ramón had brought it to the house a few years earlier. Catalina kept it covered with a tablecloth and had placed a vase with flowers on top because she mistrusted the voices of men she couldn't see. Ana removed the flowers and the cover and fiddled with the knobs past the static and the strange noises of that hulking talking box, until she found a sound they could understand.

The reports were confusing, but the story slowly emerged. A group of men, mostly university students from Havana, had attacked a military barracks in Santiago de Cuba. It was impossible to ascertain the number of dead and wounded on both sides, but one thing was clear: twenty years after the last revolution, the people of Cuba were once again rising against the government.

"What happens now?" Catalina asked Ana, who remained on her knees in front of the radio.

"I don't know, but it won't be good," said Ana.

Catalina rushed back to the kitchen when she smelled burned milk. Breakfast was ruined. Then she remembered it was Ana's birthday.

"Happy birthday!" she said as she approached Ana again to help her stand up. The two women embraced with devotion and dread.

"Thank you, my dear Catalina," she said, but her voice sounded tentative.

"What's the matter?" Catalina said, pulling back from the hug and looking at Ana's open but worried face.

"I think this is the beginning of the end."

"The end of what?"

"The end of life as we know it. These rebels won't stop here. You'll see," she said.

Despite the uprising, and Ana's worries for the future, life continued its course in Sabanilla: the men worked in the fields; the women did everything else; the children grew up.

Life took care of the rest, but not gently, not kindly.

Mara

Sabanilla, Las Villas
October 2019

The notebooks I pulled from the bag and would go on to read that long night were school notebooks, similar to the ones I used to have when I was a schoolgirl in Cuba, but with green covers made of thick cardboard.

The dates on the cover were 1939–1945, coincidentally, the years of WWII, but there was not a word here about the war. Instead, it was all about my mother, Linito, the farm, the work, and the domestic details of the Fernández and Canal families in Sabanilla.

"Lila is an inquisitive child, who has inherited her mother's features as well as her grandmother's curly red hair," it began. It mentioned among other things that my mother had been very attached to the small animals on the farm and would cry whenever her grandfather slaughtered a pig. If young girls in the 1940s could have declared themselves vegetarians, my mother probably would have done so.

From that notebook as well as the others I read that night, it was clear that my mother's childhood was marred by her own mother's constant ailments. "Carmen is always in pain, often doubled over. She says it's her stomach, but Catalina isn't sure," Ana wrote.

Ana's telling of events left no doubt that Catalina's opinion carried much weight in the household because she was a healer, able to cure people by merely placing a warm towel on their stomachs and muttering a prayer. This seemed interesting if a little far-fetched. People brought her gifts as a form of payment for her services. Once, the gift had been a beautiful red hen, which Catalina said it reminded her of the one Ramón had killed when Carmen was born. She said that if *Colorá* had returned to them in the form of a gift after so many years, it must be for a reason. Instead of killing it for supper, she had decided to allow her to procreate. Eventually, they had sixty chickens from that one hen, and Lila tried to name them all after each letter of the alphabet. Once she reached Z and named the chick Zoila, Lila gave up. There were too many and they had to begin selling them, one letter at a time.

I learned they had used the money from the sale of the hens to send my mother to the dentist for the first time when she was thirteen. She had a chipped front tooth and she cried so much over it that her grandfather took her to Quemado de Güines, the nearest town with a dentist. Because the treatment would take more than one day, Ramón left her for the weekend with a family he knew there. Ana didn't seem to know their names because she referred to them as *los chinos de Quemado*. This Cuban Chinese family took my mother to the sea for the first time, just to see it, but it was enough to leave a lasting impression on her. When she came back, my mother told Ana all about her visit to the sea, how beautiful and peaceful it seemed, how green, but also how blue. She wanted to go in, but she didn't have a bathing suit and now she wanted one, she told Ana.

"I took her by the shoulders and looked her in the eyes," Ana wrote. "By then Lila was almost as tall as I am, and I told her never to mention anything about the sea to her grandmother. She asked me why, but I didn't explain. I just said that the sea was dangerous, and she should never go in. I made her promise me. She was shaking, and her eyes opened wide. I think I scared her enough that she'll never bring it up again."

At that point, I had to put the notebook down. My mother had never told me this. I knew she was afraid of the sea. And she had told me many times this was the reason she had named me Mara. "You have to name your fears, so you can conquer them," was a phrase she often repeated. But I didn't know she had been made scared, for no reason other than her family's past traumas—traumas that were never explained to her. It must have been disturbing for my mother to receive that message at such a tender age.

Ana's entries in these notebooks included some juicy stories about people in the town. I had to smile at Ana's flair for words. She wrote about the town drunk, a man named Emilio who was a regular at *El salón de la alegría.* He would order beer after beer and would not allow anyone to take the empty bottles away. Ana once counted sixteen bottles.

She wrote about a woman named Hortensia who loved a man but married another after her brother-in-law, who was secretly in love with her, knifed her boyfriend in a fight and almost killed him. Ana added, "Hortensia is not even pretty." She wrote about a neighbor named Teresa who set herself on fire when her husband left her for another woman, and about a man who took his sister-in-law as his common-law wife after the death of his own wife. His children were appalled and moved away. Years later, the man and his wife were found dead, naked in bed, rats nibbling at their bodies.

Such drama, such horrors! I thought, and not for the first time, that people who romanticized life in the country had clearly never lived in the country. Life here was raw and difficult. I was beginning to feel sad and sleepy but reached for another book. This one had just one date on the cover: 1955.

"The doctor came yesterday. He was ashen-faced when he left but didn't say anything, at least not to Lila, who told me she feels like she lives in a house of secrets and whispers. Sometimes I feel the same way, but I know that Catalina is protecting her, just like I know I'm protecting Catalina. I, too, have my secrets."

"What? What secrets?" I said aloud, bringing the notebook closer to my face and rifling through the pages rapidly, as if, by doing so, the secrets would begin to drop into my lap like mangoes from a shaken branch.

Catalina

Sabanilla, Las Villas
1955

CATALINA DROPPED TO HER KNEES, realizing instantly that she wouldn't be able to help her daughter this time. No tincture or potion, prayer or saint could cure what ailed her. She wasn't sure what it was, but she had had a presentiment as her daughter's body writhed in pain as if possessed by a demon.

"Take it out!" she screamed. "Take it out!"

Ramón ran to her, placed his still strong arms under her body, and picked her up from the floor. Lila, who was almost sixteen, pressed her back against the bedroom wall as if willing herself to disappear. Her mother's crisis had not been a total surprise. The two slept together and at night she often heard her mother groaning in pain or calling to God and all the saints for help. A doctor had recently visited, and he had seemed upset when he left, but no one told her what was happening.

From her grandmother she had learned to place a glass of water under the bed to cleanse her mother's torment and allow her to sleep peacefully, but the water hadn't worked. And now, this.

Ramón brought his daughter to the bed delicately and laid her down. Then he rushed back to Catalina and helped her stand up, folding her limp body into his. She was pale, and her upper lip was sweating as if she, too, were in pain.

"What's happening?" he asked her because he knew Catalina had all the answers.

But she pressed her lips together and shook her head. Slowly, she walked to her daughter's bed and took her hand in hers. She felt the pulse. Too fast. She placed her ear near Carmen's nose and felt the warmth of her breath and a sour smell that made her recoil. Lastly, she dared to touch the spot on her daughter's stomach that she had pressed before collapsing. It was a bulge to the right and it felt hard to the touch. She noticed, not for the first time, that her daughter had lost a significant amount of weight and her skin had a yellowish tint.

"Ramón, saddle the horse. You need to take her to the hospital right now," she commanded.

"I better go and get the doctor," he replied.

"No!" Catalina insisted. "That doctor doesn't know anything. I'm telling you this is different. You need to take her to the hospital."

At that moment, Ana came in and immediately took in the urgency of the situation. She knew Catalina never left the house, and also knew Ramón wouldn't be able to deal alone with the ordeal she sensed was upon them. She offered to saddle her own horse and accompany Ramón and Carmen into town.

"It'll be fine," Ana said, holding Catalina's face in her hands. Catalina's forehead was cold, as if all the blood had drained from her face and had concentrated itself at the tips of her fingers, which were gently rubbing her daughter's stomach while she recited doña Elena's prayer: *Cross the bridge, my dear daughter, so you don't drown in the river or the tempestuous sea that is our tenebrous life.*

On the many occasions she had heard her grandmother utter those words and in the many times she had said them since, Catalina had never fully realized their meaning: that salvation lay in being able to walk over water rather than succumbing to it. And who, but Jesus, could walk on water?

This was her punishment, she realized. Finally, the water that should have taken her long ago, along with her first daughter, had come for her.

But instead of claiming her, as it should, it was wresting her other child away from her. Why? Hadn't she suffered enough? Wasn't her garden of dead babies a testament to the crosses she had to bear? What else did God want from her? Catalina lifted her hands from her daughter's body and brought them to her chest, making a gentle fist, as if invoking the bleeding heart of Christ himself. She raised her eyes to heaven and silently begged. Please, please, please. Not Carmen, too. Not this one. Please, please, take me instead. But immediately she took it back for she realized she was questioning God's will, and life had taught her not to challenge Him. Instead, she prostrated herself on the floor, arms open, legs closed, forming a cross, with her head down, and said this aloud, "Thy will be done on earth, as it is in heaven."

At that moment, Carmen moaned and threw up. Catalina got on her knees to clean her and then Ramón came into the room and with one quick motion lifted her from the bed. Catalina ran after them. Gently, Ramón arranged Carmen in front of him on the horse so he could hold her body and the reins at the same time. Ana had already mounted her horse. She looked back at Catalina and attempted a smile of encouragement, but for the first time in her life, was unable to do so. Instead, Ana asked her son to go and find his father, wherever he was. Catalina stood at the kitchen door as they left, with Lila behind her.

As they left, Catalina asked herself why she had not noticed how sick her daughter was. It was true that when Carmen had returned, ashamed and pregnant, a part of her, the part that Catalina treasured, had evaporated, like a puddle under the sun. Gone were her joy, her curiosity, and her spirit. Catalina had been disappointed, and Carmen must have perceived it. Now she could see that Carmen's meekness had been driven by shame. Not even the immense love Catalina felt for her daughter could make her whole again. In that, Catalina thought they were similar. She wished they could have connected over their losses. She should have realized that her daughter's heart was as broken as hers. How could she have been so blind? How could she have ignored her daughter for so long? The two were like passing ships in the house, always busy, always doing or tending to someone else, but not really talking, not really connecting as they used to before Carmen fled her home to go after Macho.

Once Lila was born, Catalina had focused all her love on the needy baby and her daughter had receded into the background, but that didn't mean she had stopped loving her. No, of course not. But did Carmen know that? When was the last time she had told her daughter that she loved her? Now it was too late. All she could do was pray.

Five hours later, Ramón returned to the house alone. Doctors had found a mass in Carmen's liver and told him she needed to stay in the hospital for urgent treatment. It felt to Catalina like a recurring nightmare that she couldn't awaken from. She went to her bedroom, closed the windows, and lit candles. On her knees, she begged the Virgin of Candelaria for help and began praying a *novena*. In all the years she had lived in Cuba she had seldom prayed to that virgin who belonged to her old world, to her old life. But now she didn't know what else to do. Though she had already entrusted her daughter's life to God's will, she could not understand why He would want to take Carmen so soon.

She would gladly have given her life for her daughter's if that would save her. She would ride the horse until she got to the town where she had first lived in Cuba, in the yellow house that Ramón's aunt so lovingly kept. And then she would find the beach nearby, the one she had smelled from her bedroom, but never wanted to see. She was ready to walk in the ocean until the water covered her entire body and her face. She wanted, simply, to offer herself to the sea. Take me, instead of her. Then her lungs would explode and she would be, finally, in the place she had escaped for thirty-six years. That would be just. That would be fair. But that, she knew, wouldn't save her daughter.

Catalina stayed put in her home, but the next day when Ana returned to get clothes and other necessities for her stay in the hospital, she encouraged Lila, whose birthday was that day, to go visit her mother. Two days later, when Ana returned with Lila alone and told her that Carmen had died, Catalina already knew, because in the middle of the night, as her child was dying, she had been awakened by the roar of angry waves.

Catalina refused to go to her daughter's burial. She stayed home, sitting on the back porch, cradling her heart, and thinking of her own mother. She wondered if her mother was still alive and if she had suffered her disappearance as much as she was suffering Carmen's absence now. No loss Catalina had ever suffered was as great as losing Carmen. She thought she should be used to it by now, but no. How can a heart accommodate so much pain?

Once again, she had the impulse to leave the house and start walking, to go to the sea, to throw herself in the water and give in. Yes, that's what she'd do. She got up and went outside to find one of the mares to ride. Should she wear boots? What does one take to the sea?

Just then, in the distance, she saw the procession returning from the cemetery. Leading them was the unmistakable outline of her granddaughter's figure, with her head bowed and her unsteady gait. That was when Catalina knew she couldn't leave. She had to stay a little longer, for Lila. And, more pressing, she had to cook dinner for the mourners.

She sighed. Bending down in a quick and fluid move, Catalina grabbed a white hen that was pecking the ground in front of her. Bringing its head close to her face, but not close enough to get pecked, she looked the hen in the eye for a second or two, as she always did before killing for sustenance. Then, placing her hand under the hen's head, she extended her arm, making wide circles in the air, twisting and twisting the exposed neck, until the bird hung limply in her hand and fluffy feathers settled at her feet. Only then, did she walk into her kitchen, put on an apron, and began to boil water for a soup. Her eyes were dry, but her bloodied hands were trembling.

Mara

Sabanilla, Las Villas
October 2019

I READ DEEP INTO THE NIGHT, until Ana's words blurred, and my hands grew numb from holding the notebook so tightly.

"On October 22, a day after Lila turned sixteen, her mother died in her arms. Carmen was only thirty-five. The day before, Carmen had me bring Lila to her room in the clinic so that she could give her a birthday present—her treasured gold mirrored compact that she had asked me to bring from her room. Lila was told her mother died of cancer, but I know her mother died of sadness and regret. No other man had ever come calling on her. In the eyes of many she was a damaged woman, judged always by the one mistake she had made when she was a teenager. She never knew love again. In fact, I'm sure poor Carmen had never known real love, for how can a man abandon a woman he had once truly loved? I know that my brother, had he lived, would never have abandoned Catalina. Although Catalina is now only fifty-five years old, she told me after Carmen's death that she feels ancient and spent."

I couldn't continue. My heart felt tender, and I had tears in my eyes, as I realized that my mother had never fully explained the circumstances of her mother's death. Suddenly I felt an enormous wave of love for my mother and a need to protect her.

The year I turned sixteen, my mother had been certain she was going to die. I remember waking up on my birthday to the feeling of someone caressing my arm. I opened my eyes and found my mother sitting next to me, crying silently.

"What's happened?" I asked, and sat up quickly, my heart beating wildly. It was the first time I felt my heart galloping inside my chest like a wild horse.

"Nothing, Mara, nothing, don't worry," she said, and dropped my arm.

"No, tell me," I insisted.

Thump-thump-thump-thump. I placed my hands on my chest and bent over. "Please," I begged. She must have noticed my discomfort, because she immediately replied with the last thing I expected to hear, "It's just that my mother died the day after I turned sixteen and today is your birthday."

Kicking the sheet away from my body, I got out of bed. I started pacing back and forth, massaging the area over my heart, willing it to calm down. I couldn't believe my mother had ruined my sixteenth birthday like this. All I could think about then was my pain, not hers. Concerned, she brought me a glass of water and sat me down, remaining next to me, saying nothing, until my panic abated. We never spoke about it again, but my heart had learned a lesson: from then on it would always react in this way when words failed me.

I turned sixteen in 1980, the year after we left Cuba. During our voyage, my mother had held on to me, afraid she'd lose me to the waves that sometimes crashed over the railing of our small vessel, leaving a trail of salty water behind, like tears. Now I think my mother was afraid that she was the one who'd be lost, that she would die, leaving me an orphan on our way to the United States.

My mother's fear was so great that one of the first things my parents did once we arrived in Miami, at her urging, was to buy a cemetery plot. Not yet forty, my parents wanted to control their final destination. Now I knew that my husband Nelson was right when he said years later that behind my mother's harsh exterior and brusque demeanor there has always been a scared little girl.

She would be eighty in a few days, and all I asked was for enough time to help her heal from her old wounds. Perhaps Ana's notebooks could help with that. Or at least I hoped so. I hoped my mother could read these diaries as I had, with curiosity and detachment, but perhaps that was asking for too much. After all, for me these were anecdotes about people I never knew, or remembered in a different way, like Ramón. For my mother, this was her life.

In a way, my mother had been protecting me from her past. I was beginning to understand that many of her character "flaws" were the product of a childhood lived in the shadow of secrets, shame, and fear of illness and death. No wonder she had fought me so hard every time I tried to assert my independence. The move to New York had been a battle; the move to Spain, a war. I couldn't wait for the morning so that I could call her, or, better yet, fly to Miami and talk to her in person and hold her in my arms.

I placed the notebooks I had read aside, took off my reading glasses, and covered my head with a pillow, the way I used to do when I was a child. I fell asleep instantly. But before I did, I remembered that the one thing my mother had insisted on bringing with us from Cuba had been a small gold-mirrored case that no longer held any powder. Etched in ornate letters were her mother's initials, *CFQ*.

Catalina

Sabanilla, Las Villas
October 1963

OCTOBER HAD ALWAYS BEEN her favorite month at home. The weather was balmy then. The worst of the summer was usually over, and a breeze used to rustle the leaves of the banana trees outside her bedroom window. At night, in the evening air, it almost seemed as if the trees were talking to each other in the pine forest, and the fragrance of the magnolias planted in the front invaded the whole house. It seldom rained.

But that was a long time ago, before October brought with it sharp memories of Carmen's death eight years earlier, and before their world had changed in ways she couldn't have imagined. Now, every month was the same, a way to mark time until the inevitable came. She would welcome it. She was ready.

Just like Ana had predicted, the rebels that had attacked the military barracks in 1953 continued their fight in the mountains and eventually brought a new government to Cuba six years later. President Batista, who seemed so strong, ended up fleeing in the night of New Year's Eve with his cadre, leaving behind a country so wounded and divided that it was easy for a band of young men with long beards, rosaries dangling from their dirty olive-green uniforms, and no experience in government to take over and begin to experiment with communism.

Catalina did her best to remain isolated from the world, but life had become so hard for her family in the last four years that it was impossible to remain immune. There were no batteries for the old radio and they still didn't have electricity, so the news rarely got to them, except what came by way of the neighbors, and what she heard wasn't encouraging. So many people had left the country since the rebels had taken control; so many had lost their businesses, their lands, even their families. It was painful to recognize that this government that had come to power with so many promises had turned out to be a disappointment. Food had been rationed and basic items were difficult to find. Catalina and Ana had learned to make soap in their kitchens and to cook with whatever limited ingredients they had available.

But Catalina was so exhausted. She lived in constant fear of the *alzados*, people who hid in the hills to fight against the government. At night sometimes she heard distant shots and saw shadows darting in the distance. Sometimes an animal would disappear, then two. They had taken to hiding their animals overnight, locking them in the shed. No one knew who the robbers were, and there was no point in telling the authorities because then the scrutiny on their own property would only intensify.

Alone with Ramón in the house, afraid of everyone and of everything, she found herself unexpectedly thinking of the past. What had become of her sisters? she wondered. Lucía, who was in such a hurry to grow up, must be an old woman by now, just like her. And Simona? Was she happy in her marriage? Had she had any children?

These thoughts and other, darker thoughts began to plague her. She thought of the sea and how she had narrowly escaped it. She could have been aboard the *Valbanera* when it sank, battered by the wind, so far from Cuba and so deep in the ocean that it had taken days to find it. In fact, she should have been on that ship, together with those she loved and who loved her. But she wasn't. And if she had, she never would have met Ramón and Carmen would have never been born and

Lila wouldn't exist today. There was no point in having those thoughts. Her survival had been useful in some ways. She had built a family, after all, even though it was out of the ashes of another family.

And who could blame her for loving again and for letting life take over? Who could blame her for allowing the grace of God to bless her with another daughter? True, her daughter had been taken too soon, but she had left behind Lila, a joy of a child. Who knew what God had in store for her granddaughter? Catalina doubted that she'd get to see Lila's children. She wished she could but knew that was asking for too much. She realized that her time was drawing to a close.

Death had been looking for her, circling for more than four decades, getting ever closer. First, it took her grandmother and her father within weeks; then, her husband, her lover, and her infant daughter together. Later, the unborn twins, ripping them from her belly when they were each no bigger than a potato. There were other losses. And then, of course, Carmen, taken so young, and leaving behind her own young daughter.

Ramón could see she was sad. Every evening when they sat together after dinner to end the day as they had started it—sipping coffee with milk, a ritual they had kept for years—he tried to engage her in conversation, but Catalina seemed to be elsewhere, lost in her thoughts. He imagined she was sad because Lila was no longer living with them. She had fallen in love and had moved to Havana with her husband. When he asked her if Lila's absence was the reason for her sadness, Catalina nodded and smiled weakly, knowingly, because it was easier that way. She could feel that her heart was tired. Sometimes she felt it skip a beat or beat slower than usual, as if alerting her or asking her to pay attention. At such times she paused and held on to a wall or to the back of a chair or the trunk of a tree for support because she felt faint and nauseous. She feared fainting, but never did. It was simply a warning.

All she could do with the warning was to acknowledge it. How does one prepare for death? What could she ask of God? Another year? Six months? What was the point of that? Every night, she slept closer to Ramón, hoping that if death came during the night, it would find her in his arms.

At dawn, when she heard the rooster's crow and smelled the coffee Ramón was brewing in the kitchen, she was always surprised and always disappointed. Another day.

Mara

Sabanilla, Las Villas
October 2019

I heard a noise somewhere in the house, and realized I wasn't alone. I tried to go back to sleep, but the smell of coffee—strong and delicious—forced my eyes open. For a moment, I felt disoriented. It was as if I were back in time and Grandpa Ramón was in the kitchen preparing a breakfast of buttered toast and *café con leche*, and my father was outside, shaving carefully in front of the broken mirror hanging from a nail on a tree, as he used to do every morning of our summers here. But, no, it was Linito. I heard him dragging his painful leg as he moved about the house.

I found him in the kitchen, where he was making breakfast with the same lopsided smile he had always had. He pointed to the outhouse and the old white enamel bowl on a stand outside the door, where I used to wash my face every morning under the stare of the original Azabeche and Villanueva oxen. I did the same this time, with the younger set of oxen nearby, pawing the dirt with their hooves, just like others used to do. The water was quite cold. When I was done washing up, Linito handed me a clean towel. It was only 6 a.m. A film of mist hung near the ground, and dew clung to the grass as I walked around the back of the house, reacquainting myself with a terrain that was once so familiar.

Sabanilla could not be more different from La Peña. Back in La Palma, lush forests framed an ever-changing sky—from azure in bright days to lead in foggy mornings. Here, palm trees, like birthday candles, pierced a land flat as a sheet for miles. Small hills punctured the sameness of the horizon, looking like camouflage army helmets, a riot of greens and browns contrasting with the bluest low sky. On the ground here, it was always chaotic: bushes and weeds and enormous creeper plants grew wild, held back only by the machetes all men carried in their belts. In the distance, I saw the low, terraced hills where my great-grandfather Ramón used to plant the rice and the black beans he sent us every year at harvest time. For short, they called that patch of earth *La Loma*, the hill.

"Whatever happened to *La Loma*?" I asked Linito once I was back in the kitchen. These were the first words I had uttered since the evening before, and my throat felt scratchy and tender as it had in the days after Nelson's death when I cried even while sleeping.

"It belongs to the government now," Linito said. "When Ramón died and no one was here to claim it, the government took it."

"But you are here," I said, looking back at him.

"Yes, but I'm not blood. Not officially, anyway."

"What do you mean?"

"Did you read the notebooks last night?" he asked by way of answering.

"Not all of them. Why?"

"Go on and eat your food. It's going to get cold," Linito said, and left the house before I could react.

After finishing my breakfast of two delicious fried eggs and coffee with milk, I quickly returned to the room to retrieve the red bag. I took it outside to sit, as I used to, under the shade of a mango tree. I cleared a space on the ground with my boot, and sat in a spot that seemed dry, and picked up a notebook with the year 1959 on its cover.

Except for Linito's father, Aquilino, this was not a family that had eagerly awaited the triumph of the Cuban revolution, as so many

Cubans seemed to have done. And, except for Ana, neither were they supporters of Fulgencio Batista, the strongman who fled overnight clearing the way for the rebels led by Fidel Castro to declare victory on January 1, 1959. From Ana's notebooks I gathered they all went to sleep early on the last night of 1958, as they always did. In the morning, they heard some distant neighbors shouting with joy. Another neighbor rode his horse to the house to tell them Batista had fled, and the rebels had won.

This is what Ana wrote of that day: "Ramón sat down, punched the kitchen table and said, 'This is communism, you'll see.' Then he asked us to hide anything of value. We didn't have much, but we put away some money. Aquilino thought we were exaggerating and became angry. Then, he disappeared. I don't really know where he goes, but I think this time he went to celebrate, and he knows I wouldn't tolerate it."

There wasn't much more that Ana narrated about the new government in that notebook, but, that same year, in August, she wrote that Ramón had taken my mother to Havana.

"Lila left for Havana today to spend a few months with distant relatives of Ramón. I didn't even know he had any relatives in Cuba until they came to Carmen's burial. He thinks it'll be good for Lila to get to know the capital. I think so, too, but we will all miss her terribly, especially Linito. She is more than my niece; she is like a daughter to me."

A few pages later, my father's name appeared for the first time. "I got a letter from Lila today. She's met a young man. Tall, she said, and very thin, like her, with wavy black hair, a long nose, small but penetrating dark eyes and broad hands with neat, clean nails. The only thing she doesn't like about him is that he's a year younger than her. She doesn't say it, but I know she is going to marry this man. His name is Ernesto Denis, and he comes from a family not far from here. Unlike ours, though, that family is complete. He has six siblings. I, on the other hand, lost my dear two brothers so long ago that sometimes I forget the details of their faces or the sound of their voices. And I know, though she doesn't speak about it, that Catalina misses her sisters as well."

In another notebook, she mentions that Ernesto Denis came to Sabanilla to ask for my mother's hand in marriage. Ramón was delighted. Catalina was quiet, but happy for Lila as well. The wedding was set for October 28, 1962. My mother had often recounted how her honeymoon was disrupted by what the Americans call the Missile Crisis and Cubans baptized euphemistically as *La Crisis de Octubre*, as if the world had not been on the brink of nuclear war. From the window of their hotel in Havana, they could see tanks rolling by as the country prepared for war with the United States.

But Ana didn't write about any of that or about the earlier, failed attempt to overthrow the Castro regime during the Bay of Pigs invasion in 1961. Perhaps these events were difficult to comprehend from a distance, in her cloistered life in the country, far from the places where decisions were made, and lives upturned. In later notebooks there were hints of how difficult things had become after the revolution and, especially, how angry Ana's husband Aquilino had become, and how he had found solace in "journeys to the hills."

"Aquilino was certain the new government would bring peace, prosperity, and equality to the country, but even he can see that is not happening," Ana wrote. I could tell she was being elusive here, for obvious reasons, but I got the impression her husband may have been involved in what was then called "counterrevolutionary activities." That was a serious offense; the punishment, if caught, was prison, or, depending on the offense, death by firing squad. But I couldn't be certain that's what Ana meant about his "journeys to the hills." She made them sound like outings to commune with nature. Somehow, I didn't think so, especially since I knew from my own earlier readings on the subject that until 1965 there had been insurgents in the mountains of

Escambray, not far from here, fighting to overthrow Castro. That uprising had been quashed by the government, which had shown no mercy. So, if Aquilino had been involved, as I suspected, he was a very lucky man, managing to avoid certain death twice, first from Franco's men and, later, Castro's.

In a book with 1963 on the cover, I found this: "I can feel Catalina slipping away. Ramón doesn't seem to notice or chooses not to. Her birthday came and went and, of course, she didn't want a celebration. At sixty-three she was too old for a cake, she said. I tried to find some *gofio* to make the foods she used to like from home, but *gofio* is impossible to find these days. *Gofio* and everything else."

There were a few pages after that in which Ana had started to write and then seemed to have given up or lost her train of thought.

"It rained today," one page said, dated September 15, 1963.

"Ramón said we might lose this year's rice crop. Rain is good, but not this much rain." That was dated September 20th of the same year.

"It's been raining for an entire week . . ." And nothing else on that page, not even a date.

There was an empty page and then this: "Catalina died last night."

Those were the last words Ana wrote. There were no notebooks dated after 1963 in the red bag.

Catalina

Sabanilla, Las Villas
October 4, 1963

ANOTHER DAY.

She got up and opened the windows to let the sun in, hoping the light would wash away the lingering shadows of the night and of her fears. Her biggest fear was leaving Ramón alone, but she wasn't sure how to prepare him. He had come into her life when she most needed him. In many ways, he had been her greatest gift from God, a complete and flawless person who had been her pillar, her strength, and her true and lasting love. Sometimes, late at night, when he held her in his arms caressing her back and catching his breath after making love, he whispered in her ear how much he needed her and how important she had been to him. He never spoke of love, but there was no need. Everything he did, Catalina knew, he did for her and their small family. And now, there was no family left. Carmen was gone and Lila had moved on. All they had was each other and there wasn't much of her left.

Her bones hurt, her hair was falling out in clumps, her skin was dry and wrinkly, and the freckles of her youth, which had disappeared years ago, had returned as tiny warts all over her face, neck, and under her breasts. She looked at herself in the mirror sometimes and wondered where exactly her young self had gone. How can a body be so ruined in only sixty-three years? She felt ancient, older than the trees and the low hills where Ramón still toiled each day to plant and harvest their food.

Today, she was outside, looking at the October sky, clear and luminous, as always. Toby, an old dog that had appeared at her door as a puppy shortly after Carmen's death, was resting at her feet, his belly rising and falling with each breath. Catalina hadn't slept well. She was tired of the daily struggle, and she was tired of cheating death. She could understand if her heart was tired, too. She touched the sore skin above her left breast and massaged her heart a little, not to convince it to keep going, but to let it know it was fine to let go.

Ana approached quietly. Her voice took Catalina by surprise. Toby jumped to his feet, tail wagging at the sound of Ana's voice. She bent down to pet him.

"The neighbors said a hurricane is coming. We should get ready," she said.

"Ready, how?" Catalina said without turning around. "What can we do?"

Ana laughed.

"I don't know, but looking at the sky won't help," she said.

"Does it have a name?"

"Who?"

"The hurricane. If they name it, it's bad. If it doesn't have a name yet, it's nothing to worry about," Catalina said.

"It's called Flora," Ana replied.

"Then we better get ready," said Catalina, who finally turned around.

She looked ashen. Her face was drawn, and Ana noticed for the first time that Catalina had lost weight. Was she eating? She didn't remember the last time the two had shared a meal that wasn't a snack. Lately, everyone was so afraid to be out after dark that Ana made sure to be home before sundown and didn't go out again unless Catalina needed her. Ana was a year older than Catalina, but she was much stronger and her lithe frame had not changed. Remarkably, her curly black hair remained black; only her face revealed the ravages of time and of a life spent under the relentless sun. She put her arm around Catalina and walked her home for an afternoon pick-me-up.

While Catalina brewed the coffee, Ana cut a chunk of guava paste into tiny, long strips and put pieces of homemade cheese on top. She placed them on a blue platter, and the two sat quietly in the dining room eating their *timbitas* and sipping sugared coffee. Through the open windows they could see a slowly darkening sky. The palm trees stopped dancing in the breeze and the leaves of the other trees suddenly stood still. The atmosphere became dense and calm, and the air around them was no longer invisible. Everything acquired a yellowish tint, as if a filter had been applied to their world.

Lightning shook the sky and made Ana drop her guava and cheese *timbita*. She hastily picked up and swallowed it before the dog could get to it.

"I better go home," she said, and after pressing her cheek to Catalina's, she ran out as the first fat drops of rain hit the roof like marbles.

Ramón was moving some of the animals to the shed when it started to rain. At first, it was a normal rain, like a spring shower, but then, it began to pour and wouldn't stop. He ran back into the house and Catalina helped him dry off with a towel.

It had been raining on and off for two days. Tired of being locked in, Catalina opened a window. The rain was falling like an unfurled piece of fabric—thick, opaque, and undulating in the wind. Ramón, still holding the towel, reached over and closed the window.

"What are you doing? You are going to get soaked! Move away from the window, woman," he ordered her.

The rain mesmerized Catalina. It paltered the roof as if wild horses had been set loose on top of their house. It rattled the doors, almost begging to get inside. And it pounded the ground with the force of a pickax. Old Toby, scared, hid under a bed.

"This is too much," Ramón muttered, and moved about looking for leaks or signs of flooding. There were none, but Catalina felt she was drowning. She started to cough, as if trying to dislodge something from her throat. Alarmed, Ramón came to her aid and massaged her back.

"Did you just eat something?"

She shook her head no and sat down in her favorite *taburete*, the one with the legs painted orange. It was so old the cowhide cover of the seat had a shiny patina and the dull bristles no longer poked through her clothes, making her thighs itch as the others did. Her heart began to throb with the old familiar pain, and she felt faint, so weak that, had she tried, she wouldn't have been able to get up. Ramón knelt in front of her.

"What's happening? Tell me!" he demanded when he saw Catalina hold her head with her hands.

Her head was throbbing, her jaw was locked in pain, her lips began to turn blue, and her teeth were chattering, as if she were cold or had a high fever. She had trouble breathing and focusing her eyes at the same time. She chose to focus. Catalina wanted to look at Ramón one last time. She took his face in her hands and got her lips close to his ear as if she wanted to whisper a secret, but she didn't have the strength. Her hands dropped to his shoulders; her head lolled to the side.

She remembered what the doctor had told her long ago when she asked how it felt to drown. Now she knew the old man had been right, except that she felt no despair, only peace, as she sank into the dark waters of her death and plunged deeper underwater, finally reaching out for her daughter's tiny hand.

"Catalina!" Ramón yelled, but she didn't hear him. She heard only the rush of her pounding blood in her ears and the distant sound of a ship's horn. Ramón buried his face on her lap, his tears drenching her thighs. It was the last sensation Catalina felt—something wet and cool, like water, running between her legs.

The wind blew open a window and rain poured in. It ran like a river on cracked concrete floors until it settled in the lowest portion of the house, the dining room, where Ramón and Catalina remained caught in an awkward embrace, a puddle of water growing at their feet.

Mara

Sabanilla, Las Villas
October 2019

I sat under that mango tree for hours, the notebooks strewn around me. A goat approached and began nibbling on the grass. I heard a horse neighing and some chickens clucking and the rustling of the banana leaves in the breeze and the buzzing insects and the unbearable din of cicadas, like chunks of meat sizzling in hot oil. And I felt, finally, that I was in Cuba. I allowed myself to feel, just feel, because this was so familiar. This, in many ways, was still my home.

Something seemed to dislodge itself from my chest and move to my throat, constricting it, and then to my face and, finally, my eyes, where tears began to flow freely. There was so much to mourn, so much, but also so much to be grateful for. I was grateful for the strength of these women, particularly Catalina, who had dared to live again, who had survived the unthinkable to create life, to live in love and with love, to cherish a child and, later, a grandchild, my mother. My mother, who had known how to choose a wonderful man, had modeled for me how to be a good enough mother of a wonderful son. Because at the end of it all there was Dylan. And I was so very glad that everything had happened in such a way that I had ended up with precisely this child, my Dylan.

I heard Linito approaching before I heard his voice calling my name. He didn't even notice I was sobbing or decided not to mention it. Instead, he asked me if I was hungry. I had to laugh through my tears, because that's exactly what my father would have said if he saw me sad. Food is always the solution for Cubans. As it turned out, I was hungry. Famished, in fact. And so, I extended my arms and Linito pulled me up with some effort but—bless him!—pretending I was still as light as the child who used to ride on his once-strong back.

We headed back to the house after gathering the notebooks in the bag, and he served me a feast. It was the best rice, black beans, and pork with a side of *tostones* I've ever had. I kept quiet, though I had a million questions. Instead, I let Linito tell me about his family. After his mother Ana died, his father had been bereft without the only woman he had ever loved, but, as it is often the case for men who depend on their wives, Aquilino soon married a widow from another town, moving away with his new wife and living happily until he died in his sleep of old age.

Linito, however, stayed. He thought his place was here, taking care of Ramón, the two houses, the animals, and, though he didn't say it, the memories of the two women who had raised him, his mother and Catalina. He married, had two daughters, and was a grandfather of five boys he had never seen, because his daughters, using their Spanish ancestry, had moved to the Galician village his father had escaped from so many years ago.

After lunch, while I dried the dishes Linito had carefully washed, he told me how his mother had died. Two months after Catalina's death, she went to visit her grave. Ana asked Aquilino to leave her there, alone, while he ran some errands in town. She lay down on the ground, next to Catalina's tomb, and apparently fell asleep. When Aquilino returned for her and woke her up, she didn't know where she was or who he was. After that, there were moments of lucidity, but they were brief and ever more infrequent. She asked for Catalina constantly, and when they told her she had died, she would cry inconsolably. Then, she would ask again, a few hours later, and the cycle repeated itself until Linito and his father decided to lie. They told her Catalina was in her house, or in the *guayabal,* or running an errand with Ramón. Anything to avoid the torture of telling her Catalina was dead. In January of 1965, Ana died in her bed, her body atrophied and curled like a fetus in a womb.

"I think she wanted to be with her sister," Linito said.

A silence followed as I processed what he had said. I thought of asking him to repeat himself but realized I had heard him correctly and that this was the revelation he had been hinting at since the day before.

"With her sister," I repeated, avoiding a direct question.

"Yes, they were sisters, half-sisters, but in the end, they lived longer together than they had with their full siblings, and they probably loved each other more than they loved anybody else in the world."

"I don't understand," I said, utterly confused. This was beyond *guajiro* speak. He was making no sense.

"Catalina's father was my mother's father as well," he said, not looking at me, but at the low hills in the distance, green and golden from the midday sun.

Here finally was a simple declarative sentence. But I was still confused or perhaps I didn't want to believe it. In the Canary Islands, I had heard so many stories about Catalina's father don José, as everyone called the family patriarch, that it seemed he was practically a saint, a man with no faults or vices, wise and smart, endlessly patient, and optimistic. Life and especially my job had taught me no human was perfect. But still, I needed proof. How did Linito know that? How could he be sure of it?

"Did I miss that somehow in the notebooks?" I asked.

"No. That was her deepest secret. No one knew that, not even my father, and especially not Catalina, but my mother told me and asked me never to tell anyone," he said, turning now to face me.

"Then, why are you telling me?"

"I don't know, but I think it can't possibly hurt anyone now. As I told you yesterday, they are all dead and soon I will be, too. Someone should know," he said.

Suddenly, everything made sense.

"Was Juan also Catalina's half-brother?" I asked, horrified.

"No, just my mother," he said, and went on to explain how Tomás and Juan had had the same father, a good-for-nothing drunk who had abandoned them, as Julián had told me when we visited the old house in La Peña. That much seemed to be true. The rest was new to me. When their mother was left alone, don José started visiting at night; the boys were quite young. No one knew, and it seemed harmless enough, until she got pregnant without a husband, and a little girl was born, Ana. No one in the town knew who the father was, but José Angel knew.

"That's why he was so opposed to the relationship between Catalina and Juan," Linito said. "My mother always felt guilty about that, that her very existence had made it impossible for the two to love each other without complications. That's a hard thing to live with."

"Do you think they were in love?" I asked him.

"Who?"

"Juan's mother and José Angel?"

"I don't know. It was probably one of those things. A woman alone and a greedy man," he said. "But they were thoughtless, and my mother bore the consequences of their sin all her life."

"But it wasn't her fault. If anything, it was her parents' fault, or even more directly José Angel's fault, for taking advantage of a vulnerable woman," I said.

"Yes, but things were different then," Linito said. "My mother was a deeply religious woman, and her devotion was really focused on the two of them, Juan and Catalina. She thought it was her way of paying back for her life."

My feelings vacillated between anger and horror, but also relief for finally learning the truth.

I left soon after that, with a bag full of notebooks, a headache, and a profound sadness in my heart. I knew that I would never again return to Sabanilla. On the way to the car, Linito showed me how to caress the oxen's hide without spooking them—gently and from the side, keeping their eyes in sight. At the last minute, when I was already halfway into the car, Linito deposited a kiss on my forehead, the same way my grandfather Ramón used to do.

As I drove away, I looked through the rearview mirror and saw him standing in a cloud of dust, waving, like people do to departing ships. I realized then I hadn't taken a single picture. All I had from the experience of the last few days in Cuba I carried in my heart and in my soul.

Postscript

But they learned the sixth moon fled against the torrent,
and the sea remembered, suddenly,
the names of all her drowned.
—Federico García Lorca, "Fable and Round
of the Three Friends" (1929)

Postscript

Mara

Key West, Florida
October 8, 2019

When I left Cuba and landed in Miami, I didn't visit my mother at first, as I had been yearning to do. Instead, I rented a car and headed south. Four hours south, to Key West.

Since I heard the *Valbanera* described as the poor man's *Titanic*, I had been mulling over the idea of coming here. The comparison was apt. The ship was mostly full of poor immigrants who had worked long hours to cobble together seventy *pesetas*, a fortune at that time, to buy a ticket to their dream life. The irony and the parallels between their story and mine were too poignant and powerful to ignore. Sixty years after the wreckage that took my great-grandfather and so many others, I had escaped the island they had once seen as their salvation. They remained in these waters, the same waters that had delivered me to a life of peace and prosperity in the United States.

Somewhere in the water, about forty miles from here, the body of Juan and that of Catalina's baby had been buried deep at the bottom of the sea for a century, along with hundreds of other bodies, interred in a bank of a quicksand so deep that no one had ever even attempted to dig them up for proper burial.

I wasn't sure what a proper burial would be for them, but I intended to go to the place where the *Valbanera* was still half buried.

As a parting gift, Julián had given me a book, *The Mystery of the Valbanera*, a treasure that I wish I had read earlier. I had been reading and marking up the book since then, and had a pretty good idea that to accomplish this mission I would need an experienced seaman, a solid boat, a Dramamine, a Xanax, possibly wine, a great deal of courage, and a $200 session with my therapist afterward.

It was seventy-five degrees outside, so I turned off the AC and lowered the windows. The cloudless sky was the kind of cerulean blue that inspires poets, and the breeze from the ocean wafted pleasantly into the compact green KIA. As I made my way through the Keys on US 1, the water on both sides shimmered endlessly. Curiously, I felt no fear or apprehension, only a sense of freedom and a giddiness I had not felt in a long time, as if I were about to open Christmas gifts or get dressed for a party. The exposure therapy must be working, I thought.

My phone rang at that moment with the distinctive dull sound of a WhatsApp call, jerking me from my thoughts. I answered, a smile already spreading on my face as I realized it was Nina.

"Nina!" I said urgently, as if I had missed an assignment and had just realized it. She heard the anxiety in my voice.

"Take it easy, woman! I'm just calling to check on you," she said, sounding relaxed. She was probably having tapas and a glass of wine. I checked my watch. It was 6 p.m. in Madrid. Yes, definitely time for a drink.

"I'm fine, Nina, but so much has happened. You wouldn't believe me if I told you."

"I'm all ears," Nina said, and we both laughed, because, in fact, her ears were too big for her small face.

So, I told her all I knew about the *Valbanera*, about Julián and the family I had found, and about my trip to Cuba, keeping to myself only the secret Linito had divulged at the last minute. I was not yet sure I was going to tell anyone, not even my mother.

When I got to the end of the story, I was already crossing the seven-mile bridge—always the highlight of a trip to the Keys—and I was only fifty minutes from my hotel.

Nina took a moment before reacting, and this is what she said, "Tell me you took a photographer with you to Cuba, even if it wasn't me."

"No, of course not," I said defensively, not sure where she was going with this.

"Then, please tell me you took pictures with your phone."

I remained silent.

"Damn it, Mara! You know better than that."

"It wasn't that kind of trip," was all I could say to Nina and to myself.

Nina backed off. She could tell she had upset me.

"Anyway, when will you be back in Spain?"

"Two weeks at the latest," I said. "Why?"

"I've got an assignment in Thailand, and I need a reporter. It's for *National Geographic*. I can give the editors your name if you are interested."

"That'll be great, thank you. Just what I need to get my mind off Cuba, and my mother and everything else. Send me an email with the details, please," I said. "I'll call soon, for sure."

"Okay, see you soon," she said, and hung up.

But before I could process the call, the phone rang again. I pressed the button to answer without taking my eyes off the road.

"What? Are you calling to apologize for the scolding?"

"Mara." It was a male voice.

"Julián," I said. "It's you. Sorry, I thought it was someone else."

"It's just me," he said.

His gravelly voice filled the car and made me inexplicably happy. He wanted to know all about my trip to Cuba. He had been counting the days, the hours, he said, because he knew there would be no internet where I was in Cuba. How did it feel? He wanted to know.

"I don't know, Julián. I have a lot to process, a lot to tell," I said after a beat.

"Can you give me the highlights?" he insisted.

"I'm not one to give out information for free," I said teasingly. "I'd need some wine, and at least one of your fabulous meals, maybe even a picnic back at the house. We never did drink that bottle of wine, you know."

"The house is yours as well, you are welcome to it anytime," he said. "In fact, I have a key here waiting for you."

I was speechless.

But he wasn't done.

"And, of course, I'd be up to discuss anything you want in person. I'd love to see you again."

Did his voice drop an octave or did my heart skip a beat? There was an awkward silence now. I had to get out of this call.

"Listen, Julián, I'm driving right now and I have to go, I'll call later, I promise," I said, and hung up before he could reply.

I placed a hand over my chest to still my heart. I wasn't used to such tenderness anymore, such thoughtfulness. Or was it something else? I grabbed the wheel more tightly with my two hands and shook my head, willing thoughts of Julián to escape through the window like a plume of smoke. It was better to put that aside for now.

I parked in front of the hotel, the same shabby old inn where Nelson and I spent our honeymoon and where I've stayed all these years. They know me by name. I left my bags at the front desk after kissing everyone hello and went for a walk. The weather was too good to waste a minute in my room.

The first time I saw Key West I had just arrived from Cuba, and we were being bused from the docks to an immigration-processing center. From the window of the bus, the town had seemed small and provincial, with most of the wooden houses run-down. Chickens owned the road. I couldn't believe that I was in an American city. Where were the skyscrapers I had seen in the movies, the fast-moving underground trains, the sophisticated people dressed in black? Where was the snow? I felt I had been duped and that, instead, we were back in Cuba, in some rural area I had never seen and where, somehow, people spoke a language I didn't understand.

But over the years my tastes changed, or the town evolved, for now it seems to me charming and quaint, though somewhat overrun by tourists. The obsession with Hemingway is real, and there are too many tacky T-shirt shops. But I can live with those in exchange for the spectacular sunsets and the feeling I get sometimes, when walking down certain side streets, that I'm in some small town somewhere in Cuba. I know it's an illusion, but what is life in middle age if not a grand illusion?

I splurged on an early dinner of a mediocre lobster and a glass of excellent white wine and went to bed around nine with a collection of Hemingway short stories I bought at the Hemingway Home and Museum I always visit. I had been looking for a story he wrote inspired by the wreckage of the *Valbanera*. It's called "After the Storm" and it was first published in 1932, only thirteen years after the ship was swallowed by the sea. It's the story of a fisherman who discovers the wreck, and hoping to find a treasure, dives in with a wrench to break the glass of a porthole. Through the porthole, he sees a woman, her long hair floating around her. He sees her face up close, even the rings in her hands, and tries desperately to break the glass, one, two, three times, but can't. Gasping for air, he resurfaces, his nose bleeding from the water pressure. He tries again. In the end, he has to leave, exhausted, defeated, and empty-handed. I put the book down with trembling hands, drank a sip of water, and turned on my left to find sleep. But I kept the light on.

The image of a floating woman through a porthole was the last thing I remembered before I finally fell asleep.

In the morning, I skipped breakfast and packed quickly for the day. I took only the seasickness pill and a small bottle of rubbing alcohol so

I could be revived in case I fainted. Out of habit, I touched the doorframe and whispered a prayer, though there was no mezuzah here. I had hired a young fisherman named Ernie to take me to Half Moon Shoal, the place where the *Valbanera*, buffeted by hurricane winds, had sunk in a bank of quicksand. Since Ernie can be a nickname for Ernest, I kept hoping his boat was called *Pilar*, like Hemingway's, but no such luck. It was called *Say Yes*. That was good enough for me. I wanted to know the story behind that name, and Ernie wanted to know why I wanted to go to Half Moon Shoal.

"It's so far! It's gonna take us more than two hours to get there, and that's if the weather cooperates," he said, squinting up at the flawless sky. "But, hey, it's your dime."

I had checked and rechecked the weather forecast several times. There was no way I was going to get in a boat without knowing I'd be in for a smooth ride.

"The weather will be fine," I said, and left it at that. I really didn't want to explain the story of my family to Ernie.

I sat down quietly, almost primly, tucking my hands under my thighs. I lowered a Miami Heat basketball cap over my eyes, trying not to appear nervous. The water was so calm, though, it seemed as if we were gliding on top of a mirror.

The last time I had been in a boat, in the Canary Islands, I had made a spectacle of myself, passing out in front of Nina, the crew, and the rescued refugees. I was hoping that would not be the case today. I tried to focus on the view, which was always bittersweet for me. I felt an unbearable angst as I looked out to the sea. Cuba was so close and yet so far: ninety miles, but it felt like thousands. My heart ached and I realized that doesn't just happen in the realm of poetry; it is possible for the heart muscle to ache from sadness. Perhaps sensing my discomfort, Ernie began whistling a tune, but the boat's powerful motor drowned out the sound. Even speaking was now out of the question, which was fine with me. Eventually, Ernie lowered the speed, the noise abated, and I could hear his whistling again. It was irritating.

"So, why do you call your boat *Say Yes*?" I asked, to get him talking instead of whistling.

"Why not?" he replied too abruptly.

"Never mind," I said, and turned my face to the sun, which was not yet strong. It was only a few minutes after nine, and suddenly I had the feeling that I had been asking questions for too long.

"It's not an interesting story," Ernie said, a little softer now. "It had that name when I bought it. I figured I'd keep it."

I felt obliged to say something, but all I could muster was a thumbs-up. I was exhausted, nervous, and a little nauseous. I swallowed hard, trying to keep it all together. My mind was going around and around in an endless loop, calculating the minutes until we got there. Why had I thought this was a good idea? I could feel a panic attack coming. I sipped some water and closed my eyes, breathing in, visualizing Dylan's face, then Nelson's, a mountain, a burning candle. It's all good, all good, I repeated, like a mantra. I focused on relaxing every muscle of my body. I knew I had to be brave for only one minute, then another.

When the moment passed, I began to tell Ernie why I had hired him to take me to the quicksand. Ernie was a good listener. He didn't interrupt.

"Then this is a cemetery for you, you are here to visit the dead," he said solemnly.

"Yes, something like that," I said, looking down.

I had come here to mourn.

Ernie shut off the motor, stood beside me and helped me up. We had arrived.

"Do you see that reddish shadow below?" he asked gently.

I didn't, but I nodded. The reddish shadow was probably part of the hull of the ship. Tears were running down my face, and I could feel the sun burrowing into my scalp despite my Miami Heat cap.

"Where are the flowers I brought?" I asked Ernie.

He gave me a blank look.

"They were in the bag I gave you . . ." But I stopped talking because I could tell he had no idea what I was saying. The lilies I had picked out that morning on my way to the docks had been left behind. A prayer would have to suffice. I tried to think of one, but Ernie interrupted.

"I'm going in," he said, taking off his blue long-sleeved T-shirt in one quick motion. He was wearing red swimming trunks. "And you?" he asked, pointing at me with his chin.

"Me?"

My mouth was dry, my palms sweaty. If I couldn't throw flowers in the water, would my body be enough?

"Can you swim?" Ernie asked, squinting a little.

"Not really. I used to," I said, and swallowed hard again.

"Come on, I won't leave you alone. Besides, it's not very deep," he said.

"I didn't bring a bathing suit," I said, walking backward, away from him, my hands holding on to a thick rope behind me.

"I have towels, and the sun will dry you off in no time," he said.

"Will I be able to touch the bottom with my feet?"

Ernie laughed.

"No, no, it's not that shallow, and you wouldn't want to. It's quicksand down there, but I promise, I won't leave you alone. Come, give me your hand."

It was a beautiful day, a perfect day for a swim, as Nelson used to say. The water was flat and clear, like an endless turquoise pool. Here and there silver fish leapt from the sea and hungry pelicans dove in for their meals. In the distance, tiny bursts of deep green interrupted the view of the water like wild weeds in a manicured lawn. The sun was nearing its highest point, making everything shimmer in hues of gold. All was quiet around us, except for the gentle tapping of waves, like my father's soft kisses, against the hull of Ernie's boat.

I thought of my great-grandmother and how she died afraid of the sea; of my grandmother, who died without ever seeing the ocean; of my mother, who had waded at a beach for the first time during her honeymoon and had never learned to swim; and I thought of my son, who had taken to the water like a fish from the time he was four months old and was probably somewhere in the middle of the Atlantic right now in a training exercise. I was the missing link. There was a reason my mother had named me Mara, and here it was now right before me—a thing so beautiful and placid I could no longer understand why I had always feared it.

I needed to honor my dead and honor my name.

"Mara, your hand, come on," Ernie repeated, extending a surprisingly beautiful hand with a tiny tattoo of a conch. He smiled, showing a row of flawless white teeth. His dirty blond hair fell like a curtain over his creased forehead, and his blue eyes crinkled with encouragement.

But I didn't take his hand. Instead, I kicked off my white sandals, held my breath, and jumped in.

Author's Note

THE STORY OF THE *VALBANERA* is a historical event detailed in several nonfiction books and novels inspired by it. I could not have written this book—indeed, I would not have had the spark of the idea that became this novel—if I had not found, serendipitously, in 2006, *El Misterio del* Valbanera, written by Fernando José García Echegoyen, who, years later, graciously discussed with me his work on shipwrecks from his home in Málega, Spain. His book is a deep and highly readable investigation about the doomed ship and the circumstances that led to its sinking off the coast of Key West.

When I was writing this novel, I had not yet visited any of the Canary Islands. In fact, I didn't go to La Palma and Tenerife until a few months ago, when the manuscript was already in the hands of the publisher. During my trip, I followed the steps of the characters I had created and visited places that I had imagined after reading travel guides and several books about the islands. By far, the most helpful of them was *The Canary Islands: A Cultural History*, by the renowned Canarian journalist Juan Cruz Ruiz. His description of topography, flora, fauna, food, culture, and significant historical events imbued my own work with the kind of details writers hunger for. But this is a work of fiction, and, as such, I've taken liberties to change a few things to fit my narrative. The town of La Peña, for example, is imaginary, but I'd like to think that my description of it mirrors the way real towns on the island looked and felt at the beginning of the twentieth century. And Gladys & Claude, the B&B where Mara stays in La

Palma, is really located in the village of Chardonne, in Switzerland, but it seemed appropriate to remember it in this context.

Though some readers will find elements of my life in this novel, this is not my story, but it could have been. Like Mara, I'm a journalist and reported on immigration issues for a long time. Like Mara, I came from Cuba in a boat when I was a teenager and made Miami my home. Indeed, portions of Mara's fictional story as a child in Cuba and her journey to the United States were first published in my memoir *Finding Manaña*. My maternal grandmother's name was Catalina Quintana; her father, Antonio Quintana was from the Canary Islands, though I don't know which island. I know very little about her life, in fact, but I know she had five children, of which my mother was the oldest. I know she died of stomach cancer at forty, the day after my mother turned sixteen. And I know she was in pain for most of her life. Much like the fictional Catalina, she was courageous and entrepreneurial, and a much sought after healer. While her husband, Juan Muñoz, my beloved grandfather, was away cutting sugar cane, she opened a bodega in her own home and, soon after, a dancing saloon, *El salón de la alegría*, as the fictional Catalina does. During my childhood and adolescence in Cuba, I visited the house where she lived and died every summer in Sabanilla. The stories my mother told me then and up until the last day of her life, November 7, 2021, are the backbone of this book, dedicated, of course, to them both.

April 15, 2025

Acknowledgments

Without a doubt, this is, for me, the best part of book writing—the place where I finally get to thank everyone who has helped me in this most solitary endeavor of writing a book. First, my forever gratitude to Leslie Nolan and the Canterbury Shaker Village, where, in the late summer of 2021, I finished the first draft of this book as an artist in residence. The residence gave me mental space and idyllic surroundings to finally finish a story I had been carrying around since 2006 when I bought, for $10, a coffee table book called *El Misterio del* Valbanera. I must thank its author Fernando José García Echegoyen, for his excellent research and his willingness to discuss his findings and share his archive of photographs.

My thanks also go to Armando Correa, for believing in the story so early on and helping me find the time to write it. Every writer should have a friend like Armando, a selfless bestselling author who has been by my side on every step of this long journey, including the reading of a very early draft. I'm also indebted to Carmen Lamas, for giving me the idea that unlocked the writing and, along with Kristina Arriaga, for being such thoughtful and careful early readers. To Carlos Verdecia, for his enthusiasm from the first draft and his editing skills. And to my sister, Mabel Junco, and my friends Ana Rabel and Fabiola Santiago, for reading the manuscript as it was meant to be read, not as editors, but as readers. I'm indebted as well to Elaine Colchie, who edited my last draft before submission and made the novel stronger with her sharp eye, gentle comments, and general life experience. Her generosity and good spirits are boundless.

My gratitude extends to those on the other side of the Atlantic who helped me immensely. In the Canary Islands, my dear Javier Sordo Letang, for answering all my questions about the islands and providing me with important research material; to Victor J. Hernández, in Santa Cruz de La Palma, for sharing with me his passion and knowledge of the slice of heaven he calls home. To Carlos Verdecia, hijo, and his wife, Naty, for correcting my mistakes. And to all the kind and warm people of the "fortunate islands" who shared their time and experiences with me.

Closer to home, I'm indebted to my fierce and savvy agent, Johanna Castillo, who took me on when all I had of *Deeper than the Ocean* was two chapters. Her wise counsel and friendship steered me in the direction of Union Square & Co. I couldn't have asked for a better home for my debut novel. My editor, Claire Wachtel, a wise woman, was truly a joy to work with; always kind, always smart, always available to answer my endless questions. The entire team at Union Square was supportive and professional. In particular, I'm grateful for the help of Mika Kasuga, editorial director for fiction; Alex Serrano, publicity manager; Chris Vaccari, director of school and library and retail marketing; Juliana Nador, assistant editor; Barbara Berger, executive editor; Christina Stambaugh, project editor; Patrick Sullivan, art director; Jared Oriel, jacket designer; Rich Hazelton, interior designer; and Sandy Noman, production manager. Copy editor Hayley Jozwiak and proofreader Margaret Moore, who, with their sharp eye and sense of narrative, perfected the work of so many others.

Every writer is a collector of stories, experiences, and passing phrases. Here, I've taken the liberty to quote others whose ideas have stayed with me. The words I attribute to a fictional editor about the importance of details are those of a former national editor of *The Miami Herald*, Bill Rose, who taught me to pay attention. The quote Mara finds in a memoir about the importance of the sea for islanders comes from Juan Cruz's *The Canary Islands*. I first heard the description of immigration as a human drive older than the word in a lecture by Professor José C. Moya, a renowned historian at Columbia University. The phrase "filaments of trauma" is from the poet Peter Balakian. The description of how the *Valbanera* may have gone down was first imagined by Fernando José García Echegoyen in his book *El misterio del Valbanera*. The doctor's description of what it feels like to drown was inspired by Sebastian Junger's exquisite research in *The Perfect Storm*. The line from a memoir of a Syrian writer comes from *The Return: Fathers, Sons, and the Land in Between*, by Hisham Matar. The lovely verse that Catalina hears the night of the concert by the sea is from the poem "Tide-Water" by Canadian poet Kate Seymour Maclean. I found the prayers Catalina recites in *El diálogo*, a book about the teachings of Santa Catalina de Siena.

It is never easy to write and publish a book, but it is especially difficult for those of us with full-time jobs. The encouragement and support of my colleagues at NBC News and Telemundo was crucial during the last stages of this process, particularly the enthusiastic response of Brian Caravillano, NBC Head of Standards, and of Luis Fernández, Chairman of Telemundo Enterprises.

There were days in the journey when I was ready to give up, but my children—Juan Arturo, Lucas, and Marcelo—wouldn't let me. I'm lucky to be surrounded by artists at home, and equally lucky to share my life with a pragmatic man who shored me up when I thought I would never finish this book. I'm grateful to them for making my life so interesting and full of love.

And, finally, I must thank my late mother, who, as a child, used to climb an old orange tree on the family's tiny farm and, sitting on its branches, dream of being a writer. She never wrote a book, but she was a great reader. It is my great sorrow that she didn't live long enough to find her stories on these pages. Mima, this is for you.

Bibliography

Barry, John M. *The Great Influenza: The Story of the Deadliest Pandemic in History.* New York: Penguin Books, 2004.

Cruz Ruiz, Juan. *The Canary Islands: A Cultural History.* New York: Duckworth Overlook, 2017.

Dillon, Paddy. *Walking on La Palma.* 2nd ed. Cicerone, 2011.

Feltwell, Dr. John. *The Story of Silk.* New York: St. Martin's Press, 1990.

Ferrer, Ada. *Cuba: An American History.* New York: Scribner, 2021.

Fornés-Bonavía Dolz, Leopoldo. *Cuba Cronología: Cinco Siglos de Historia, Política y Cultura.* Madrid: Verbum, 2003.

García Echegoyen, Fernando José. *El misterio del* Valbanera *(desaparición y naufragio).* Madrid: Agualarga Editores, 1997.

García Ramos, Juan-Manuel. *El Zahorí del* Valbanera. Tenerife: Baile del Sol, n.d.

Gjelten, Tom. *Bacardi and the Long Fight for Cuba.* New York: Viking, 2008.

Hemingway, Ernest. *The Complete Short Stories of Ernest Hemingway.* Foreword by John, Patrick, and Gregory Hemingway. The Finca Vigía Edition. New York: Scribners, 1987.

Junger, Sebastian. *The Perfect Storm.* New York: W.W. Norton & Co., 1997.

Larson, Erik. *Dead Wake: The Last Crossing of the Lusitania.* New York: Crown Publishers, 2015.

Le Canarien: Crónicas francesas de la conquista de Canarias. Introducción y traducción de Alejandro Cioranescu. Santa Cruz de Tenerife: Ediciones Idea, 2004.

López Isla, Mario Luis. *Valbanera: Naufragio, Misterio y Leyenda.* Miami: Editorial Primigenios, 2020.

López Isla, Mario Luis. Valbanera: *Requiem por un naufragio.* Gran Canaria: Tepemarquia Ediciones, n.d.

López, Calixto, and Rosalia Rouco. Valbanera, *1919.* Columbia, SC: 2020.

López Pérez, Alessandro, Mónica Pavía Pérez, and Iván Díaz Pelegrín. *Cronología de los Naufragios de La Habana Colonial.* La Habana: Ediciones Boloña, 2011.

Stone, Olivia M. *Tenerife and Its Six Satellites or The Canary Islands Past and Present.* Vol. 2. London: Marcus Ward & Co., 1889.

Stone, Peter. *The Canary Islands: A Cultural History.* Oxford: Signal Books, 2014.

Santa Catalina de Siena. *El Diálogo.* Translated by Ivory Falls Book, 2015.

Sánchez, Orlando Martín. *El éxodo canario: Una historia real de los inmigrantes canarios en la Cuba del siglo XX.* 2016.

Yáñez Gallardo, César. *La emigración española a América (siglos XIX y XX).* Colombres, Spain: Fundación Archivo de Indianos, 1994.

About the Author

Mirta Ojito is a journalist, professor, and author of two previous non-fiction books. She is the recipient of an Emmy for the documentary *Harvest of Misery* as well as a shared Pulitzer for national reporting in 2001, for a series of *New York Times* articles on race. A refugee from Cuba, her work often explores the complexities of identity, belonging, and the quiet power of resilience. She lives in Coral Gables, Florida, where she is endlessly inspired—and occasionally outnumbered—by her three grown sons and too many plants. *Deeper than the Ocean* is her first novel.

RAISING READERS
Books Build Bright Futures

Thank you for reading this book and for being a reader of books in general. As an author, I am so grateful to share being part of a community of readers with you, and I hope you will join me in passing our love of books on to the next generation of readers.

Did you know that reading for enjoyment is the single biggest predictor of a child's future happiness and success?

More than family circumstances, parents' educational background, or income, reading impacts a child's future academic performance, emotional well-being, communication skills, economic security, ambition, and happiness.

Studies show that kids reading for enjoyment in the US is in rapid decline:

- In 2012, 53% of 9-year-olds read almost every day. Just 10 years later, in 2022, the number had fallen to 39%.
- In 2012, 27% of 13-year-olds read for fun daily. By 2023, that number was just 14%.

Together, we can commit to **Raising Readers** and change this trend. How?

- Read to children in your life daily.
- Model reading as a fun activity.
- Reduce screen time.
- Start a family, school, or community book club.
- Visit bookstores and libraries regularly.
- Listen to audiobooks.
- Read the book before you see the movie.
- Encourage your child to read aloud to a pet or stuffed animal.
- Give books as gifts.
- Donate books to families and communities in need.

Books build bright futures, and **Raising Readers** is our shared responsibility.

For more information, visit **JoinRaisingReaders.com**

Sources: National Endowment for the Arts, National Assessment of Educational Progress, WorldBookDay.org, Nielsen BookData's 2023 "Understanding the Children's Book Consumer"